Into Darkness

Jonathan Lewis made award-winning documentary films for thirty years. He, his wife and their dog now split their time between a cottage in Oxfordshire and an old motor yacht. *Into Darkness* is his first novel.

Into Darkness

JONATHAN LEWIS

arrow books

This paperback edition published by Arrow Books 2011

10 9 8 7 6 5 4 3 2 1

Copyright © Jonathan Lewis 2010, 2011

Vicki Hearne quote on page 189 from 'A Taxonomy of Knowing: Animals Captive,
Free Ranging, and at Liberty' – paper delivered at the New School for Social Research,
New York, 1995

Jonathan Lewis has asserted his right to be identified as the author of this work under
the Copyright, Designs and Patents Act 1988

First published in Great Britain in 2010 by Preface Publishing

20 Vauxhall Bridge Road
London SW1V 2SA

An imprint of The Random House Group Limited

ww.rbooks.co.uk
www.prefacepublishing.co.uk

Addresses for companies within The Random House Group Limited
can be found at www.randomhouse.co.uk

The Random House Group Limited Reg. No. 954009

A CIP catalogue record for this book is available from the British Library

ISBN 978 1 84809 258 7

Mixed Sources
Product group from well-managed
forests and other controlled sources
www.fsc.org Cert no. TT-COC-002139
© 1996 Forest Stewardship Council
FSC

The Random House Group Limited supports The Forest Stewardship
Council (FSC), the leading international forest certification organisation. All our
titles that are printed on Greenpeace approved FSC certified paper carry the FSC logo.
Our paper procurement policy can be found at http://www.rbooks.co.uk/environment

Typeset in Times by Palimpsest Book Production Limited,
Falkirk, Stirlingshire

Printed and bound in Great Britain by CPI Bookmarque, Croydon CR0 4TD

For Eee

Prologue

I am running along streets.
Running fast.
I do not know what to do.
I do not know where I am going.
The metal thing is broken and clattering.
Nothing I know is of use now.

I am very frightened.
Getting tired.
Slowing down.
No one is behind me.

And that is what scares me the most.

1

IT WAS A HORRIBLE PLACE to die.

The body was face down on a strip of mud in a disused dock basin that reeked of raw sewage. Ned Bale kept his distance as usual, and watched the flock from Forensics converge on their prey. Bloody stupid, wearing white. They looked as if they were about to star in a TV ad. The ultimate test for our soap-suds: wading waist-deep in muck and death. From the tide marks on the quayside, the level in the basin clearly went up and down. Easy to see why. One of the sluices in the lock gates was open, and beyond ran the great tidal river. Was the body dumped onto the mud, or did he fall in at high water, drown in the shit and get beached as the tide went out? First impressions are always bollocks, Ned thought, and turned away.

The place was made even more unnerving by a nasty whistling noise. Wind in the what? Ned looked up. A wide walkway snaked out high across the lock gates. It seemed to sprout from the Victorian Gothic offices of the adjacent dockyard, but where it went, he couldn't see. The wind didn't stoop low enough to blow away the stink from the basin. Time for a clamber. Maybe some fresh air up there.

It wasn't easy getting onto the walkway. There was no access from the stinky basin. He had to find a way into the dockyard and flash his warrant card at the dragon in the office before she'd let him out through the fire exit onto the catwalk. Or rather, catwalks. It looked wide from below because there were two: a modern one running alongside an ancient one. He stepped carefully; no good trampling a possible crime scene. The closer he got to the lock gates, the more rotten the planking on the old walkway. The sound of jollity wafted up. Ned looked down. The team was having a tea and fag break. One of them held up a cup and pointed at Ned, who smiled a little bleakly and shook his head. That gave them all a good laugh. The running gag was that the ace Detective Chief Inspector was squeamish – the one exception to Fatso's rule that a copper was no use to man or beast if he couldn't watch an autopsy eating a bacon sarnie smothered in tomato ketchup. Given half a chance, he'd set it as a test.

Ned was just above the basin when he saw the gaping hole in the old walkway. The closer he looked at it, the clearer it was that the hole was fairly recent. The tops of the timbers around it were a slimy greenish black, but the edges of the broken planks looked a few shades lighter. He felt among the splinters. Almost dry, crumbly. When had it stopped raining? Late yesterday afternoon. Had our man fallen through here? Or been pushed? And what was that? A matchstick. Dry. Burnt at one end, pointy at the other. Bag it. That's what he was doing when he heard the commotion below.

Forensics had finished their ghoulish tea break. Again, odd phrases drifted up. Very nice coat. He had a bob or two, this one. What was he doing round here? Dying, mostly. Tide's coming in. Almost lapping those natty shoes. Time to flip him over. Stretcher boys on cue. One, two, three. Bugger me, you see who it is? Can't be! Fucking is! Fucking hell!

Fatso was in his element. He pretended it was routine, but they could all see he was as high as a kite on it. Pigs in space. Cheese roll in one paw, unlit fag in the other, crusted egg where there'd once been a tie, eyes abulge, matching beads of white scum at the corners of his mouth. He was an acquired taste, Detective Superintendent Fullerton, and no mistake. Few wanted to do the acquiring, but few who did regretted it. Not just the crack of the man, but he was good and cunning. And he'd back you, even if you'd done something wrong. Then, a bit later, he'd get shot of you. Funny, that. He didn't much like wrong 'uns. And he really didn't like losers – didn't like losing. And he wasn't going to lose this one. It was huge and it was all his. Except Spick and Span would do the legwork, natch. Extra Bilge would sort the technical stuff. And Ned the Yid would do all the brain work, as per usual. He'd work out who had actually bumped the bleeder off. But Fatso's in charge. Wild boars in hyper space.

'. . . sending over a gang from the Celeb Squad? Evenin' all, darlings? No chance. They couldn't nail Her Nibs's bent butler or the nonce with the ponce in the pool . . .'

Ned's attention drifted as Fatso waded through a catalogue of unsolved celebrity crimes, whose perpetrators were known to absolutely everyone in the world except the denizens of the Yard's Special Enquiry Team. He, like Fatso, wouldn't want anyone muscling in on this one, if they really were dealing with murder. But were they? For the moment, it was as likely to be tragic accident as crime. Spick put it into words.

'No sign of foul play yet, boss.' There. Someone had said it. They all looked back at Fatso. He seemed a little disappointed, but only for a moment.

'Early days, cock, early days. The great man's croaked, and it's up to us to sort out the how and why.'

The team was fleetingly reassured that the cause of death had not been prejudged, when Fatso added a coda.

''Course. Much better if someone done in the National Treasure, innit. Got to be. I mean, we don't do "accidentally slipped on wet cobbles", do we? We do coshed, pushed, drowned. We do murder. So let's all be hoping that's what we got.'

They went through the little they knew. The National Treasure's office had him at a retrospective at the Film Theatre which he'd left just before 11 p.m. saying he wanted some fresh air and would walk back to his hotel. The Metropole said he never got there. Doc Bones was up to his elbows in the autopsy. The widow Angie Best was on the redeye from LA to identify whatever was left after Doc Bones had had his fun. Loads of people to talk to, things to do, better bloody get on with it. Fatso gave his favourite detective the crooked finger as the meeting broke up.

They sat in Fatso's ashtray of an office while he thumbed through Ned's first briefing. Fatso hadn't smoked in there since the ban. The fag in his mouth was never lit. Merely renewed when it got too soggy to maintain structural integrity. But it didn't matter a damn; Ned still felt he breathed in a year of secondary smoke every time he went in there.

'Who found him?'

'A crane-driver saw him from his cab. Apparently he keeps a pair of binoculars up there to identify the birds that light on his crane . . .'

Fatso shook his head, incredulous at the ways of others.

'And you say the basin's tidal?'

Ned nodded. 'A sluice has jammed open. We tried to close it.'

'Big enough for . . .'

'Suzy.'

'. . . Suzy to slip through?'

Ned nodded again.

'Keep the divers on all night, then. Hang the overtime. Don't want to lose the baby with the bath-water. You better get down there and keep an eye on them. Brave gits, divers, but daft.'

Ned nodded yet again and made for clear air. As he reached the door, he heard Fatso ask something, but it seemed to be more to himself, so Ned kept going into the sunny uplands of the outer office. It was a good question though, and one Ned would have to crack. What were the great man and his famous little friend doing down at the Docks at midnight?

It had been a nasty place in the morning. By night, it was deeply unpleasant. The stink had built up over the heat of the day, and with the tide in, the nostrils were a lot closer to the turgid, rotting surface. Floodlights bathed the basin in a dull steamy glow. The scummy black surface was broken as a diver bobbed up or slipped down. No one said anything. There wasn't anything to say. And after a night of plumbing the grim depths there wasn't anything to find. Maybe she had already been sucked out by the ebb through the sluice. They had to find her. She was part of the story. Part of the legend.

'. . . *the Queen has sent a message of condolence to the family of Sir Thomas Best, whose body was found in the Alexandra Docks yesterday morning. "My thoughts and prayers," she told them, "are with you." Sir Tommy, as he was usually known, had been a particular favourite and friend of the Royal Family for over forty years. Her Majesty is understood to have written privately to Sir Tommy's widow, the film star Dame Angela Dalkey, who is flying back from . . .'*

The river police blew a fortune in diesel not finding her body, before a newsagent a mile from the Docks rang in to say he'd got her – alive. He'd been offloading papers from the van at 5 in the morning when he saw her in a corner of the shop, panting and shivering. He had no idea who she was. He gave her something to eat and some-where to rest, and almost forgot about her. It was only when his daughter stopped by and saw her, fast asleep . . .

'Christ, Dad. It's Suzy! It's been all over the news, about the old boy drowning. They said they were doing a door-to-door search for her . . . Look, she's got that thing hanging off her. Oh, isn't she lovely? You got to ring 'em, Dad. Tell them she's here.'

Spick led a mob out to work the streets between the newsagent and the basin, looking for a witness. By lunch they'd found one. A man had heard her go by. He'd hurt a leg playing football and was sleeping downstairs in the front room. Said he'd been woken by a tinny clattering past his window. Someone running like the clappers, dragging something metal . . . he couldn't make it out. He was half-asleep. A sort of patter – like a child running barefoot. Scampering for its life, it sounded like. Heavy panting. Funny thing was, there didn't seem to be anyone in pursuit. He looked out the window, but there was nothing to see. Dark street. Dead silence.

Small wonder he couldn't make it out. It was a sound you don't hear every day. The sound of a guide dog running from the death of her blind master.

2

'WHERE'S THE DOG TART?'

Fatso squinted at the packed room. There was the usual pause. She always needed a few beats to summon the strength to speak out in public. A pause during which a few of the younger men would turn round to see her. The older hands didn't bother, rare sight though she was. They knew there was no point. Ned was the exception. He always looked at her, even though he swore to himself he wouldn't. He'd made a lot of these sorts of promises, mostly before he met her. In the street he'd glimpse a woman approaching he knew he wanted to stare at, and would force himself not to. He'd tighten a shoelace or scour a shop window. Sometimes he'd look the other way, knowing she'd come through his field of vision. He didn't want to be impervious – didn't want to be cured. He just didn't want to get caught ogling.

'I'm here, sir.'

She was half-hidden behind a pillar. Slight and fearless. Sharp and funny. Overalls four sizes too big for her. Hair scrunched into a cap, head lowered just enough for the peak to hide her face. Her face. That face. The chin. The mouth. The cheek-bones. The skin that never got made up and never needed it. The eyes. That extraordinary, precious face. Ned dug a fingernail into his palm to distract himself. He knew her story. He even believed bits of it.

He'd promised himself. He'd sworn. He'd really, really tried. But he'd totally failed. Ned was hopelessly in love with the Dog Tart.

'What's the story, then?'

'Dunno, sir. Physically, she's not too bad. But she's in some sort of shock. Barely eats. She's dead jumpy.'

'Any sign she was in a scuffle? Separated from him by force? What do the claws tell us? Had she been in the water? Have you done swabs? Any way of telling if she was trying to get help?'

She didn't glance across at Ned during his string of questions. Just as well. Everyone knew you couldn't look her in the eye without dying an exquisite death right there on the spot. Medusa reborn.

'Her harness was hanging off. Broken away on one side. But there's no sign of struggle on her. No cuts, torn fur, nothing. No claws broken. No, she hadn't been in the water. Yes, we've done swabs. Of course, I assume she was trying to get help. That's what she'd have been trained to do.'

'We've got to hold onto her, Boss,' Ned said, without looking up from the notes he was writing. 'She's our only witness.' He ignored the rumbling in the room at the idea that a dog could be a witness, and carried on. 'Is the family insisting on having her back right away?'

'Dunno. You can ask Dame Angie yourself. You and me are seeing her this afternoon. We're certainly holding onto her for the mo. If that's all right with the Dog Tart?'

Ned winced again at the nickname. Oi Fatso! She's WPC Kate Baker.

'It's fine. Only I've got leave booked in a fortnight . . .'

Fatso was immune to the eyes. Teflon pig.

'I've got every bloody rag in the country trying to get to that effing mutt. The *Guardian* wants to use "regression hypnosis" on her, whatever that is. The *Star* wants her minced into cat food for failing to save the National Treasure. I don't want her out of your sight. Take her on holiday if you have to. I hope we don't pay you enough for it to be foreign?'

She shook her head. Meeting over. As usual, she slipped away without anyone seeing her go.

Doc Bones whistled while he worked. It wasn't that he was happy. He was rather a miserable sod. But he whistled for exactly the same reason that his father used to stick his tongue out when reversing the Riley. Doc Bones aged 6 would be losing the fight against car sickness in the back, when suddenly this great moon-face would swing round like a searchlight towards him, tongue clamped between teeth. This heralded a crashing of gears and a major shifting of the contents of Bones Minor's stomach from bow to stern. What made this routine so peculiar was that it always seemed as if his father was turning round to look at him – perhaps to ask how the dicky tummy was going, old chap – but what he actually did was stick out his tongue and stare right through him. Didn't he know sticking out your tongue was rude? It took young Bones a while to understand that his father was simply concentrating on not flattening the vicar or a pillar box. It took a further decade before he realised that his father suffered from malocclusion, but it was a direct hit on his field hospital in Korea that did for Doc Bones Senior, not a dodgy fang/jaw interface. The son was as unaware that he whistled as the father had been that he stuck his tongue out.

The Latin was something else. Ned had once tackled him about it after Extra Bilge announced he had been tracking Doc Bones's increasing use of Latin, and by 2019 he would only be uttering one word of English a fortnight. The team all reckoned they'd quite like that, as it would give them the excuse they craved for not understanding a word Doc said.

'*Ecce, Nedice! Quid novi?*' said Doc Bones, who always liked a visit from people who might not be total buffoons.

'Doc Bones, what's with all the Latin?'

'Ah. That then.' The Doc put down his ghastly probe, sat back on his stool and placed the tips of his fingers together in an open-weave prayer.

'As you know, young Nedicus, Latin is a dead language.' He glanced down at the corpse on the slab. 'What more appropriate language for this *locus horribilis*? For my ghastly and sinister work? Indeed for me, surrounded from dawn to dusk by drawers full of *cadaveres croakati*?'

Doc stood for a bit more probing. Ned turned his back, as he always did at such times.

'Doc. There's no such word as *Nedicus*. Or *croakati*. Or *telephonis mobilis*. Or *subpantes*.'

Doc waved his probe triumphantly in the air.

'There is now! Never heard of "life after death"?'

Anyway. Doc Bones whistled. It was the kind of whistle where the tongue forms a reed against the roof of the mouth, and it sounds like a kettle wondering whether to boil. There were occasional tunes, some of the masculine-Christian persuasion. This trapped newcomers to his charnel-house into mistaking Doc for a religious man, but no one who saw it piled high with the remains of a school-bus crash could ever forget his muttered mantra: 'See? No God whatsoever. See? No God whatsoever. See? No God whatsoever . . .' There was no whistling that first morning, but by late afternoon the word went round that Doc was whistling again, and everyone seemed much relieved. He stuck to simmering kettle versions of Cole Porter and Gershwin for a long while after that.

Tommy Best was by no means his first celebrity corpse, but he was the only one Doc Bones actually recognised. Doc had little interest in popular culture, and he'd happily turned a number of famous footballers, rock stars, snooker champions and television personalities inside out without having the foggiest who they were. But Tommy Best was different. Doc Bones didn't just recognise him – he knew him. They had sat on the same table only a few months before at a WHO fund-raiser to eliminate leprosy. Doc Bones spent two weeks every year working at a leprosy hospital in Mumbai – something he successfully kept secret from his colleagues – so he and Tommy had plenty to talk about. He was impressed. Tommy was a good listener, and when it came time for the keynote speech, Doc was surprised and pleased to hear Tommy recounting a story the Doc had just told him. Telling it with added wit, and fitting it artfully into a cogent rallying cry for earlier diagnosis and more public information. So when Doc Bones stood over the late Sir Thomas brandishing his junior hacksaw, he felt what he was about to do was, to a fraction of a degree, personal. Not nearly enough to excuse himself; the connection was too fleeting and the stakes too high for that. Besides, within minutes the identity was being almost literally stripped from the *croakatus*, to the tune of 'Always True to You in my Fashion'.

The road wound through unscuffed countryside. Goodbye dirty docks, the scream of Doc Bones's Black & Decker, the office fug, 360° squalor. Hullo gated communities, daytime sex and designer chickens. And hullo hacks. There was a scrum of them outside, with nosy great lenses and shiny stepladders unsplodged by paint. While Ned waited for Security to buzz them through, the hacks crowded round the car. Fatso wound down the window. Gave a little belch. Begged their pardon. Closed it again.

Ah Fatso, thought Ned. What's not to like?

They were taken through by a PR woman with kitten heels, and calves to crack coconuts. 'She's in the morning room,' she said, and pretended not to hear Fatso mumbling 'Best place for her in the circumstances' as she clip-clopped over the parquet. Dame Angie was sitting at a small desk, reading a letter. Tiny little woman. Perfectly proportioned. Perfectly still. They waited. Ned took in the two Oscars being used as doorstops. The photos of her and Tommy with JFK. King Hussein. Onassis and Callas. Hitchcock. The Dalai Llama. Jack Nicholson. Angie with Andy Warhol and Robert Mapplethorpe. The famous Jane Bown photo of Tommy with Laurence Olivier and Ralph Richardson in a Soho salt-beef bar. Angie on stage in Nashville with Dolly Parton and Johnny Cash. Dancing with John Travolta. Tommy sailing with Uffa Fox and the Duke of Edinburgh. Sitting at a piano with Noël Coward. Having a picnic with Charlie-boy and Camilla. In a hammock with

Sean Penn, Angelina Jolie and a baby chimpanzee. He took in the Modigliani nude. The Benin bronze. The orchids. The full mail sack at Dame Angie's feet. The sobbing. And then that marvellous voice.

'Don't cry, Chippy darling. We've got the police here.'

Whoever Chippy was, the sobbing stopped and someone scuttled out of the conservatory beyond the morning room and into the garden. Dame Angie slowly put the letter down on the desk, wrote carefully across the top and placed it in a folder. Her shoulders sagged, just a little and just for an instant. Then she stood and turned. She looked exactly like herself.

'Good afternoon, gentlemen. First, tea or coffee? And then, please tell me who murdered my husband?'

Ned told her what they knew. It didn't take long, and it didn't include the name of Tommy Best's killer. There was a bit of question and answer, and then she started to talk. The room was pretty quiet from the off. By the time she fell silent an hour later, Ned felt he was in an acoustically dead coffin with her disembodied voice inside his head. Then the silence became absolute. She just sat in the gloom, motionless. Talked out. Ned and Fatso waited. Five minutes went by. Nothing. Then Fatso gestured towards the door and they stood. Whispered their thanks, and left. For a big man, Fatso moved surprisingly lightly. As Ned gently closed the door behind him he looked back and saw Dame Angie lift her face to the ceiling. It was like a scene from one of her films. A fitful shaft of sunlight caught the famous profile: the arch of endless neck, the tumble of golden hair. It lit up the flawless diamond pendant Tommy had won for her at a Live Aid charity auction, which Ned and 100 million people had watched Mandela himself fasten around that oh so elegant neck. If it had been a movie a close-up would have picked out a filigree of tears on perfect cheeks. But this wasn't a movie. The sun went in and Ned tiptoed away.

Fatso was propped up against the car, fag in face. Ned had almost reached him when he stopped. Felt his pocket and turned back into the house. The PR woman was nowhere in sight. He retraced his steps, silent as a thief. He paused only a beat outside the morning room door, then barged in. The chair was empty. She had moved. She was standing framed by the arch into the conservatory in someone's arms. Someone's long brown arms. Ned went to the sofa and bent to feel under a cushion or two. As he straightened, he saw the oval face of a girl in her late teens peer round Dame Angie's quivering shoulder. Her agonised eyes darted from Ned to the door, imploring him to leave.

They had been driving a while before Fatso shifted his bulk and glanced across at Ned.

'Left yer notebook behind, my arse. What did you see?'

Ned shook his head.

'Not a lot. She was with a girl. Maybe that Chippy.'

'Dying duck in a thunderstorm still? Or were we having a laugh?'

'Genuine grief, I'd say.'

Fatso pulled a face.

'Come off it, Ned. We're talking about a bleeding actress. That's what they do. Laugh, cry, flirt, fuck. Just because it fools you doesn't mean it's true.'

Ned had a think.

'She clearly adored him, she's seriously rich in her own right, and she's distraught. I don't think she had him pushed in.'

Fatso also had a little think.

'Nah. Nor me.'

They bowled along for a bit.

'"Distraught", Ned the Yid? Where'd you get 'em? Where does he get 'em? Why don't you say "in pieces"?'

'Distraught's her kind of word. I like thinking about people in their own . . . language. It helps.'

'Pompous git,' said Fatso affectionately. 'Must have a bleeding field day thinking about me.'

'Wouldn't dare, sir.'

'Wouldn't fucking dare, Ned.'

'Yes, sir. No, sir.'

Fatso promptly fell asleep, which suited Ned just fine. He could replay Dame Angie's stream of consciousness in peace. Sort it. Break it down. File it under headings: Death. Dog. Mood. Motives. Enemies. Secrets . . .

First, the death.

'You say you don't yet know the exact cause of death? Well, I can tell you, he was as fit as a fiddle. You'll find out for yourselves . . . I suppose you're going to poke about in him. God knows, I've played enough forensic pathologists. My poor Tommy. Those awful saws . . . can't bear to think of it. You'll find no noxious substances in Tommy. Rarely drank to excess. Drugs an absolute no no. Look elsewhere, gentlemen . . .'

Yes, Dame Angie, thought Ned. We will. He suddenly had a flash of her in a bloodstained apron, with Julia Roberts stretched out, not quite dead, on the mortuary slab and Denzel Washington's gun to her neck. That neck again.

Then there was the dog.

'They were inseparable. I am sure she'd have died for him. And he . . . except, did you know, Tommy couldn't swim? Stupid. I gave up trying to persuade him. No, Suzy was terribly important to him. Well, she was the best bloody guide dog in the country. They had this nationwide competition on *Blue Peter* . . . There's no way she'd have failed her master. Not Suzy. She was utterly bomb-proof. If they were separated, it was because someone forced them apart. No question. You have the proof of that in the broken harness.'

Funny how she spoke as if the dog was dead. So there's no possibility the harness was already damaged?

'I don't recall seeing anything wrong with it. But I wouldn't necessarily have done. Look, Chief Inspector, I wasn't turned on by Tommy's blindness. We didn't all sit round of an evening saddle-soaping his harness and repainting his white stick. That wasn't a family pet, you know. That was a working dog. Part of his operating system. Like his laptop, or his mobile phone. I didn't recharge his phone battery, and I didn't feed Suzy . . . I don't want her back.

I couldn't even bear to see her . . . Tommy turned me on. Not his bloody blindness . . .'

She doesn't like the dog. That imperfect tense, good-as-dead dog. Chilly words hiding even colder thoughts. Resentment? Constant reminder of his disability? Even jealousy? Spends more time with her than me? That goddess, jealous of a mutt? If so, then what else might she have been jealous of?

Mood.

'Hah! You mean, did he top himself? 'Course he bloody didn't! Greatest advocate for life anyone could ever meet. Just look at his work, for heaven's sake. My husband was a patron of the Samaritans for donkey's yonks. And long before that he'd done his share of manning the bloody phones. And doesn't the word "Sunburst" mean anything to you in connection with Tommy? I don't know where you've been the past thirty years . . . You must have seen him often enough on television: with the blind, the sick, the disadvantaged, the dying. They're re-running the Amnesty film on Sunday at 8 p.m. BBC1. I suggest you take a look at it. And, as it happens, he was in a singularly jolly mood on Thursday. He rang me twice. Unicef had finally fixed his Burma visit, plus he'd just been invited to play Pius Thicknesse in the final Harry Potter. Jo Rowling had asked him herself. He was as happy as a sandboy.'

Fatso hadn't meant, did he kill himself? thought Ned, but rather, was there anything on his mind? Still. Same answer, I suppose. Not a cloud in the sky. Everyone a winner. It was like the *Sun*'s black-edged front page: Tommy with a ruddy great glowing halo. Grinning. That 'it may all be ghastly, but let's find the light somewhere' grin. Then there was the cartoon in the *Telegraph*. Tommy is shown arriving at the top of a staircase made of cloud to a vast welcoming host of angels of all ages and colours. The caption: Tommy's old catchphrase: 'Who's your best friend then?'

Secrets. Hmm. With secrets, the questions are always slightly daft. Did your husband keep any secrets from you? How would I know? Did *you* tell *him* everything? Course not – do you tell your wife everything, Chief Inspector? I'm not married, ma'am . . . and that's *Detective* Chief Inspector – but who cares. It's not like I'm doing much detecting . . . Bollocks questions, bollocks answers which slam more doors than they open. Now if someone wants to tell you a secret, that's an entirely different kettle of fish . . . Let's try motives. A few enemies, perhaps?

'Haven't a clue. Ever since that bastard at United Artists died, I don't think Tommy had an enemy in the whole world. He once had a flaming row with Bing Crosby on a golf course, but so what? I deduce that my husband was murdered, not because I can think of someone who wanted him dead, but because there's no other possibility. I refuse to believe he killed himself, and he had absolutely no reason to be down at that dock in the middle of the night. You are looking for a junkie in need of money for a fix, or some young thugs. The kind of little wretches who tie up and rape old ladies and then steal their gas money. A life for two pounds fifty. And what a life . . .'

It was Fatso who quietly broke into her grief, with a surprisingly well-informed thought.

'Sir Thomas must have got a few backs up in the Third World, Dame Angela. I remember seeing him on telly having a good go at the Nigerians when they tried to top that poor woman. Then wasn't there a scene with those Burmese generals a year or two ago? And that whaling business . . . If terrorists can wander about blowing up buses, then how difficult would it be to take out a seventy-six-year-old blind man on a dark night?'

Never mind that Japan isn't conspicuously in the Third World – Fatso had pulled the widow Best up sharply. She started to frown. Stood. Walked to the window. Walked back. Sat. Peered at the para-doxical blob on her sofa, with its rancid jacket and its shortness of breath and its piercing bright eyes.

She then launched into a laundry list of tinpot dictators whose regimes Sir Tommy had had a swipe at directly or in passing. His charity work had taken him to the grimmest places on the globe, and Tommy was not one to keep quiet in defence of the weak. She talked, transporting Fatso and Ned to arid wastes whose rulers studded their estates with grandiose fountains while the people perished from thirst. To sweaty republics in South America whose football stadia needed constant white-washing to blot out the blood splatters. To crucibles of tribal bigotry and slaughter. Hotbeds of persecution. Forced famine. Corruption. Torture. Crimes against children were a particular hate: slavery, child soldiers, sweated labour. The list grew, the shadows lengthened. At one point Ned was convinced that Fatso had fallen asleep, and became desperately worried that he'd start to snore. He tried to slide close enough to him for a surreptitious prod or kick, but the sofa was too big, and Fatso too far away. Not that Dame Angie was likely to notice a wake-up nudge. She was becoming increasingly unaware of anything outside her as she worked through her husband's long fight for freedom and justice. Ned realised that Fatso could probably snore as loud as he liked, could take his trousers off and stand on his head and it wouldn't make a jot of difference to Dame Angela Dalkey. She was lost in Tommy's campaigns, like a general's loyal widow. The list of suspects expanded beyond the noting. The dockyard became peopled with assassins, blow-pipes behind every bollard. Polonium sprayed from gratings. Bullets from gantries. Just before he realised he was himself starting to nod off, Ned had a vision of a queue of killers, like the water-carrying broomsticks in *Fantasia*, marching in grotesque step behind a blind old man and his faithful dog as they groped in utter darkness towards a gaping hole.

Ned and Fatso turned into the hospital car park to find Doc Bones sitting in his car by the barrier. Fatso leaned past Ned, nearly suffocating him.

'In one word, Doc, what was it?'

'Drowning. *Indicia nulla theatri gallinarum.*'

'That's ten words,' Fatso bellowed. 'And nine of 'em are crap!' He turned to Ned for a translation.

'He says there's no sign of the theatre of chickens. He means foul play, sir.'

'What about the crack on the back of his head?'

Doc Bones shrugged.

'Bounced off the woodwork on the way down, I'd say. Still doing matching tests with the timber fragments . . . But it wasn't the cause of death.'

'The water he drowned in – was it the same as the water in the dock?'

'*Non dubium est.*'

Fatso turned again to Ned.

'He says definitely.'

'Ask him about the time of death.'

Ned blinked, but put the question to Doc Bones.

'*Quando . . . tempo mortis . . . erat*?'

'With the body in water, can't be categorical. Sometime between midnight and 6 a.m. Give or take.'

Doc Bones started his car.

'*A fronte praecipitium, a tergo lupi.*'

And Doc roared away. Fatso sat back waiting; Ned had to think about this one.

'"Precipice ahead, wolves behind," I think. Not sure who Doc means.'

Fatso yawned like a hippo. They were back on the main road before he spoke. Slow. Definite.

'Drowned doesn't mean it wasn't murder. Drowning doesn't mean that. It just describes something that happened to Tommy after he hit the water. Tells us fuck all about what happened in the moments before. Drowning's Doc Bones's business. But what happened in those moments, eh? That's *our* business. What did Doc say? "Precipice ahead and wolves up your bum." Nice one. Poor old Tommy. We've got to find those bastard wolves. Drop me off at the boozer, old cock.'

Ned got to the Docks early. Cold, sunny, dead quiet. Just a few Scene of Crime bods sniffing about. Time to think. Spring tide. Mud strip under water. Not so smelly today. Matey's crane on the move, swinging a cement mixer through a flock of starlings. Given that Doc Bones had failed to find any stab wounds or bullet holes – that the evidence from the victim himself was entirely consistent with an accident – then Ned had to find out if such an accident were possible. They'd rigged a ladder from the quayside to the walkway, and up he went.

The walkway was now tented over. Planks straddling the girders to make sure no one walked on the timbers. Right. Let's not fuss about what Tommy's doing here. Let's just try to piece the event together. We know just one thing for sure: Tommy drowned in this cesspool. Work backwards from that. Man flies up out of the shit through a crumbling hole onto the rotten catwalk. Steps backwards. Freeze. Is dog up there with him? Let's say: yes. Ah. Dog has pulled up smartish. Has spotted gaping hole in the dark at the last moment. Run it forward. Dog tries to stop master. Bit of a tussle. Don't know why master doesn't obey dog. Need to know more about seeing dogs and the blind. Harness suddenly breaks. Man jerks backwards, falls through hole. Dog, distraught, legs it for help. Hmmm. Stop. Does man turn to have his tug-of-war with dog? That would be the obvious thing to do. If so, cannot have clipped his head on this side of the hole. Or does he stay facing forward and pull dog with arm stretched out behind him? Isn't that a bit awkward, or do blind people prefer to stay facing the direction of travel? And would the harness just break like that?

Ned stared at the hole for a bit, then spotted a familiar face from Forensics taking photographs below.

'Billy?'

'Coming and running, sir.'

'Do you know if samples were taken along each of these edges?'

'Did it myself, Mr N. Doc Bones had 'em day one. If you're going to talk to him, do you want my sketch map?'

Ned nodded and Billy hared off. Ned stared down through the hole at the murk of the basin. Wonder if they should just have drained the whole thing? Probably valueless now. With the sluice gaping, no one could be sure that what's in there now didn't float in after Tommy's death. Thanks Billy. Right, Doc. Let's be having you.

'Hullo, Doc Bones. Any point in draining the basin?'

Doc wasn't convinced. 'It's not as if we're looking for a gun, Nedicus old chap. Or a dead dog.'

'On another tack, Doc. Did you play "I Spy" with the scrapes from along the edges of the hole?'

'*Certe*. Just emailed the stuff to Extrus Bilgus. Sir Tommy passed though your hole all right. You say you're there now? Hold hard . . . B6 is your bit. Yes. B6.'

'What's special about B6, Doc?'

'It's got traces of Sir Thomas's skin and blood on the upper outward edge of the *plankus*. Ties in with that abrasion on the back of his bonce.'

Ned orientated Billy's sketch map with each plank carefully labelled. So if Tommy had come from the Lassiter Street end, he'd have to have turned through 180° so as to crack the back of his head on B6 as he fell. Or been manhandled round.

'By the way, Doc, isn't *tabula* the Latin for plank? Not *plankus*. Doc? Doc?'

Next puzzle: what were they doing on the rotten, as opposed to the new catwalk? Note – this is not the same question as: what were they doing up there at all? It's about *how* they strayed onto the wrong catwalk. Again, let's assume the most innocent scenario.

Ned walked away from the hole and almost immediately bumped into Span. Span looked very pleased with herself. Span's tail was all awag. Morning Jan Span. Morning sir. What've you got, Jan Span? Span had money. Or rather, didn't have money. Span didn't have a thousand pounds that the National Treasure had withdrawn from several city-centre holes in the wall in the afternoon and was not on his person when he plunged into the Styx that night. Tommy hadn't had to fork out for dinner – that was all paid for by the organisers of the retrospective. His PR person had been with him when he took the money out and was with him right through till he said he'd walk back to the hotel. No way could Sir T can have spent it without – and Span had to check her notes here – Zara Canley-Carlton noticing. Or C-C as Tommy used to call her.

Ned examined the printout from one of the banks. The frame-grab from the security camera of Sir Thomas at the cashpoint. The photo-copy of the credit card Sir Thomas used to take out the money.

'Before you ask, sir, C-C is filthy rich. Really unlikely she rolled the old boy. Plus she's got the barman at The Metropole and half Real Madrid giving her an alibi for the hours in question.'

Ned nodded and smiled.

'Spick and I reckon his killer or killers must have recognised him. See, they left him his credit cards. All sorts. Platinums. Even an Amex Black. Well, they'd have been useless. Got to be one of the most recognisable faces in the world.'

'You've done good.'

She gave a broad grin. Replaced the papers in her folder. Was just turning away when . . .

'He had other money on him, didn't he?'

Span stopped and checked in the folder.

'Yes, he did. He had . . . £17.60 in a tenner and coins. Sixty euros in twenties. And a hundred-dollar bill.'

'Why not nick that as well?'

'I dunno. Maybe he handed them the thousand and they thought, fair play . . .'

'. . . and then they pushed him through the hole. Maybe. One more thing. How often did Sir Thomas withdraw sums like that? Was it unusual?'

'Dunno. An' now I owe Spick two drinks. He said you'd come back with things we couldn't answer. We're onto it.'

Ned followed the turns, rises and falls in the two walkways. According to Extra Bilge, the old one was built by Thomas Telford himself a million years ago and so was listed. The council couldn't pull it down, but if they simply closed it, they'd be chopping a chunk out of the Great River Towpath and that would never do. The Docks were at the heart of the city's regeneration scheme. Though the National Treasure drowning in them might put a bit of a crimp in that. Maybe not. Maybe it'd be good for ghoul tourism. Anyway, the council had built a new walkway alongside the old.

The twins rose behind the Bonded Warehouse in Lassiter Street. Snaked around a gasometer. Over a dry dock. Past the old Ropery. Eventually both dropped down adjacent flights of steps into a cobbled terrace street of old dockers' cottages. 'Police Line Do Not Cross' tape blocked the foot of both staircases, but Mr Telford's was also heavily gated, with signs warning of dangerous structures, sheer drop, doom and death. At which end of the walkways had Tommy Best started? Either way, his presence on the old one must surely have been against his will. Ned had seen no easy way to slip from the safe new walkway to the fatal old one. The dog would have to have led her master under two sets of handrails. Made no sense. Didn't fit. Ned was staring at the gate when who should pop up to disturb the peace but Extra Bilge.

Extra Bilge had buck teeth and wild eyes. He looked like a mad horse. He'd been banned from every pub quiz in a radius of a hundred miles, ninety-nine of which were overkill as Extra Bilge didn't get out much. Except to crime scenes, and Extra Bilge LOVED crime scenes. They didn't have to be gruesome. He didn't get off on shards of bone and saliva. He wasn't a sicko – what he liked were boring details. It came in handy if they told a story about a crime, but if they didn't, that was fine too. Extra Bilge had all but moved into the betting shop by the station during the case they called Big Bill's Bookie Blag. In fact, the team thought he had. One day Spick found a bed-roll under the counter that no one claimed but had a well-thumbed copy of *Bus Route Monthly* for June 1977 stuffed down the foot. Then Extra Bilge said he'd have the mag, if no one else wanted it, 'cos he was missing that one. It's all yours, son.

How do, Extra Bilge. Hullo, Mr Ned, sir. Phone networks dodgy today? Pardon, sir? Getting a lot of visits, that's all. Oh. Anyway. And Extra Bilge got out his notebook.

'We've had a good go at the swabs from the dog's paws. There's no way of saying for sure she was on the walkway . . .'

'Which?'

'The old one. We don't think she was ever on the new one, because the red oxide is starting to flake. Shoddy job, clearly.

23

Should have used an etch primer. Needs a repaint. Now we did find minute traces of algae that match samples we took along the old walkway, but they also match samples taken from the footbridge over there . . .'

'You're saying we can't place Suzy definitely on the old walkway because there were other places round here where she could have picked up this algae?'

Ned knew he had a nasty habit of interrupting Extra Bilge and felt a bit bad about it. Extra Bilge, for his part, loved interruptions because they were almost always invitations to get deeper into details. Lovely scrummy details.

'Precisely. I don't know how much you know about the design of dogs' paws, Mr Ned sir, but I've worked up some 3D drawings from a set of casts Miss Kate took. Now, if you'll just take a look, you'll see that there are four pads on each paw. Now we walk on our soles, as do bears. By the way, this part is called the *metatarsus*. You'd know it better as the rear pastern. But dogs walk on their toes. Like the horse. The equivalent of the human heel is the hock, here, but that doesn't touch the ground. Do you see? You've got all the weight forward on these pads. Four pads means three gaps, with four paws per dog equals twelve potential zones in which particles can be trapped by all that downward pressure. Now what makes this even more gripping, Mr Ned, is the figures. Three gaps averaging 22mm in length and 8mm in depth with a mean expansion of 6mm. This expansion gap is of course triangular in plan, given that the toes splay outwards, but I've pro-rata'd it. Times four. That's a total paw particle catchment area – what I call the TPPCA – of a whopping 12,672 cubic millimetres per dog.'

Ned shook his head in wonderment. At the information. At Extra Bilge. At himself for not dashing his own brains out on the cobbles there and then. Extra Bilge might have preferred an interruption, because he still had some details up his sleeve, but he settled for Ned's wonderfully affirmative headshake.

'Now, sir. I'm sure this has already occurred to you, but then there's the fur.'

'Ah, the fur.'

'Exactly, you see. It isn't just what we call pad and gap. There's also the fur. Now I've had this detail magnified by two hundred and you can see that the hairs work in a much modified version of the way Velcro does. There's a doggy connection here, Mr Ned, because Georges de Mestral, the Swiss gentleman who invented Velcro, got the idea from a close examination of the burrs that became adhered to his dog's fur during their daily walks in the Alps. There are no clues, incidentally, from the historical record, what kind of dog this was, but a St Bernard must be a candidate. Did you know that the leader of the pack at the hospice of Menthon on the Great St Bernard Pass was by custom always called Barry?'

Ned needed to sit down and drink a bottle of absinthe. Supposing all this stuck in his brain? He'd have to go for a lobotomy. Then he realised Extra Bilge had fallen silent.

'Extra Bilge?'

Extra Bilge had lapsed into a daze. Perhaps he'd over-detailed. He really did look even more like a mad horse today than usual.

'Yes, Mr Ned?'

'I want to make sure I've understood . . .'

Extra Bilge's senses sharpened. He smelled the possibility of a recap, with all a recap's opportunities for digression.

'. . . the dog never set foot on the new walkway, because if she had, the furry gaps in her paddy paws would contain traces of oxide paint.'

Very clever, our Mr Ned. Got it in one. No chance of re-explaining it all a slightly different way.

'Precisely.'

'Now what I'm really interested in, is this old walkway. That's why I was standing here, at the foot of it, when you came along . . .'

Ned detected the rising impatience in his own voice. Veer away. Stay calm.

'. . . which was very timely, because I need to know if they went up these steps to the rotten old walkway. Or did they get onto it from Lassiter Street?'

The mad horse lifted his head and bared his teeth in excited anticipation. This was the question he had been praying for.

'Well now, Mr Ned. It seems they used to load lime into railway wagons along here. And sure enough, we've found traces of lime and ash and iron oxide – rust to you – in Suzy's TPPCA. The really interesting thing is that we haven't been able to find this particular combination of elements anywhere else in the Docks. So we know Suzy must have come this way. Plus there are matching traces on the soles of Mr Best's shoes. Albeit very much on the faint side, though, owing to the shoes being in very dirty water for several hours.'

Getting somewhere, at last. Ned looked round. They *had* been here. In this nothing little street with its rundown houses and its mossy cobbles and its engineers' blue-brick wall. This may have been where – sinister scenario – Suzy was separated from her master by enough force to break her harness. What about the harness?

'Yes, Mr Ned sir. You've guessed it. There are prints on the harness: Mr Best's for sure, and those of several other people. We've found no match on the Police National Computer.'

'You'll need to eliminate everyone: family, closest friends, the PR woman. The organisers of the retrospective . . .'

And yet, even as he was saying it, Ned found himself remembering the photo of Suzy on the Incident Room wall. The printed yellow cloth on her back: *Do not pet me – I am working!* Touching the dog harness of a blind man. Bit intimate? Or just insensitive?

'Thanks, Extra Bilge. It's very helpful. Great.'

Extra Bilge whinnied appreciatively.

'Thanks, Mr Ned. Do you want me to leave you this stuff? About the paws? There's another full set on your desk.'

'On my desk is fine. Thanks again.'

Ned resolutely turned back to the gate, but couldn't focus on it until he'd heard the last of Extra Bilge's hoofbeats. The more he looked at it, the less obvious it was that the gate, for all its forbidding appearance, was actually locked. So he decided to give it a tug. Enough slack in the police tape. Gloves on. Go for it.

'It's not locked, you know.'

A man was peering at Ned over the blue-brick wall. He was about forty, with a green woollen pom-pom hat, smoking a roll-up.

'You with the rozzers?'

Ned nodded.

'Like I say, it's not locked. There was a chain an' padlock, but they 'ad that off, day one. Then every time the council chains it up again, they 'as it off.'

'Who is it who takes the chain?'

'They call themselves the Psycho . . . I dunno . . . Psych . . . iotrists. See them knobs all along the new rail? Well the old one's smooth, innit? They can cycle from the far end all the way down to here.'

'What – cycle along the railing?'

The man nodded and took a drag.

'On the rims, of course. No tyres. Only I 'aven't seen you before.'

Ned examined the cobbles at the foot of the steps.

'You won't see nothing. They use mattresses, to break their fall. Otherwise they'd cattle their wheels, wouldn't they?'

'Are these "Psychiatrists" local lads?'

'All over. Come from all over. Not round here so much. Well, it's a competitive sport, innit. They've done a video – trying to interest Sky an' that. Seen loads of your mob. Just not you.'

Ned wandered over to him.

'So does the gate normally hang open? Before. When we didn't have our tape across it?'

'Does an' it doesn't, if you get my meaning. It'll wodge closed, or you could look out an' find it gaping. If them . . . Psyches 'ave been through. With the rozzers, eh? Only you don't look like one. What d'you do, then?'

'Poke about a bit,' said Ned.

The man nodded.

'Only I'm not as tall as this usually. I'm standing on a milk crate.'

'I wondered,' said Ned with a smile and turned back yet again to the gate.

''Ere. You're with the rozzers. Do you know Terry Press?'

'No,' said Ned over his shoulder. 'What does he do?'

'He's a thief.'

The man nodded at Ned and sank out of sight.

Fatso wanted to see him when he got in. Face full of lardy cake. I'm under pressure, Ned, to release the body. Big pressure. It's not the Westminster Abbey thing the *Mail*'s on about – Dame Angie wants him back sharpish for local planting. Family and close friends job. No sweaty hacks. Place for you – see if you can pick the murderer out of the mourners. The Dog Tart'll go with you. They want the mutt there. Suits us. Murderer spots the only witness to his cold-blooded crime sitting on a tomb licking its balls, freaks out, breaks down, confesses. What do we know?

Ned told him. About the way Sir Tommy fell, facing forwards. The missing money. The trick cyclists and the open gate. The possibility that the dog never got as far as the old walkway. That it wasn't quite adding up.

'Bits and pieces they may be, Ned the Yid, but they nudge us closer. National Treasure bumbles off the end of the pier all accidental? Naagh. Dogs don't abandon their masters, let alone blind dogs. He went through that hole alone, his dog ripped from him, light a grand in cash. This is murder, Ned, murder. And the choice is rich. One: ugly toe-rags mug the National Treasure for his dosh, or two: old mucker with a grudge, or three: loony Arabs got him down for a Solomon Rusty. Bit stumped? Phone a friend!'

Ned suggested that the best person to phone might be Doc Bones. Check he'd finished with the body. Fatso rang him there and then. A moment's thought and Doc Bones cleared Sir Thomas Best for take-off. In that case, Ned said, he had no objection. After all, the one thing they were sure of was the cause of death. Exactly, said Fatso, plus we can always dig the bugger up later when no one's looking. Get Span to sober up the coroner and it'll be lardy cake all round.

On his way out of the office Spick added to Ned's growing sense that he was wading in treacle. He was compiling a list of people, states or organisations with possible grudges against Sir Thomas Best. Ned should have it by the end of the week. It was already three sides of A4: tin-pot dictatorships, corrupt companies screwing the Third World, exploiters of children, of animals, of the environment, of the air, of the planet, of you, of me. Apparently absolutely everybody adored Tommy, except for those who hated his guts.

So Ned went home: to an empty fridge, nothing on the telly, and a death-enhancing call from his mum on the answer machine. That really irritating mix of pathetic bleating and dishing out the guilt. So he poured himself a stiff drink and thought about Kate.

3

NO ONE KNEW WHO SHE was. No one knew who they were. They were invisible. And they kept out of people's way. Every morning they'd get into her unmarked van and drive to the edge of the city, park and walk deep into the countryside. The dog ran free now, with just the occasional stop and look back. Major triumph. At first, she wouldn't leave Kate's side. She wouldn't do anything to please herself. She looked as if she was punishing herself, hard. That first day, she just sat with the saddest look, waiting. Waiting for what? Certainly not food – not at all hungry. Didn't want to go out. Wouldn't play. Then when she realised that whatever she was waiting for wasn't going to happen, she put herself to bed, panting a little. She panted herself asleep, but it took hours. Kate sat on the sofa, watching her. After a while, she realised that tears were trickling down her cheeks.

She left the bedroom door open so she could watch the dog. They woke within minutes of one another in the early morning. For a moment, the dog seemed back to normal. A lick, a scratch, a shake, a wag. Then, a moment later, it was as if she had remembered her burden. Her shoulders sagged, her head drooped as though the emptiness was beating her down. She had all the usual readjustments that seeing dogs – and people – have to make in the early days of retirement, acclimatising themselves to the loss of timetable, of responsibilities, of others who need you. But this was worse. This was bleak. Kate knew all about reading human responses into animal behaviour. Her veterinary nurse training had sorted that. But you didn't need two years in college to see that this dog was in a mess. So she cuddled her, rubbed her tummy, spoke soft words into those lovely ears. You're a poor broken dog, she said, and I'm going to help you put yourself back together. That's what I had to do for myself, and now I'll do it with you.

Kate took the news about the funeral badly. About having to attend it. Her worst thing was to be seen. She had a carefully chosen wardrobe of ill-fitting clothes and nothing much for best. She lived in baggy coveralls. She had a seminal childhood memory of a film on the telly one wet Sunday afternoon. Black and white and doom-laden. It wasn't a cosy film to curl up in front of. She watched it with her Nan, sitting almost formally by her side on the sofa, gripping her hand tight. A brave man parachuted into occupied France. She and Nan knew the Germans were waiting for him behind hedges, but all he could see were the fields of his beloved France coming up to meet him. He landed and quickly gathered in the parachute. For a moment, the wind gusted and enclosed him in silk. She thought, seeing it then, that it would make the man invisible. If only he could stay like that, wrapped in the billowing white cloth, the nasty men in black leather coats with guns would never spot him. He'd be safe.

Baggy coveralls were brilliant. Not only could no one get any impression of her body from the folds and bulges; she couldn't feel herself. No waist, no hips, no breasts. Just air and the occasional brush of material. Nothing binding. But could she wear saggy baggy coveralls to the funeral of the decade? Her colleagues in the Dog Team were adamant. No way, DT. You gotta wear black, girl. Pencil skirt, black stockings. Like you're really the grieving widow. Remember that pic of Cate at Heath Ledger's funeral . . . great sunglasses . . . Yuh, right. As if the DT is going to do that. Get real. The plot wasn't to get the Dog Tart to show a leg, but scare her off. They had a lottery as to which of them would squire Suzy once the DT bottled out. It was all about the celebs. Being there with fantasy figures like Mick and L'Wren, Elton, Sienna and Chelsy and the Princes . . . with half of them coming up to stroke the poor bereaved pooch, standing so close you could smell their aftershave.

Millie rehearsed a range of dialogue responses, appropriate to Jude Law and Lewis Hamilton and Daniel Craig. She crafted them on the bus and in the bath. She'd got up to thirty-seven bespoke exchanges, without the foggiest idea who in fact would be at the funeral, before Kate stopped by the unit to say she was going to take Suzy herself. Definite. Yeah, DT. But wotcha going to wear? Easy peasy, said Kate. I'm going to wear my uniform. And she turned on her wellington-booted heels and tripped away with Suzy. The prospect of all those dazzling celebs had blinded them to the obvious: uniform. They felt a bit daft as they busied themselves with mucking out the vans, and doing paperwork and checking the puppies. Well, makes sense, her going in an official capacity. It's not like she is in mourning. Nah. She's representing the Force. That's the only reason she's going.

The backlash came later as they ate their lunch in the tack room. Lucky bitch. Not as if she cares about celebs. They'll be wasted on her. We could always give her my camera. It's dead tiny. We need photies and lists and autographs. And then there's who she's going with. That Ned. He's sexier than all them celebs rolled together. No foreskin, Jewish men. Less sensitivity. Keep going all night. Jammy Dog Tart. She's gotta tell us everything . . . There was a long pause while they munched their sarnies.

'That true about Jewish men?' asked the new girl who handled one of the sniffer dogs.

'So my auntie always reckoned,' replied Pauline, dreamily. 'She done her gap year on a kibbutz. Didn't get a wink of sleep.'

It was Ned who suggested uniform was appropriate to the occasion. He'd rung Kate to ask how the dog was, and she slipped in a breezily innocent question about dress code for the funeral. He said he'd be in a dark suit – what he called his funeral suit

– because he wasn't uniformed branch. Uniform for her then. It wasn't billowing parachute silk, but it would have to do. Anyway, there was something about being ordered to do things – it took away the burden. Probably why she'd joined the force in the first place. Her job had a framework of discipline, but with bags of leeway. The clincher, though, wasn't the uniform, but the dog. She couldn't bear the thought of anyone else having her, not even for a couple of hours.

When she took charge of Suzy, Large Sarge removed her from all other duties. The others didn't resent it. They knew Kate was the best they had. The Dog Unit never accepted a puppy without her approval. If a puppy walker was having a problem, send in the Dog Tart. Dog feeling a bit peaky? A case for Dr Kate. Specialist training needed – cocaine, Semtex, firearms? She'd work with the handler to get the spaniel sniffing right, or the German Shepherd happy to go into dodgy buildings with a camera on its head. She'd taken a rescue spaniel puppy and trained her on explosives to such a pitch that the pair had virtually joined the Royal Protection Squad. They used to say Her Majesty wouldn't open a new hospital without Banshee's bark of approval. Kate put her foot down over one Border Collie who passed his tests with flying colours. Said he wasn't to be trusted. Large Sarge reluctantly backed her and pensioned off the mutt. Nothing happened for a year, and then the owner took it to watch his kid playing football. For no apparent reason, the dog went wild. It broke away and took chunks out of several young legs flashing by. Since Banshee, Kate hadn't had her own dog; she worked across the whole unit, wherever needed. But now she had Suzy.

Ned and Kate went their separate ways to the funeral. He'd wondered about picking her up, but she left a message to say she was bringing Suzy in her van and would see him there. So he drove into the countryside with just Tommy Best for company. Tommy Best on a *Desert Island Discs* repeat.

'. . . *and there was just a sea of corpses. I had never seen anything like it. Everywhere you looked, dead people. I couldn't believe there was no one alive, so I walked out into this . . . landscape of death. I'm not trying to be poetic; it's just that words are all you've got, and words aren't up to it. Not mine, anyway . . . I've tried to describe it before, and I'm always stumped . . . The people who were with me tried to stop me. Called me back. Disease, contagion . . . I don't know. Balderdash, I thought, and walked on.*

It wasn't easy finding a place for my feet. At first that really bothered me: trampling the dead. Then I thought, what the hell. If I trigger a cry of pain, I'll have found a live one. I don't know how far I walked. I didn't look back. It was extraordinary. And extraordinarily beautiful. That's an odd thing – I've never thought that before. But it was. They wear such flowing, colourful clothes, and there was a light wind, and it shimmered. It was like a psychedelic ocean. And they were all dead. With one exception . . .

I heard it before I saw it. It wasn't crying, you know. For some reason people always say it was the crying that alerted me. Don't know where they get that from. There wasn't any crying. It was making that gurgling, chortling, happy sound that babies make. Why not? It was curled up in its mother's arms, next to its dad. It was happy. It had no idea it was an orphan. I picked it up. It was a little girl. Then she saw the look on my face. I don't know . . . I thought I was smiling at her, but that's obviously not how it seemed to her. Her expression changed to the bleakest I've ever seen on a human being . . . devastating. And then she let out this truly terrible wail. I turned, and that was the moment when the photograph was taken . . .'

'*. . . the famous photograph . . .*'

'*The famous photograph. He must have been following me . . . at a distance, because in the photo you can see the dead rippling all around me. I thought I was alone. Just me and that tiny baby . . . And then click! . . . So I carried her back . . . Before, I said "one exception", but if you think about it, Kirsty, how could I know there weren't others alive, further on? Only I never went further on. I had the baby. They got their snap. End of story.*'

'*Remarkable story, Sir Thomas, and a remarkable life. Now, I'm*

*going to maroon you on a desert island – how do you think you'll
cope without family – and without an audience . . . ?'*

By Fatso's standards, the funeral was very discreetly policed. Ned
half expected snipers on roof tops, SWAT teams pretending to mend
the road and bogus undertakers with earpieces talking to themselves.
But no. The emphasis was on keeping the press and public behind
crash barriers; inside the churchyard Ned saw plenty of people he
recognised but no one he knew. He went back outside and waited
for Kate and the dog. It was a day of bright light, but strangely little
heat. The whole place looked like a foreigner's impression of an
English village, and the church played its part to the hilt. Ned's
attention wandered to the ancient yews and the stocky tower with
its gleaming dolphin weather-vane, and he completely missed Kate
arrive. She'd almost reached the lychgate and safety but then
someone shouted 'Suzy!' and a swarm of photographers and news
cameramen darted over the barrier and buzzed around her. Ned saw
the commotion, thought it was yet another movie star, and was about
to drift back into his Pevsner reverie when he realised the hacks had
watched half Hollywood plip-plopping out of Rolls-Royces without
lifting more than a shutter-finger. The centre of the storm had to be
something else. Must be the dog. He dived across the road and was
about to get rugged, when the swarm parted of its own accord.

Ned had only once before seen her in anything but her trademark coveralls, and was as knocked sideways by what he saw as
the press was. If she'd been on a police recruiting poster it would
have been rejected as total fantasy. Dazzling as she was on the
outside, on the inside she was frazzling. It took all her will-power
to keep walking and not turn with Suzy and run. She stopped,
looked straight into the bristling lenses and very quietly said the
word 'Please', and the hard hearts melted. Or maybe they'd got
their snaps of the nation's favourite pooch with the wet dream of
a WPC. Either way, they retreated to squat again like vultures on
their stepladders. Revealed as they parted, was a familiar face.
Thank God.

Seeing Kate's utter vulnerability, and sensing how much this must be costing her, Ned seized her firmly by the elbow and, showing their invitations to the security guards, walked her into the sanctuary of the churchyard. As he did so, he realised he shouldn't be touching her. Hoped the television cameras hadn't caught the gesture. Dreaded the crop of innuendoes and rash of screen-savers. He pulled his hand away and bent down to stroke the dog. Kate was fairly shocked to have been touched by Ned, but reassured to see how he was greeting Suzy. It was a way of judging people, how they were with animals. He seemed fine.

'Look, Grangie! It's Suzy!'

He looked up and there was a boy of about six with Tommy Best's eyes and Tommy Best's forehead and Tommy Best's mouth. In fact, he looked exactly like his grandfather in that 1937 black and white Dickens film, the tiny figure standing in the doorway of the factory staring at the whirring machines, with a look of bemused awe. Just before Charles Laughton sends him flying. Dame Angie glided over and greeted Ned with surprising warmth. Kate received a regal nod, and the dog a brusque pat. She looked the epitome of svelte in mourning as she glided away with her grandson playing tugboat.

The two police officers and the dog joined the crowd funnelling into the church. Ahead of them Ned saw the brown-armed girl – Chippy, was it? – being supported by a brace of ancient theatrical knights. He could see her skin whitened around their gnarled fingers. They held her so tightly she looked as if her feet weren't touching the ground. More gliding, thought Ned. At the door they were handed an order of service and an envelope for donations. A well-meaning usher asked if they would like a pew at the back, 'so the dog can get out if it needs to' but Kate shook her head. Her instinct would have been to embrace the obscurity of the back row, but the idea that Suzy might need to be removed suddenly offended her. They moved down the aisle and tucked themselves into a pew which contained most of the actors who have ever played James Bond. Not that Kate cared. Out in the throng, Suzy had gone unnoticed, but as soon as she sat down at the edge of the aisle whispers started and heads turned. Kate suddenly felt even more protective. Most of the looks were of happy recognition followed by 'aaahs' and sympathetic smiles for the dog who had lost her master. But Suzy also received a couple of hard stares and small, slow shakes of the head as if to say 'There's the dog who let down her master.' Kate stroked the nape of Suzy's neck, subduing a blush of indignant anger.

It wasn't the first murder case funeral Ned had attended, but for some reason the sight of Sir Tommy's coffin gave him a start. What if Doc Bones had failed to stitch everything back up? He got a sudden, ghastly vision of a trickle of blood coming from a corner. Then there was the central mystery: what had happened to the old man? What were they missing? Had they learned absolutely everything from the body, or would they be doing a Burke and Hare at dead of night? And then there was the dog. What if she could smell her master through the mahogany, silk and formaldehyde? The undertakers got closer. Suzy had stood when the congregation rose, and she now turned her head as Sir Tommy was carried slowly past. She watched, but didn't move. Ned felt Kate's tension compounding his own. The coffin receded down the aisle and was lowered onto its trestles. They gave tiny sighs of relief. The dog-lead was slack, but Kate gripped it in both hands, so he held the order of service for them. 'Immortal, Invisible, God Only Wise'. He liked that one. '. . . Thy justice like mountains high soaring above . . .' Kate relaxed a little, and as she did, became aware of him singing the hymn. He knew the tune and he knew the words. Barely looked down. Funny. What was he doing knowing a Christian hymn, and him Jewish. Mind you, the Jews believed in the Old Testament, didn't they? It was the New Testament which was just for Christians. Perhaps it was an Old Testament hymn. She scanned the words. No mention of Jesus. That was probably it. She didn't know much about Judaism, and the same went for Ned. All through school he'd gone to assembly with everyone else, not wanting to stick out, not wanting an exemption like Joey Abrams and the

Mendozas. They'd file in, very self-consciously, for the notices at the end, along with Bunny Singh and the Moslem Mob. The irony was, he alone of the Jews in school became the school Jew. Became known as Yid. He was sharp enough not to fight it, though Big Towaali from Uganda told him that if any of them ever called him Nigger, he'd rip their balls off. Ned let it ride, and in time it became clear that he was accepted in a way that the Mendozas never were. '. . . *O help us to see, 'Tis only the splendour of light hideth thee.*'

When everyone sat, so after a moment, did Suzy. Ned's eyes darted around the church. Evidently the Prince of Wales had slipped in during the hymn, because he was now sitting next to one of the theatrical knights bookending Chippy. If you weren't at this funeral, you were nobody. The fashionable end of show business rubbed padded shoulders with royalty and the great and the good, in a rippling sea of black hung over with a haze of expensive perfume. The sea was studded with islands of poor taste: an excess of veils, priceless but garish baubles, a forestful of fox around emaciated necks. Then there were the berets, scarves and bow-ties – worn, Ned presumed, in the bohemian pretence that film is the legitimate child of Impressionist painting and revolution. Or perhaps it was just that these people were, for once, wearing their own clothes – with all the attendant risks.

So Chanel No. 5 and Monsieur de Givenchy, astrakhan collars and Jimmy Choo shoes knelt. Stood. Sang. Sat. Listened. Ned swore a binding oath with himself on his mother's life that he would not look down at Kate's legs during the prayers, and kept it fairly well until his attention wandered during a particularly dull Senegalese invocation for the dead. On balance he felt that trading his mother into the fires of hell, to which she was going anyway, for that glimpse was worth it. So he did it again.

Kate's grip on Ned's religious convictions slipped completely during the *Nunc Dimittis*. She could understand he might approve of a light to lighten the Gentiles, and might well want to vote for an abundance of glory to the Father, but shouldn't he have stopped there? Where did he get off glorifying the Son? Let alone the Holy

Ghost? What if his rabbi found out? If he even had one. Perhaps he wasn't Jewish. Just clever. Suzy was lying down now. That's better. Home stretch. She hoped they didn't have to go to the graveside. Probably just be close family. Nearly there.

But they weren't nearly there. During the final blessing, a screen was lowered silently in front of the altar. They were obviously going to give Sir Tommy the last word. Kate should have taken the usher's kind offer. She nudged Ned and gestured down at the dog.

'I don't know how she'll react. If she hears his voice. It could really upset her,' she whispered.

'Should you take her out?'

'I don't know if I can . . .'

She hivered and hovered, and was about to make her move, when the coffin was lifted to begin its slow journey to the grave, with Dame Angie and close family ranged behind. She could hardly get up now and walk with the dog ahead of the coffin. Then the screen sprang to life, filled with images of Tommy Best. The first clip was the exact moment from the film that Ned had recalled in the churchyard: the urchin staring into the factory and getting the kick from Laughton. Suzy didn't react, didn't recognise her master's voice in the child's yelp and his famous tirade which followed it. But Kate guessed the clips would span Sir Tommy's life. She pulled Suzy out of the aisle and tucked her down at her and Ned's feet. The coffin went by. As the clips ran, Suzy grew more and more alert. She looked up at Kate, then tried to turn around. On the screen Sir Tommy brought his battered destroyer through the Western Approaches, tangoed with Sophia Loren by moonlight in the Piazza Navona, swung a punch at John Wayne, cross-examined Bruce Willis and walked Sandra Bullock to the altar. Suzy started to get agitated. She whimpered. She tugged at her lead. The nearest James Bond tried to distract her with a peppermint, but in vain. The end of the family procession was just going by, when Kate made a decision. She stood, straightened her skirt, and led the dog out into the aisle, bringing up the rear. She carried it off with such cool that everyone thought it must have been planned. While Sir Tommy

harangued and fought and laughed and played everyone from God
to a DreamWorks walrus, his seeing dog stepped slowly from him.
She and Kate had just reached the doorway when Sir Tommy's
voice boomed out from his last film: 'Here, girl. Don't go! I need
you!' The congregation knew he was addressing Keira Knightley,
but those who had seen his dog leaving – and that was half the
church – looked back. And then everyone turned. Dead silence.
Suzy stopped, silhouetted in the open door. She turned her head
the merest fraction. 'I didn't mean it, girl,' said her master in a
broken voice, and his dog walked away into the light.

The montage ended, almost inevitably, with the still of Sir Tommy
standing in the sea of corpses holding the baby. 'Dear Chippy. Poor
wee scrap,' murmured the 007 with the mints, confirming Ned's
guess: she of the brown arms was the baby Tommy had rescued
from the charnel desert. So what was the chronology, Ned asked
himself as he waited to file out of the pew. How old is Chippy?
When did Tommy lose his sight? When did he get Suzy? Who are
the parents of the little spitting image? This was a job for Extra
Bilge. A family tree and chronology. And not just when did Tommy
lose his sight, but how much of it did he lose? He didn't know
nearly enough about Sir Thomas Best, and if they continued to
draw blanks with a stranger as killer, that would become more and
more important. The Bonds all rose to their feet beside him, and as
Ned was hardly going to get in their way, he stood too and started
to shuffle out.

'Angie says you're on the case,' came the familiar brogue in his
ear. 'We need your best shot.'

Ned turned and had to look up.

'Did you know him well, Sir Sean?'

'Well, we had a bit in common: a couple of movies, golf, a girl
or two – before Angie and Micheline, of course. And we must have
got through a still of malt together. Don't waste your time, Inspector
– it is Inspector? No one who knew Tommy could have done it.
You find the guy, Inspector, you find him and give us a call. Just
need five minutes with him.'

He squeezed Ned's shoulder hard to seal the arrangement. Once out of the church the Bonds were claimed by a trio of *Avengers* girls, and Ned looked for Kate and her charge. They were on a slight rise, watching the scene around the grave from a distance. People kept coming up to see the dog, stroke her, talk about what was going to happen to her now. Several even offered to have her themselves. Kate handled the string of repetitive questions well. She's a Labradoodle. Yes, they call them designer dogs, but they were actually bred as seeing dogs. The best bits of a Poodle and Labrador: really clever, and non-allergenic. One old actor remembered Tommy's allergies. Recalled a ghastly sneezing fit on a David Lean picture in Ireland. Lovely. Missed their scene, and had two days off dapping for trout on Lough Corrib. No, Suzy was too old at 11 to have a new partner. Strictly speaking, she should have retired already, but apparently Sir Tommy had been putting it off. Yes, she'd be looking after her for now. Yes, she is the dearest thing.

A particularly well-heeled, well-spoken old couple drifted over. The woman ran her cane down Suzy's flank.

'She's still jolly distressed, isn't she. Well, not surprising, is it? Tommy was her whole life. To lose him like that . . .'

The man asked Ned if he was 'with the Constabulary'. Ned said they both were.

'Well? Any closer to catching the blighters?'

Ned said they were still trying to piece it together. Did the old gentleman have any direction to steer them in? The old gentleman gave a little harrumph.

'Haven't the foggiest. Sorry. Probably turn out to be a bloody fool accident. You couldn't help him, you know. Tried to steer him once down the Strand, but he wasn't having any of it . . .'

'. . . "if I fall, I fall". . .' added his wife. The old man nodded.

'"I got my dog," he used to say, "Who could ask for anything more?" That's how he was. Pity anyone who tried to mug him. Well, there was all that fencing, riding and tumbling in his youth and then the cycling before he lost his sight. Raised an absolute mint for charity. Then hours in the bloody gymnasium. Fit old bugger, was Tommy . . .'

The old woman broke the silence, with another poke of her cane: 'She knows the answers. Just aren't saying, are you, old girl?'

The knot of people around the grave was starting to disperse. A slight figure broke away and darted over: Chippy. She didn't say a word, but bent down and gave Suzy a huge hug. For a moment Suzy responded like an ordinary dog, wagging her tail and licking Chippy's face. Then, as if trying to get back to the fold before anyone noticed she'd escaped, Chippy scampered away, and the dog's shoulders sagged and the tail went still.

Probably time to make a move. The line of waiting limousines stretched out of sight. The photographers were poised for their second and best chance. Now the famous would be walking towards them through the lychgate. Dame Angie walked briskly past, with the boy in tow.

'. . . Grangie, what's it mean, "lorum" . . . ? What the men were saying . . . ?'

Ned glanced in the direction they had come, the direction of the grave. A small huddle of men stood around the coffin, each throwing something down onto it. Not earth: something small and green. A clattering and popping drew Ned's gaze to the gate, where Dame Angie was slipping elegantly into her Rolls-Royce, haloed by a cannonade of flash guns. By the time he looked back, there were only the grave-diggers filling in the hole.

4

'...*AN ENTIRE EVENING DEVOTED to the life and achieve-
ments of Sir Tommy Best. His extraordinary career spanned the
worlds of film and theatre, campaigning for children's rights and
protection through Unicef, his roving role as Britain's sports ambas-
sador and of course all those charities to which he gave so much.
The highlight will be a celebration, live from the Royal Albert Hall,
in the presence of Her Majesty the Queen and Prince Philip, with
all proceeds going to Sir Tommy's favourite charities. There'll be
music from Damon Albarn and the Africa All-Stars and from Nigel
Kennedy and the LSO, with comedy from Mitchell and Webb,
Stephen Fry, Victoria Wood and Rory Bremner, and song and dance
from Darcey Bussell, Katherine Jenkins and the Royal Ballet
School. Paying tribute to Sir Tommy will be a galaxy of stars and
surprise guests. Presented by Jonathan Ross and Kylie Minogue,
that's* Our Best Friend Tommy, *this Sunday at 7 p.m. on BBC1 and
Radio 2 ...*'

The day after the funeral, the telly went Tommy Best bonkers and
the weather turned. The nation watched his old fifties films with
old fifties rain filling the brims of old fifties hats, while it tipped
down outside. By the time they got on to the sixties, with a polo-
necked Tommy in Montmartre holding umbrellas over Audrey

43

Hepburn and Leslie Caron, there were floods in Gloucester and Cornwall. Kate wanted to watch the films, but didn't in case Suzy had a panic. Ned recorded a long compilation documentary, but didn't bother with the films. He had an extra that would never be included in the boxed set: Sir Tommy's final appearance before the cameras. Extra Bilge had put together in sequence all the relevant sections from that night's CCTV tapes. On the front he'd stuck the rushes of a local news piece shot outside the Film Theatre after the retrospective. Fans crowd around the great man, while Zara Canley-Carlton watches protectively. A few autographs, a few photos. Someone passes him a cell phone, so Sir Tommy can surprise and charm a fan from another era: white-haired now and bedridden. There's a bit of fuss around Suzy, then Tommy and Zara go into a little huddle. He shakes his head adamantly – according to Zara C-C's statement, that's when he refused a lift to the hotel. Told her he wanted some air. A bit of trying to say goodbye but getting waylaid: Sir Tommy infinitely patient, very relaxed. Then he sets off with an elderly pair who seem to be going his way. A succession of CCTV cameras picks up the three of them, chatting and laughing. Timecode races inexorably in the corner as the view switches to a distant one that shows the couple at a corner bidding Sir Tommy farewell. He and Suzy walk onto a zebra crossing. Then, a bit further on, they stop and Suzy sits. He glances around, then faces the wall for a while, silhouetted by a street light beyond. Ned didn't have to watch this twice to know what was happening. Sir Tommy Best's last pee. The light reflected in the puddle at his feet.

Off they go again. Getting gloomy now. Dimmer streets. This was the bit Ned watched a dozen times, virtually frame by frame. Sir Tommy ambling along with that unmistakable gait, dog's harness almost slack in his hand. In and out of the occasional splosh of light from a street lamp. The first time he saw this section of the tape, Ned had a sudden flash image: of doomed little Jamie Bulger being led to his death, somehow transposed into an Edward Hopper painting. Now every time he reached that point he had the same ghastly vision, but Tommy was definitely alone apart from Suzy. They are lost for a moment behind an articulated lorry, but are picked up again as they clear the cab and turn down Mission Street. The baton is handed to a camera high and wide on top of a warehouse. They walk down the middle of the road, and then, in an odd moment, they stop. Sir Tommy seems to stoop and do something. Extra Bilge had zoomed in on this section and treated it, but there just wasn't enough picture to work with. Ned loved those bollocks moments in Hollywood films when the cop tells the geek to enhance the image, and dim blur turns like magic into crystal clarity. The licence plate can now be read, and the puzzle is solved in a pixel. Ho ho. So what was Sir Tommy doing? Stroking Suzy was a possibility, but no one was sure.

He's moved off now, towards the camera. It's hard to see the expression on his face. Certainly doesn't seem agitated. A spring in his step, if anything. He gets nearer and nearer until he and Suzy slip silently out of the bottom of the frame. The scene holds for a beat or two, then freezes with the timecode reading 11:09:05:17. The next time Ned sees Tommy Best, he'll be face down in the mud, dead as a dodo. In between . . . nothing.

The area of the Docks where the great man died was one huge blind spot.

'They aren't due to stick the cameras up till the site's clear,' the man from Traffic Surveillance told Spick. 'That's all part of Phase 5. Well, there's not much going on down there now, and no crime to speak of . . .'

'Yeah . . .' said Spick, '. . . murdering Sir Tommy Best not being a traffic offence . . .'

But Traffic Man was not in playful mood, and rang off.

Ned glanced for the hundredth time at the map on the wall with its arcs and sweeps showing the camera angles and its dotted line marking Sir Tommy's route. From the end of Mission Street there were a dozen ways he could have gone, and still met his killers on the walkway. The neighbourhood around the Docks was a warren. And then there was the timing. Ned pressed Rewind and made notes. They left the Film Theatre at 10.51 p.m. He did his stoop at 11.05. They went off the radar at 11.09. And what did Doc Bones say was the time of death? Ned checked his notebook. Between midnight and six. Hmm. Can't be more than about a fifteen-minute walk from the Film Theatre to the Docks. If that's where Sir Tommy was going, as opposed to where he wound up. Bloody mystery, the whole thing. Ned slumped in the chair. Yawned. Pencil rolled off the table. Didn't bother to pick it up. He pressed Play as Loop and let the thing run.

It wasn't the kind of soupy doze you have in front of the telly after a meal, when you know you should go to bed, but how could bed be more comfortable than this? It was the kind of jumpy doze you have when you're on a train and don't want to miss your station. Fitful, and uneasy; spiralling half thoughts, punctuated by starts into consciousness. It was in one of those that he realised there was something slightly odd happening on the screen, but he couldn't work out what. On the face of it, there was nothing out of place. The shot was taken broadside on across Harty Street. Big, dirty old Harty Street. There was a row of small shops with residential above, and an articulated lorry parked in front, stretching across much of the frame. The man and the dog walked in from the right, disappeared behind the truck, reappeared and walked out left. What's the problem?

He looked at it again at half speed. Nothing. Nothing was wrong. Must have dreamed it. First impressions are bollocks, yeah, yeah. Ned watched it again at proper speed. He hadn't dreamed it after all. There was something wrong, or rather, there was something different about the man and the dog on one side of the truck and the man and the dog on the other. Despite the fact that they looked absolutely identical. Sir Tommy hadn't swapped hands on the dog, or changed his scarf, or slipped behind the truck holding a bunch of flowers, and popped out with an umbrella. But something had changed.

Minehead. He was on Minehead beach riding a donkey, and his mother was eating an ice-cream. A man was leading him, and holding some candy-floss. Little Ned's candy-floss. He couldn't grasp the reins and the candy-floss, so the man said he'd take it. His mother looked as if she couldn't be arsed about his candy-floss. She was too busy with the ice-cream. She ate it with mock lasciviousness. Licking right into the camera. Ned was fairly appalled when he saw it. When he found the rolls of film in the box with his dead dad's projector. It took him a while to work out what was wrong with the film, apart from his mother's absurd flauntings. He couldn't remember whether she had been eating the ice-cream at exactly the same time as he had taken the donkey-ride, and the film was no guide because the intercut shots of the two scenes were in fact complete. His father, who fancied himself a bit of a Fellini, had simply cut the two shots into pieces of equal length, and alternated them. It looked weird. While his mother was seen fellating the 99, little Ned on his donkey should have moved along the beach a bit. But when the shot next cut to him, he was at exactly the same point he had been the last time we saw him. The same applied to his mother. It was as if she froze, with her pink tongue curled round the white peak, waiting for the donkey to jerk a few more yards across the sand, before she could unfreeze and go down on Mr Whippy one more time. He remembered asking himself if it really was his mother. He'd never seen her like that. Then he started to wonder if, as a child, they'd hated him for being in the way. Were they dying for his bedtime so that they could get at one another? That's presumably why the neo-Fellini had wanted to drag out the time it took his son to get across the beach on the donkey. To make the artful point that he was always bloody there – the little twerp who couldn't even hold his own candy-floss.

What was wrong with the Harty Road scene had nothing to do with how it looked, and everything to do with timing. He watched it again and again, beating time on the desk-top for every one of Sir Tommy's footfalls. He kept them up while the great man vanished behind the truck, and invariably when he reappeared he was out of step. For some reason, while he was out of sight, the old boy speeded up.

Had he heard someone? The next shot was from a camera down the road doing a sweep, but it caught Sir Tommy just after he cleared the truck. Ned watched frame by frame, almost willing a shape to appear out of the darkness beyond, stalking Sir Tommy. But the man and his dog walked alone. The dog. Perhaps Sir Tommy quickened his pace because of the dog. Because it was now the dog that needed to pee. After all, she'd been stuck in the Film Theatre for hours. And do dogs have to have grass, or will anything do? Ned studied the map. There was a small park off Caledonia Street, but when did it close? Would Sir Tommy have known about it? It also looked as if there was a verge along Albion Road opposite the main dock entrance. Was that why Sir Tommy was going that way in the first place? Back to the map. Between the Film Theatre and his hotel there was a patch of grass in front of the Council Offices, but Victory Park itself was only three hundred yards off his route. When did Victory Park shut? Time for some help.

He dished out the jobs. He gave Extra Bilge the dog pee questions. Extra Bilge said he'd work up some graphs showing canine bladder control across an average of breeds arranged by sex on an hour by hour basis with affecting factors to include temperature, age and diet. Ned said why not just ask Kate, then he grabbed Span and jumped in the car.

The deal with Zara Canley-Carlton was that they'd have to interview her at the airport. She was on her way to Los Angeles. To Hollywood. Apparently there was already talk of a biopic. Ned bet himself that Span would not get through the day without saying the words: 'It's another world.' He glanced across at her. She was thoughtful and very meticulous, with one huge advantage. She had absolutely no gut instincts. She played no hunches. She caught the guilty by catching them out. If Ned had done something wrong, she was the one he'd least like to be questioned by. She was aquiline of face and sturdy of body. Her husband was a schoolteacher and they had two tiny children. She and Spick weren't an item.

His real name was Sam Pick. A few years back, Fatso had set them both at some indescribably dirty doings at a waste handling plant, and they came out of it smelling of roses with a bunch of convictions. Spick and Span it became.

'So, Detective Sergeant Jan Span. What do your gut instincts tell you on this one?'

'To turn off at the next junction and park at Airport Security, sir.'

Zara Canley-Carlton was a hell of a gel. She was sitting at the bar in the deserted First Class lounge with a bottle of champagne in front of her, looking as if her divorce settlement from Donald Trump had just dropped onto the mat. When she opened her mouth though, what came out was the authentic nose-pinched, buttock-clenched strain of a fifties deb.

'Good of you to see us, Miss Canley-Carlton. We really need some help. Frankly, we are in a bit of a muddle.'

Jan Span knew that opening as 'Ned Three'. It disarmed. It invited mothering. It tempted show-offs. She often thought that, if she ever did anything wrong, the one colleague she'd most like to be interviewed by was Ned, because she knew his gambits. She also knew that this wouldn't help her much, because the trick with Ned was not so much the questioning, as what he made of the answers.

'. . . never saw. You know how one looks away when chums are using holes in the wall. "Pin drift", I call it. Just didn't see, I'm afraid.'

'You were with him at both machines. He didn't say anything the second time? Make any reference to what he was doing? The amount he was withdrawing?'

She shook her head and looked girlish.

'I'm awfully sorry, Detective Chief Inspector, but no. It wasn't Tommy's way. The old darling could jaw for England, but he gave nothing away he didn't want to. And remember, I don't know how much he took out. I thought his card had been refused the first time. Which, I suppose, would have been odd.'

'Was he secretive?'

She smiled a little, then stopped, as if she could get Ned to fill the gap and castrate the question. But Ned kept silent. She tried another smile.

'Well, I don't know. Yes. I suppose so. It's an awful thing to say, and I loved him to pieces, but . . . it wasn't always easy to read him. His eyes . . . being blind . . . you know.'

Tea arrived for Ned and Span. C-C sipped her champagne. Ned's turn to smile at her. And what, he wanted to know, was Sir Tommy's mood that evening? Jumpy? Tired? Tetchy?

'He was as sweet as sweet could be. He had a word for everyone. Everyone. You know those dos; there's always some ghastly person who bores on about a continuity error in the trailer for the Albanian version of *Bunyan's Blade*, and there were two or three of them that night, but he handled them beautifully. Made everyone feel special.'

Ned saw the eyes moisten.

'He was on vintage form, bless him . . .'

Careful dab of hanky, reckless dab of champagne.

'He told you he wanted some air . . .'

C-C nodded, and shrugged.

'You couldn't argue with him, Detective Chief Inspector. Only Dame Angie could do that, and she rarely bothers . . . bothered, unless it really mattered. I don't know if either of you saw it, but I got a fearful pig-sticking from the red-tops for letting a blind old man wander off alone into the Docks at night. I mean, what they just have no concept of is that to us Sir Tommy wasn't really blind – or old for that matter. He'd made such a thing of his independence and mobility from day one. And he and darling Suzy just got themselves wherever they had to be. You'd say, see you at Pinewood at sparrow's fart or the Ivy for dinner at 8, and the two of them'd bloody be there. On the dot.'

'You speak of wandering into the Docks; did you in fact know he was going there?'

'Hadn't the foggiest.'

'He went off with an older couple . . .'

'Yes, the Harrisons. He always liked seeing them. Peter Harrison wrote the BFI booklet, and Vona had been in the script department at Gainsborough when Tommy did those films with Phyllis Calvert and Patricia Roc. So they always had something to talk about. I actually thought they'd all go off for a drink together . . .'

Span wrote down the Harrisons' phone number while Ned toyed with bailing out. Then it occurred to him to ask Zara C-C how she had got back to the hotel that night. Taxi. Not the Rolls? No. Definitely a taxi. Where was the Rolls? She didn't know. The chauffeur Cyril had dropped them off at the Film Theatre, and that was the last she saw of him until the funeral. So how did Sir Tommy think they'd get back to the hotel?

'As I say, Detective Chief Inspector, by taxi. In fact now we're talking about this, it comes back to me. He said he wanted his bit of air, and asked me if I minded getting a cab.'

Ned's next question evoked a peal of laughter.

'Walk with him? Me? Walk? The old sweetie knew better than to ask C-C to walk anywhere. No, Detective Chief Inspector. I always said to him: If it's walking, Tommy old love, you're on your own. Well. Apart from Suzy, of course . . . By the way, what's happening to her? All sorts of people keep asking . . .'

'I just can't see Michelle Pfeiffer as Dame Angie, can you, sir?' said Jan Span as they reached the car.

But Ned wasn't listening.

'We need to find out when exactly Sir Tommy decided to give Chauffeur Cyril the rest of the night off.'

'Yes. I mean, she ought to be English. I think Helen Mirren would be perfect. Or Julie Christie. She's so beautiful. Still, imagine having breakfast with "Michelle" at the Beverly Hills Hotel tomorrow morning. I'll ring him when we get back.'

She started the car and headed back into town.

'Egg-white frittata with freshly squeezed carrot juice. That's what they'll have. In the Polo Lounge. With skinny café macchiatos to follow. Decaff, defo.'

'It's another world, Jan Span. A completely other world.'

* * *

51

This took her back a bit: watching *Blue Peter* on the box. All she needed was a cup of tea and a Wagon Wheel and she'd be round at her Nan's a decade ago. Except this wasn't a few moments of precious release from the hell of home. This was work.

'. . . *for that crucial first meeting. We stayed a little way off, because we wanted to give Tommy and Suzy a chance to get to know one another. At first it seemed as if Tommy was the nervous one! There. He's giving her a stroke. Now a little tickle under her tummy. Nick explained that since we last saw them both, he'd taken Suzy back to the railway station and the market, and that she'd heard a lot of loud noises and traffic, and she'd seen all sorts of different . . . ah, now they're off. They seem to be getting along really well. Earlier I asked Nick what he'd expect out of a first meeting between a guide dog and her new owner, and what we should look out for when Tommy meets Suzy . . .*'

Kate instantly recognised the painfully handsome man on the screen, even after the gap of ten years. The high cheek-bones and luminous black eyes. Can't have been more than thirty then. She must have seen this when it was first on. Funny. There was Suzy as a teenager: all legs and ears, with a nose like a black snooker ball. Really adorable. She realised she knew Suzy the minute she saw her at the newsagents – knew her in some deeper way, but couldn't remember how. Now she understood. She'd followed the story on children's television, about how Sir Tommy Best was going to have to have a guide dog now he couldn't see, and how she'd been trained by this man . . .

'. . . *I don't know . . . I suppose it was an extension of just loving dogs. I've always been gripped by seeing a guide dog. You're told by your mum that it's rude to stare, aren't you, but . . . I bet lots of you children out there . . . just like me, gawping at the wonder of it. I mean, how does the dog know what to do all the time? Not just the occasional trick when it feels like it, like our old family dog Chewbacca, but* all the time, *with someone's life depending on it? I remember as a kid on Waterloo Station, we were going down to see my grandma in Poole one Whit weekend and there were tons of people and a real din, and this dog was threading her way through the crowds, leading her blind owner to the right train, along the platform edge – you know, that sheer drop with trains hurtling by . . . And people just sort of parted when they saw her. You know, it was the dog, almost more than the blind person, they were making way for. And I thought, if I could ever train a dog to do that, it would be the most fantastic thing I could ever do in my life . . .'*

. . . by this incredibly sexy man that the gang at school all fancied. They'd pass notes about what they'd let him do to them, and what they'd like to do to him. She pretended to herself that she only watched the programme because she loved dogs, and that was the reason at first. But then she too got hooked on the eyes, and the soft, expressive voice, and his tender way with animals. She was fifteen. She didn't write any notes – she wasn't in the gang – but she read the one about the bath and the bar of soap, and keeping your little fingernail trimmed. She barely understood where the pleasure might be, but it made her blush when she thought about it afterwards, and she found herself thinking about it more than she ever expected to. She knew he'd never want her to do that to him. Maybe Chrissie Legge, but not her. He'd not fancy her. She already kept her nails short, but not for that reason. It was to avoid scratching herself when she stuck her fingers down her throat after meals.

'. . . to spend time at the Blue Peter *studio so Suzy could get used to being around lights and cameras, and being really quiet and still, and see what happens in studios, because they're the kind of place she'll have to go to with Sir Tommy.'*

'You've got a lot of obstacles round here, Katy, like these cables and scaffolding and these brace things on the back of the scenery that you could easily trip over . . . like that!'

She glanced across at Suzy, but she was asleep in her basket at the end of the sofa. Head turned well away. Couldn't have heard a thing even if she'd been awake, because Kate was wearing headphones. The man's voice, deep inside her head . . .

'*. . . people talk about bonding. I mean, bonding's really import-*
ant, but you've also got to understand that the dog is professional.
This is her or his job. She'll have this sign on her back . . . can
you read it? Do not pet me – I am working! *And it isn't just people.*
She's going to see and meet other animals. No good if Suzy suddenly
decides to chase a cat. And she'll meet dogs in the street all the
time, including other guide dogs.'

'*That's why Stuart's brought Bonnie in, to give Suzy more prac-*
tice with other dogs.'

'*Hi, Stuart. Hullo, Bonnie, how lovely to meet you, big star that*
you are. Meet Suzy . . . Ah . . . all girls together . . .'

The pencil test. Took one into the bathroom and tried it before
her shower. The test the gang was talking and laughing about when
she went over at break, slipping in at the edge of their circle. It
was in this magazine Carmine Bright had brought in. Her big sister's.
So Kate stood like the article said, head, shoulder blades and bum
up against the wall. She tried as hard as she could. Tried the left
one and the right. Hopeless. Wasn't as if the pencil slipped out
after a moment or a wiggle – it wouldn't begin to stay there. She
silently joined the gang at lunch the next day and waited for a lull
in the conversation.

'You know that pencil test?' she ventured. 'Tried it last night.
Really hopeless. I couldn't manage it at all. It just kept falling out.'

There was a horrid pause. Agnes looked at Chrissie and then
across at Amy. Kate knew she'd blown it. Didn't know what she'd
done wrong, said wrong. But knew she was done for. Carmine
Bright leaned in and hissed right in her face: 'You stupid fat ugly
slag. You pathetic piece of shit. Little Miss Upturned Top Tits.
Little Miss Perfect Pants. Little Miss Cocky Cunt. Why don't you
just fuck off.'

Kate didn't say anything; she didn't know what to say. She
stood and turned and walked, hoping they didn't see the hot, hurt
blush and the tears. She wasn't showing off, for God's sake. She'd
told them straight out she'd failed. Why the wish to crush her?
Why the hatred? How are you meant to learn the right thing to

say, anyway? You've got to know all about boys' bodies and girls' bodies and sex and make-up and thongs and Brazilians and music. Last week it was what boys' stuff tasted of . . . and all she really knew about was . . .'

'*Dogs. There's no other animal in the whole world as clever and as teachable and as obedient and as utterly devoted.*'

'*And what about Labradoodles, Nick? It's such a funny name . . .*'

'*I know, it's a fantastic name for them. It all started in Australia with someone asking for a guide dog that wouldn't trigger an allergic reaction . . . you know, Katy, if someone has sensitive skin, the fur, dog fur, can sometimes give them a rash or other reactions, or it can affect their breathing with asthma . . . now Poodles are used as guide dogs though you see more Labs . . .*'

'*And you also get Retrievers and German Shepherds. I don't know if you can see them up on the screen . . . aaah, aren't they gorgeous!*'

'*. . . so this breeder had the bright idea of putting the two together for this person, knowing that Poodle fur doesn't shed so much and is less of an irritant . . .*'

'*Now we thought it'd be good to test this out, Nick, so we're going to do an experiment with Suzy and Bonnie to see whether Labradoodles are really any better at holding onto their fur . . .*'

'*OK . . . so Nick, you take Suzy, and Katy's got Bonnie . . . and here are your combs . . . and I've got these two trays which I've lined with black paper so the hairs will show up really well . . .*'

'*I don't reckon Nick's really trying 'cos he wants Suzy to win!*'

'*. . . Oh, she really likes that, doesn't she?*'

'*OK, in there . . . a bit's floated away . . . must be the heat in the studio . . . Gotcha! Now let's have a look. Who's first in the Fur Stakes . . . ?*'

Kate lay back on the sofa as the inanities bubbled out of the past, washing into her, around her and over her. She was getting drowsy now. Very drowsy. That delicious doze just before full sleep. Then, ear-splitting barks! She looked at the screen but there was no barking dog there. Just Sir Tommy, a decade younger in a denim jacket and T-shirt, talking to Nick and Katy and Stuart, with Suzy and Bonnie curled up at their feet. Close-up of Sir Tommy now, face full of expression, eyes blank. He was talking about the darkness. About how even if he looked up into the lights, he could only see black. The barks grew louder. They weren't coming from the television, but from the room. She sat up, pulling off the headphones. Suzy was sitting up in her basket, staring at the screen and barking and barking.

He must have looked a little funny, but he didn't care. At that time of night there was hardly anyone around to see him. He had a clipboard in one hand and a stopwatch in the other and he was trying to walk at exactly a step every 0.6 seconds. One by one he checked off the waypoints: the bus-stop at Meriden Road: 10.53. The zebra crossing by the Whalley Way school: 10.56. The corner where they had stopped and talked before the Harrisons went one way and the old man went another: 10.59. Stop 42 seconds for a pee. Then along Harty Road where Sir Tommy had gone behind the lorry. Where he'd speeded up. No lorry there now. Hard to see the point at which Ned should speed up. Was this boarded-up café the one he saw on the edge of the frame in the wide shot? And hold on a moment. What's this? A pawn shop with a load of clocks in the window. For a fleeting, foolish moment, Ned wondered if Sir Tommy really was blind – if he'd noticed the time, and realised he was late for something. Just then, a church bell struck eleven. He checked a carriage clock in the window and then his own watch. It's late. The time's 11.02.58. He checked the timings on the map. The old man disappeared behind the truck at 11.02.37. A difference of just twenty-one seconds. Interesting. Extra Bilge will have a whole lot of fun up that clock tower working out exactly how much time it's losing. If it's wound and corrected at the same time on the same day every week, that would be about right. Leave it to the Bilge.

He restarted the stopwatch, adjusted his pace to 0.5 seconds and moved into the dark section he had studied so closely.

He wondered if anyone was watching him on the monitors at Traffic Surveillance: a lone figure following a dotted line on a sketch map. At 11.05 he stopped in the middle of Mission Street to tie his shoe. Then he walked on. Four minutes later he vanished off the screen of the last monitor of the last camera before the Docks. He was on his own.

It was windier and chillier than he thought it would be. It was also eerie. He didn't particularly feel like a Detective Chief Inspector with an entire police force a panic button away. He felt vulnerable. Handy as he was at unarmed combat, he knew he looked like a weedy bloke in the wrong place at night. Plus, he couldn't see particularly well. The street lighting was patchy. 'As dim as a NAAFI candle' his grandpa used to say. There was a smudge here and there of sodium, but the deeper he went, the darker it got.

He'd chosen the most direct route to the place where Sir Tommy fell. Eleven hundred yards. It started by crossing a succession of big approach roads to the Docks, but a right turn off Albion Road took him into a maze of back-streets and unlit alley-ways. He gingerly made his way along a narrow stinking canal, slowing for safety, though he had no idea if Suzy and Sir Tommy would have done. In front was the old footbridge leading to the cobbled terrace which Extra Bilge reckoned Suzy must have walked down because of the lime gunge on her paws. What did he call it? The TCPA? Total paw . . . particle catchment area . . . the TPPCA. Mad as a hatter. Wish he was here now, though. Maybe not. He'd probably fall in the canal trying to measure the phosphorus levels.

Far side of the bridge now, and down into the terrace. No one about. Walkway ahead. Nearly there. Hullo. There's a pile of mattresses at the foot of the stairs and the gate's open. Those trick cyclists must have been here, damn them. It's a bloody crime scene, not a playground. Check in the morning. Get security tightened.

Up the new walkway. Really windy up here. Longer walk than he had remembered. Past a clutch of warehouses. Matey's crane towering above. Decrepit railway line below. There's the fire exit he'd clambered out of that first day. And there it was. The hole.

Click! 11.32.19. A bit later than he thought it would be, but it still gave Sir Tommy at least half an hour to spend with his killers before they pushed him through the hole. He looked down at the water, but it was too dark to see anything. The smell was there, though, and the nasty atmosphere that Ned had sensed from the beginning. Horrible place to die.

He put away the stopwatch and went back to close the gate and re-tie the police tape. Wasn't a wasted night. He had another tiny clue. He now knew why Sir Tommy speeded up behind the lorry. He'd heard the clock strike eleven. Either he just realised it was getting late. Or else he had an appointment to keep. With his murderers.

The word was out that Fatso was on the rampage. Those who could, stayed clear of the office. The rest tried to look scarce, because pigs weren't happy. They were grumbly, edgy, sulky pigs. So far from being pigs in space, they were down-in-the-dumps pigs. Shovelling shit pigs. Up to my arse in incompetence pigs. Sometimes they quietly languished in their sty, gazing fretfully at reports and underlining things with a huge puce magic marker in huge puce trotters. Sometimes they had people in, to snort solutions out of them. To wheedle answers to riddles. To go over it again on the off-chance that the crucial bit had been missed. And occasionally they strode around the main office: angry, roaring pigs. Pigs had been Thwarted. Some people had failed to Please. Some people didn't know Stuff, and the Stuff they didn't know was exactly what a pig needs to hear. Like Who Fucking Dunnit, eh?

It wasn't ostensibly about the Best case. In fact, it was never about the Best case. Fatso's rants were aimed at every case but Sir Tommy Best's. The team recognised the signs. The longer one of Ned's mysteries dragged on, the more pressure Fatso put on everyone else. The quicker they'd have to sort out the Carstairs rape case. The Grievous Bodilys at the ice-rink. The bike bomb. The bread and butter, rain and shine, come as you are mayhem and violence that filled their days and nights and charge-sheets no matter what. There was a permanent level of civil insurrection which pigs had to put down, and which, however successful a pig and his cohorts might be one day, would all be back the next. If Fatso had known about Sisyphus, he'd have commandeered him as St Porker.

Some of the team didn't like it much, and a few resented it. Resented being expected to buy slack for Ned. They knew he was cleverer than the rest of them put together. That Homicide Command, Counter Terrorism and the Security Service had all tried to poach him. That he was a bit of a star. Ned did his damnedest not to take advantage or appear a cut above the rest. But inside he knew that others were suffering for his privileges. Knew to tread carefully with them. Felt bad he hadn't cracked it. The irony was, that when Fatso roared at everyone but him, Ned felt as if the roars were aimed only at him.

In one of Fatso's quieter moments he went for a pee, and cornered Ned. Frightening stuff – not what Fatso said, but being alone in the loo with him. He was very civil to Ned. Realised, or so he said, that it was a tough one. That tough ones are slow ones. That if anyone could crack it, it would be Ned. More time, Ned? Take more time. No one on your back. That's what I'm here for. Take the flak. Run interference. Hold the bastards off. Buy you breathing time. Buy you space. As the pig grunted all this out, in Ned's imagination the loo seemed to shrink and the pig seemed to swell so that Ned felt himself pinned to the scummy tiles by a wild spraying monster. No breathing time. No space. Not a dry shoe in the place. It was only after Fatso waddled out through what seemed an impossibly slender doorway, that Ned realised he had dried his trotters on the towel – without bothering to wash them first.

On his way home Ned stopped at the Light of Kerala for a take-away *thali*. He had a *lassi* while he waited, and tried to catch the seeds with the straw while wondering if he had enough excuse to ring Kate. He didn't. One day he'd just ring her anyway. But not tonight. He agreed with Hindal that this made four sets of the trays with little dishes he'd taken and not returned. Hindal said he might have to set the police on him. Big laughs from old Raj and Selima at the till. He'd bung them in the dishwasher tonight and pop them back tomorrow. Honest. It was turning dark and very windy, and he had to run home. By the time he reached his front door, it was monsoon time and the spicy poppadoms were sodden. He ate at the kitchen table, not putting the light on so as to see the lightning better. Giant jagged darts got closer and closer until there was no gap to count and the house seemed to shake. He reached for the phone.

'Just wanted to see how the dog was, with all this thunder.'

'She's fine. She seems bomb-proof with the obvious things: other dogs, loud noises, carrier bags in bushes, toddlers pulling her tail. Really well trained. It's the other stuff . . .'

'What other stuff?'

'Sir Tommy was on the telly. In the repeat of some *Blue Peter* thing. I had the sound off, but she saw him. She recognised him. Went barking mad.'

'What did it mean? Can you tell? Is it fear, or anger, or distress or what?'

'I don't know. I'll think about it. It was really . . . bad.'

Silence. He didn't say anything, so she did.

'Thanks for calling. For asking about her.'

If he answered her, she never heard it because the thunder erupted again over his house.

'Are you OK? That sounded really close.'

But the line was dead. She went to bed, wondering if he'd been struck by lightning, but not having the nerve to ring him and find out. And he went to bed wishing like a little boy that he could crack the case and win the girl. Hindal's trays didn't get a look-in.

As he slept, Ned's problems got tougher. The crime scene took a severe beating, and not just from the weather. Firstly the high, wet winds tore away the police tape and tenting over the walkway adjacent to the hole. Then early in the morning – one of those still, clear mornings after a storm – an enterprising photographer climbed up, contaminating the scene, and banged off a load of snaps before he could be chased away. Up till now, the public had no picture of the exact place where their beloved Tommy had died. The next day, the flowers started arriving.

It began with the local school. Evidently the history teacher had been a 'Sunbeam' – an orphan in one of Sir Thomas's Sunburst Homes. When the *Mail* stuck the black-framed photo of the death scene on its front page, he led the whole school out at lunch-time to place a wreath at the foot of the steps up to the fatal walkway. The PE teacher emailed the local rag a photo of them standing in the drizzle, singing 'Always Look on the Bright Side of Life' and the next thing everyone knew, a grotty run-down cul-de-sac in the Docks had turned into the Mall the week Diana died. Ned, Spick and Span watched aghast as all hope of keeping the area virgin vanished in a sea of bouquets. 'Police Line Do Not Cross' tape was used to tie up banners: 'Tommy we love you'. 'Our Tommy'. 'You were the Best'. Photos. Flags. Kids' drawings. Candles in the wind. People kneeling in prayer. Singing. Hugging one another. Crying their eyes out. Fast-food pushcarts pitched up flogging doner kebabs, DVDs of Tommy's Oscar triumph and boxes of tissues. The PM was said to be on his way to lay a wreath. Maybe a Royal. Maybe Elvis.

Ned & Co. couldn't get within twenty yards of the gate across the old catwalk from the street side. Fatso wanted to clear the whole lot away, but orders from on high declared the area sacrosanct. It was the 'focus of national mourning'.

'Fuck arse of national mourning, more like,' was Fatso's retort.

Slowly, the crime scene degenerated, the fragile messages from its few undiscovered clues – including a crucial twisted black pipe-cleaner – trampled by wallowing, mawkish masses and then washed away by more rain.

5

SHE LEFT BEFORE THE SUN came up. Dog in dog cage. Dog cage in the back. Small suitcase. Tent. Sleeping bag. Walking boots. Weatherproof coat. Some books. Thermos. More stuff for Suzy than for her: food, blankets, bedding, dishes, toys, leads, brushes, shampoo, treats. She shared the plan with the dog: up betimes (her Nan's phrase), a quick walk before the off, then away to be on the hills by dawn. They were, too. She pulled her van off the road at the first cattle grid, and drank coffee while the dog loped about. The city behind was in a fuzzy shroud. The way ahead lay sharp and golden. It was lovely to see Suzy relaxed. That's just how it should be, dog of mine, when you're on your holidays.

The road led east, and was squinted at beneath the sun visor until the culprit rose high enough and wheeled far enough south to leave her undazzled. The moment of liberation coincided with their passage from a route she knew well – the old road to college – to ones she knew not at all. She could have taken motorways, but they would have sent her around three sides of a square. So she pressed on past strange place names, through forgotten villages, across increasingly featureless landscapes. They stopped for petrol and a loo break, and she could barely understand the accent of the witch at the till. She had jet black hair scraped back from a bone-less white face on which streaks of mascara doubled for absent eyebrows. The roads post-witch grew narrow and high-hedged, so that for a while she couldn't see the countryside at all. Then a great river was crossed, followed by a lattice of drainage ditches. The road now perched on an embankment allowing the sun, seven hours and 3.4 million miles later, to attack through the rear-view mirror. Muddy canals struggled to absorb the seepage from sodden fields. Clusters of diggers and bulldozers showed where the battle was being fought. New sluices and trimly lined channels marked recent victories. Getting tired now, dearest of dogs. Getting late, too. Stop for the night. Press on in the morning.

They did not get up betimes. No need. They were on holiday, and she'd just have to hope he was in when they got there. Anyway, there was a chilly-sounding wind and the tent was snug. Having the dog curled like a cat on the end of the sleeping bag gave her warm toes and the perfect excuse to lie in: it seemed such a shame to shift her. By nine, Suzy was restless. It was time for thick socks and a brisk walk over muddy fields. They were moving by ten, soon reaching a small town on a tidal river with sandbags in doorways and whey-faced inhabitants. She took the right fork at the off-licence, following the river-side road till she reached a swing-bridge. It was a strangely industrial sight, so deep in the countryside. It also seemed to her to muddle what properly belonged to land and what to water, what to trains and what to ships. The railway line seemed to be floating on the reeds, which rippled like waves across a lake. The bridge itself had once been painted grey like a battleship, but foul weather had gnawed at it, dribbling rust. A dull brick signal box presided over the scene on the far bank, and was itself dwarfed by a flag pole, tall as the mast of a galleon, but bare save for a wind-torn red flag.

Kate cut the engine and watched as an old sailing-barge crept close, its crew trying to lose way in the hope that the bridge would be open by the time they got there. But it remained firmly closed, and the crew swung the barge about, sails billowing, curses flying. The reason for the delay clattered over the bridge soon after: a stubby train in garish blues and yellow, carrying no one. Nothing seemed to happen for an age, while the barge drifted back the way it had come. Then, amid a grinding of gears and a wincing of metal, the bridge started its swing out.

The bargees brought their craft round and as they did so the wind suddenly remembered them, filling the big brown sail, sending the barge towards the bridge so quickly it looked touch and go if it would open in time, or slice off masts. The crew looked to their lines and their blocks and their wake – in fact at everything except the bridge, as if to give no satisfaction to its keepers. The bridge juddered to a halt in the open position just as the barge reached it. Only then did a man appear on the signal-box gantry, and he in reply affected to show no interest in anything nautical, but sauntered around and, with his back to the barge, peered at the one direction in which there was neither rail nor water to be seen, but only undulating reeds and scudding clouds.

'There you have it, Suzy. A silly men stand-off.'

Such a waste of a day and a boat and a good wind. Part of it was the things themselves. The boat. The bridge. The gantry that allowed the signalman to parade his indifference. What was that counsellor's phrase? She wasn't very nice, but she was dead clever. Eileen. She had a good phrase for it, to do with those things to lift the car when you've got a puncture. 'Vanity jacks'. When men – and not just men – use a thing or a gesture to pump themselves up. Or use a person. It's bad if you're the vanity jack.

She moved off, watching the bridge close in the rear-view mirror as she drew level with the barge. The men were clustered around the helmsman, an old man of the sea with yellowing white beard. They were laughing. She pulled ahead. A young crewman was alone at the prow, coiling a line into a neat hank. He caught her eye and smiled. She did not smile back. She never smiled at strangers. In fact, she pretty much only smiled at dogs.

The road hugged the river for another couple of miles until she reached a decapitated windmill. No sails, no turret. It had been heavily gentrified, with a sitting area on the roof, but it still looked stunted and wrong. There was the track behind it, the rough farm track. Hold on tight, dog. Bumpety-bump. The further she went, the wilder the landscape. There seemed to be fewer trees, and those there were looked hunched and gnarled. Hedgerows laden with sloes and blackberries spilled across her path. Stone walls had fallen down. A scatter of logs almost blocked a passing place. At one point she had to negotiate a gush of water inexplicably crossing the track. The drive seemed much longer than two miles. It was partly because she had to slow so often for obstacles, but also because the track was taking her into wilderness. It wasn't just wild. It was anarchic. She didn't associate him with anarchy.

The house looked reassuringly normal if dilapidated. An old stone farmhouse with a slate roof and a fearful amount of ivy and crawlers. It was perched on a rise overlooking a horseshoe bend in a river. Maybe the same river. Hard to tell. No sign of the barge. She stopped just past the house and let Suzy out. The dog bounded away, making a loop around the rough lawn in front of the house before coming back to sit and scratch an ear. The garden looked a mess, but it smelled lovely. There were tobacco plants and autumn clematis and witch hazel. Along the gravel paths she spotted *Sarcococca*, with its glossy green leaves. Her Nan had some. Kate remembered going into her garden one New Year's day, and her nostrils filling with the intense perfume. All the more beautiful for flowering in the dead of winter. God's breath, Nan used to say. If it hadn't been animals for Kate, it would have been plants. She knocked on the door. Nothing. She tugged the bell-pull. Still nothing. A louder knock. A harder tug. Silence. They walked around the side, disturbing some chickens. They wandered over to an open, ramshackle barn. No sign of a car. He must be out. I don't know, doglet. Wait, or walk? Walk first, then warm up in the van.

The old Land Rover was moving fast. Very fast. It was being driven by someone who knew the road well and expected to find no one coming the other way. It swerved around the logs and did not slow for the rogue stream. It let up a bit as it neared the house, but not by enough. It hit Kate's van broadside on, pushing it fifty yards through a hedge and old greenhouse. The driver just managed to stop the Land Rover, but the van tumbled down the slope into the river, rolling over in the water before sinking. Bubbles streamed up for a while, then stopped. The driver of the Land Rover lay with his bleeding head against the steering wheel. Nothing moved.

Suzy heard the Land Rover first. They were picking their way across a meadow about a mile from the house when she suddenly stopped with head in air and front paw raised. She looked like the water dog in the old print that used to hang in reception at college, with the hunter lying in a punt beside her squinting down an endlessly long gun. She turned and gave a new noise: the faintest of growls. They walked on for a minute or so before the distant crash made them turn back. From the angle at which they hurriedly approached the house, nothing seemed changed. Then she saw that her van was missing, and the dog suddenly took off over a track that had not been there before. Beyond the smashed plum hedge and broken window frames the Land Rover had come to rest against the last few feet of embankment before the slope down to the river. Suzy was up on her hind legs, head through the window, licking the face of a man with a wild beard. A man who looked dead. Why on earth is Suzy licking him, she wondered in shock. And then it came to her: Suzy knew him. That's why they were there.

Even with all the prying resources of the police force, it isn't that easy finding someone if they really don't want to be found. Not if they are clever about it. Kate had taken the problem to Extra Bilge. He was the only man in the whole place who seemed to treat her as a colleague, rather than a sex object. Apart from Mr Ned, of course. She couldn't imagine any of the rest of them being with her for the whole funeral without once glancing at her legs. In retrospect she didn't know how she had the guts to wear that skirt. Presumably it was because she knew Mr Ned was above all that. It was one of the things that made her feel comfortable with him.

Not that she felt comfortable with Mr Bilge. I mean he was weird. Everyone knew that. But it was a different kind of weird. She didn't know why, but whenever he spoke to her, she found herself thinking about something else within seconds. Even if he was telling her what she really wanted to know. Like how to find Nick Parsons. The man who had trained Suzy for Sir Tommy Best.

'You've got your National Police Computer which is brilliant if your target has had a criminal process initiated against him . . . which he doesn't seem to. Or we can access the Central Social Security Computer via the Comtel uplink at Droitwich. Now if that draws a blank . . . within MI5, which strictly speaking we need a Form B779 signed by . . . or the HM Revenue and Customs database which runs off an Atlas Mainframe Mk 8 at 58.2 teraflops per second. If you put a mug of soup on the master modem diffuser it'll boil in 37 seconds. That's a metal mug, mind. Thick mushroom would be slower than chicken because of the viscosity . . . or else we could look him up in the telephone directory. Where does he live, exactly?'

The harder Extra Bilge looked for him, the more elusive Nick Parsons became. His *Blue Peter* fame had led to appearances on *Parkinson* with Sir Tommy and Suzy. It turned out he was a television natural. He went on *Have I Got News for You* and *Never Mind the Buzzcocks*. The BBC hailed him as the latest Barbara Woodhouse, and announced they were giving him his own show, *Walkies Talkies*. And then, suddenly, it all stopped. He cancelled his phone, gas and electricity. He sold his flat, with no evidence of him buying anywhere else. He stopped paying rates, National Insurance, tax, council tax. His parking permit, subscriptions to the RAC and a number of dog and blind associations lapsed. He cancelled his membership of the Kennel Club. His passport expired and was not renewed, but there was no evidence that he had left the country. Extra Bilge checked with Interpol, FBI, Homeland Security and the Central Customs Agency. Nothing. It was as though Nick Parsons had never existed.

The speed of his disappearance added to the mystery. From the date of the BBC press release about *Walkie Talkies* to Nick Parsons dropping off the radar took barely three months. Perhaps he became petrified at the idea of success. Or failure. Or just fame. Kate decided to ring the BBC producer and find out what went wrong. It took an awful lot of courage. She'd never made a call like that before. She toyed with the idea of pretending she was a detective, but didn't think she could carry it off and, anyway, didn't feel comfortable about it. She told him she was from the Dog Unit and that she was looking for Nick Parsons, and the producer, who was now in the Natural History Unit, seemed interested and happy to talk. He had no idea why Nick had changed his mind. It all seemed to be on course, and then Nick rang him. Late one evening. Said he wasn't going to be able to go through with it. He'd really have liked to, but it wasn't possible any longer. '*Force majeure*,' he had said. She got him to spell the phrase out, writing it down carefully.

She found Extra Bilge in the canteen, sitting with Dr Bones. It was like being back in school, sidling up to the gang.

'Mr Bilge, what does "*force majeure*" mean?'

But it was the formidable forensic surgeon who answered through a mouthful of macaroni cheese.

'Aha! "*Vis major*".'

Extra Bilge looked impressed. Doc Bones was someone to listen to, not talk at. He knew an awful lot of stuff Extra Bilge needed to know.

Oh God, she thought. It's Carmine Bright cross-dressing as a barking-mad quack. Think. Breathe deep. In through the mouth. Out through the nose. Or was it the other way round? Well she certainly wasn't going to ask Doc Bones which. Nor was she going to turn and flee. She was on a mission. Her mission. She drew up a chair and sat down.

'Look, Dr Bones,' she said. 'I don't do Latin. I do dogs. I believe our best witness to what happened to Sir Tommy Best is his guide dog Suzy, and the best person to unlock it is the man who trained her ten years ago. Except he suddenly went missing owing to "*force majeure*". If you know what it means, I'd be really grateful if you could share it with me in plain English I can understand. If you can't or won't, then I'm really sorry to have disturbed your lunch.'

Doc Bones put down his fork. Wiped his mouth. This has to be the one they call the Dog Tart. He looked at her, in her shapeless, muddy overalls. Took in the high cheekbones, flawless skin, huge eyes, glorious hair. Ravishingly beautiful. Sharp, feisty mind. Delightfully self-confident and clearly as nutty as a fruit-cake.

'It means a superior force, a force that cannot be resisted. This could be what some call an "act of God", others a natural cause, like a hurricane or an earthquake. It could also be an uncontrollable power, such as that of a military enemy. Lurking at the back of all these definitions is the idea of irresistible violence.'

There was a moment's silence as she sat writing, her head bowed and slightly to one side, with tiny tip of tongue peeping. Irresistible violence. She then looked up from her notebook, smiled a devastating smile and slipped away. Extra Bilge was gobsmacked. He had never heard such a sustained burst of English from Doc Bones, and he'd never heard the Dog Tart stand up for herself before. She was obviously a bit of a *force majeure* herself.

'Tartus treaculi, O Bilge? Custardo cum?'

It was his car which gave him away. An old Land Rover. The DVLA in Swansea simply reported that the road tax had lapsed in 1998, and that since then they had received no 'off-road declaration' or notification of change of ownership. But Extra Bilge smelled a lead and Land Rovers were his kind of anoraky vehicle. Particularly, as he told Kate when he phoned her in a state of barely controlled delirium, Series I Land Rovers with 4.88–1 ratios on the spiral bevel differentials. Which were of course unique to axle numbers up to 861371. Of course they were, thought Kate. Everyone knows that, stupid.

'It seems the front transmission failed, and our Mr P had to give his address to a specialist supplier. Now, I'm not sure how up to date you are on the Series I front axle, but the drive goes via enclosed constant velocity universal joints . . .'

She had worked out her entire Christmas present list except for

Auntie Ida by the time he said the magic words: '. . . it's in the middle of nowhere. Have you got a pen and paper?'

She sat in the front of the ambulance with Suzy, trying to make sense of what had happened. Why had he hit her van? Was it anger at his privacy being breached? If so, what would he do when he woke up? If he woke up. The paramedic said he had severe concussion, as well as a broken arm and leg. They raced past the stunted windmill and the swing bridge, through the sandbagged town and onto the main road. The personal disruption was another thing. She had lost her transport, clothes, tent, food, all of Suzy's stuff . . . There was insurance, but that'd take ages. And then she started to feel the enormity of it all. It was her fault. If only she hadn't parked there. If only she hadn't gone there. What if he died?

'He doesn't mind the siren, then?' asked the driver.

'She doesn't seem to. She's a guide dog.'

The driver reached a hand across to stroke Suzy.

'You training her up, then?'

'No. She's retired now.'

'Done her bit, bless her.'

They let her wait with Suzy in the paramedics' mess-room. It helped that she was police, but they also took pity on her, realising she was in shock. Cup of sweet tea. Bowl of water. Her worries multiplied the longer she waited. She'd lose her job, for sure. Fair play, it was her holiday, but Fatso would see it as her messing about with his murder case, and now it looked like she was responsible for a second corpse. Spiralling panic was overtaken by sudden fatigue. She clambered out of a jagged sleep to find a woman her age with ponytail and stethoscope shaking her shoulder.

'Hullo, did you come in with Mr Parsons? I'm Dr Kim.'

The next few minutes were muddled and frustrating. Dr Kim insisted on knowing Kate's exact relationship with the patient before telling her how he was. No, she wasn't a relative, and she wasn't his girlfriend. In fact she had never met him. She had gone to see him out of the blue. To ask him about the dog. He'd trained the dog. A long time ago. She needed to ask him about her. It's . . . sort of in connection with some police business. She told Dr Kim where she worked and showed her ID. Dr Kim peered at the Dog Unit warrant card, and then glanced down at Suzy. She then did a very old-fashioned double-take.

'That's . . . that's . . . whatsername! Isn't it? The dog! Sir Whatsisface's dog!'

They sat quietly together, while Dr Kim explained that Mr Parsons was alive and very lucky. They'd done a CAT scan, and there were no penetrating injuries. There was a fracture of the tibia in the right leg. The shinbone. The right arm was also cracked just below the elbow. He'd have a load of bruises. Dr Kim paused a moment and looked at her a beat before speaking again.

'He's blind, you know.'

Kate's relief at the comparative lightness of the injuries dissolved into an agony of guilt. He'd hit her bloody van and lost his sight. She'd blinded the poor man. Must have been shards of glass from the windscreen. Probably so old it wasn't safety glass. She hadn't seen any blood coming from his eyes, but then she hadn't looked that close. And Suzy was up there, licking him . . . probably licking the blood off . . . Oh God . . .

'. . . all he'd say was that it happened quite suddenly, about ten years ago. He has absolutely no light perception whatsoever. He is totally blind. It's amazing he was still driving. Unbelievable. I assume – I hope – he never went out onto public roads. The paramedic said it looked like he'd got a bit of land. We can only guess he knew his way around it, just as he knew his way around his own house. But you parking your van there sort of moved the furniture.'

Ah, Kate thought. Suddenly and totally blind. That'll be the irresistible violence, then.

The van hung in the air, drizzling like a colander. She imagined it would look rusty, or be smothered in weeds. In fact, if anything it seemed a little cleaner. She'd never felt sentimental about it – never even given it a name – but it suddenly looked vulnerable and she was a softie for that. She was about to say something about it not looking too bad and couldn't it be mended, when it swung round lazily on the hook, revealing the other side. The side the Land Rover hit.

'Lucky you weren't in it.'

The loss adjuster spoke without looking up. He reminded her of a stoat. He was perched on the Land Rover's front bumper with his head buried in a book illustrated with lots of little photos. Probably one of those guides to used car prices.

'Very nearly was. And the dog with me.'

He sucked in some air and clattered his teeth. The barge-crane started to lower the van onto the embankment.

'So does that tell you how much it's worth?'

He shook his head.

'Nah. Footwork.'

All this with his head buried in the book. Then he said something under his breath which sounded to her like: 2-3-4-1 – turn.

She was about to say 'Pardon?' when the van landed with a slight crash. The crane men made a soaking, smelly pile of her belongings, got her to sign a greasy docket swearing that they hadn't added to the van's desperate state, then chugged away down the river. The stoat finally put the book down and showed an interest. She let him get on with it while she took a look at the opponent. Rather unfairly, she thought, the Land Rover was pretty intact. A lot of broken glass and a slight twist in the bumper, but otherwise rudely fit considering the havoc it had wreaked. The stoat's bible, lying on the bonnet, turned out to be *Latin Rhythm A Go Go – Advanced Dance Steps*. It was open at the page on the Carioca. The little photos were of strutting feet encased in patent leather.

'Regionals next week,' said the stoat blithely as he noted down the van's terminal mileage. 'You ever seen the Carioca? That's not the same as karaoke, mind. It's a dance, not a drunken sing-along. The wife and me, well, it's sort of our signature theme.'

He started to take pictures of the crumpled wreck.

'They say the secret of marriage is low-grade telepathy. Well, in the Carioca, you and your partner dance with your foreheads actually touching. The rest of you's going wild, but your heads are glued together. First time we tried it the wife used double-sided Sellotape. Now it's second nature.'

It was only when he was packing his things away into an old music case that he ventured some thoughts about the van. It was a write-off, of course. He'd put it in at £1,500. Because of the mileage. Favour to her. But, word to the wise, she might have to watch her back a bit as our blind friend can't have been insured. It might take a bit of time to sort out. Did she want a lift back to the hospital, or was she staying here?

They had given him a room to himself 'for safety's sake', the ward sister said. He was doing really well medically, but was in a foul mood. Visit him at your peril. He'll be glad to see his dog again, though. Well not see, but you know what I mean . . .

She put her nose round the door and paused, looking around, smelling. She went in a little gingerly. She walked up to the wheelchair, sat and stared at him for several moments. Then her tail began to wag, and when he did not respond she made a little whimpering sound. He stirred. Lifted and lowered his head. Looked puzzled. His good arm was hanging over the chair and she found his hand, licking it, then burying her nose in the palm. His face was screwed up, wrestling with questions and mysteries. He felt her face, with its tight curls, and long eyebrows. The ever so soft, silky ears. The shaggy folds at the neck, and the soft flanks. She was standing now, and he ran his hand down her back and up her tail, with its smoothness at the front and its flared fur at the back. His fingers darted to an ear again, and found its wispy tip. His face started to relax.

'Suzy?'

She gave the softest of barks. The bark he had taught her to give, so that when she was off the lead at home Sir Tommy would know where she was. The trick was in how her name was called – the intonation. Easy for a great actor. Pitch up on the second syllable and she'd tell you she was listening. Pitch down and she'd come running. He smiled.

'Suzy, old girl. What are you doing here?'

There had been no way of getting the dog into the hospital without lying. The bits were true enough. The man was blind. She was a guide dog. But put together it was a lie. She was not the blind man's guide dog. Suzy would have to look the part. Kate had dug around in the sodden remains from her van until she found a *Do not pet me – I am working!* vest. She got the stoat to put his car heating on full whack to dry it out, but it was still damp when she slipped it around the dog. She didn't bother with a harness – thought it might freak Suzy out. Suzy wasn't crazy about the vest. She stood stiff and uneasy. Kate walked her around the visitor's car park until Suzy started to relax. Right, dearest of dogs. Let's go for it. And just remember: no telling jokes and no laughing. You're working again now.

'Who's that with her? Eh? Who's there?'

He turned the wheelchair away from the window. What Kate could see of his face for the bandages and plasters looked older than she expected. The beard had been shaved off. The hair was almost all grey. He seemed somehow to have slipped into her father's generation. It was a delicate one that: the difference between being fanciably older and embarrassingly ancient. And the eyes – those piercing eyes which had given her the first delicious squirm of her life – were dulled.

'I'm a police dog handler. I brought her to you, Mr Parsons, because we need your help.'

He was in a filthy temper. And the news that it was her van he'd hit only made it worse. She didn't want an apology from a blind man for not seeing it, but she didn't expect fury. She might have killed him. She had no right to be on his property. No right to invade his privacy. To hunt him down. He'd broken no law. He'd done nothing wrong. He'd just wanted to be forgotten. It was bad enough being as blind as a bleeding bat, without now being a fucking cripple as well. The room slowly filled with furious self-pity until she felt she might drown in it.

'I'm going to get us a cup of tea, Mr Parsons, and I'm leaving Suzy with you.'

She dropped the end of the lead onto his lap and walked out. He let fly again, but she kept going. It was only when she was in the lift going down to the cafeteria that she realised what it was that felt so weird. It wasn't being bollocked by someone who'd bloody nearly drowned her. No. This was the first time she had been separated from Suzy since they met. No problem, she thought. As the vest says, she's a working dog. Time she did a bit of work. On old Misery Guts.

She didn't go straight back with the teas, but went to see the ward sister in her cubicle. Sister was well peed off with Mr Parsons. She'd asked him for his next of kin so they could come and get him, and Mr P said he hadn't anyone within ten thousand miles. Didn't know if he was telling the truth. He said he wanted to go home, but they couldn't send him back by himself. The OT had been in and offered home help, but he wasn't having strangers there, pushing him and pulling him. Kate gave Sister his cup of tea, and went back to the room, bracing herself for the onslaught. He must have heard Kate come in, because she made sure she did so noisily, but the anger was all spent. The room was still and almost silent. Suzy's head was resting on his knee, and he had wrapped her lead tight around his good hand. So tight the skin was white. As if he never wanted to be separated from her again.

'Do the blind cry?' She'd Googled that weeks ago, when this all started and she decided to mug up about blindness. Yes, the answers screamed from the computer screen. Our eyes may be buggered but our tear ducts aren't and neither are our emotions. Kate sat down and said nothing while the tears rolled down his cheeks.

The road unspooled yet again. It was becoming familiar, in the strange way of holiday roads. One minute you're groping for them in the dark, the next you know every cat's-eye, every passing-place, every chip shop. A month later the brain's wiped the lot. Proves this is a holiday, though the rest of it doesn't feel much like one. The closer she got, the crazier she thought she was. Why was she doing this? Why had she suggested it? He'd already shown himself to be fairly loopy, driving blind. What if he were a mad axeman? Or a rapist? She glanced across at him. He had his face by an open window, and was drinking in the fresh air. Some of the bandages were off, and he seemed marginally less tense. As long as she locked her door at night and kept Suzy with her. She didn't want her beloved dog getting too attached to him.

'We're passing the swing bridge.'

Just how blind was he?

'I can smell the oil and machinery.'

The ambulance driver treated them like a couple. They must have looked a bit cosy, with her handing him his crutches and the dog busying between them. She thought any minute she'd be addressed as Mrs Parsons, and had a snappy response ready. The driver walked them to the door, but Nick made it plain that was far enough.

'We'll manage from here, thanks very much.'

We? Who's this we?

Her fears grew with every step she took inside the house. It was quite the weirdest place she had ever been in. There were no decorations, no pictures, no ornaments, nothing personal. There was precious little furniture. And then there were the walls: splashed with great daubs of paint in clashing colours. There seemed to be no pattern to it. The paint had been applied between waist and shoulder height, with no attempt at even coverage. Where it had dripped onto the floor or across light switches, it had simply been left. The effect was nightmarish. Some rooms were simply dark holes. Others had a crack of daylight squeezing through drawn, cobwebby curtains. She tried the lights. None worked. She couldn't see if this was because there were no bulbs, or no electricity. And then she saw that locking herself in her room was no option. There were no doors. No doors anywhere.

Nick was still in the kitchen where she'd left him, but had worked his way over to the range where he was laboriously trying to lay a fire with his good arm. He was clearly in pain. It was only with the greatest difficulty that she got him to sit down and let her do it. She reminded him of their conversation in the hospital. Of the deal they had struck. She left him simmering while she went to find their supper. He called out after her not to move anything. He didn't want to break his fucking neck as well. She didn't feel great sticking her tongue out at a blind man, but at least she felt better.

The more of the house she saw, the more she understood why it had been so difficult to find him. She went round to the far side, where she'd not been before. Hidden from outside eyes were solar panels, wind generators, wood stores, an extensive orchard and vegetable garden, rainwater collectors. Pipes snaked from lavatory and bathroom windows down to holding tanks for irrigation. A well with a pump provided water, but she also spotted a semi-hidden pipe coming up from the river. There was a wash-house, with tin bath, clothes-horse, drying racks and mangle. And next to it was the food-store. It looked a bit like something from one of those glossy country lifestyle magazines. There were jars of preserves, chutneys, jams. Bunches of drying herbs and peppers. Racks of apples, sacks of potatoes. Plastic dustbins full of growing mushrooms. Eggs from the chickens. Goat cheese hanging in muslin. How did he know what was where – what was jam and what was pickled onions? Could she have told looking at it that it was a blind man's world? There was some broken glass, some spillages that hadn't been cleared up. But there wasn't nearly as much chaos and mess as she'd have expected. Perhaps he wasn't so alone after all. The freezer contained no brands. Nothing familiar. No oven chips or fish fingers or ice-cream. It had two compartments: the smaller was full of meat: bags of chicken legs and wings, steaks, chops. The bigger was divided into home-grown vegetables and home-prepared meals. She grabbed something and went back outside.

It wasn't just a case of what there was, but also what there was not. He'd said in the hospital that he lived 'off-grid' but she hadn't really known what that meant. Now she was starting to understand. There was no television aerial. There was no telephone line. There was no mains electricity. There was no pile of newspapers. Nick Parsons wasn't just frighteningly self-sufficient. He didn't exist to the outside world, and the outside world didn't exist to him. So what, she wondered in mounting dread, did he do for loo paper?

She wanted to flee. To grab Suzy and run back down that bloody road all the way home. She suddenly missed Fatso shouting 'Where's the Dog Tart' and Extra Bilge talking crap, and taking Raffles out sniffing for explosives and finding dead bodies on waste ground and having a giggle with the gang over coffee and mucking out the puppies. It was all so lovely and safe. And Mr Ned.

'It says it's 'Veggy Tag . . . tag . . .'

'Tagine.'

'How do you read the labels?'

'I don't. I can't.'

She emptied the contents into a saucepan and set it on the range. He said nothing. Time passed. She wondered if he remembered she was there. She felt more and more uneasy. That Sunday evening feeling when you've got school the next day, or worse still, an exam. She had become, she knew, the prisoner of her own rituals for survival. Had learned a raft of coping devices, many interlocking. Some were bound up with her space and her things: her belongings, her flat, her van. Many were to do, of course, with food. But she had lost her van – her mobile sanctuary – and most of what was in it. She was adrift. Over the years she had made herself independent of others, and particularly of men. She too was off-grid, but in her own way. Now she was in a strange man's strange house with no doors and no lights, preparing to eat the strange man's strange food. She was on his grid, big time.

'I should have said, Nick. I'm a vegetarian.'

'So am I.'

'But there's chicken and stuff in there.'

He gave a snort.

'They're my sister's. She has to have meat when she comes.'

'Why don't you make labels in braille? They have a thing, don't they? Like a typewriter?'

'Won't use braille.'

Neither spoke for a while, and then he spelled it out like a mantra.

'No braille, no cane, no dog.'

She responded without thinking.

'No blind?'

'No, not "no blind".' He was shouting now. 'Totally fucking blind. But I'm fucking meeting it head on, not trying to trick my way around it.'

'You're upsetting the dog.'

She gave Suzy a calming stroke and murmured into her neck: 'There's absolutely nothing tricky about a dog.'

He sank back into the chair. She put the rice on. Another ugly silence. She didn't want to say anything else, but she had to.

'Another thing. In the loo. There's no paper. Just a big basket of leaves.'

He tried to sound civil, but she could hear the clench in his jaw.

'They're very soft leaves. Chosen specially. Hand-picked.'

'I . . . I can't . . . I'm sorry, but . . .'

He didn't reply immediately, leaving her to flounder in her panic. Then he tossed a lifeline.

'The room you're in, the big room upstairs at the front, it's my sister's room. There's a built-in wardrobe. You'll find various things . . . She calls it her "anti-Nick cop-out kit".'

She fairly raced upstairs. The 'cop-out kit' was heaven-sent. There was soft loo paper, soap, tampons, toothpaste, shampoo, dry skin cream, torches, batteries and candles, as well as spare clothes. The reassuring smell of cedar wood and lavender. Inside one of the doors was a full-length mirror. She held a pair of jeans against herself. Sister was a good two sizes larger, but that suited her fine. She didn't have to wonder long to see what Sister looked like. There were photos stuck into the mirror frame. Nick and Sister as children in a dinghy, pleasing and happy. At his graduation. She had cropped hair, an irrepressible smile and her brother's once luminous eyes. A handsome older man on a tennis court. A handsome woman serving a green rabbit-shaped jelly at a children's party. Nick and Sister and the tennis player and rabbit server all in hiking gear sitting on a stile. Sister and a man in a kilt feeding the chickens. Nick and Sister picking plums. Big smiles all round. There were more photos on the inside of the other door, but Kate only saw one. It was a large, glossy publicity still of Nick and Suzy in the *Blue Peter* garden with Sir Tommy Best. She stared at it, letting it plunge her back into the reason she was there. Nick, suave and dated – a world away from the battered, angry man in the kitchen. Suzy as a wistful puppy: fluffy and edible as candy-floss. Sir Tommy, timeless and easeful. Half a smile and a ton of twinkle still to spare in those dimming eyes. A face more familiar to Kate than her own grandfather's. When she finally closed the wardrobe doors and went downstairs, she almost felt dizzy, as if the photo had sucked her into some dark vortex.

Supper took place in the wake of their bickering. Brittle pauses flecked with banalities. The food was good – the tiny mouthful she ate. More daring tastes than she was used to, but the whole experience was like that. Just got to hold on tight. The kitchen was warm now, and she'd lit one of Sister's candles. Suzy had been lying on the rug in front of the range but the heat had got too much for her and she'd taken herself off to another room. They sat with mugs of tea, and he smoked his pipe. His own tobacco, apparently. The smell was rather nice. Like wood chips and vanilla. He'd tried one of the green leaves for loo paper, he said, but it seemed a shocking waste. The conversation beached itself shortly after. Right. Painkillers for him and bedtime.

She tried to persuade him to sleep on the settee in the kitchen, but he wouldn't hear of it. The idea wasn't just to save him the struggle; she also wanted more distance between them. He started to work his painful way up on his bottom. He wouldn't be helped. Fine. She left him on the third step and took Suzy for a quick walk. By the time they got back he was near the top. She flashed the torch up at him. For a second, into his eyes. She had to be sure. He didn't blink. The slashes of paint up the stairs, red and green, looked particularly garish. What would he do at the top? Could he stand by himself? He struggled for a while, before she slipped behind him and helped him up. He mumbled grudged thanks and limped into the darkness. His room was directly opposite hers down the landing. She'd checked it out when there was still some daylight around, and knew he could see straight into her bedroom. If he hadn't been blind, that is. So what. Don't have to see to rape. Treat him as if he could see.

First she pinned a thick blanket across the doorway, using some pegs and a length of cord she'd picked up in the wash-house. Behind that she put a chair with an enamel water-jug perched on the edge. Tripping over that would wake her up. She settled Suzy between the bed and the chair. She kept her clothes on. She only blew the candle out when she heard the bedsprings take his weight. She thought about tiptoeing in and stealing his crutches, but what if he had to use the loo in the night? She only allowed herself to fall asleep when she heard his breathing deepen into a snore.

6

NED'S KNEE FELT WET. The left knee, not the right. Less his knee; more the bit just above it. So wet that he actually looked down to see if there was a stain on his trousers. Bone dry. So it was back again. He knew better than to mention it to Doc Bones. You had to be 100 per cent dead for the Doc to show the slightest interest in you.

Ned was used to medical minimalism. The family doctor of his teens had never, he believed, got any further in the medical encyclopedia than the letter A. He was a dab hand with Asthma and could spot a case of Angina on the horizon, and if by chance Ned were to be let down by his Adrenal glands he had no doubt whatever that the good doctor would nail it in seconds. But try him with anything connected to the Bladder or the Cervix or matters Duodenal, and Dr Perkins would start to bluster and mumble. It didn't matter what other letter of the alphabet you were dying of, he'd only manage to collect himself by remembering the letter A again. Ah! he would say, like a chain-smoker lighting up after a flight to Australia. Best try some Antibiotics.

Doc Bones had reduced the practice of medicine to an even more negligible state than Dr Perkins. Some unkind members of the constabulary, ignorant of his secret services to leprosy, wondered playfully whether Doc Bones really was a doctor, or if he'd taken a parallel career path which exempted him from knowing anything about the living whatsoever. Either way, word got around and soon no one ever took their ailments to the Doc. He was perfectly safe in lifts and at parties. No one ever showed him their scars or their tongue.

Ned eventually found the key to Wet Knee Syndrome when he was referred by his GP to a neurologist. Years ago when Ned was in uniform, he'd been shot in that same leg, just above the knee. It was an incident for which Ned subsequently received a commendation for bravery, but about which he could remember almost nothing beyond a picture in his mind of a piercingly bright day, a woman with a baby on the balcony of a block of flats, and a dark shape behind a wheelie-bin. Its legacy extended, it seemed, beyond a fulsome section in his personal file and a silver spray of laurel leaves he kept in a jar along with his grandfather's Africa Star and his dad's old CND badge. The neurologist used some words Extra Bilge would have drooled over, but the upshot was that the nerves in Ned's leg had been bished and boshed in such a way that at certain times the endings, perhaps remembering that bloody morning, sent a message to the brain that the skin was wet. The perverse thing was that he'd always meant to watch out in the shower to see if the nerves reported an arid dryness in the region, but once in there he never remembered to think about it. Anyway. He was off to Dame Angie's again, and he didn't have to worry that it would look as if he'd peed down his trousers.

The weather was nothing like the last time, but at least the hacks had vanished along with the sunshine. No sign either of the fearsome PR woman; Dame Angela opened the door herself. She was wearing jeans and a chunky sweater and a very sexy pair of spectacles. She took him into the kitchen and put the kettle on.

'You haven't "got them", have you Chief Inspector?'

Ned freely admitted he had not 'got them'. He couldn't even see a neck in the distance he'd like to breathe down. He realised what he'd said and made sure he didn't catch her eye. He could hear the smile in her voice as she asked him what he knew.

He told her that he believed Sir Tommy had an appointment that night. That he'd slipped out at 9.05 p.m. during a long film clip to ring the chauffeur Cyril to say he was not needed any more that evening. That he had been picked up on CCTV cameras leaving the Film Theatre . . . At this point Dame Angie gasped and leaned for a second on the back of a stool. If she had thought about it, she would have realised . . . Of course. Bloody cameras everywhere. She wanted to know how he seemed. If they showed anything of the attack. Of his death . . . Ned reassured her that he seemed perfectly fine up until the pictures ran out. Coverage in the Docks was patchy, but what there was definitely suggested Sir Tommy knew he was late.

'Late for what, Chief Inspector?'

He'd known this moment was coming. That she'd ask that. He had designed his narrative to lead up to it. He made sure he had a clear view of her face. If she had turned away to make the coffee, he'd have played for time. Delayed the trigger line. He had to see how she would react. The trouble was, she was one of the finest actresses alive, so when she asked the question with some curiosity and no hesitation, he had no idea if she was being genuine. It wasn't that Ned suspected her. But he was very curious to know if she suspected Sir Tommy of something.

'Late to meet his blackmailers?'

She looked exasperated.

'Oh for God's sake, Chief Inspector! You're thinking about the thousand pounds Tommy took out? Well it's absurd. Doesn't mean a thing. He hated using credit cards. Always feared someone would rip him off. Much preferred cash. Treated it like confetti. Plus he had expensive, impulsive tastes. He'd suddenly spend a fortune on malt whisky. Or Havanas. Or something for Chippy. Or me. And it wasn't just his own tastes he indulged. He'd sit down with any beggar or *Big Issue* seller on the street, particularly if they had a dog. Natter away like old pals and then give them twenty pounds, fifty pounds. "Save some for dog food" he'd say with a grin, although I told him enough times his money was going straight to the drug dealers. Give them tea and a sandwich and a tin of Chum, I'd say, but not cash. He was immensely stupid about it. Sugar's in the bowl. Milk in the jug.'

They drank their coffee in silence. He was busy trying to work out how to get the conversation back on track, when he became aware that she was shaking her head. And smiling. He looked at her questioningly.

'Do you know, Chief Inspector, I once drowned my husband. At night, in a swimming pool. I knelt on the edge – it was very hard on my knees – and I held his head under till he just sort of sagged and floated away.'

Ned stayed very impassive.

'It was in a film I did for Melville in '67 at the Victorine Studios in Nice. Well, all went fine until the Inspector came to see me. He was played by lovely Jean-Paul Belmondo. And – it's too silly for words – I did to him what I've just done to you. Except we were sitting on a sunny terrace in Provence, not a wintry English kitchen. Jean-Paul tried out some silly theory which didn't implicate me at all, and I flew off the handle at him. And my manner alone aroused his suspicions. Up to that moment he had no idea that I might have done it. I had a wonderful alibi, you see. I was supposedly having supper with the Inspector's own wife. Perfect. Except she was having an affair with my brother, which I was . . . facilitating. It was all very French. But from that moment on, darling Jean-Paul had me in his sights.'

She stirred a few grains of sugar into her half-finished coffee. Slightly absent-mindedly.

'I killed myself in the end. Jumped in front of a train.'

'The way you do.'

She nodded.

'And who were you having an affair with?'

'With Jean-P–'

She suddenly went bright red, and turned sharply away.

'I meant in the film . . .'

But that conversation was dead. Ned finished his coffee. When Dame Angie turned back, she looked very serious.

'How do you know he was late for something?'

He explained about retracing Sir Tommy's steps and him speeding up behind the truck, and about the church clock in Cathcart Street that gets wound on Fridays, and by Wednesday runs an average of 2 minutes 45 seconds late. Sir Tommy died on a Wednesday. She shook her head.

'It's not a lot, is it? You haven't got a lot.'

Ned agreed he didn't have a lot. There were other leads in progress, stuff he and others were working on, but no, it wasn't adding up to much. Which was why he needed to know if there was a chance that Sir Tommy was being blackmailed.

She went over to the door and switched the lights on, and when she came back she was not cross, but calm. The truth is, she told Ned, she had no idea if Tommy was being blackmailed. The reason she'd flipped was because she couldn't believe that darling Tommy was capable of doing anything that would put him in that situation. And to be honest: not just couldn't believe. Couldn't face the possibility.

'Almost certainly no need for you to face it. It's just a process of elimination. I'm as likely to be wrong as right. You say yourself he treated money like confetti. It may not have been blackmail. It may have been someone touching him for money. An old Sunbeam. One of those beggars in the street with a dog. Some out-of-work actor friend.'

Dame Angie nodded. She supposed so. 'The Inspector must follow every possibility.' She remembered saying that to Belmondo.

'Now if only you'd had that attitude from the start, you wouldn't have had to throw yourself in front of the Blue Train. And it was 1969. *La Belle en Noir*, 1969.'

She broke into a broad grin.

'What do you need, Chief Inspector?'

The DCI needed shoes. Sir Tommy's shoes. They might be able to tell from the soles if he had ever gone that way before, or if it was a one-off. He'd checked with Cyril, and Cyril had never driven him there. But it was best to eliminate the possibility. Fine. She'd get Chippy to sort out what he needed from Tommy's dressing-room. It was everyone's day off today, and she had to go into town. But Chippy would help.

'One last thing, Dame Angela.'

She was quite close to him when she turned. She smelt of musk rose.

'That's a bit of a cliché, Chief Inspector. It's never really the last thing, is it?'

'No. It's just something we say.'

She looked from his left eye to his right and back again. It was almost shocking to be so near her.

'Time for a new line, perhaps. Well?'

'Sir Tommy's call to Cyril. We can't find a record of it.'

'That's not surprising. He had a . . . what do you call it? Pay-as-you-go phone.'

'Why would your husband have a phone he'd have to keep topping up?'

'Don't you mean, why did he have a phone that leaves no trace?'

He could feel her breath on him. Warm. Sweet.

'I'm curious about that as well, Dame Angela.'

'So he could make calls without leaving any trace.'

She didn't wait for the follow-up question.

'That way, Chief Inspector, a bored kid in accounts at a phone company wouldn't be able to flog Johnny Depp's cell phone number to the *Sun*. Or Prince Charles's. Or Carla Bruni's.'

Ned nodded.

'Dame Angela, do you know where his cell phone is? It wasn't in his clothes.'

'No idea, Chief Inspector. In that ghastly mud at a guess, or on some murderer's trophy shelf.'

She turned and strode away, winding a cashmere scarf around the perfect neck he'd just breathed down, and calling out Chippy's name.

He was getting gloves, plastic bags and labels out of the boot of his car when she came round the side of the house with Chippy. Quick kiss on the cheek, then into a midnight-blue BMW and away. One of its blackened windows opened just enough to let an elegant hand slip out, flutter for a moment and then withdraw, though whether it was a farewell aimed at Chippy or at him, Ned could not guess.

The rich are indeed not like us, thought Ned. Even in their darkest corners they have no fluff. He knelt, bewildered by the choice: boots, brogues, daps, tap, black, suede, loafers. What to choose? He turned a couple over. A bit of mud. Some grass. A tiny stone jammed in the tread. He knew the tell-tale traces could be minute, so just picking the dirtiest ones wasn't the answer. The question was, what shoes was Sir Tommy likely to wear for a stroll around the Docks? No. That wasn't it. If he was paying someone off, he might have to go down at short notice. Couldn't always put on the ideal shoe first thing. Then again, no reason to believe that the drop-off would always be in the same place.

'He liked these. Reckoned they were really comfortable.'

Ned looked up. Chippy was holding out a pair of battered trainers. He bagged them up. Anything else? She shrugged and shook her head.

'I know those trainers because Mum always gave him a hard time if he tried to wear them to go out. Said they were a disgrace.'

Ned smiled and went back to the array. Look for favourites across the spectrum, from formal to casual. Why was it so odd hearing her refer to Dame Angie as Mum? Ned dismissed age. These days you could be using your free bus pass to pick up child benefit. Besides, she wasn't the child he thought she was when he first glimpsed her. According to Extra Bilge's exhaustive chronology, she was nineteen years old. Old enough to be their child – though ten years younger than their son, who turned out to be a vapid actuary with no motive and a solid alibi. Colour? Ned knew that as a rootless cosmopolitan he ought to be terribly sensitive to race questions, but (a) adoption and melting-pot marriages made it impossible to say who could or could not be a child's parent and (b) he couldn't be arsed. What was the statistic? White people have on average 21 per cent black blood in them. Whatever the hell that means. Wasn't sure how his lot had kept their quota up. Tough on his pogrom-dodging Great-Great-Grand-Booba Ruth to have the added burden of finding black lovers on the Lithuanian–Latvian borders in the 1880s, though she had a reputation for managing well during trying times. No, it was all about intimacy. He found a well-worn pair of black shoes and popped them in a bag. Hearing Chippy refer to Dame Angela as Mum reminded him how gripped he had been as a teenager wondering what Dennis called Margaret Thatcher in bed. The brogues looked likely. Bag 'em.

Then another memory. Another shaft of intimacy. A body covered by a green sheet. His first autopsy. They all had to look at the body. Twenty or so medical students and three fast-track police graduates crowded round. Ned was already dreading it, and then the attendant removing the sheet dislodged an arm, which swung down over the side of the table. She was a woman in her early forties. He hadn't seen that many naked women in his life, let alone dead ones. Up strode the mighty consultant pathologist, triggering a headlong rush for the best seats. Ned bagged one at the very back, turning his chair round to face the wall. The others craned their heads to see better. Ned jammed his fingers in his ears to shut out the screech of saws and used his lower palms to squeeze his nostrils shut to block out the nauseous smells. During a lull, he relaxed his hands and heard the consultant pathologist boom out: 'So, ladies and gentlemen, we have established cause of death as myocardiac infarction. On to Mr Plod's second favourite question. What was the time of death?'

Without having seen a slice or heard a word, without understanding the science a jot, without turning round, young Master Ned Plod piped up: 'Between 6 and 7 in the evening.'

There was an aptly dead silence, broken by more booming. This time a whole lot closer.

'You! Boy at the back! Turn your bloody self round!'

You're a fine one to talk, Ned thought as he reluctantly turned. The star had abandoned his spotlit stage and was leaning his bloody aproned paunch on the rail at the front of the observation seating and staring at him. Along with everyone in the room apart from the corpse.

'You've clearly blundered into the wrong lecture, boy. I teach flower-arranging here on Thursdays, not Tuesdays.'

There was a round of nasty sycophantic laughter, which the great butcher chopped off.

'However. You also happen to be bang on target. Our woman perished around 6.30 yesterday evening. Assuming it wasn't you who called the ambulance, and given that you've failed to do me the courtesy of paying a blind bit of notice to anything I've said or done all afternoon, how the hell did you guess so bloody accurately?'

It wasn't, Ned assured him, a guess. It was a deduction. He pointed out the arm, still hanging down, and the fingers, with their nicotine stains and very showy, shockingly fresh nail varnish. All except for the little finger, which had not yet been done but which had a smear of red from cuticle to first knuckle. No wedding ring, but a mark where one had been, indicating a fairly recent divorce. All of which suggested that she'd just started to paint the last nail before going out for the evening. Before the massive, fatal heart attack. Sir.

He sat on the floor making out a receipt for the dead man's shoes.

'I remember you from the funeral.'

Ned looked surprised.

'You were with the policewoman holding Suzy. Is she your girl-friend? She's really exquisite.'

Ned laughed and stood, handing her the receipt to countersign. No, she's just a colleague.

As they walked downstairs, Ned asked her if it was difficult when she was young, having a dog that wasn't really a pet.

'She wasn't a pet at all. He wouldn't even throw a ball for her.'

Chippy suddenly stopped.

'Mum said you'd try and ask me questions. And that I shouldn't get "drawn in". She said you were very clever.'

'It wasn't a clever question, and it doesn't matter. Thanks for your help with the shoes.'

She held the door open for him.

'He once caught me dressing her up in my ballet clothes. Tutu, leg-warmers, headband, the lot. She looked wicked. He went ballistic. I was in deep shit. Deep dog shit.'

They grinned at one another. And then it was Chippy's turn.

'If she's just a colleague, why were you looking at her like that?'

'I mustn't get drawn in, Miss Best. By your clever questions.'

She nodded and closed the door.

'Where's the Dog Tart?'

'Still on holiday, sir.'

'She got that mutt with her?'

'Yes sir. Still got the mutt.'

'Lucky fucking mutt.'

And away to the canteen Fatso waddled. Ned saw no reason to mention that Kate was trying to track down Nick Parsons. He had the impression she didn't even want Ned to know about that. She hadn't reckoned on Extra Bilge's compulsive dissemination of trivia. Except this might not be trivia. Given time, he might have a few questions for Mr Parsons himself. If she managed to find him. Thus far he'd managed to resist the urge to call her. One day at a time. One day at a time. And then his phone rang. It was a voice message from Large Sarge. Young Kate had had some sort of bother with her van. The Dog Unit wasn't too pressed, so he'd given her an extra week. She'd said to pass on to Mr Ned that 'the witness was safe'.

'*. . . he rang me up after the Oscars and said: "'Ello, Tommy. You done really well, winning the gong, making loads of dosh, only I've got some advice for you. It's sumfing that not many people know . . ."*'

The studio audience laughs at the Michael Caine impression.

'*". . . by all means race out and buy Angie a diamond tiara, or a ski chalet in Klosters. But whatever you bleeping well do, don't bleeping buy a bleeping yacht." Best advice I've ever been given! Bob Hoskins told me years later Michael had rung him up after . . . I think it was* Who Framed Roger Rabbit? *. . . and said exactly the same thing – only with even more bleeps! . . .*'

Ned pressed the Pause button and put the kettle on. He was watching the tribute programme *Our Best Friend* recorded the week Sir Tommy died. Wasn't exactly sure what he was looking for. To know him a bit better, certainly. To glimpse the man behind the fame. Clichéd as that sounded, it was important. If Sir Tommy had been mugged to death by a stranger acting on the spur of the moment – perhaps not recognising him in the dark – it wouldn't matter what he was like deep down inside. But if he had a more sophisticated relationship with his killer, then knowing who Sir Tommy Best really was could become pivotal in the solution of the crime. Ned wondered about the objective corollary: if Sir Tommy was every bit as good as his surname suggested, then did it argue for a casual killing? Hardly. Otherwise no one would ever slaughter innocents. Ned stirred the tea and pressed Play.

'. . . *you know the sort of thing – the kind of star who gushes on about having "*. . . *the most extraordinary experience. I mean, you go to the men's room at the Academy Awards, and there's Robert de Niro* . . . *you know* . . . *and I'm thinking like, oh my God! I'm standing next to Travis Bickle* . . . *Vito Corleone* . . . *Jake LaMotta* . . . *This guy is a living god. I mean, he's created people I know better than my own family, and I'm thinking like, what's a little nobody like me even doing here?"'*

Sir Tommy drops the slightly effete West Coast accent.

'*To which the short answer is: having a pee.*'

Big laugh.

'*Now, you'll never catch me carrying on like that* . . .'

He holds the pause perfectly.

'. . . *because I use the disabled loos, and the only star I ever meet in there has four paws, a cold nose and a bushy tail. Say goodnight, Suzy.*'

The huge Comic Relief audience roars with laughter and shouts out 'Goodnight, Suzy,' then erupts into tumultuous applause as Sir Tommy and Suzy go off-stage. That clip seemed to answer a question that had been nagging Ned: was there – heresy of heresies – a sense of connivance in his modesty? Answer, no. Sir Tommy came over as a thoroughly decent man. A *mensch*.

'. . . *Ah, yes. Never forget that. The wind caught the bloody thing and it billowed up around me. Felt like forever while I struggled to pull the damn thing in. But you know the strange thing – I'm no method actor, Jonathan, but I actually felt – for real – that if I didn't get that parachute down, the Germans would have me. Ridiculous, I know. I mean, for heaven's sake it was just a day-for-night shoot in the dear old Vale of Evesham, not Nazi-occupied France, but of course I couldn't see a thing. Couldn't see Micky Powell. Couldn't see Bobby Krasker. Couldn't see the sparks standing around with their mugs of tea. Couldn't see anything. I was blinded by all that white silk. For a few seconds I felt sheer, utter panic. It's the only moment in my entire career I've ever had that feeling – of actually living the emotion rather than putting it on, and, of course, the irony is that this one moment when I'm not acting, you can't see me! Can't see my face! There I am – absolutely petrified – and all you can see is that great white shimmering shroud signalling to the Germans: "Here's the man you're looking for! Quick! He's over here!"*'

'*It is an extraordinary moment in the cinema. Let's have a look at it, the famous parachute scene from* The Fields of France . . .'

But Ned never saw it. He was out the door. He had a date with the Psychiatrists. At the dogs.

The attraction of the Greyhound Stadium to the guerrilla trick cyclists was white, a metre high and 410 metres long. The railing ran around the inside of the track, angled slightly outwards over the smaller rail on which the much-mauled mechanical hare ran for its life four nights of the week and all day Monday and Friday. Ned arrived in time for the last race. He was met at the staff entrance by the Head of Security, who happened to be Fatso's cousin. It was hard to think of them sharing anything, let alone two grandparents. It wouldn't have mattered so much him not looking like a pig if only he'd resembled a greyhound. Unfortunately Doggy Dave, though tall and thin, had a totally flat face with a rim of curly orange hair. He looked like a sunflower, but he did not beam. He glowered. He ushered Ned up to the VIP box in silence, leaving the detective to muse on what the medieval schoolmen would have made of a man with a face like a child's drawing of the sun, but whose cold and morose temperament had been determined by the great ringed planet.

The other occupants of the box were a sleek and tanned man in his fifties who looked as if he managed a football team, and a bubbly woman ten years younger with a mass of blonde curls and thigh-length boots who probably managed a beauty salon. Although, it occurred to Ned, it might be the other way round. As soon as the last dog cleared the post they downed their champagne and hurried off giggling into the night. After a minute or so of silence Doggy Dave morosely volunteered the information that he was the Professor of Medical Ethics at the University and she was some-thing senior in Customs and Excise, thus confirming Ned's belief that first impressions were bollocks. He occasionally wondered if this wasn't just a no-blame way of saying that he was a dreadful judge of the relationship between appearance and character. He certainly had no idea if people were well or badly dressed. He couldn't tell by looking at them if they were rich or poor. Far from making him a bad detective, he had decided, his shortcomings forced him to be a better one. He had to know things in order to decide. Yuh right, Ned, he said to himself, staring at the rim of tax-deductible lipstick around her empty VAT-paid champagne flute. Keep telling yourself that.

As the greyhounds were led away from the track, Ned pondered on the sheer dogginess of this case. He had wanted a canine mystery to solve ever since he first glimpsed the Dog Tart . . . er . . . Kate. It was three years ago. A joint operation with the Security Service. They had forty minutes top whack to find a bomb factory in a gaunt four-storey terrace house behind the railway station. It was an in and out job. No arrests to be made. No trace of police pres-ence to be left. The tenant had been delayed in a pub car park by the old puncture stunt. There were just two others going in with Ned: a middle-aged explosives expert from the Security Service who looked like a bank manager and this girl who looked like no one Ned had ever seen in his entire life. Even the bespectacled Bang Boffin, as Fatso called him, who had seemed so totally single-minded at the briefing, kept glancing at her in the rear-view mirror as they drove over to the house. She only had eyes for her orange and white spaniel, Banshee, whom she'd trained to sniff out a penny banger in a Thermos flask buried three feet under concrete from a moving train a mile away. Well, that was how Ned described it to the team the next day.

So in they went. Ned's job was to watch out for trip wires, non-exploding evidence and a sudden return. He didn't really see much of the Bang Boffin, who spent his time taking snaps and notes, but he saw plenty of Banshee and her handler as they sniffed and swished from room to room. Ned also made himself responsible for tidying up behind the dog team – to eliminate all signs of their presence. Apart from replacing the occasional chair, he had little to do on that score. Kate and Banshee slipped like a pair of eels though the warren of rooms. Eel. That was a funny word to use in the light of all those stories he had heard about her trademark baggy coveralls. Eels have notoriously unshapely figures. Most unlike her. No, eel was apt because, as the song went, of something in the way she moved. Funny, he thought, as he followed her slim, curvy, sinewy, darting form. Her perfect bottom. Physically she seemed totally assured, totally un-selfconscious. Not at all like the Dog Tart of gossip and legend. And here's the thing. That night, on that tense operation, in that house of dangers, her overalls were as tight as skin. You see, Ned? You aren't as blind to appearances as you make out.

When they got back, the first thing they had to do even before the debriefing was to take their overalls off. Overalls they had been given by the Security Service, that left no traces. They shed nothing, but retained any dust they had been in contact with which could then be vacuumed off and tested. The reason the catsuit fitted Kate so perfectly was that it wasn't her own, and the less danger of snagging on something the better. When she returned with it bagged up and in full shapeless mode, Ned started to understand what people had been on about.

It turned out they were all heroes that night. The house had enough in it to take out half the city. Banshee won a no-publicity PDSA Gold Medal, the Bang Boffin stepped back into the shadows, and Ned awoke to the realisation that he was enthralled and in thrall. That was why this was so bloody perverse, he thought, as he sat in the VIP box at the stadium watching the floodlights going out, bank after bank. Here is the dog case to end all dog cases, and I've been as tongue-tied as ever with her. I haven't been able to 'shine and solve' as my bloody mother would say, and even if I could, Kate isn't here to see it.

The stadium was absolutely dark now. Doggy Dave had gone off to keep an eye out for the trick cyclists. Silence now. What was in the fridge for when he got back? That pasta bake. Would he feel like it? And would he feel like heating it up, or would he wander around the flat, eating it cold out of the bowl as he so often did. Strange, that leathery translucence of melted parmesan when cold. A real fall from grace. What would it be like to live with someone again? It had been so long. Was his isolation becoming entrenched? Should he pull himself together now, and start eating hot food at a table with a napkin, in preparation for settling down with Kate? God, he said to himself, you don't half think a load of bollocks. And then the lights in the VIP box went out.

Ned had a torch, but didn't want to use it in case the cyclists came in by another entrance and saw the light flashing about. He sat a while for his eyes to acclimatise. Except they didn't. The overhang of the stadium roof blotted out the city lights and there was no moon. Pitch black. Hmm. He was getting seriously peckish. Hadn't he seen a bowl of nuts on the table where the Prof and Revenue Queen were sitting? And maybe some grissini sticks. Or were they cheese straws? Where were they? He stood and took a tentative step forward. Then another. Why do we stoop when we can't see, even when there are no doorways or low chandeliers? He straightened up, then crashed into something that he tipped forward over, landing on his back on the floor. A sofa. What sofa? Was there a sofa? He felt about a bit. No, it was a padded armchair. He remembered that, a bluey-grey one, but it should have been over there. He must have got the room wrong by ninety degrees. And now he had lost all orientation.

This was turning into a bit of a mission. He wasn't driven now by the siren song of the wild cashew but by pride and curiosity. He was not a clumsy man. He'd played Danny Zuko in *Grease* at school. He was a judo black belt. He stood, banging his head on some springy-armed floor lamp. A hunched step forward and he hit his shin on the sharp edge of a coffee table. His respect for Tommy Best was growing. He felt around gingerly. What was this? His hand was suddenly dripping wet and freezing cold. Champagne bucket. Great. Now for those nuts. He carefully edged around the chair she had been sitting in. Felt ahead over the table. Glass one, check. Glass two, check. A bowl. At last. Hunger over. He grabbed some and – a second later – spat the mouthful out in utter horror. It was a bowl full of olive stones and pistachio shells. God, how vile. Wash mouth out. Quick. Where's that fucking ice-bucket? He turned, took a step, crashed his other shin, sent the coffee table flying.

Doggy Dave's torch beam caught the crack detective sitting in a pile of upside-down furniture, soaking wet, with his face screwed up in lingering disgust.

'It's wheels within wheels,' said Doggy Dave lugubriously as they stood in the dark watching the cyclists career round the railing in the now floodlit stadium. It wasn't apparent what the rules were – overtaking was clearly a no-no – but it didn't look random either.

'You're here because Benjamin's your boss, like. And they're here because the dad of one of the cyclists is buttering the catering manager's muffin. It's like I say, wheels within wheels.'

Benjamin? Hearing Fatso's real name unfailingly tripped Ned up. Someone misjudged a joint in the railing and was jolted off in a

bone-crunching crash-landing. As for buttering people's muffins . . .
proper Poet Laureate, our Doggy Dave.

''Ere, Mr Ned. What you call old Benjamin, then? You lot. Must
call him something. A nickname.'

A cyclist going like the clappers deliberately bumped the one in
front, who was then pulled off the railing by a couple of what
seemed to be race stewards. They reminded Ned of the targets at
his Taser training awayday.

'"Sir",' he said, quick as a flash. Any delay would be highly
suspicious. 'We call him "sir".'

Doggy Dave nodded.

'He done well, has the Lump. That's what we call him at home.
The Lump.'

'Sir,' repeated Ned dreamily. Bumps. That's what it was. Bumps.
They all started the same distance apart, and you eliminated the
others by catching them up and nudging into them. Last one on
the circuit, won. Simple and clever. But how did that work on the
walkway in the Docks? With a sheer drop, rather than soft grass?

'Right,' said Ned. 'I'm going to say hullo. You stay here, Dave.
Best if it's just me. Somewhere in this room there are some cheese
straws, if you get peckish. Only no using your torch. It's cheating.'

He was walking down through the seating on the ground floor
of the stand, vaguely wondering how to play it, when he noticed
two figures, warmly dressed against the cold, enjoying the action.
One introduced herself as Marjorie from New Events, the other as
Phyllida from New Media. Ned mumbled something about being
more on the research side . . .

'Audience or programme?' asked Marjorie.

Ned was saved having to answer because their attention was
suddenly split between a catastrophic multiple pile-up on the railing,
and the appearance of a bionic woman in her early forties bearing
a Thermos, some paper cups and a plate of brownies. She had
plump lips, long eyelashes and blonde hair, none of which she
owed to nature. It turned out she was the catering manager at the
stadium. Ah, thought Ned. Our lady of the buttered muffin. He

tried not to look down. They watched the cyclists hurtling past the semi-inert and bleeding bodies of the fallen.

'That answers Derek's big worry then,' said Phyllida through a chocolatey mouthful. 'About it not being violent enough.'

Big relief, agreed Marjorie. My problem, Phyllida confided in Ned, is do I care? Ned wasn't sure whether to shrug or nod, so he did both. She turned to him with an earnest little expression.

'I mean, you must know Jason tons better than I do, but wouldn't he be worried about Profile Definition?'

'That's exactly what I was thinking,' said Ned, going for thoughtful concern-sharer, rather than clever-dick second-guesser.

Phyllida nodded furiously. 'Are you going to tell him? I don't want to double up.'

Ned stretched his back, as if he'd just driven a long way.

'Well, I've got to do a report on all this. Whether he'll see it . . .'

More furious nodding.

'Given Jason's . . . you know . . . I mean, it wouldn't hurt, you simply expressing our concerns,' Ned suggested in a brotherly sort of way, wrinkling his forehead and speaking soft.

'Thanks for that. Bless you.'

They watched for a bit. The thing about trick cycling was that if you went too slow or too fast, you fell off the track. But get in your groove, as Ned murmured to his new friend, and you had something almost tantric going on.

'Oh, my God!' cried Phyllida. 'Wouldn't it be great to get David Bowie to present?'

Ned was just starting to enjoy himself dreaming up riskier banalities, when they were joined by an entirely new player who shattered the atmosphere and shunted the night on. He was wearing a black duffle coat and a grey Russian fur hat with ear flaps akimbo. He had the wispy black beard of an anarchist, the wire-framed spectacles of a poet and the manner of a pretentious git. He didn't give his name. If these were, he waved expansively at the mayhem before them, the Psychiatrists, then he was their Chief Consultant. He then launched a bid to impress the representatives of Sky Sports – naturally including Ned. There was talk of IP rights and secondary windows, of 'beside the line' marketing and 'licensing out', of feeds, intakes and uplinks – all of which went down a treat with Marjorie and Phyllida. He then walked them closer to the excitements at the rail, pointing out the star cyclists, the indefatigable first aid team, the pit mechanics. He talked of it as a 'cross-over' between counter-culture and mainstream . . . the appeal to teenagers as a guerrilla sport . . . the bicycle as green statement . . . the stellar growth of cycling as consumer market . . . the zen of balance on two wheels . . . the yin of business . . . the yang of violence . . .

'You're operating a bump system here, aren't you?' Ned interrupted. Black Duffle Coat agreed.

'That's great for a circular track, but how do you manage on a linear, A to B rail? You must have some like that?'

Phyllida looked terribly impressed. Terribly proud.

Black Duffle Coat said indeed they did. There was a brilliant stretch of railing over grass at the airport, but security there was too tight. But the best was at the Docks. Really dramatic. What they did there was bigger staggers on the start and rate it on course speed, not bumps.

'So you keep . . . er . . . written records?' asked Ned vaguely, his eyes fixed on a pair of cyclists zipping past only inches apart.

Black Duffle Coat assured him that they kept meticulous records of all their meets, whether 'circuits and bumps' or 'line and time'. That way, if they had to leg it at any point, they'd know what the pecking order was, and how to place the cyclists when they resumed. He pointed at two men in kagouls sitting on folding fishermen's chairs with a laptop, exercise books and a six-pack of lager. One of them had his hand up our lady of the muffin's ivory Puffa jacket. Ah. The butterer revealed.

'Could we have a quiet word?' asked Ned, in a tone of voice the others had not yet heard, and he led the man away with the gentlest of touches on his black duffle sleeve.

Time passed. Cyclists crashed. Marjorie texted. Phyllida jigged from one varnished-toed, fur-encased foot to the next, hugging herself against the cold, and maybe as the closest substitute she had for her new best friend. He meanwhile showed Black Duffle Coat something he produced from an inner pocket. Small, like those things you keep credit cards in. Black Duffle Coat peered at it, and started to fidget. They were too far away to be heard, particularly over the crunch of bones and aluminium. She could tell even at a distance that Ned was doing most of the talking, because of the little wisps of hoar breath that streamed from his lips, caught in the stadium backlight. Black Duffle Coat spoke little. His breath looked more like the fitful puffs of an Apache smoke signal, and what it was saying was 'Get me out of here!'

Ned spoke of murder, of accessory to murder, of trespass, of breaking and entering, of behaviour likely to cause a breach of the peace, of health and safety violations, of endangering the lives of others, of the destruction of property, of public liability and insurance offences, of failure to report crimes, of theft in the matter of electricity for floodlights, coffee and chocolate brownies. Ned listed breaches of laws ancient and modern, bylaws, bike laws, dock laws, the Children's Act, the Unauthorised (Temporary) Closure of Public Walkways Act of 1877, the Organisation of Public Sports Regulations of 1935 and 1955. And then back to the wilful destruction of evidence in a murder case.

Black Duffle Coat tried excuses, tried bluster, tried spluttering. Eventually he alighted on surly contrition and stuck with that. It was as well that he did, because from time to time Ned glanced round with a smile at the emissaries from Sky, reminding Black Duffle Coat that his plans for the globalisation of Trick Cycling were hanging in the balance. The Coat agreed to come in the next day with the names and addresses of everyone present on the walkway the night Sir Tommy fell: racers and officials. But Ned had some questions he wanted answers to there and then.

Phyllida saw them waiting for a lull to step over the rail. Then they went up to the two scorers. The one who was scoring with our lady of the muffin withdrew his hand and stood sharply. He listened to Black Duffle Coat for a bit, then rummaged in an exercise book. He showed the open pages to Ned. Then they summoned a couple of cyclists. One was sitting in a heap having his shin bandaged. The other had to be yanked off the track. Big huddle now. Ned listening. Taking notes.

'You know, Phills,' said Marjorie mid-texting. 'I reckon he's not from Research at all . . .'

Phyllida's china-blue eyes widened.

'Just look at him. Pinning them down. Asking the tough questions. Making them jump. The way he's carrying on . . .'

More texting. The race was grinding to a halt as other cyclists joined the scrum around Ned. Phyllida could barely stand the suspense. Her little brows furrowed. She fairly bobbed up and down.

'. . . he's just got to be Business Affairs.'

Phyllida gazed round at her new hero with even more respect; hugged herself even tighter. At that exact moment, he broke away from the throng and walked towards them, holding the exercise book. He paused, fixing Phyllida with his huge brown eyes and deep, gentle voice.

'I'm off now. Tell Jason it's about packaging it with free-running, parkour, bungee-jumping, scaling public buildings and guerrilla gardening. Edgy. Urban. Sexy. Brand it as Bandit Sports.'

'Oh my God – Bandit Sports!' wailed Phyllida. 'That's soooo brilliant!'

'But then,' Ned added, 'what do I know? I'm just a murder squad detective.'

Marjorie did a perfect double-take and looked around in a panic as if caught in a sting operation, but it took Phyllida a moment for the truth to sink in.

'Does that mean you won't be at Jason's Mind Munch on Thursday?' she called plaintively after Ned.

But he just kept walking. Doggy Dave was lurking by the car. He was relieved to hear that all had gone well. It was hard to tell in the gloom of the car park, but Doggy Dave looked faintly dishevelled. He seemed to have a fresh cut on his cheek and what looked like bits of cheese straw in his hair. But it could just have been the glint of sodium on ginger.

'Say wotcha to the Lump for me,' said Doggy Dave.

Ned said he would, and went home.

'Seems like we're getting some traction,' said Chief Superintendent Larribee. They were in Meeting Room 1 as Fatso's office was in particular need of mucking out. For weeks the cleaners had refused to go in there after sighting a rat in the debris banked up around the waste bin. Chief Superintendent Larribee had no nickname. You've got to like someone a little to give them a nickname, but everyone referred to her in full as Chief Superintendent Larribee. She pitched up for monthly Case Review, and no one knew where she spent the intervening time. There had been talk of putting a tail on her, but the consensus was that the truth would be even duller than they imagined.

When she had first taken CR, Fatso asked Span to look her up and check out her mighty feats of coppering. How many professional criminals were rotting in hulks, crying revenge on the woman who had cut them off in their villainous prime? Did she have a nose for poisons? An eye for a swindle? An ear for the lie? Did she have the chops for hard questioning, or did she fillet out the truth without you knowing? Was her forte reading blood-spattered crime scenes or corrupt balance sheets? Was she instinctive or technical? How was she in the muck and bullets? In the lab? In the witness box at the Bailey? Up the Dog and Vomit for the Christmas party? What trail of gnarled old coppers, of pining Dr Watsons had she left behind, devotedly recalling with rheumy eyes her firework displays of deduction, tenacity and intuition? What pimply constables pounded the beat driven on only by the solemn mantra: 'When I grow up, I want to be just like Chief Superintendent Larribee'?

Answer came there none. She had risen to her lofty rank with no visible justification. She had solved no crimes that anyone could recall. She had apparently run no teams that had ever solved a crime. She was a very senior police virgin, and far from that attracting derision, it won her huge respect. She had, after all, managed effort-lessly what many others worked so hard for: maximum promotion for zero achievement. The rest had to graft and risk failure. Not so Chief Superintendent Larribee. Huge respect, no liking.

It didn't help, on Planet Fatso, that she had a face like an elderly croissant. He enjoyed the attractiveness of others, male and female. He could be – and was – as ugly as he pleased, but it was his ugli-ness. All his. He hogged it and wouldn't share his last ugly with anyone. Some unkind souls would say that Chief Superintendent Larribee had no need of Fatso's generosity. Her skin was tan-coloured and flakey. Her jowls were desiccated, her lips cracked, her eye bags voluminous and leathery. She had unerringly poor dress-sense. Plus, she outranked him. So twelve times a year, for an hour or so, Fatso seemed ever so slightly wrong-trottered.

Last month's buzz-phrase was 'ping me'. Extra Bilge kept a list inside the coffee cupboard door. Others included 'caught in the eddies', 'helicopter view', 'socialise the issue', 'thought show-ers', 'warm and fuzzies', 'customer-centric', 'parking lot issues' and – the only phrase to appear seven times – 'totally inappropri-ate'. The day before CR, they had a sweepstake to guess the next cliché. No one had won it yet. Evidently some thought the chances of Chief Superintendent Larribee choosing 'suck my lolly' or 'mois-turiser regime' were, though remote, worth the 50p punt. Anyway, this month it was 'traction', and Ned was starting to get some of it.

He told them about last night's admission by the trick cyclists that they had definitely left the way onto the old walkway open that evening. It was part of their urban 'right to roam' guerrilla philosophy: city land should be trespassed, rails ridden, and gates left gaping even if they led, as this one did, to a sheer drop. One cyclist, incidentally, had mentioned seeing the hole and thinking it would be a bad place to come off his bike. All in all, their evidence suggested that Sir Tommy, feeling like a stroll on a nice night, simply took a wrong turning and fell through the hole in the rotten planks to his death. He wasn't to know at ground level that one of the walkways was safe and the other dangerous. Tragic accident.

But other evidence fresh in – forensic evidence – gave the lie to tragic accidents. This wasn't unfamiliar ground to Sir Tommy Best. He hadn't wandered there at random. He had been down to that part of the Docks before.

They had taken samples from the walkway and from the terrace which led up to the steps. That stretch had been the old Lime Quay. It was linked to the rest of the harbour railway system by a line which crossed the cobbles in front of the terraced houses. There they identified a unique mix of lime, ashes and iron oxide. This odd cocktail was only found in this specific area of the Docks – and on the soles both of Sir Tommy Best's favourite trainers and a pair of black dress shoes. Together with the night he died, that made three visits they now knew about.

Ned decided not to pause to let Chief Superintendent Larribee and Fatso wallow in the revelation. After all, it was dramatic but intrinsically meaningless. It could simply have been a place where Sir Tommy liked to walk. So he reminded them that the great man was not alone. He had his faithful dog with him. If they had simply been on a regular stroll and gone up the wrong flight of stairs, Suzy would have fallen through the planks into the water with him. But when she was found she was bone dry and very distressed, and her harness was broken. Whatever had happened on the walkway required them to be separated. And they knew she had been with him at least as far as the terrace, because swabs taken between the pads of her paws the morning she was found showed traces of the same lime, ashes and iron oxide mix. Ned knew that they must have come from that night, because earlier in the day Suzy had been to have a bath, shampoo and nail clip. To make her beautiful for the Film Theatre that evening.

He did not let up. He pushed Chief Superintendent Larribee straight into the rendezvous hypothesis: the speeding up behind the lorry/church clock/call to Cyril scenario. Then he threw in the strange case of the missing £1,000, and let her get there for herself.

'Are we perhaps looking at blackmail, Detective Chief Inspector?' asked Chief Superintendent Larribee, with a smug glint in a bloodshot eye. She liked 'we' an awful lot. And she was welcome to it, according to Fatso, if it kept her off his back for 353 days in the year. He let out a delightfully ambiguous 'Aah!' noise that suggested she'd just cracked the case on her own, and at the same time hinted she was barely keeping up.

Ned said they could not rule out blackmail.

'Best cut along, then,' said Fatso before Chief Superintendent Larribee could come up with any other screamingly obvious ideas. 'We don't want it happening again.' And he gave Ned a fleeting wink on her blind side.

Ned went back to his office to drop off the files. For all the recent breaks, he did not have a spring in his step. The evidence in the Best case was mounting, but against whom or what was, if anything, less clear. The notion that Sir Tommy had gone down to the Docks – three times – to bail out a friend in need was a bit unlikely. There lay one of the big mysteries: were his wanderings at the Lime Quay directly related to his death or coincidental? It was certainly easier to imagine the mugging-gone-wrong scenario: ruffians light upon old boy on a regular walk – than the blackmail-murder caper: slaughter in the pay-off zone. More likely the blackmailee would try to bump off his persecutor. Perhaps the National Treasure had declared the £1,000 to be his final payment, and the blackmailer wasn't amused. And if blackmail, what exactly had Sir Tommy done? Dame Angie didn't seem to know. It was certainly easier to maintain the idea of Sir Tommy's innocence than build the idea of his guilt. Not that an affair or whatever it was, amounted to big-time guilt. The break on this was as likely to come from a prying tabloid as a murder squad line of enquiry, but so far there was not a whisper. If Chief Superintendent Larribee wanted to see it as traction, fine. Ned just felt stuck in the familiar, essential process of elimination. Where to next? The canteen, he reckoned. Didn't they do rock cakes on Thursdays?

7

KATE WAS HAVING AN ODD time with him. Not in the seedy way she feared: he showed no sexual interest in her. Didn't matter; barricades were never wasted. They saved her having to make a calculation as to whether someone was predatory, and she was a hopeless judge. Plus she dreaded giving anyone a sign that she welcomed their attention. Barricades worked both ways. She could stand on tiptoe in her elephantine coveralls to change a lightbulb in the puppy kennel, and no one could see the arch of her back or think she was showing it off. But Nick Parsons couldn't see her at all, and that was a big relief. After a couple of snore-filled nights she took a gigantic risk and removed the water-jug.

The longer she stayed with Nick, the more gripped and puzzled she became. How do blind people manage without all those things that mean so much? The big things, like making judgements about people from the way they look. Who do you trust? And the little things – knowing the Cheddar's off because it's got blue bits. Seeing if it looks like rain. How did they manage without being able to decide anything on appearances? And what about the effect that their blindness had on those around them? How easy could it be to treat them as normal? She became aware as she watched him moving around the kitchen range how fixated she was becoming on his safety. Will he burn himself? Does he know he's dropped the oven glove? What if he trips over it? What'll he use to take the pan out of the oven? Should she help? This wasn't like helping blind people cross the road. That had more in common with buying the *Big Issue*. It told the world she was nice and gave her a tiny little buzz. Both acts also saved having to engage with a strange, incomplete person. This was different. This was in her face, and Kate had spent years keeping things out of her face. Being with Nick was forcing her to empathise with a human being.

'What are you thinking about?' she wanted to ask him as he chopped onions. If she'd been blind, she'd have been thinking, is this slice too big? How close is the blade? Don't they make onion flakes? Where's my finger? She wanted to ask, but she didn't. The question would sound too intimate even with the word 'about' on the end, however banal the answer. It was used in films where the soon-to-be-lovers start to speak at the same time. You have to talk simultaneously several times before you have sex, then the morning after you've had sex you go to the market together and feel melons. Often the man feels the melons, to show that he is caring and discerning and sensuous. You know. Melons. Then later on, when it's time to introduce some wistfulness, with the possibility that a love like theirs cannot survive in the real world, one of them asks 'What are you thinking?' She watched quite a lot of films.

Anyway, she just knew looking at him that he was not thinking about chopping onions. And then he started to talk.

'I used to eat the lot. The brains and the balls and the livers and the lights. Raw oysters, foie gras, veal. I didn't give a stuff for other people's squeamishness. Nor for their meaningless distinctions. What's wrong with eating veal? Why is it OK to nosh on lamb, but not veal? Roast veal with almond sauce – lovely. Schnitzels. Veal chops. The lamb is no less dead. Or the cod with chips. Sure, force-feeding isn't very nice, but neither is suffocating to death on the deck of a trawler in the North Sea. Or wading through blood, prodded along with electric shocks, waiting your turn to receive a bolt in the head. None of it's very nice. So why split hairs? Eat and enjoy, I thought. Then, one night, I had a dream.

'I was in a big white room, with white skirting boards but no furniture, and in this room was every animal I had ever eaten. Not just the steaks and roast chickens, but all the soups and the gravies. I hadn't thought about it before, but there can be bits of twenty dead cows in one stock cube. Perhaps the most shocking thing was the calves. There were calves as far as I could see. And I couldn't work out why until I remembered the cheese. All the cheese I'd stuffed myself with over the years set with rennet made from the linings of calves' stomachs. And the jellies. So there they all were. The room was now enormous like an aircraft hangar, just to get them all in. They were alive and they stood there, not jostling or fighting or shitting or doing anything. Just standing about. Occasionally one would give a snort or that lowing sound. Mostly they just stared at me. There were some animals I had no idea I had eaten. There were several horses, plus a few dogs and a cat. God knows when I ate the cat. And there were still smaller things sitting between all the hoofs and paws. I don't know what they all were. Guinea pigs or rats. Rabbits for sure. The little beasts weren't scurrying away, frightened of being trodden on or anything. They all knew they had nothing to fear from the other animals. Just from me.'

And then he cut his finger. Kate rushed over and led him to the sink and washed the wound and wrapped it in kitchen paper and sat him down while she hunted for plasters and antiseptic cream. Then she dressed the cut, which was a bit deep and bloody. She told him he was lucky he'd just had a tetanus jab at the hospital, and that at least this injury wasn't down to her. He said the others weren't really, because he knew blind people shouldn't drive cars. She looked at him to see if he was joking, and he wasn't. It didn't feel particularly intimate, but it wasn't impersonal either. It was surprising how open he was about his feelings. She'd have betted on him being all uptight and closed in, him living so totally alone. Maybe it all just got pent up, and then she had showed and out it all tumbled. Bet his sister couldn't get a word in for days.

So they talked some more about food, and she nudged it round to food and being blind. Turned out he didn't care about mould on cheese. Reckoned all cheese was slightly off anyway – and as long as you ate it up within a few weeks, it wouldn't kill you. In fact, blindness was a bit of a liberation from what he pompously called 'the tyranny of trivia'. He said he used to fixate on the appearance of food. He'd decide to make a salad which was entirely red. Then he'd find himself hunting through the peppers to find one with not a single streak – or even hint – of green or yellow in it. Bonkers. He didn't care now. Couldn't control it; didn't want to. He and his sister had four big sessions a year filling the freezers with food for every season. He knew the layout of the compartments and where the stews were, and the frozen vegetables, and the puddings. He still loved good food but he didn't care what it was, as long as no animal had died to make it. Then he asked about her vegetarianism. Her reasons. Kate never talked about her eating habits, so she brushed it away with her old formula: mostly health, tiny bit moral. It seemed to do the trick.

And then there was Suzy. He suddenly asked her what exactly she needed him to do. He knew she'd started to explain at the hospital, but he hadn't taken much in. Big understatement, she thought and said she didn't know a whole lot more than had been in the papers, but she strongly believed that if anyone could help them find out who had killed Sir Tommy Best, it was Suzy . . . She broke off. Nick's jaw had dropped. He looked ashen-faced. Oh my God, she thought. He doesn't know. He's got to be the only person in the whole world who doesn't know Tommy Best is dead. Didn't know.

'. . . When did he die? How . . . did it happen . . . ?'

As she tried to answer him, tears welled up in his eyes.

'But murder? He was murdered?'

She reluctantly mumbled yes, not wanting to upset him any more.

'It looks that way. We don't know for sure. That's why Suzy and I are here.'

He got up and tore some kitchen paper off the rack by the dresser. He mopped his eyes, blew his nose, and slumped back in his chair while she told him the little she was allowed to about what had happened that night. They sat quietly for a while, and then he called

Suzy's name. She came and sat by his side, and he ran his fingers through the fur at the base of her neck.

'I just thought Suzy was with you because she was retired . . . It never crossed my mind . . .'

He tried to pull himself together. It took a while.

'I really loved that man. When I was first diagnosed, I didn't go to see my own father. I went to Tommy. He was so amazing to me . . . I was OK at first. Calm, together. Then, I just seemed to fall apart. It was awful, what I said to him. Told him I couldn't stand the thought of going blind. Told him I dreaded the helplessness, but I detested the aids. Hated how blind people looked: the white sticks, the dark glasses, the guide dogs with their harnesses. The sheer, fucking ugly surgical truss feel of it all. It was crazy. I'd been working with blind people for years. Had no idea I thought that way until I heard myself blurting it out to Tommy. Unforgivable . . . He was great about it. Said he had felt exactly the same at first. He just couldn't understand that I didn't want a dog. And that was the one thing I couldn't explain to him. He even offered me Suzy back. Imagine! He knew how I felt about her. That she was the best I'd ever trained. Said I could have her, to make it as easy for me as possible. As easy to go blind as possible.'

He sat, stroking the dog, shaking his head. Fuck me, Kate thought. He's done nothing but shout and sulk and cry since I met him. Really high-maintenance. All that emotion. Who needs it?

She was playing tennis with Suzy in the meadow where they had heard the crash. She was bashing the ball as far as she could and Suzy was running and fetching, when suddenly there was Nick behind her. She had no idea how he'd found them. He stood still and silent while Suzy chased the ball and brought it back to her. Then Kate hit it away again, and as Suzy dashed off, he spoke very calmly.

'Tell me how she returns. Does she come back reasonably straight, or does she make an arc – a bigger arc than she needs to?'

Kate watched, intrigued. Suzy caught the ball on the first bounce then went into a slow, expanded turn. She went almost as far to the

111

right as she had gone to retrieve the ball. Nick nodded when Kate told him, and asked her to do it again. Again Suzy made a large sweep before turning towards them. The next questions were about her tail wagging. How high was the tail? How low? How far from side to side? Then her posture. Sagged? Bent-backed? Droopy? Now the eyes. Bloodshot? Dilated pupils? Glazed? Whale-eyed? Her behaviour. Her mouth. Her paws. Her fur. Tell me everything.

Then, when he knew all that Kate knew and could see, he wanted to know whether Suzy had been like this since she was found that morning. Had any of these characteristics developed since then? Had any disappeared since then? Questions, questions, questions. Answers, timings, details. And he wasn't jumpy and self-obsessed or emotional. He was focussed on Suzy, and Kate found that much, much easier.

That night Nick seemed to wait until Suzy had left the kitchen for the cool of the sitting-room, and only then did he tell Kate the thing he couldn't tell Tommy Best: why he didn't want a guide dog. Not even Suzy herself.

'Stress. I couldn't any longer bear to subject a dog to the stress levels guiding the blind imposes. It had been creeping up on me, I suppose. I'd seen some academic work on it – various tests: cortisol, blood pressure – but I knew I'd been seeing it on the ground for years and denying it to myself. It was only when the blind person needing a guide dog turned out to be me that something clicked. Or snapped. I couldn't put another dog through it, and I couldn't take Suzy not just because it would deprive Tommy, but because . . . Some dogs cope better than others, but even the very best – and Suzy was that and then some – can sometimes struggle in the job. It's so demanding, what they have to do.

'I'd seen the faintest, earliest signs of stress in Suzy when she came to me from the puppy walker. Maybe I should have pulled her out. It didn't take the usual form of nerves or temper or volatility. It wasn't something you could really put your finger on. The longer I had her in training, whatever it was seemed to go. The only sign of it left was . . . I don't know. I know it sounds crazy, but she took things almost too seriously.'

They sat in the darkening kitchen. She hadn't lit the candles, and perhaps wasn't going to bother. She listened to the sounds that were becoming familiar: the dull rumble of the fire, the chortling of the boiler, the scratch of cotoneaster on the window pane. So how much of what she was now seeing in Suzy had been there all along? The earnest look was there in the puppy in the photograph on the wardrobe door upstairs. Her mind went back to her first days with her. The difficulty of getting Suzy to play, to do anything for her own amusement. She accepted Kate's cuddles, rather than seeking them out for pleasure. She lacked energy. She moped. She dawdled. She had little interest in food. Kate had put it down to grief, but wondered if there was more to it. It was almost as if Suzy was beating herself up. She had been unable to save her master's life; could dogs feel anything approaching guilt?

Kate had taken Suzy to her vet, a formidable cross-eyed woman in a pleated skirt who had known Suzy for as long as Tommy had had her. The vet had given the dog a thorough check-up and said she was in pretty good shape. Slight weight loss. Fur mostly seemed to be staying put. Never ate much at the best of times. Not a young dog, ye know. She put Suzy's listlessness down to unemployment. 'Tommy kept her blessed snout to the grindstone,' she barked, 'and now she's got time on her paws.' Grief? Overrated, human bloody emotion. Guilt? Don't be a damn fool, my dear. She's a dog. Bow-wow.

Kate had come away from the encounter resolving to fill Suzy's days with doggy activity. She had spent her life with humans, doing human things, being responsible for a human. It was time for her to be a dog again. Time for bones and ball games. By the time they went to find Nick, Suzy was doing pretty well. She'd bring a ball back, and run and play, but only up to a point. It was as if she hit a barrier. Her heart wasn't in it. Kate couldn't help but feel that Suzy saw it all as some form of work. Her new job: being a dog of leisure. Or was it that she was doing it as a favour to Kate? Either way, Suzy was somehow keeping part of herself closed off. She may be a dog, but try telling her that. Bow-wow my arse.

She did light a candle. Nick stirred at the strike, smelling the

113

sulphur in the match. She turned to a clean page in her notebook and started writing out the questions she needed Nick to answer. She flipped to the notes she'd scrawled at the first Fatso session she'd attended on the Best case. And as she looked at the page she saw something she hadn't remembered. Something she wouldn't have guessed she'd done, but there it was like a truth uttered in drunkenness, quoted back at you the next day. Something which intrigued her and made her blush. She had written down and circled the phrase 'She's our only witness.' and drawn a line off to the margin. There she'd squiggled the word NED and around it she'd doodled the tiniest garland of flowers.

No one guessed quite so many people lived in the Docks. When Ned set the team on it, he assumed they were talking about perhaps fifty or sixty households. It turned out there were a thousand plus. Developers had set up shop at Baltic Wharf, and over half the apartments in the warehouse complex were inhabited. The India Basin had been residential for a decade; it was where the city's great and good had penthouses. There was the world famous architect's practice with its submarine conning tower on the roof, and the kind of restaurant that is written about so much Ned felt he knew how the food tasted without having to risk the disappointment. Let alone a month's salary. Apparently the celebrity owner-chef lived over the shop. Wonder if he fixed himself up with a freeze-dried Arbroath smokie lozenge on a disc of caramelised seaweed with daiquiri foam on his night off? Or did he have egg and chips? Extra Bilge would soon have the answer to that and countless other riddles. Then it would just be a question of seeing if any of the Dock dwellers knew Sir Tommy Best and/or had criminal records and/or had a motive for black-mailing/bumping off the National Treasure and/or were without an alibi for the night in question . . . Piece of piss, said Spick as he readied a team of rozzers to bang on doors and frighten the horses.

Fatso walked into the Incident Room and stared at the gigantic blow-up of the Docks from the Ordnance Survey along one whole wall. He peered at the nasty little basin where Sir Tommy had been found, the spot marked with a body outline. He ran a porky pinky along the streets that fanned out around it. He breathed black-pudding fumes over the converted warehouses and bijoux developments. His penetrating piggy eyes stared at Lime Quay, with its giveaway cocktail of dirt that winds up on dead men's shoes. He stepped back and took in the storm of activity, revelling in the invigorating atmosphere. The constables marking the households for which data was in. Extra Bilge running cross-checks on the National Police Computer. The clatter of printers and the clamour of phones. Somewhere in this he smelled a solution. He didn't say a thing. He didn't have to. All he had to do was trust Ned and wait.

For a man who famously felt no pressure, Ned was feeling a little pressure. He'd yanked all these people and resources onto the case, not because he suddenly had a tantalising lead, but because he had the exact opposite: a vacuum, a hole, a nagging mystery. Had Sir Tommy gone to the Docks to visit someone he knew? If so, why hadn't Cyril driven him there? Why did he go to them? Why didn't they ever come to him? Or did they, and no one knew about it? Why did Dame Angie not seem to know the answers? Who was ashamed of what? Was there anything to be ashamed of? Indeed, why was it a mystery at all? That, in a way, was the key question.

He wasn't in the Incident Room when Fatso came a-calling. He was scarfed up against the cold; head into the wind along the new walkway. His path was strewn with dead flowers and soggy messages. Matey's crane was still. Perhaps cranes weren't safe to use above a certain wind speed. Extra Bilge would know. Better not to ask him. Ghastly to think of all he'd tell you. The tide was out in the basin. Light glistened off the mud. He stopped and looked out towards the great river. A battered old tug was easing a laden container ship off the wharf on the south bank. It had a line onto the ship's bows, and was leading it into the tideway. Simple image. Sudden connection. Cartoon lightbulb above Ned's bonce. Why not let Suzy loose in the Docks, and see where she goes? Whose door she takes us to? For a moment it seemed like a grand idea, but chasing along just behind it was a pack of problems, and by the time the idea had come to a halt in Ned's brain and the caveats had all caught up with it, Ned could barely glimpse the grand idea for the trouble it would cause.

He got back just as Extra Bilge was printing off the list.

'It's just a first trawl . . . It hasn't been checked . . . The Aspex data isn't in yet . . . It's still raw . . .'

Yeah, no worries, Bilgey Boy. What was it Dad used to say? 'Let the ferret smell the rabbit.' Ned got a sudden, flash memory of his father, who'd taught Politics and Art at the College of Further Education and had been allergic to authority and animal fur. He wouldn't have recognised a ferret if one had bitten him in his flares. His regular barber had, early in their relationship, mistaken him for someone who knew all about whippets and greyhounds. Thereafter the barber would turn to him and say: "Ere, sir. You're a doggy man, ain't you? What should Horace do about this distemper that's going about?' Having missed his chance to admit his total ignorance, he was committed to giving non-committal advice. Mmm, he'd say. Tough one, that. For a time, Young Ned used to go with him to have his hair cut and he fancied that his father almost acted as if he was at the dentist, not the barber. He knew the answer, and would love to impart it, but unfortunately – mumble mumble – he couldn't. There was even one occasion when Ned wondered if his father was being wound up, when the barber thanked him for the excellent advice he'd passed on to Horace. Sir'd be pleased to know Costello had quite got over the kennel cough and was back on his fodder. But the barber seemed really sincere. Maybe Dad had been boning up on doggy ailments between haircuts, or maybe he had a double. Maybe somewhere out there was a genuine doggy man who was the spit of his father. Given the way his mum carried on, maybe it was the doppelgänger who was really his dad. It was a mystery Ned never solved, though the allergy helped explained why he was never allowed to have a pet.

Ned thanked the team, and sent them all home. Then he sat alone in the Incident Room in front of the giant map, looking from the printout up to the wall and down again. Then he got up and made a note of an address at the centre of the map. He rang Spick, and called off any idea of mob-handed house visits. For now. Then he dressed up warm and went back down to the Docks. Alone. To smell the rabbit.

Doc Bones was troubled.

Everything had been going swimmingly for him. Not too many *croakati*, but not too few, either. Too few was no good. Got to ply one's craft. He'd solved the jolly interesting puzzle posed by an almost complete ear they'd found in an allotment after a nasty spat between two gangs. Mrs Bones had lost a couple of pounds which always pleased him. He could again place the balls of his thumbs on either side of her waist, with his middle finger tips meeting at her spine, just as they did that first night. Mrs Bones, incidentally, could not nowadays set Doc Bones any such physical test that he would pass with the ease shown by that raffish medical student thirty years ago, but he still made her laugh. Miss Bones had been vindicated in her decision to stay in the army by getting a rather natty promotion as Military Attaché somewhere *sur le continent*. Doc could still tell his *cisterna chyli* from his inguinal nodes but was pushed to remember the difference between Slovenia and Slovakia. The garden was looking a bit ratty, but then it always did at this time of the year. And he'd soon be off for two weeks at the leprosy hospital in Mumbai, so that was all right. Except it wasn't. That was what had triggered his unease.

It was a bit, only he didn't of course know it, like Ned's father and the barber. If you miss the moment to tell someone something, then the longer you don't tell them, the more difficult it gets to tell them. He'd almost forgotten it himself, and then he checked his diary and realised he'd be knee-deep in *myobacterium leptae* in a fortnight, and that reminded him of the evening he met Sir Tommy Best, and that reminded him of the autopsy he'd done on Sir Tommy, and that reminded him of the tiny thing he knew which he should have told dear old Ned, but which he'd kept to himself because it wasn't relevant, was it. Or should that be, 'was it?'

117

To answer that question, he had to do a bit of research. On the QT, of course. He didn't want the chaps to know until he was sure. Surprising research it was too. It took him into the railway station bookstall, not to earnest magazines explaining the downturn in the economy or the secrets of collecting Georgian daytime jewellery, but to the rack of rags offering insights into what Charlene does in bed to keep her man, and why Razza bought a Bentley station wagon with a bidet in the back. Doc Bones hadn't a clue who Charlene or Razza were. His guess about the bidet was bang on, as it were, but he was way off-beam on bedtime man-keeping. Indeed, as a medical professional he doubted it was anatomically possible. None of this mattered a damn. He'd only bought the celebrity magazines to find out the publishers' addresses. It was back numbers he was after. He needed the editions that had come out immediately after Sir Tommy's death. And the more luridly complete the detail, the better.

The Dog Unit was out on the edge of town, a hotch-potch of buildings backing onto fields with hills beyond. They had once been the kennels of a great estate's hunting dogs. The family had made a killing in the slave trade and yearned for respectability. Landscape gardeners and dancing masters did what they could, but the family soon realised that hunting down the terrified was what it did best. The pianoforte fell silent, the flower beds were grassed over and the locals grew used to the din of incessant barking. The grand house was razed to the ground in 1942 by a lone Heinkel. Some claimed this was a desperately brave precision hit upon a heavily defended ultra hush-hush unit designing death-rays; others said the cowardly pilot couldn't face the flak over the Docks, his assigned target that night, and dropped his bomb-load short before wheeling safely back to Germany. There was even a rumour that on the fiftieth anniversary of the house's destruction a white-haired old gentleman in a Merc with Düsseldorf licence plates had been seen, map in hand, peering out across the vacant fields. Either way, if it was him, he'd got away with it. The Dog Unit had added a cluster of sheds and dog runs around the original, Grade 1 listed kennel courtyard. Two hundred years on, and the locals were still stirred from their beds and serenaded to sleep by a chorus of barks.

It was the first time Ned had been there. He'd wanted to see Kate in her natural habitat, of course, but he'd never had the excuse. Wouldn't do to just pitch up and gawp. No such inhibitions for the women dog handlers. The men didn't bother. The new girl saw him first. She'd just put her bitch Davina through recognition exercises on a new Semtex variant. The explosives safe was in the old building, so she'd stashed the phial and was on her way back when she saw this majorly fit guy perched on the low wall by the water trough in the courtyard. She dashed off to the mess-room to tell the others.

Next thing Ned knew there were faces staring at him through every bottle-glass window in the wall opposite. Then, strangely for a secure police dog kennel, a puppy somehow escaped and suddenly the yard was filled with WPC dog handlers trying to catch a bouncing ball of fur. Except they couldn't – or didn't – and it was Ned it ran up to and Ned's lap it jumped on and Ned's face it licked. The WPCs giggled with vicarious pleasure, and imagined. This would probably have gone on for hours if Large Sarge hadn't bustled into the court-yard. The WPCs and the puppy suddenly remembered a load of things they were meant to be doing elsewhere, and went off to do them.

Large Sarge's office had a pot-bellied stove and a mess of team photos on the back of the door. While Large Sarge made coffee, Ned played spot Kate. She was there, of course, but only just. She did not mug for the camera like the others. Indeed, she made sure it rarely caught her. She hid behind someone else, or held a puppy in front of her face, or looked away. Sometimes she was just a blur – as if she'd timed a head turn for the exact instant the shutter clicked. There was just one perfect photo of her: emerging from a pile of smouldering rubble with Banshee and the remains of an IED – totally unaware of the camera, covered in dust, radiant and ravishing.

'That's on the range up at Cannich. They'd just halved the record, bless 'em. Black no sugar, Mr Ned, sir.'

They sat by the stove and sipped their coffee. Large Sarge looked

119

a little surprised when Ned told him he hadn't come about Kate and Suzy.

'Tell me about Grace Talmadge.'

'Blimey, Mr Ned. That's a blast from the past. Mother Talmadge. Is she still with us?'

Ned nodded. Large Sarge didn't look pleased with the answer.

'I ain't heard her name for twenty year or more. Don't want to, neither. Horrid bit of work. Should 'ave been dead by now.'

'I need to know what you can remember about her, Sarge. It's important. It's to do with the Best case.'

Large Sarge rocked back in his chair to think. It looked a bit dangerous, him teetering there. He was very big. He'd always been big, but he hadn't always been with the dogs. He had spent his formative years in the Vice Squad, and then one day decided he'd had enough of the tawdry ways of man. And woman. That's how he explained it to the Vice Squad Gaffer. The truth was, he'd had his head in porn and paedophilia so deep he'd started to worry about himself. The Gaffer didn't want to lose him, but could see in a flash that he'd lost him already. Only way to keep him in the force was find him a bit of innocence to manage.

The Dog Team fitted the bill perfectly. Large Sarge had a two-year-old Bichon Frise he doted on – he was unmarried – and he wasn't afraid of dog shit on the soles of his shoes. He'd thrived, and so had the team. But Ned had just thrown him back. Two decades of good, hard, innocuous work wiped out. His face suddenly looked drawn. Being so big came in handy for ageing, but the plump pink face didn't look so smooth and safe now. There were lines on Large Sarge which Ned hadn't noticed before he mentioned the name Talmadge.

The night before, Ned had stood a long way off watching her house. No one could have seen him; he'd made sure of that. He was just a dark shape in a dark doorway on a dark night, but his night vision monocular was locked onto her blank, say-nothing walls. Her roof, with its satellite dish – everything coming in, nothing going out. Her windows, with their ruched, muffling curtains. Her door.

Heavy mahogany. Brass fittings. A spyhole, two deadlocks and a rim lock, with probably a brace of bolts on the inside. Had the bolts ever been thrown, the locks ever turned, the door ever swung open for Sir Tommy Best? And not once but three times – at least? And did he close that door behind him as he went to his death? Or did somebody do it for him? Who?

He watched. Nothing stirred. Then a light went on in a room at the side, lobbing a dull glare onto the white wall of the next house. Several minutes went by. Then the sound of rushing water, and the light went out. It was a sign of life inside, but what kind of life, Ned could not guess. That's why he went to see Large Sarge.

'She started out as an actress and dancer, under the name Tally Grace. 'Ad a bit of a success as a Bluebell Girl, then did her ankle in. So she took the weight off 'er feet, as you might say, an' went on the game. Knew all these stage-door johnnies, as they used to call 'em. Men who wanted their evening to end well every time. Plus she knew the girls who needed extra cash and weren't too fussy. Mother Talmadge, they called her. The whole time I was with the Vice, she was a fact of life. Other madams, they'd have some give and take. You could get some information, use them a bit within reason. Not Mother. She gave us nothing. And she kept her toms on such a short leash, they gave us nothing neither. We couldn't use her, and we couldn't stop her. Our trouble was, we couldn't get anyone in there, whether as a punter or a tom or a maid. Trust – that was her whole thing. She had to know you. You had to come with a personal recommendation. No good just breezing in, wedged-up and grinning. No chance. You 'ad to be a friend.

We tried breaking in – her gaffs were like Fort Knox. We tried taps – she did no business on landlines; she had a bent little ex-Nokia bastard do her mobiles for her. Once, we got her with a Mk 1 'man-in-the middle' scam. This was way before IMSI-catchers. It lasted about three days, tops, and during that time we got absolutely stuff-all. She and her toms never said a dicky bird. She didn't use banks and she was never flash. And she never, ever, wrote anything down.'

'So why didn't you like her?'

Large Sarge threw Ned a short smile and shifted his weight, bringing the front legs of the chair crashing down. He used the momentum to stand up. He refilled the coffee cups, paced around the room, adjusted the date on a doggy calendar and sat down again.

'The word was Grace Talmadge wasn't just providing a little slap for the lonely. The thing about Mother was, she liked her friends to 'ave exactly what they were after. Whatever that might be. And the way she saw it, she was catering to friends, not to nonces. But some of her friends were nonces – as well as being cabinet ministers and rock stars and merchant bankers. So we had this 'orrible, nagging sense that some of her girls were underage. But we never saw hair nor hide of them, and we could never get her for it.'

Ned asked what it was that had given them the horrible, nagging sense.

'It was partly in the air, around town. Like a smell in the street. You don't know where it's coming from. You can't find the source. You can't see it. But you know something or someone's cooking up a stink. Then you retrace your steps, and the smell's gone. A lot of Vice is like that. Or was in my day. Vague stuff, fair enough – but then her name came up in a bit of loose talk on the Nonce Wing at Parkhurst. The social worker was worried enough to phone it in. But this man, a City solicitor, topped 'imself before we could get to him.'

Large Sarge had stopped rocking in his chair. His great frame had sagged forward motionless against the desk. The body message was, Ned thought, 'Big as I am, I couldn't protect them.' Large Sarge. Large failure.

'We done her bins regular. Terrible thing, going through bawdy-house bins. No one makes rubber gloves thick enough. But, like I say, she wrote nothing down. Every now and then there'd be blood and stuff in there, but – so what? Even DNA can't tell you a girl's age. Leave alone if it was spilled with her consent.'

The conversation petered out shortly after. Ned thanked Large Sarge for his time and the excellent coffee. Large Sarge said it was always a pleasure seeing Mr Ned, and hoped he'd been of some service. He guessed Mr Ned would rather he kept their conversation to himself, and Mr Ned said he guessed right. They walked to the car via the dog runs. The sight of the puppies tumbling over themselves, all paws and ears, went a little way to restoring his colour. He told Ned he expected young Kate back any day now. With the precious witness. And that reference to Suzy must have set Large Sarge brooding about the Best case and thence to Mrs Talmadge, because as he was closing Ned's car door he came up with a last, rather poetic thought.

"'The pride of a whore surpasses that of a ploughman in his best clothes." It's something the Gaffer used to say. I always thought we'd get Mrs Talmadge with her pride. But we never did.'

The door slammed shut, and Ned drove back into the city.

Doc Bones was waiting in his office. He looked a bit like a deflated balloon. Seemed atypically deferential. Something wasn't right. He had something to tell Ned, but not here. Could they perhaps go out? Ned didn't see why not. He grabbed his warm coat and rang down for a car.

Ned gave the destination to the driver without thinking. It was only as the car turned onto the approach road to the high bridge across the river that he realised how the Docks had become a magnet for him. Given the Talmadge angle, he didn't want to be seen there for a while, so he had the driver stop and let them out to walk across the bridge and pick them up on the far side. The tide was in. The wind was up. Nothing moving. No one around to hear them. They stopped and stared at the murky turbulence below, while Doc Bones chose his moment and his words. Ned guessed he must have made a mistake, and wondered just how big a mistake it was. He had a sudden vision of digging Sir Tommy up again. Of floodlights around the grave. Of rain like stair-rods. Of trying to hold the world's press back. Of having to explain the unforgivable. His mind started racing. Supposing the coffin was full of stones? Supposing . . .

'Nedice, *mea culpa est*. I found something during the Best autopsy I should have told you and failed to. There was semen in the urethra.'

To Doc's surprise, Ned greeted this not with anger, but with questions. How long before could the ejaculation have occurred . . . how long could it have stayed there . . . what would the effect of the water have been . . . was it possible for semen to be present without orgasm . . . ? Doc Bones was prepared. It seemed unlikely the semen can have been there for very long, given the flushing effects of urination. Obviously hours not days. You'd need to know when Sir Tommy had peed last and that might not be easy to find out. On the contrary, Ned thought. As Spick would say: it'd be a piece of piss. Just after 11 that night. He remembered the CCTV image: the dog sitting patiently while her master faced the wall. The glowing, growing puddle.

The semen/orgasm question was more complex. It was technically possible to experience emission without ejaculation, and ejaculation without orgasm. The presence of semen in the urethra was not categorical evidence that orgasm had taken place. But it was hard to believe there hadn't been orgasm, given the impressive quantity of semen for an older man. Which was sort of why Doc Bones had kept quiet. He launched into a rambling account of having met Sir Tommy at the charity fund-raiser, about what a decent sort he was, how he'd first seen Dame Angie years ago in that film with the bonnets and cornfields and thought she was an absolute poppet. Well, given all that, he'd sort of decided that if Sir Tommy and Dame Angie had had a pre-brekker roll in the hay on his last day on earth, it was no business of anyone's.

They walked on a bit to the halfway point, where the pavement widened to accommodate two benches and a coin-in-the-slot telescope. Doc Bones knew every last thing was their business and carefully avoided catching Ned's eye. He couldn't face disapproval from the one person in the whole set-up he really respected. Ned made things easy for him by popping in a coin, swinging the telescope round and putting his eye to the eyepiece. Matey's crane still. Lime Quay, with its whitened flagstones. And, in between the warehouses, glimpses of the twin walkways snaking through the Docks.

The Doc started to talk again. About how the science had started to bother him . . . the unlikelihood of the semen hanging around all that time. So he did a bit of digging around, and there it was in black and white in some ghastly rag, that Dame Angie hadn't arrived back in the country until the Thursday after Sir Tommy died. So it could hardly have been her . . . you know . . . on the receiving end that morning.

For a medical man, Doc Bones was unbelievably prudish. There were people up on the walkway. Perhaps going to pay homage at the sacred site. Perhaps just ramblers on the Great River Towpath. Hard to hold it steady in this wind. Ned fervently hoped Miss Bones had had her sex education from her mother.

'Well,' the Doc explained. 'That left me with a bit of a brain teaser. Because that same scandal sheet warbled on about how very much in love Sir Tommy and Dame Angie were after thirty years of marriage. I felt like a bit of a rat coming up with the evidence that the National Treasure had been playing away from home right at the very end. On the other hand, if that was the case, you of all people had to know about it, Ned old chap. In case the girl bumped him off or whatever . . . whatever . . .'

Doc Bones couldn't have felt worse. Of all the chaps to let down, dear old Ned. And not a single word of reproof or reproach from him. An exceptionally decent man. The Doc blinked hard and blew his nose. The shutter on the telescope suddenly clattered shut. It was getting too dark for Ned to see much anyway. Dark and cold. Bloody Doc Bones. He could have saved them a ton of time and effort if he hadn't kept that nugget to himself. It might have got them to Mother Talmadge weeks ago. Ned felt his anger rising.

He thrust his hands into his coat pocket and was about to give Doc Bones the major bollocking he deserved, when he felt something. Something plastic, sealed at the top. A small evidence bag. He'd last worn this coat when? Oh, bugger! The morning the body was discovered. He knew what was in the little bag without having to look. Big buggers! Best not bollock the Doc. *Et ego, Brute?*

'Don't beat yourself up, Doc. Better late than never. It ties in with a new lead on the place where he might possibly have experienced that very orgasm. Just over there. By the way, Doc. Could you get your people to run a test on this matchstick? It seems to have a faint pink tinge at the pointy end.'

Ned's tone then changed. Having started out all nonchalant, honesty now took over.

'Oh, and don't bother looking at the date on the bag. You're not the only late developer on this case.'

Briefing Fatso wasn't easy. The problem wasn't covering for Doc Bones; that was easy and had the merit of some truth: 'The Doc's had another look at something that's been bothering him . . .' No, the tough bit was stopping the wild boar from charging up Mother Talmadge's mob-handed with blues and twos and search teams and arrest warrants and a bolt-together gallows from IKEA. He only resigned himself to keeping within the confines of his sty when Ned pointed out that even if they found the National Treasure's dabs on Grace Talmadge's bedposts, it still wouldn't prove anything. Hauling her off for questioning was unlikely to work as she was notoriously on the taciturn side, and there was simply no evidence yet that she'd committed a crime.

The fun had begun with Fatso wanting to know what Ned had that tied an elderly brothel-keeper into the Best murder.

'A cocktail of dirt and a 1950 musical.'

Fatso settled his bottom into his battered and stained revolving chair, with that snuggling-in wiggle that children do when they are being told a bedtime story.

Well, said Ned. They had run a cross-check on people living in the Docks whom Sir Tommy might know, but whom he might not want anyone else to know he knew. Now he and Dame Angie had had Sunday lunch with the famous architect two months ago. Similarly, they both knew the celebrity chef of the fashionable restaurant – he'd hosted their silver wedding party – and the surgeon and his MP wife who lived in the converted Customs House. But why keep visits to these people quiet? They were friends of Dame

Angie as much as of Sir Tommy. And why not just get the chauffeur to drive him there? Why walk? And why go via the cobbled
terrace near Lime Quay? It would have been positively perverse
to have gone that way from the Film Theatre if he was bound for
his architect pal or the Customs House or the swanky restaurant,
all of which you got to off the main Docks entrance. From where
the Harrisons left him, Telford Street would have taken him straight
there. Lime Quay wasn't just the long way round. It made no sense.
Unless perhaps, rather than being en route somewhere, it was Sir
Tommy's destination. And we believe he had an appointment with
someone, or for something. But who? What?

Pause, like the tantalising one when the page in the bedtime story
is being turned. Fatso loved these moments, loved these delicious,
private sessions with Ned. More wiggle-bottom and an eager little
nod for the tale to continue.

Well it just so happens that slap bang in the middle of the cobbled
terrace where they dish up a unique cocktail of lime, ash and rust,
you also find the residence of Mrs Grace Talmadge, vile and ancient
brothel-keeper of this parish. And we can connect her to Tommy
Best, because at the age of eighteen he played Will Scarlett in *Yew
and Me*, a musical comedy about Maid Marian. At one point Robin
Hood's men sneak into the palace disguised as minstrels, and to
check out if they really are entertainers King John plucks Will from
the troupe to perform a number with the Court Dancer . . . played
by Tally Grace. Aka Grace Talmadge. Also eighteen. She sported
a mass of auburn hair, a willowy body and endless legs. The show
ran at His Majesty's for 114 nights – curtain down at 10.15 p.m.
That still left plenty of night for a pair of over-sexed teenagers.

If at that moment Fatso loved Ned, it was as nothing compared
to the moment of adoration Ned had experienced when he had read
Extra Bilge's report in which the connection was first made. Of
course, he wouldn't have felt it if the revelation had been made in
person. He probably wouldn't have been awake to hear it.

Fatso fleetingly in love was, however, no fool.

'What's old Mother Talmadge doing in a crappy terrace down

the Docks? She must have made a fortune over the years; how'd she do all her money?'

Ned didn't know, and Large Sarge was too long out of it. When he switched to dogs, Mother T was still riding high. Perhaps Fatso could ask his old mucker, the now-retired Vice Squad Gaffer, if he'd see them. Fatso said he'd ring him in the morning, and trotted away. A few minutes later, his disembodied voice rang out across the darkened main office. The sentences were broken up; Fatso was struggling into his filthy tarpaulin of a raincoat.

'Funny the old boy shooting his wad, innit? . . . Maybe he thought it would shut her up . . . from blackmailing him . . . Or maybe he just gave her one for old times' sake . . . a mercy fuck . . .'

It was late. Ned took the bus home, and popped into the Light of Kerala for a takeaway *thali*. Hindal wouldn't give him any more metal trays with the little dishes. While Ned waited for polystyrene boxes in a plastic bag, he found himself digging deep into the pockets of his coat, to make sure nothing else had lingered behind. Bad if he found some crucial clue from an ancient, unsolved mystery. But nothing. The matchstick was enough for one coat. For one day. And what a busy bloody day it had been. He started off home. He was just going to eat and sleep. He knew he needed a shower and a hair wash, but that'd have to wait till tomorrow morning. And he must get someone in to fix the washing-machine. With all that water in it, he couldn't force the door. He was running out of clean clothes. Starting to look like Fatso. God, he was hungry. Hadn't realised. He was so absorbed with these thoughts that he didn't glance twice at the ancient Land Rover with the slightly twisted front bumper that was parked outside his house.

He was on the telephone in the kitchen with his coat still on, trying to calm his mother's latest panic, gulping down the *thali* between bursts, when the doorbell rang. He went to answer it, mouth full and spluttering. Standing outside, sparkling-eyed and shatteringly beautiful, was the one person in the world for whom he would want to be spotlessly clean in the freshest of clothes. Preferably without a dribble of *dahi vada* down his chin.

8

FOR A HUNDRED MILES SHE'D known she was driving to see Mr Ned. It made sense; his place was on the side of the city she was coming in on. She knew that, because of a job she'd done years ago with him and Banshee in some bomb factory near the station. He'd been really nice. She was terrified: that the place was booby-trapped, that the terrorists were still at home or that they'd come back and catch them at it. Mr Ned was utterly cool. At first she felt really uncomfortable having someone so close on her tail, particularly given the skin-tight clothes they had to wear, but she had no time to brood and after a bit having him so close just made her feel safe. She thought he must have a gun, though she didn't know where he'd hidden it. For a man, he moved really gracefully and silently. Kate could tell everyone was really pleased, because for the first time ever she'd had a car drive her home. It had dropped Mr Ned off first, so she knew where he lived.

Taking the Land Rover had been Nick's idea. He reckoned it'd stop him from changing his mind and going for a spin when no one was looking. You for starters, she'd added, but he didn't have much of a sense of humour. She was glad to be leaving. He'd been clever about Suzy and the stress, and she'd learned a bit about blindness and guide dogs, particularly one aspect, but Nick Parsons was the sole subject of his own song. She didn't admire him one bit.

Not like Sir Tommy Best. He'd shown you could be blind as a bat and still make a real contribution to people. And it wasn't just Sir Tommy. Kate had had a brilliant English teacher at school who was blind. Loads of lessons were like being in a war zone, but when Mr Booth taught them *Paradise Lost* you could hear a pin drop. Her mum's cousin was blind. He worked for the Citizens Advice Bureau during the day and did shifts for the Samaritans at night. And Nick had actually known Sir Tommy. Had cried on his shoulder. Why hadn't he followed Sir Tommy's amazing example? But then Tommy Best had been a wonderful person before he went blind. Nick must have been insufferable. She didn't believe losing his sight had anything to do with it, though it allowed him to add self-pity to self-adoration. Maybe it was precisely because he had loved himself so much that he felt so sad and angry when the object of his passion was suddenly afflicted.

She kept wanting to tell him to get over it and get a life. I mean, how bad was it going blind? OK, really bad, but at least he was alive, in his own place, with money. All he did was look after himself. He did nothing for others. Nothing that made use of his other senses. He could have listened to the radio and read lots using braille. He could have learned and then taught languages. He could have blended perfumes, or practised aromatherapy or grown medicinal herbs or sold his fruit at a farmers' market. But no. Nick insisted on tucking himself away, cutting himself off. If he hadn't been so hung up on himself, he could have had a relationship. She'd reluctantly decided he was still quite good-looking. In a way. That was the night she reinstated the water-jug.

Only in the act of doing that did she realise that Nick's behaviour was a mild version of what she herself had done so self-destructively for so long: focus on a specific part of her body, worry at it, become depressed and anxious, obsess about it, hide herself from others in case they saw it, allow it to dominate her life, to make her think she was ugly, unlovable, without value, and then hurt herself trying to 'fix' it. It had taken her four terrible years of pain, drugs and therapy before she could start accepting herself as she was. To lower enough of the barriers to live in the world. Part of the key to it was that just as she was emerging from under her own shadow, she made a vital external connection that pushed her outwards and onwards. Nick was nowhere near that point. He was still trying to pretend he wasn't a blind man. That's why he'd pared his life down the way he had. That's why he refused to use a stick or braille. Why he'd been driving. Funny that the one thing it was most surprising that he'd shunned was the very thing that had worked so spectacularly for her: a dog.

He was a mangy old collie called Saul. The owner became too decrepit to walk him, and for some reason she decided to pounce on the self-absorbed, screwed-up teenager passing her door on the way to the flat above. She handed over the dog-lead, gestured towards the park, and hobbled back inside. So the teenager walked back down the stairs with Saul and across the road into the park. An hour later, and the scars from her Cognitive Behaviour Therapy session were healed. Not that she was cured, but she was absorbed. It didn't matter that Saul couldn't run fast or do tricks. It did matter that he accepted her, and responded to her, and wagged his tail, and cocked his head on one side as he looked at her, and gave her his paw to hold while she waited for him to get his breath back.

When they got back to the flats, his owner wanted to know if he'd 'done anything'. Kate didn't know what was meant by this, and replied rather proudly that Saul had done lots of things. The old dear said she'd best take a bunch of bags with her next time and here was a quid for today and another for tomorrow. The offer of money was refused; the teenager was no good at valuing herself. Funny thing was that almost immediately she got home, she started missing Saul – for all his bad breath and fleas. Next day, at school, with her counsellor, in the chemist picking up her Zoloft, he kept coming into her mind. Where they'd go together. What they'd do together. How she'd tidy him up. Get him a new collar. Twenty-three hours to the second after handing him back, she was knocking on the old dear's door. The Dog Tart was born.

She left Suzy in the Land Rover. It'd only take a minute. She rang the bell. Long pause. Perhaps he was asleep. What time was it?

Late, but not too late. Besides, it was important. The door swung open and there he was: on the phone and chewing. He seemed a bit surprised, didn't say anything, swallowed hard several times, wiped his hand first on his chin, then on his jumper, told someone he'd call back. Then he gave a slightly daft smile. Well, she thought, he's so brilliant at work – he's got to let go a bit when he's off duty. Besides, he probably can't remember who I am. Then he sort of shook himself together and said hullo in his honey voice. She hadn't planned to, but she then heard herself asking if she could come in. And did he mind the dog, because she didn't want to leave her in the car?

He stood on the step, watching her fetch Suzy, his mind racing on a virtual tour of the downstairs of his house. Just how messy was it? Had he left any underwear lying about? No, it was all submerged in the washing-machine. How bad was the sofa? Had he done the washing-up? What if she wanted to use the bathroom? If he'd known she was actually coming into his home he'd have taken a week's leave and got in one of those firms that French-polish out all your blemishes. He'd have replaced all the carpets, of course, and redecorated. New lights in the living room. Put up that painting he'd bought in Wales last summer. And his kitchen had far too much patina for its own good and his health. Plus he was out of coffee. Then he saw Suzy.

She had only met him once before at the funeral. And yet the moment she climbed down from the Land Rover she went up to him and placed her head between her paws with her bottom in the air.

'You should be honoured,' Kate said. 'She's bowing to you. It means let's be calm. Let's connect.'

Ned gave her a little bow back, and as she stood up, bent down and rubbed her tummy. He then showed his precious guests into the house. Kate was a green-tea person, which was fine. He put the kettle on and set a bowl of water down for Suzy. Kate sat on the sofa, and Suzy went for a brief wander before lying down at her feet. It all felt strangely natural.

She gave him the short version, concentrating on the stuff Nick had told her about Suzy that was relevant to that night. She could definitely swim. In fact, he'd trained her in life-saving because Sir Tommy and Dame Angie used to have a place on the water near Hamble. As soon as her master had fallen in, she'd have barked loudly, and then jumped after him. Nick had said that if she didn't go in, then it can only have been because someone or something was restraining her. Ned had wondered whether he needed to take notes. Now he knew he did. Check if anyone interviewed in the initial house-to-house trawl mentioned hearing any barks. Next, peeing. She did not need grass to pee on. She preferred it, but it wasn't essential. Similarly, although trained to pee off-lead, she'd go in the gutter in harness if she had to. Nick reckoned that as she got older, this would have happened more often. So Sir Tommy wasn't in the Docks looking for a dog lavatory.

Then there was the question about the walkways. Assuming for a moment no third parties were involved, could she have accident-ally led Sir Tommy onto the wrong one? Theoretically, yes. Guide dogs are not infallible. Generally, the handler sets the direction and the dog sets the specific route along the pavement to avoid people and obstacles. Sir Tommy may just have indicated they had to go up the stairs; Suzy chose which side. But it could be that Sir Tommy had never been there before – at which point Ned told her they now knew he had – in which case, Kate went on, it could be that he had not been there since they built the new walkway. Furious writing by Ned. And a growing realisation that Kate was really, really smart. Either way, she went on, the dog would've seen the hole ahead of them, stopped and turned. It's common for good guide dogs to retrace their steps. Nick had trained her with Sir Tommy to get back from the lavatory to their table in a restaurant, even when it was the first time they'd been there. Reversing the route she'd taken was standard stuff for her. And Sir Tommy wouldn't have thought going back was at all strange. He'd have trusted her absolutely. Which brought Kate to what she thought was the most interesting stuff she and Nick had talked about.

'Does the phrase "intelligent disobedience" mean anything to you?'

Ned thought for a second, and then shook his head.

'It was something we touched on in college, but don't use with our sniffers and trackers. It's pretty much a guide dog thing. It's when a dog uses his or her initiative to ignore an unsafe command. Nick said there was a case in Florida where a dog totally refused to let her blind master cross a road. He tried to make her; he couldn't hear any traffic and thought she was being bolshie. She wasn't. She could see what he couldn't: this huge alligator sprawled across the road in front of them.

'It's complicated, because the dog's got to be obedient to you in principle. It can't become the boss. You have to be able to re-direct them, and they have to be up for quickly changing their thinking, like we were saying: retracing steps. Really good guiding dogs learn when to use their initiative, when to disobey intelligently. The key thing for the blind person is to trust the dog's judgement. Nick says Sir Tommy and Suzy were brilliant at this. Apparently he was so independent, not wanting to rely on other people, always off somewhere new, that Suzy learned to be really assertive if he was taking them both into danger. And he learned to trust her completely.'

They sat for a while without talking. She stroked Suzy's silky ears, while Ned tried to apply what she'd just told him to what might have happened that night. He remembered the CCTV pictures, eerie and fuzzy. This almost impenetrably complex partnership making its way over the cobbles into the darkness. The impos-sibility, as Kate explained it, of Suzy obeying his order to move forward if she sensed danger. The mad anguish she must have felt as someone held her back. Did they let her see her beloved master plunge through the walkway? Make her watch? Did she howl? Was that the last sound Sir Tommy heard as he hit the water?

Ned wasn't sure how long he'd been lost in the horrible reverie. Kate was now standing, putting on her coat. And he noticed some-thing new on the coffee table in front of him, with the shape and feel of a credit card. On the front it had that text in dog Latin which printers stick in while waiting for the real thing: '*Lorem ipsum quia*

134

dolor sit amet, consectetur, adipisci velit, sed quia non numquam eius modi tempora incidunt ut labore et dolore magnam aliquam quaerat voluptatem.'

And it was green.

'Nick gave it me. Sir Tommy gave it to him. Apparently he had a sort of club for his friends. For people who'd really helped him, whom he really trusted. He told Nick that it would get him in places. Special places where they all had a great time. Nick remembered him mentioning some hideaway island in the Bahamas with amazing scuba-diving. There were posh restaurants where you have to be A-List . . . I don't know. Nick said he started going blind before he got a chance to use it. And after he went blind, he didn't want to. He's kept it ever since though. 'Cos he thought Sir Tommy was just the best.'

She gave a deprecating laugh at her silly pun. Her nose wrinkled ever so slightly as she did so. Normally that would demolish even Ned's legendary concentration. But not tonight. Not now. He picked it up, turned it over. There was no magnetic stripe on the back. Just the number 8.

'He says he'd like it back some time. I thought you ought to see it. It's probably nothing. '

And she and the dog left. As he went to bed that night he couldn't actually say whether he'd even got up to show them to the door. He may just have sat there, staring at the card, remembering that puzzling moment at Sir Tommy's Best's funeral when he glimpsed the group of men around his grave, and a fluttering of green onto his coffin. And then Sir Tommy's grandson walking past, asking Dame Angie in his piping, prep-school voice: '. . . Grangie, what's it mean "lorum" . . . ? What the men were saying . . . ?'

Short answer: ring Grangie, find out. Ned called her the next morning. Dame Angie sounded pleased to hear from him. Wanted to know how he was doing. Unfazed by the question. Ah, he meant the Basle Club. Tommy's special cronies. It was their excuse for heavily cushioned excessive behaviour. They used to be a bit wild:

early on she'd had to bail them out of the police cells in St Moritz for some nonsense involving six girls from the Holiday on Ice *corps de ballet*, the hotel swimming pool, a sack of potatoes and a baby elephant, but these days it was all pretty innocent stuff. They didn't have the lungs or the livers for their old capers. Plus there's not much room on a snowboard for a guide dog and Suzy never took to scuba-diving.

Why Basle? It was after Tommy played Johannes Froben in *The Printer of Basle* for darling Alain Tanner. Or was it Goretta? Anyway, Froben had a close circle of high-achievers, though Tommy's gang didn't quite sport a Holbein. *Lorem ipsum*? Some nonsense Latin Froben used to fill in with while waiting for Erasmus to cough up the next chunk of New Testament. Was that all? – because she had to dash. Oh, some names and contacts? Certainly. She'd email the ones she'd got the minute she rang off. She wished him luck. Praised him for his patience. Said she'd be away for a week in Los Angeles. Something to do with this film about Tommy. She'd have her phone with her. Only please don't wake her up. Goodbye. Click.

Ned sat there for a moment, thinking. She sounded so normal. It was as if she was telling him that Sir Tommy had just popped out, and would ring Ned back the minute he returned. Given her acting skills and assuming she wanted to conceal the truth from him, she'd have sounded the same whether the Basle Club was for mass murderers or mothers and toddlers. He wasn't going to crack this case by reading something clever into the tone of Dame Angie's voice.

Back to the evidence. He took himself down to the basement. After a brief wait the grey metal box was placed in front of him, together with a pair of gloves. He never went straight to the thing he was looking for. Stay open, his first governor had taught him. Let the evidence speak to you. You may notice something whose significance you've missed. Like this: the once-sodden contents of Evidence Bag 5b, retrieved that first morning, according to the tag, from Sir Tommy's coat pocket, outside right lower. It seemed to be a small yellow cardboard box, with patches of green and red and a strip of sandpaper along one crumpled edge. A matchbox. On one side he could make out a bar code and the word DANGER! On the other side was a white swan against a green background. A Swan Vestas matchbox. He shook it. Nothing, but that didn't mean the box was empty. It had gone mushy in the water and then dried; the match-heads may have stuck together. He asked for some tweezers and a small torch. He tried to ease out the tray, but it was all part of the box now. He carefully bent one end of the tray down, and shone the torch inside. The box was empty.

On to the credit cards. Sir Tommy kept his in a crocodile-skin holder, with his initials in gold. Just like you and me, thought Ned. Inside he had a fair old selection of the fanciest plastic around, including an American Express Black and a Coutts' purple. For the man who puts a quarter of a million dollars on his card a year. Just like you and me. And there at the very back was a green card: '*Lorem ipsum quia dolor sit amet.*' Not at all like you and me. Like just seven other people in the whole wide world. He flipped it over. Sir Tommy was Number 1. Nick Parsons was Number 8. So who exactly were Numbers 2 to 7? Back upstairs.

Ping. You have email. Six names, one of whom she'd marked as deceased, with contact numbers. Evidently Dame Angie did not know that Nick Parsons was in the Basle Club, perhaps because he'd not activated his membership. Ned wondered if Nick was the last to be so honoured. His memory was of no more than four around the grave. They'd soon know. He called Spick in, wound him up and set him going. Next . . . But Ned's next was already decided for him. The buck teeth came through the door first, closely followed by the rest of the mad horse.

'Mr Ned sir, would this be a good time to talk about your matchstick?'

Extra Bilge did not wait for an answer, just in case it was no. He plonked himself down and waited patiently, jaw slightly open in a vacant smile. Then he made a long arm over his back and scratched his withers. Ned was about to ask him if he could stick to bullet points, but couldn't face the hurt look. Besides, it was like the old governor said: stay open. No it wasn't. It was more like being bludgeoned to death.

'First, the wood. Almost certainly *Populus tremula*, which you and I know by the name of Common Swedish Trembling Aspen.'

Of course we do, thought Ned. Those are the kind of madcap, live-for-the-moment, butterfly-brained people we are.

'By the way . . .'

That must be a record. A digression so soon. This was going to be a slow one.

'. . . the aspen's quivering habit is said to be the sign of its remorse for being the only tree at the crucifixion to have doubted the divinity of Jesus Christ. Unlikely, I've always thought, given that the tree is not native to the Holy Land.'

It probably got exiled for its heretical beliefs, thought Ned. Wish I could get exiled for my heretical beliefs. Right now. He slowly slumped while Extra Bilge droned on about the aspen's suitability for making matches because of its low flammability and its application in animal bedding manufacture because of its low phenol content – Ned would know, of course, that phenols such as are found in juniper and pine can trigger respiratory problems in some species . . . Of course Ned knew that. That's why he was building Extra Bilge a new stable out of juniper in his spare time. Ned missed the next bit about the history of the Swedish Match Company, but started coming to at the point when Extra Bilge identified the match as being a tenth of an inch square in section, which together with being hewn from *Populus tremula*, made it an odds-on cert to be a Swan Vesta. In which case it would have had an unburned length of exactly one and a half inches. Note the Imperial dimensions, Mr Ned. And it just so happened that Sir Tommy had a Swan Vestas box in his coat pocket when he died, which Extra Bilge had bagged and tagged himself – 5b, as he remembered. Better not say anything, said Ned to himself, or it might just draw attention to the fact that he'd kept the pointy match in his own coat pocket for weeks. At which point Extra Bilge handed Ned a new box of Swan Vestas.

'Incidentally, Mr Ned, the swan on the box used to swim from right to left. Then at some point in the early 1950s, for reasons that are still obscure I'm afraid even to phillumenists, the swan was turned from left to right. It helps us in a way, because we can tell at a glance from the swan's orientation that Sir Tommy wasn't using a fifty-year-old box of matches.'

Yeah, thought Ned. That clears up that confusion. That, and the bar code on the back. Phillumenists? Then there was another slump in Ned's concentration while Extra Bilge rambled on about phosphorus sesquisulphide, the interesting use by shoe salesmen in the 1960s of crushed Swan Vesta heads as bait for mouse traps, and the origins of the word Vesta, which led him onto a major digression about the cross-dressing music hall star Vesta Tilley. She apparently retired from the stage when Sir Tommy was two, which neatly explained why Extra Bilge could find no record of them ever working together. You could say the same about Amy Winehouse and Galen of Pergamon, thought Ned. Or Ben Stiller and Alaric the Goth. At this point Extra Bilge started fidgeting in his chair and scratching his lower back. Ah, thought Ned. Saddle sores. Perhaps he should see the vet. Certainly one of us should see a vet, if only to pick up an overdose of ketamine.

'Now, about the DNA . . .'

Ned was wide awake.

'We found traces of both blood and saliva, and some yellow dust particles on the matchstick. No decomposition had taken place, presumably because according to your tag it was dry when you found it on the walkway. Therefore it had been dropped after the rain stopped and the timber dried off. So no problem getting a DNA match – if you'll pardon the pun, Mr Ned . . .'

Mr Ned would happily have strangled him at that moment, if there was a way of combining it with still hearing the punch-line.

'. . . definitely Sir Tommy Best.'

Extra Bilge took a match from the box, lit it, let it burn a bit, blew it out, and then twizzled the end in his fingers. It produced a taper, he explained, but not sharp enough. Plus a match that's been lit leaves black smears on your fingers, and Sir Tommy was a bit on the fastidious side, they say. Extra Bilge fished out his own Swiss Army Knife. It was one of those with everything including the hook for getting stones out of his own hooves. He then took another match, and started to whittle the end to a point.

'You'll find his in bag 4a, if I remember right. It's a Victorinox Spartan. Simple, classic. I checked, and found minute slivers of *Populus tremula* on the smaller of the two blades.'

He handed his finished work over to Ned.

'There you go, Mr Ned. The yellow dust was dried plaque. Sir Tommy used to make his own toothpicks.'

'That's an unusual last request, sir,' said Jan Span when Ned told her about it. '"I'd just like to pick my teeth."'

There was a pause while they thought about it. Then they looked at one another. Then a race to the door and down to the basement. Out came the long metal box.

'Did you look inside it?' Ned asked as they went through the bags. Span shook her head.

'I don't know that anyone did. There's nothing on the inventory log about it.'

The cigar case was in the palest buff leather: one half sliding over the other, with one of Sir Tommy's initials on each of the tubes. Ned carefully pulled the two halves apart. The remains of two small cigars were stuck deep inside. The third tube was empty.

Back upstairs to check Zara C-C's original police statement. Sir Tommy had popped into his (unnamed) tobacconist just before 6 p.m. She had hung about outside. Made a few calls. They'd locked up as Sir Tommy left. Dig out the chauffeur's statement. Thank you, Cyril: Snaresby Lovell, purveyors of coffin nails to nobs. Span dropped Ned off at Merriman Lane and went on to check the walkway and hole for the hundredth time.

The address was initially apt, if sexist. As Ned turned up, a very happy chap bumbled out with a glossy maroon carrier bag full of smoker's swag. Inside, an elderly cleric was delighted to be buying Cuban coffee which the emaciated, bald and be-suited young man behind the counter was equally delighted to be selling him. But at this point the merriment stopped. In the walk-in humidor was a couple in matching fur coats having a row. Luckily the door had a good seal and the humidifier made a bit of a racket, so no one in the main shop could hear what it was about. Ned watched the arm-waving and got the occasional flash of angry face through bursts of mist. Her blonde hair flowing down over all that fur, somehow suggested to Ned mutton dressed as lamb. Wrong. A few moments later, she stormed silently out: lips pursed, colour high. A livid lamb. What the French call *jolie laide*. Monsieur – definitely an old goat – stayed behind, vengefully raiding her tiara allowance to buy half a dozen boxes of Cohibas.

Ned flashed his warrant card at the shop assistant and asked if he had served Sir Tommy Best on his last visit there. The young man shook his head and said he'd been on his holidays, in the tone of one for whom giving alibis came naturally. Besides, it was Mrs Lovell who always served Sir Tommy. He flicked his eyes heavenwards as he mentioned her name, so that Ned fleetingly wondered if devoted tobacconist had joined sainted customer. Then he was taken around the counter to the foot of a spiral staircase which evidently led to Mrs Lovell's lair.

Mrs Lovell was in her fifties, round and trim. She was absolutely fine during the initial small talk: she was the fifth-generation Lovell in the shop . . . the first woman to run it . . . they hadn't seen hide nor hair of a Snaresby since the war . . . no, the smoking bans hadn't harmed the top end of her business . . . but as soon as Ned began to ask her about Sir Tommy she began to cry. And showed little readiness to stop. He sat there in the cramped garret with its ancient cabinets and scents of cedar, cherry and vanilla, and watched the tobacconist sob. Then she mopped herself up and shook her head and chastised herself for being so soppy, and then she sobbed some more.

In his total concentration on the circumstances of his death, Ned had lost track of what an extraordinary, intravenous effect Sir Tommy had had upon people. He'd been, like Diana and Churchill and perhaps John Lennon and John Peel, somehow in the nation's bloodstream. It wasn't a place where conscious striving could get you, or money or PR people. No one decided it, or voted on it, or pressed the red button for it. You were just there. And when these rare people die, it takes a while for their cells to die off in us. Longest for those they had touched in person.

On the cluttered table between them Ned noticed an open packet of Turkish cigarettes. He waited until she hit a mop-up phase, and then offered her one. She accepted it with a tiny, grateful nod. He lit it for her with a table lighter. Again, the little nod. She took a deep pull on the cigarette then let the smoke drift out of her mouth, drawing it back in through her nostrils. Ned's Auntie Annie used to do that. The air between them hung with blue, still smoke, behind which Mrs Lovell recovered herself. Then she made a small move to her side and switched something. An extractor fan went on and sucked the screen away, revealing a calm, composed tobacconist.

'He arrived just before we closed. He often did that, so he could have the shop to himself. Rang to make sure I'd be here, of course. He didn't want much, as I remember.'

She reached behind her and pulled an old-fashioned ledger off a shelf.

'He bought a box of Bolivar Inmensas to go to the house. Some pipe cleaners. And he picked up three cigars for his case: two Montecristo Robustos Reserva del Milenio and a Partagas Seleccion Privada No 1.'

What, Ned wanted to know, did those cigars look like? The ones for his cigar case? The Robustos were small, just under five inches, and the Partagas six and three quarter inches. Could Mrs Lovell show Ned a similar cigar case and put those same three cigars in it? Similar, yes. The same no. She had supplied the case herself for Dame Angie to give him on his birthday some years ago, and it was rather special leather. Some kind of antelope. But the same size, yes. She took herself down the stairs and busied about.

Ned had last smoked at a family wedding about five years ago, and all he could remember about it was the sight of the cigar sticking out of a bowl of trifle, where a health-conscious second cousin had buried it. Before that, he'd barely smoked since his teens. There was a bit of a difference between sharing a roll-up behind the bike shed and this panelled, clubbable luxury. It was a tiny bit tempting, leaving price and lung cancer aside. Yet he knew that you never get that aroma outside a smart cigar store. Like car showrooms: inside, the car is perfect, like a new-born baby. The second you take it outside, the nappy needs changing. The best bit is before. Before you buy. Before you light up. After that, it becomes something else.

Mrs Lovell returned. It wasn't antelope, and it wasn't initialled in gold, but it looked the right size. Ned slid the two halves apart. The little Montecristos were way down in their tubes, whereas the top of the Partagas was almost level with the rim of the case. So sometime before he died, Sir Tommy had smoked the big one, assuming he didn't give it away or lose it. He hadn't lit up in the shop, and Mrs Lovell said smoking was absolutely *verboten* in the Roller. Dame Angela had put her foot down. According to Zara C-C, Cyril had taken them straight from the tobacconist to the Film Theatre to check the clips. No smoking there. He didn't light up afterwards, or with the Harrisons, and he wasn't smoking in any of the shots recorded by the CCTV cameras. So if indeed he smoked the Partagas Seleccion Privada No 1, it must have been one of the last things he did on earth.

'Mrs Lovell,' Ned asked gently, 'if you were in a hurry. Under pressure. Perhaps only had a short time left . . . to do something. And you wanted to smoke a cigar . . . Well, let's say, Sir Tommy wanted to smoke a cigar. You knew him in this context better than anybody. Which of these cigars would he have chosen?'

She didn't hesitate. She turned the case over and slid out one of the little Montecristos. Why? he asked. Because it's small? Mrs Lovell shook her head.

'No. It isn't just the size. The Robustos will deliver an incredibly creamy richness almost from the first puff. But the Partagas needs time. It doesn't come into its stride until the middle two or three inches. It isn't a cigar to rush.'

So, Ned recapped to make absolutely sure. If time was tight, Sir Tommy would have gone for the Robusto. But if he was taking a stroll, with no rush on . . .

'Oh, if he was going for a walk,' interrupted Mrs Lovell, 'he'd definitely choose the Partagas. It has a very steady, consistent burn, even outside, even in wind. Many cigars don't. That's why it was always Sir Tommy's choice on the golf course.'

'And to light it?'

Mrs Lovell laughed. Swan Vestas. Nothing else. He'd been bought lighter after lighter. Couldn't do with them. Particularly since he'd, you know, lost his sight. Said he never knew how big a flame a gas lighter would shoot out. Reckoned he'd be torching his eyebrows every five minutes. But he knew exactly where the flame was on the end of a Swan, and how long he could leave it before blowing it out. And had she sold him any boxes of Swan Vestas matches that last day? No, she said, he didn't ask for any. And how had Sir Tommy paid? In cash? The Bolivars were on account, she replied, with a nod at the ledger. The three in his case he'd paid for long ago. She kept them for him in his own humidor in the cellar. When he was in town and needed a smoke, he'd pop in. Ned picked up the Partagas and looked at it. Smelled it. Cedar and earth.

'There's one other thing,' said Mrs Lovell volunteering a bit of a clincher. 'He asked me to cut the Partagas. Just the Partagas. That usually meant he was planning to smoke it the same day.'

She looked at Ned holding the cigar to his nose.

'Would you like to keep it? To remember Sir Tommy by?'

He smiled at her. He would like to buy it – but more as evidence. Though it would remind him of Sir Tommy, of course. She shook her head. She had none for sale. They were no longer obtainable. The one he was holding was one of the last from Sir Tommy's private humidor. She was sure he wouldn't have minded the detective having it. He was a very generous man. And, of course, if it could be of the slightest use in catching his killers . . . Ned held his hands up in submission. He gratefully accepted her generosity on Sir Tommy's behalf. Could Mrs Lovell possibly cut it for him, as she'd done for her best customer? She almost blushed. Sir Tommy had indeed been her best customer. It would be a pleasure. She reached for a cigar cutter, and adroitly sliced off the tip.

'There,' said Mrs Lovell putting it into an aluminium tube lined with cedar and handing it over to Ned. 'That's a real gentleman's cigar.'

Her eyes suddenly looked watery again. As soon as Ned started down the stairs she lit up another Turkish, hiding herself in blue smoke.

Kate knew it was coming. In a way, she'd brought it on herself. She'd sat in the meetings, hearing about the squeeze on resources while the national threat level was stuck on Severe. She knew experienced sniffer dog trainer/handlers were at a premium, and that a request had gone out for volunteers to join an inter-service pool – prepared to go out to trouble spots with their dogs at a moment's notice. It would be dangerous, but exciting. And she knew she couldn't get away with nannying Suzy indefinitely. But the real catalyst was her unerring eye for a winner and a small ball of fur called Jiffy.

She was one of five puppies born to a Cocker Spaniel called Jammy, who had earned her place on the honours board by absolutely refusing to leave the hold of a fully laden 747-400 bound for Bombay, despite the fact that Security couldn't find a thing. She had sat down in front of a cage full of catering boxes and canisters, and wouldn't budge. The contents were checked and cleared, replaced, checked again, cleared again. The assumption was that the dog was just wrong. The plane was now heavily delayed and in danger of missing its slot yet again. Security gave the all clear and the handler was asked to remove his dog. Jammy started to growl and bark. The handler explained that this was out of character and the dog must be trusted, but no one was very interested. Except the pilot. He'd come down from the cockpit and was sitting at the foot of the internal stairs, gripped by the dog's certainty. He insisted Security resume the search.

Forty minutes later, they found that one of the struts on the cage itself was lethally full of RDX. The explosive had been mixed with stearic acid which in turn had been mixed with turmeric, fenugreek, cumin and garlic. To throw any dogs off the scent. But not Jammy.

So there was Jammy's first litter. All adorable. A few possibles. One potential star. Jiffy had high energy. She played hard and long – essential, since dogs treat the hunt for explosives as a game. At the same time, she seemed to pant less than the others when tired. The more a dog pants, the less it can sniff and the less it concentrates. If Kate suddenly found herself somewhere in the Middle East looking for an IED under the noonday sun, Jiffy might be just the dog. When Large Sarge strolled over to J Kennel, he found all the puppies asleep except for one, and young Kate sitting in the straw playing with her. He watched for a moment.

'So that's the one, is it?'

'I think she might be, Sarge. I think she thinks she might be.'

He nodded slowly.

'You'll have to hand Suzy back. You know that.'

This was the bit Kate didn't know if she could handle. The thought of that fragile, vulnerable . . .

'I know, Sarge.'

Jiffy tried a daredevil leap from Kate's stomach onto her shoulder, missed, and rolled all the way down again.

'I'll tell the circus to keep looking.'

Kate smiled, and then looked up at him with those huge eyes. He wished she wouldn't do that. He knew he wasn't good at holding the line against her when she was hurt. Felt a bit fatherly to them all, but she was special.

'They don't want her, Sarge. Her family doesn't want her back.'

Large Sarge squatted down beside her, looping his chubby old

146

fingers through the chicken wire. They had waiting lists of people wanting retired dogs, he reminded her. Good people. Folk they knew and trusted. The Cartwrights would have her at the farm, or Mrs Gemell. And the Addisons had lost their malinois two months ago now. They'd rehome her easy. She was a star, was Suzy. Famous. They'd have to fight 'em off. Hold a raffle. It'd be like that show on the telly.

'They'd be kind to her, but they wouldn't understand her. She's not ready, Sarge. She's not free of it.'

He poked a finger through low down, bringing Jiffy darting over – all snout and tiny wagging tail.

'OK. But we're only talking weeks here, young Kate. Not months. Ow! Leggo, you little bruiser!'

Large Sarge staggered to his feet and went back to rejig the rosters yet again. It's the truth that'll free Suzy, Kate thought, drawing her knees up under her chin. We can't help much until we know what really happened to her. Ned will find out. Then it'll be OK. She looked at her watch. They'll be back any time now, she said to the puppy, scooping her up, perching her on her knees and peering into those serious little eyes. Then your mum'll sort you out. You see. What is it, little Jiffy? What can you hear? The puppy turned her head, listening to the distant barking and scampering of paws on cobbles.

Home from their walk, Millie and Joe popped Jammy, Blossom and Magic back with their puppies. A mighty tumbling and an eating and a licking ensued. Suzy lay down outside the wire watching the reunited families from a distance.

They drove out into the suburbs. Span at the wheel, Ned clocking the charmless panorama. The fake half-timbered laundrette. The building society in which you can't actually make a deposit at this branch, sir. The mall with its Huts and Shacks, but without the authentic overhead cables, bunched and radiating over beaten-up pick-ups. Thirties houses ruined by bad double-glazing and satellite dishes. New houses ruined by carriage lamps and bogus brick driveways. Neither one thing or another. Blah. Mustn't wind up here, thought Ned, when I'm an old copper. Me and Kate and a horde of pongy old dogs. Dun Nabbing, I'll call it. I might take up bowls. And every sentence'll begin with 'When I . . .' And no one'll give a damn. Will some eager beaver young detective trek out past all this crap to ask me about some case I never solved, which has reared up to bite him in the bottom? Politely masking his contempt for my past failures and current naffness?

Ned knew himself well enough to know that this line of thought led way past his retirement. He had a recurrent morbid wonder. Had the person yet been born who would, one day, lay out his dead body? Tie up the bits that leak? Stick corks in where necessary? Was he or she already in Infants, playing at pirates? Dreaming of a life of Riley on the Spanish Main? Imagine taking the child aside and saying: forget growing up into Captain Jack Sparrow or Ann Bonny. You'll be wrapping dead corpses in their shrouds. Me included. And remember Balzac's advice: 'If you don't lay out a body while it's warm, you'll have to break the joints later on . . .'

'Sir! This is it. We're here!'

It was always said of the Vice Squad Gaffer that he was a safe pair of hands since he only fancied older women, they being the last thing you find in the vice game. Young women – no problem. They are the stuff. The fodder. The battery hens. Pick 'n' Mix. Fire and forget. Bio-degradable. But it's no country for old birds. The locker-room gossip was that the Gaffer's tastes were more likely to be satisfied at a Silver Threads Saturday afternoon tea dance, than at 3 a.m. in a live-sex club. So when the mock-Gothic door was opened by a woman who wouldn't see eighty again, both Ned and Span wondered if she was the Gaffer's missus or mum. Ned had a bash at the mental arithmetic as did Span, it turned out when they compared notes in the car afterwards. The Gaffer had retired at sixty, which must have been about five years ago. So, if mum, she'd have to have had him at seventeen, which was pushing things. Except it might have been wartime, and these things happen. A brave lad on leave – hard to say no. Maybe less stigma during the war, being an unmarried mum?

And then there was her habit of calling him 'Sonny'. 'You've come to see Sonny?' 'Do you want the door closed, Sonny?' Addressing your child as 'Sonny' was something Ned associated more with fathers than mothers. And when he thought about it, more 'Son' than 'Sonny'. Both were terms he associated with elderly desk sergeants, rather than parents. Or was she saying 'Sunny'? Against all that were the faint signs of intimacy when the Gaffer did appear. In a reference to something they were doing that evening. A glancing touch on a shawled shoulder. Why can't one just bloody ask? Ned wondered. Here, Gaffer, who's the bird? Only it's doing my head in and I've a ton of work to do . . .

'. . . and good to see you again, sir. Thanks, black no sugar. You make a jolly good advert for retirement . . .'

The Gaffer looked like an old schoolmaster: chalky and ageless. It was hard to think of him knee-deep in vice. Trigonometry and equatorial rain forests – yes. Troilism and trafficking – Ned couldn't quite see it. Except the Gaffer looked like those tweedy old boys who used to get caught with their pants down in ancient tabloid sex scandals. Maybe his strength was knowing the mind of the punter. But then where did the penchant for old dears come in? Is that a grievously under-reported national fetish? On cue, the Gaffer's Whatever She Was appeared with a seed-cake on a flowery plate. The Gaffer patted her arm almost absent-mindedly as she bent over him to put it on the coffee table. He waited till she'd closed the door behind her before getting down to business. He knew what they'd come about. Mother Talmadge had been a blot on the landscape virtually his entire career. A blot shaped like a question mark. In the end, he'd just had to get used to her. Like backache. But how worrying was an ageing brothel-keeper to the Squad? Ned wanted to know. Surely there were much bigger criminals and much nastier crimes to worry about? Trafficking, sex slavery . . .

'Oh, I couldn't agree more. Over the years we stopped seeing it as our core mission to shut down every common or garden bordello in the city just for the sake of it. Unless they were unruly, or covers for something else. We didn't have the manpower or the time. Or the energy. We kept that for the real stuff. The ugly stuff. But Mother Talmadge's wasn't – as far as we could tell – common or garden. Rumour was that she provided a particular service to men with a penchant for virgins.

'You know, a century ago, it wasn't at all unusual to find virgins in their thirties. You could probably even find one in her twenties in the Rue Saint-Denis in 1920s Paris, if you were prepared to pay for it and assuming you weren't being cheated. In Fanny Hill's day it was blood-soaked sponges in hollowed-out bed-posts. Thai girls now use pellets of pigeon blood, cut with anti-coagulant. But these days, for the real thing, virgin almost certainly means underage. If truth be told, it often meant that in the past, but it depended on your definition of underage. Anyway, our predecessors weren't as squeamish as we are, and Mother apparently had no qualms whatever. The trouble was, as Large Sarge must have told you – how is he, by the way? – we couldn't get a thing on her. Tight as a drum. She ran me ragged. More cake?'

After a coffee and cake-shaped lull, Ned resumed with a question. Had the Gaffer ever actually met the lady? The Gaffer gave a laugh. As a matter of fact he very nearly had. In the early '70s, as a fast-track graduate in Vice, he'd been invited by Lord Longford on a fact-finding tour of Amsterdam. Red-light district and all that. On the *Who's Who* of fellow travellers was the name Grace Talmadge. She was there supposedly representing the interests of some women's study group. They took the ferry from Harwich to give time for some bonding and briefing en route, but no Mrs Talmadge. She was said to be on board – the purser had her on the passenger list; the steward said he'd actually seen her – but she never showed at the dinner or anything. We joked that she was there watching us. Know your enemy and that. Bit bizarre, all told.

And what did the Gaffer know of her these days? Had she retired? Why was she living so modestly in the Docks? Ah, said the Gaffer. You don't know about her son? The infamous son on whom she dotes. No one knows who the father was. A son with a terrible gambling habit. They say he went through all her money; that's why she kept in the game. To keep him out of the gutter or prison or the canal. He lives abroad now. Spain, or Portugal. I can't think she's still working, but who knows? If her beloved boy needs money, all he has to do is ask his mum. Span, who was taking notes, asked how old the son was. Must be fifty by now. Went under various names. The Gaffer referred her to a very patchy intelligence file.

Ned left the best till last, until they were standing in the light and he could see the Gaffer's eyes. Had he ever heard the name Tommy Best in connection with Mrs Talmadge? Never. He'd have remembered that. But there was surely nothing Sir Tommy needed he couldn't get at home. What was it Paul Newman had said? Why go out for hamburger when you have steak at home? What a very stupid man, thought Ned as he thanked him for his time.

'By the way,' said Span. 'That cake was brilliant. Could you thank your . . .'

'. . . sister. My sister. I'll tell her. She'll be very pleased. Good hunting.'

Ned threw Span a glance as they walked back to the car. Funny how juniors slip bids for promotion into the most innocent conversations. Still. Neatly done. His sister, eh? Well, you can take the man out of the Vice, but you can't take . . .

Then Jan Span blew it.

'So what do you think, sir? Do you reckon the secret father of Grace Talmadge's son is the Gaffer, after a one-night stand on the Harwich ferry? And that's why he was careful never to catch her, because if so she'd have squealed? I mean, it fits his profile: Mrs Talmadge's gotta be ten years older than the Gaffer . . .'

Doc Bones sat at his computer, wrestling with the latest problem Nedicus had lobbed at him. He'd had a nasty double drowning off a sailing charter – with vital questions to answer about how long they'd been in the sea before dying – so hadn't got near it till now. Cup of builder's to flush the formaldehyde from his lungs. In the old days he'd have had his pipe. A good blast of Mick McQuaid or Tom Tough always cut through nicely. Now then. *Lorem ipsum*.

'It's Latin, Doc. Right up your *via*.' Thus ran the scrawl under the photocopy of what looked like a credit card. Doc had taken himself down to the basement to study the two actual examples they had: Numbers 1 and 8. The first, Sir Tommy's, was scratched and faded. The second, belonging to this doggy chap Parsons, was pristine. But what was immediately fascinating was the Latin. Doc had always been intrigued by *Lorem ipsum*, but had never bothered to dig and delve. It was stuck in his mind along with ETAOIN SHRDLU and QWERTYUIOP. Yet familiar as the text looked at a glance, there was something odd about it. Where was that word that always stuck out: *adipiscing*? And what was the word *quia* doing in there? Surely the old printers' placeholder text begins *Lorem ipsum dolor sit amet*? But on the green cards it read: *Lorem ipsum quia dolor sit amet*.

So Doc Bones dug and delved. And the answer he came up with tallied absolutely with Ned's note on the photocopy, and explained the differences. The Latinate guff used by printers was exactly that: nonsense. What was on the cards was genuine Latin: the original text from which some inky-fingered Swiss had nicked what he needed to set out his page layouts.

The Doc had actually been taken by Mrs Bones to see *The Printer of Basle* at the Film Club, but had dozed off early on during a lengthy argy-bargy between the printer Froben played by Tommy Best and Philippe Noiret as Hans Holbein, over whether it was OK for Martin Luther to marry some Catholic nun. Doc Bones's view was that the audience should at least be given a glimpse of the gel so they could make up their own minds – and promptly fell asleep. He thus missed the scene in which the gel in question revealed all anyone might wish to see of her and a bit more, halfway up a church tower. Sinewy contortions on spiral stairs were involved as well as black silk and bell ropes. Mrs Bones was fearful she'd get piles, with all that cold stone under her. Doc Bones came to during the credits, just as Mrs Bones was drying her eyes. Whether from sorrow or laughter he knew enough not to ask.

So where did the Latin come from? Cicero, it turned out. From the great man's *de Finibus Bonorum et Malorum*, aka *The Extremes of Good and Evil*, written in 45 BC. Unbeknownst to the slumbering Doc Bones, Johannes Froben's choice of the text arose precisely out of the ethical debate in the film over Luther's love life. Needless to say, Luther, played by Gerard Depardieu, didn't give a stuff for Froben's priggishness and naturally married the bendy, red-headed girl, whom he oddly called 'My lord Katie'.

Next, Doc started to wonder what the Latin sentence on the green cards actually meant. He struggled with it himself, aided by his battered *Smith's Shorter Latin–English Dictionary*, before retreating to the Internet, where he pulled up Rackham's 1914 translation. He had to reread it a couple of times to see what old Cicero was on about with those double negatives, but what knocked him for six, Nedicus old boy, was the last sentence. In those words, he started to see less a reference back to the film than some sort of hidden mission statement for the Basle Club itself. And if that were the case, then on the face of it, old chap, it didn't sound as if the mission was always entirely pleasant. He read it aloud to Ned when he pitched up late in the afternoon. And as Ned listened, leaning against the door-frame into the Doc's inner sanctum, he too started to frown.

'Nor again is there anyone who loves or pursues or desires to obtain pain of itself, because it is pain, but because occasionally circumstances occur in which toil and pain can procure him some great pleasure. To take a trivial example, which of us ever undertakes laborious physical exercise, except to obtain some advantage from it? But who has any right to find fault with a man who chooses to enjoy a pleasure that has no annoying consequences, or one who avoids a pain that produces no resultant pleasure?'

9

NED MADE SOME ARRANGEMENTS and then worked his way with Spick through the Basle Club's members. The first two were rich men. Public men. Civic-minded men. They were vain men. They kept their tans topped up and the manufacturers of expensive grooming products in profit. They drove the latest Bentley and the latest Aston Martin. One was on his second wife, the other on his third. Maintained them in a state of luxurious uncertainty. Laugh. Just a joke. One man advised the Prince's Trust; the other the Conservative Party. They gave heavily to charities. They put indoor pitches and gymnasia in their old schools. They were patriotic. Neither would ever move abroad. High taxes were fair dos for the privilege of living in this country. Besides – pause – they didn't actually pay that much. Laugh. They played harder now than they worked, but both recalled a time when work was all they had and playing was a big dream. They were self-made men and were mighty pleased with what they had made.

They had done their National Service with Tommy. They'd been in some unpleasantness in Korea together. It had all got a bit sticky, and they'd had to bail one another out. They were out on patrol, and turned right when they should have hung a left. Well, one forest track looked much like another. It seemed they'd dropped themselves right in it. Couldn't raise HQ on the radio. Then the bally jeep got stuck in the mud. Then they started hearing these horrible noises. Ruddy gooks making monkey sounds. Bit eerie, that. Then the bullets started whizzing about. It can be a terrifying thing, war. There was a chunk in Tommy's book about the incident. About them. Old Toms laid it on a bit thick; gave them more credit than they were due. It's just what mates do, isn't it? Help themselves out of a jam. All for one and one for all, as the saying goes. Anyway, they got back in one piece. That was the main thing.

Oh, he'd seen them by the grave, had he? *Lorem ipsum* and all that. He was with the popsy holding the dog? Right. Gotcha. No offence, but they hadn't really noticed him. Or the doggy. Laugh. Well, no point keeping it going without Tommy, they thought, so call it a day. Bunged the cards in the grave. No need for them. They said the *Lorem ipsum* for old times' sake. No, the words didn't actually mean anything. Just some Latin mumbo-jumbo from one of his films. It was more this idea of a man with bags of charisma – inspirational really – and his circle of closest friends. That was it in a nutshell. One of their ex-wives described it as a silly boys' club. Well, so it was. And why not? It had been huge fun while it lasted. Lovely, silly, innocent fun. But it could never have been the same without Tommy. He was what united them. They were *his* friends, first and foremost. His best friends. There. They were proud to say it. Not ashamed to shed a tear as they did so, either. They all did, when they met. Which wasn't so often, now their best boy was gone.

Some names? Certainly. Try us.

D – possibly standing for Dan or David – Hawley? G – maybe Gail – Talmadge? Paul Whitten? Fred or Freddie Kapinski?

Sorry, Chief Inspector. They don't mean a thing. Sorry.

Next!

Next was easy to find. He was a toff. A real toff. He had the cut-glass accent and title to prove it. He'd inherited both from his father, who in turn had been given them by his father and so on back to ancient times. Well, sometime in the eighteenth century. The first earl was the king's illegitimate sprog; the king so loved the lad's mother that he showered them with titles, estates and dosh, and his descendants had spent every waking moment since then making sure no one took any of it away from them. Ever. Except for the Toff. He'd lived his life rather differently.

If Ned had heard him on the phone, he'd have given him a pudgy red face and a game-pie paunch underpinned by those wretched salmon-pink trousers. But he was wiry and weather-beaten and he wore old clothes. He'd lied about his age and sneaked into the Navy at the end of the war and had a lively time on carriers in the last knockings against Japan. Kamikazes and whatnot. Wouldn't have missed it. The colours were so magnificent. Orange and crimson flames against that piercing blue sea. He and Tommy were old sailing companions. They'd been introduced by Uffa Fox in the Fairey yard in the mid-'50s. They raced International 14s, if you know what they are? He and Toms had particular success after they allowed the trapeze. No? Doesn't matter. That was in '69. They were pretty bloody good at it. Won the Prince of Wales' Cup twice. One day they dodged across to France, took on the Froggies, thrashed them and came straight back. Sixty hours at sea with a bloody tense race in the middle. Couldn't do that these days. Probably get done for Health and Safety.

You get close to a man on a small boat, particularly when you're up against it. Toms was jolly good company. None of that show business nonsense. A decent, decent man. Head turn. Handkerchief.

The Basle Club? He was more of an occasional member. He and the wife had spent half the year over the past fifteen in the Caribbean on a rather nice old schooner, so he'd not seen that much of them. And then Toms would be off on one of his pictures. Once a year the club'd all pile over and cruise around the islands. Eat and drink far too much. Lobster, rum punch and wonderful artisanal cigars from Cuba that never go for export. Huge fun. But not so much fun for Toms after his eye trouble. Before then he'd come out on his own – sometimes with Angela – and they'd crash about the Caymans, up to Cat Island. Scuba-diving off the Corn Islands. Bliss.

Once his sight was gone, Toms wasn't so keen. Not the sort of chap to sit back. Not a passenger. Had to be up and doing. He tried it once or twice, but since he couldn't see his footing or anything coming his way, found it all a bit difficult. Frustrating. Tried to persuade him to stick in the cockpit, but he wanted to be out there hauling down the canvas in a blow. He was safe as houses in a dead calm, but Toms wasn't a big fan of dead calms. Laugh.

Toms couldn't swim, you know. 'Course you knew that. Probably wouldn't be here asking questions if the old bugger had ever bothered to learn. Complete mystery why he didn't. Not the first sailor who couldn't swim, though, and won't be the last. Meant he always had to have a jolly good lifejacket and harness, even before the bother with his peepers. Must have been his worst fear, going like that. What he thought as he hit that water, God alone . . . Incidentally, Detective Chief Inspector, he'd never have taken his own life that way. Well, he'd never have taken his own life, full stop. Not Toms. He *was* life, that man. Handkerchief again. Blow. Better now.

He had absolutely no idea what possessed him to go to the Docks that night. In fact, now he came to think of it, he and the wife had been down there once with Angela and Toms for dinner at some restaurant owned by a pal of theirs. Not his kind of food. The sort you needed to eat with tweezers and an encyclopedia, rather than a knife and fork. But that night? Not a clue.

Had no idea the Latin had any meaning. Thought it was just stuff printers bunged in to mark time. Old Cicero, eh? Certainly Toms never talked about it.

Names? Of course, if I can.

No, sorry. You're sure that Talmadge is correct, are you? There was a splendid girl we used to know years ago named Tallent. Jill Tallent. Then she met a chap who farmed a good slice of Western Australia. Married him and went off the plot. No, absolute blank, I'm afraid. Is it important?

Not many, Toff. And you know it. That's why you came so far out of your goalmouth, mentioning Talmadge. To boot her away as hard as possible.

Next!

They didn't have to worry about the next. Number 5 was dead.

157

He had been dead for five years. He'd been Sir Tommy's dentist. Heart attack. Widow died two years later. No children.

Next!

Different kettle of fish, was Number 6. For a start, he wasn't rich or posh or dead. Well, not rich like the others. And not at all posh. He was a taxi driver. He was small and stocky and wore a red-check shirt and a grey leather waistcoat. It was a story he'd told before. On *Parky* and *This is Your Life*. About how he'd been doing an airport run in the early hours of the morning, and was on his way back when his headlamps caught a glint of something in the trees. He stopped, turned and went back to have a look. It was a motorbike, all crashed and twisted. He couldn't see its rider, but the bike had smashed through the undergrowth, so he simply followed its track back towards the road and halfway there, off to one side, he found a body. Still breathing.

He'd done first aid at youth club, so he gave it the old mouth-to-mouth and the bloke came to. Sat up. Well, he didn't recognise him in the darkness, and he knew he shouldn't be moved, but the man staggered to his feet so he thought, may as well get him to hospital. By the time he drove off and found a working call box and got an ambulance out there, he'd probably be a goner. It was before mobile phones and that. So he got the car over as close as he could and got him into it and drove him at ninety miles an hour to the nearest hospital. Well, they got stopped by the police for speeding, but then the officer shone his torch in the injured man's face and saw who it was and the state he was in with blood all over him and so they bashed the sirens on and escorted them all the way. He popped the geezer into Casualty and thought no more about it.

Then about a month later, he had a pick-up at the hospital, but from the private side, and who do you think it was but Tommy. Tommy Best. Blimey. He'd got on to the police, got his name and number at work off them, rung up the taxi firm and asked for him specially. So he drove him home. And Tommy invited him in. And they talked and talked and talked. Apparently Tommy had been on his way back from the theatre, and had swerved to avoid a deer. That was his story, anyway. Laugh. They got on really well. And as he left very late that night, after a good few over the eight, which he shouldn't admit to, he knew, but it was thirty years ago this June, Tommy said to him: 'That's the last time you drive for me. I want to see you again, but as friends.' And friends we were. Until the end.

He got up and left the room. Distant sound of another Basle Club nose being blown. Back again.

But it wasn't the same as before, now he'd told his story. Now it was a string of questions. How were the investigations going? Had they got any leads? Who else had they seen – which of the other boys? How was Angie? He'd tried to ring, but Chippy said she was in the States. Had the general public given them any good leads? They must be snowed under with tip-offs. If anyone asks him how it's going, what should he say?

That last question gave Ned the drop on his character. He was the kid in school who guards the big boy's new bike to make sure no one touches it. He was the plover, picking the crocodile's teeth. And the pickings were good. It turned out that Numbers 2 and 3 had bankrolled him in a transport business which had taken off big time. He had trucks criss-crossing Europe. They even made a toy lorry with his name on the side. That was a hell of a result. The expression on his nipper's face the day he took that in to school . . .

Supposing he hadn't stopped that night? Well. None of this would have happened. Not for him, and not for Tommy. Not given the state he found him in. Afterwards, nobody owed nobody nothing. That's what being friends is all about. Like Tommy used to say, who's your best friend then?

The boys had told him he'd be asked about some names. This Kapinski – if that's how you pronounce it – was vaguely familiar to him, but he couldn't for the life of him remember where from. The rest? No. Really sorry. If there was ever anything, anything he could do to help catch Tommy's killers . . .

Clever answer. You know you need help to pull off the lie, so you mention the others to muddy the water. And partially copping to Kapinski was good. Pick the croc's teeth and get your beak out before the jaw snaps shut. Smug, secretive, loyal unto and beyond the grave.

Before they'd started going through the Club, Spick had argued forcefully for questioning them simultaneously. Due respect and all that, governor, but it's no bleeding use just asking them nicely not to talk to one another. They were all Boy Scouts together. Masons. Dib dib dib. *Lorem ipsum* and all that crap. Ned let Spick blow his gasket, and then quietly pointed out that he knew they'd talk. He wanted them to talk. That's why he'd told them not to.

'But you've got her name wrong, governor. It's Grace, not Gail. And who the hell are Hawley, Whitten and Kap . . . Kapinski?'

'Well,' said Ned. 'David Hawley is the infinitely honest estate agent who sold my mum her house. Whitten was the name on the doorbell outside my last flat, which I never bothered to change. And Ferenc Kapinski is the brilliant Polish electrician who's just rewired my place.'

He left it at that. Work it out, Spick. Work it out. We can't tip them off that we're majoring on Mother T. We need some fudge and mudge. A bit of slop in the system. Dumb plods and proud of it. Maybe Gail wasn't quite dumb enough. Maybe should have said Lola or Carmella or Molly.

Two miles down the motorway Spick started nodding. Nice one, governor. For Spick to make Detective Inspector one day, Ned thought, he needed to have got there in yards, not miles.

There was another reason for the smoke and mirrors with the names, beyond not wanting to flush Talmadge out. He had to put the wind up the Basle Club ever so slightly. A plan was forming in Ned's mind. A bit nasty, and a tiny bit dangerous. But it would only stand a chance of working if he could be fairly sure that Mother Talmadge had stayed doing her ugly little business. And the easiest way to find that out was to see if they took steps to prevent him finding that out.

Next!

Number 7 was Span's responsibility. She'd been on the pessimistic side at first.

'You'll get nothing out of Mervyn, governor,' she said. 'He's on a life support machine. Can't move. Can't talk. Could die at any time.'

Perfect, thought Ned.

Getting the warrant was made slightly easier because, alone of the Basle Club members, Number 7 had form. He'd been arrested half a century before for his part in a robbery at a diamond merchants. An old boy had been coshed and died. Young Number 7 was done for murder, but got off on a technicality. He took his chance, turned himself around, and spent four decades working in and then running a youth hostel in one of the poorest, toughest neighbourhoods of town. It came to public attention because they started putting on shows to raise money. They kicked off with *West Side Story*, then *Guys and Dolls*, then *Grease*. Gradually they worked their way out of the street musical idiom, and transformed themselves from a hostel for wild kids into a nationally acclaimed youth theatre and talent school. Sir Tommy had entered the picture well before that, as guest of honour at the first show. He became a patron, gave money, did a masterclass or two, invited the kids onto his movie sets. He got on like a house on fire with the reformed bad boy, and gave him card Number 7.

Fast forward, and Number 7 was not a well man. He was permanently hooked up to machines that sucked and blew and pumped stuff in and out of him 24/7. He could do nothing for himself whatsoever, except think and blink. Communication, Span reported, was through a flat-screen television suspended over his bed. He spent most of the day watching old films and sport, but whenever anyone needed to talk to him or ask him something, they typed the message or question on a keyboard, and it would appear on the screen in front of him. He'd reply by means of a low-powered infra-red beam pointing just below his eye. When he blinked, the slight movement of his cheek muscle was enough to deflect the beam. This in turn was hooked up to the computer and allowed him to communicate, very slowly. He had some short cuts; he didn't have to blink out the phrases he used a lot; just a letter followed by a number. C stood for comfort, so C4 meant 'I'm too hot.' C17 – 'I have an itchy nose – please scratch.' T was for talk, so T1 was 'Hullo, nice to see you.' S(for sport)3 asked 'Did you see the game last night – what did you think?' S8 was 'The ref was shite.' The F series was for feelings. The staff or his visitors would just check the crib sheet.

'You get the idea, sir.'

Ned got the idea. Extra Bilge handled the technicalities. He started to explain in such detail how his box of tricks would work that Ned feared he'd have to delay his own retirement by a year or so just to hear it all. Not wanting to shave a minute off precious time to be spent with Kate raising puppies by the seaside, he just ordered the Bilge to get on with it. Naturally when he was doing the rounds of Numbers 2 to 6 with Spick, he made sure they all knew he was going to visit their very sick friend. 'I want to feel I've met all Sir Tommy's best friends . . .' was the formula.

As he drove cross-country Ned toyed with marching into the old murderer's room and asking him point blank if he knew the brothel-keeper Grace Talmadge. If there was an F number for 'Fuck off,' that's when he'd find it out. But F69, or whatever it was, would tell him a lot, but not everything. It wouldn't tell him what had happened to Sir Tommy. To find that out, he needed the old witch not to be tipped off into doing a bunk. Alternatively, did they need to show up at the home at all? Yes, he supposed so. To allay suspicion that they'd already learned what they needed to know by another method. By the same token, only the Director of the Pines of Rome Private Nursing Home was told the real identity of the white-coated, whinnying technician who'd gallop in to tweak Number 7's computer one day, and canter back a few days later to untweak it.

So Span and Ned spent a desultory hour with a pathetic and repellent old man. He lay and lived in a cantilevered, ducted, wired, blipping world. Yellow and brown and red and white goo in clear plastic tubes raced one another to get into him and then raced one another to get out. Banks of apparatus surrounded him; it was hard even to glimpse him, let alone assess the quality of his current life. You have to be in a man's moccasins to know that, and this man had no call for moccasins. He did have shockingly pink old feet. They hadn't touched the ground or cultured sock fluff or stepped in the cat litter for so long that they had become like the appendix:

no discernable function. Most of him was like that. But not his eyes. They had loads to do. Everything. So it became hard not to stare at them. They were very small and dark and bright, like the boot button eyes on an old teddy. But he was no teddy bear. Ned knew first impressions were bollocks and so was Cesare Lombroso, but Number 7 looked really evil. He was an ugly man. There was a kid's painting of him taped below one of the machines facing him. A grandchild's daub of poor, brave grandpa being strangled by cables and tubes. And the old devil was better-looking in the kid's appalling likeness than he was in real life. Lucky Number 7. He couldn't see himself.

Ned and Span asked about Tommy and the past and the Basle Club. And all they received were pre-baked, F-number platitudes. Tommy was a saint. The past had been hard at first, but then absolute magic. The Club was brilliant. He was sorry; he knew none of the names. It was an almost entirely vacuous hour, until Ned, out of idle curiosity just as they were about to leave, asked him what it had been like for him to be told that Tommy was dead. There was a long pause and then the eyes did something they had not done before. They shed two tears. And then two more. Then a flood. Ned was transfixed. He had got so used to translating F-number banalities that seeing all that emotion pouring out of the only bits of the man that were still working visibly and autonomously was shocking. Then he and Span became worried. Was Number 7 allowed to eject matter from his own body like that without it going through official channels? They pressed the alarm button to fetch the nurse, made their apologies and hurried away.

It was so good getting out of there. So lovely seeing fields of winter wheat and a pheasant and pylons and plastic bags in hedges and pampas grass and a pub car park and wheelie-bins and chefs out the back smoking and Extra Bilge again. Extra Bilge was grinning from ear to ear. He'd got Mr Ned the whole thing. Here was a printout of the text: everything that had been typed on Number 7's computer for the past five days. It was pretty dull stuff – first news Ned had that Extra Bilge found anything dull – until Day Three at 5.17 p.m. That's when he had a visitor who told him all about a meeting the visitor had had with Mr Ned and Spick. What they had been saying. How the investigation seemed to be going. How they were clearly flailing about and didn't have anything really, except a garbled version of Mother's name. They had her as Gail. Whatever happened, under no circumstances must Mervyn let on that he or Tommy or the rest know anyone by that name. Let alone had ever visited the Happy House. When they type their list of names out on the screen which they will do, just answer T7; T43: 'I don't know; I'm sorry.'

'Happy House.' Jan Span spat the words out, appalled. 'Bastards.'

Ned had wondered who the Basle Club's messenger would be. Who'd be the party whip? The enforcer? The plover – Number 6 – was the obvious answer. The picker of teeth. The truck-laden errand boy. But it was too obvious. Probably be 2 or 3, relishing the chance for a spin in the country. Hood down; 'The Boss' on full blast. Born to Run.

Wrong! It was a thin, rangy man in an old waxed coat. Surveillance had got him coming and going. Extra Bilge showed Ned a selection of frame grabs. Tanned, weather-beaten. Unmistakably the Sailor Toff. A very long way out of his goalmouth.

Extra Bilge was escorted into the winner's enclosure – in this case the saloon bar – and graciously accepted a nose bag and a bucket of lemonade shandy. Did the favourite want a lift back?

'No, Mr Ned, many thanks. I've studied the timetable, and I can get back entirely by bus. There's a stop over the road, and I calculate I'll be home by 2.20 a.m. There's a rumour that in this part of the world they're still using AN69 Atlanteans with the Leyland 0.690 engine. Which, given most went for export plus the age of the unit, makes this a pretty rare opportunity. But thanks all the same.'

Ned naturally deferred to an AN69 with a 0.690, though he did notice Extra Bilge eyeing up a blackboard welcoming newcomers to the pub quiz there that very same evening. He could barely imagine the anguish Extra Bilge must have felt as two great passions battled for his body and soul.

* * *

The day after they got back, Ned, Spick and Span had a catch-up lunch with Fatso. It wasn't a good idea to eat with Fatso. Granted, Ned was famously squeamish, but Attila the Hun would plead hair-wash night rather than break bread with the big man. You were reasonably OK to the side of him: out of the line of fire and you didn't have to watch. But opposite . . . Some said an umbrella was the answer, but that would have been impossibly rude. You can't sit opposite someone at lunch with an umbrella up to shield you from projectile gobs of half-chewed food. You've got to be able to look him in the eye. No, the thing they needed was one of those round spinning glass devices set into the windscreen on a ship's bridge that deflect rain to provide perfect visibility in a storm. A portable version of that, placed on the table between Fatso and the unfortunate sitting opposite him would have greatly enhanced the experience.

There was a private upstairs room at the boozer they had made their own over the years. It was dark and slightly sticky, but very quiet. Fatso sat at the head of the table and worked his way through a yellow slag-heap of *nachos*, which he insisted on calling 'cheese 'n' crisps'. Ned sat judiciously to one side of him, with Spick and Span on the other. No one sat opposite. They ordered but didn't touch a plate of rubbery sandwiches. Ned wondered if it was the same plate of rubbery sandwiches they'd not touched at the last Fatso lunch. It would make sense. Next time they should ask if they could rent it by the hour.

Ned talked about the Basle Club. About the evidence they had from Extra Bilge's computer tap that Grace Talmadge had been providing Tommy and them with the kind of service they really didn't want anyone to find out about. He took them through the tale of the toothpick match and the cigars. It was probable that, since the match was found right by the hole, Sir Tommy had lit his last cigar there. A cigar he fully expected to be smoking as he walked back to his hotel. What happened a moment later was still a mystery, but it must have involved physically restraining the dog. That was Nick Parsons's judgement, backed up by the crucial evidence of the broken harness. More than that . . .

Fatso pushed the plate away and wiped his mouth on his sleeve.

'OK. So the great man has a bang, then strolls out of the whore house onto the walkway and sparks up a burner. But then what? Mother T has her bully boys boot him into the drink for not putting the top back on the KY Jelly? Makes no sense, cock.'

Ned agreed. They had to face the possibility that his death had nothing to do with any visit to Grace Talmadge's. Muggers still couldn't be ruled out. There was no telling who'd pocketed the £1,000 in cash. Could have been Talmadge. Could have been muggers.

Fatso shook his head. Muggers just happen to pitch up on the walkway while the National Treasure's quietly sucking a Castella? Nah. He reckoned there had to be a connection between him getting his ancient end away and him getting bumped off. Fatso didn't like coincidences.

'There's stuff going on here,' he said vaguely and emphatically. 'It's just we aren't spotting how it connects. We need to know for sure if Tommy Best visited that cow Talmadge the night he was croaked.'

Ned agreed. They all stood and started putting on coats. Fatso gestured the others down the stairs ahead of him, then turned to face Ned.

'I've had the coroner on at me. Miserable old sod wants to book his holidays. Wanted to know if he can "pencil something in".'

Fatso pulled out the last three words and gave them a tight-arsed, effete voice. Then he peered up at his smartest subordinate with a hopeful, questioning, faintly dependent look.

'You got a plan, haven't you, cock?'

Ned nodded. He did. He had a plan. Tricky to pull off, but with luck it should tell them what had happened that evening. Whether Sir Tommy had indeed visited the Happy House. And what exactly happened after he lit that cigar. A glint appeared in a piggy eye, but only fleetingly.

'Are we going to piss on the National Treasure? Because if we are, he'd bloody better have been up to something. If not, we might as well leave it. Sometimes, Ned the Yid, we take a good hard look

at something, and then we put the stone right back how we found
it. If there's no third party involved in his death, if it's just a fuck-
happy old git falling through the floorboards . . .'

Fatso shook his head. Ned held his eye.

'I don't like coincidences any more than you do, sir. And I don't
think Tommy Best's death was an accident. Not with the evidence
from the dog.'

It was Fatso's turn to nod. He turned and started heavily down
the stairs.

'I told the coroner to unchock his bleeding caravan. I said to 'im,
"Charlie, hold off. Our Ned is still at work."'

They went in the Land Rover. Its carbon footprint rivalled Godzilla's,
but the track to Nick's house was a sea of mud in rain, and they'd
had monsoons on that side of the country. Kate had fitted a cage for
Suzy into the back, but when she came round to pick Ned up the dog
was beside her on the passenger seat. Suzy seemed pleased to see
Ned; she licked his hand and wagged her tail. Given the plan, it was
just as well. He opened the back and tucked his little Globetrotter
and laptop between Suzy's sack of food and toys and Kate's big
canvas bag. Bunney-Fluff's moving day. It felt a tiny bit intimate,
which was very nice. She drove and she knew the way, so they didn't
have to argue about that. It felt like going on holiday. There was a
Thermos flask and mugs and apples and nuts and raisins. They had
his and her iPods and a radio-link, but didn't use them, so there was
no peeping into the knicker-drawer of the other person's playlist. Not
yet, anyway. The city fizzled out behind them. Was this how Mr and
Mrs Coroner did it with their caravan? Or did Fatso's homophobic
voice suggest Mr and Mr Coroner? Wonder if they had a dog?

'Are we there yet?'

Kate smiled politely. The old jokes are the best, his father used
to say. Dad could be so wrong.

It was funny him ringing her like that. She was about to ring him.
And she was going to suggest to him something not a million miles

from what he proposed to her. Her plan wasn't nearly as full on and she'd be the one doing it, not him, but the idea was the same: take Suzy back down to the Docks. He told her he'd seen a tug leading a ship off its mooring and out into the river, and it had reminded him of a guide dog leading a blind person. Made him think about what they might learn from Suzy if they took her back. As soon as the idea came into his mind he kicked it out again. Just taking a wander with Suzy over the cobbles could produce very misleading results. Suppose she doesn't turn in to Mrs Talmadge's of her own accord? Does that mean she'd never gone there? A guide dog walking down a shopping street would hardly take her master or mistress into every shop, just because she had at some time been into the butcher, baker, candle-stick maker, etc. No, the only way to use the dog was as part of a plan. A plan in which the owner knew exactly where he/she wanted to go and went with the dog. For example, to Mrs Talmadge's, and then up onto the walkway.

Kate didn't say anything. This Mrs Talmadge's was a brothel, and the walkway had a gaping great hole in it which had already claimed one life. And now Ned wanted to go to both these horrible places at night and with Suzy. This is the reason they say one should never get involved with people at work.

'. . . are you still there? I was saying, if you haven't eaten yet we could meet up and talk about it over a bite . . .'

There was a cosy little wine bar halfway between them. On the way, she wondered whether to be more surprised that she was having a date with Ned at all, or that she was having a date with Ned in which she'd have to eat in front of him, or that she was having a date with Ned in which, over a meal together, they'd plan how best he might visit a prostitute and then go and drown himself and the adored dog. She was lucky she didn't know his full plan, or she'd never have gone. And actually, when she got there, it was really lovely.

It was that late, lazy hour on a slow night. It had rained and the streets glistened and glowed. Someone was playing jazz quietly in a far corner. She felt all grown-up with him and relaxed. They sat in the window and made a ridiculously handsome couple. She knew that because she could see people staring at them. And because she could see their candle-lit reflections in the glass. She had a glass of Armagnac and he had a glass of Rioja and they shared some *tapas*. He ate all the mushrooms, which she didn't like, and she ate all the *patatas bravas*, which he did like.

He watched her. He didn't know she ate. He didn't know she drank. He didn't know she went out in the evening to bars. He didn't know she wore clothes that went with the flow of her amazing body rather than smothering it in bagginess. He didn't know she could be such good company. He didn't know that she didn't know these things either, and that they were both finding them out at the same time.

Another funny thing was that they didn't once talk about anything they were meant to. No walk at night back into the Docks with Suzy. No Mrs Talmadge. No prostitutes. No gaping holes over swirling black water. No death. No plan.

The good thing about having a dog in an old Land Rover is that about the time you really need a break from having your bones shivered and shaken, the dog needs a walk. So no one need be exposed as a wuss. You take her, said Kate, while I sort the coffee. So Ned took her. It was a bit like holding a baby for the first time, when you really fancy the single mother. Ned tacked the word 'single' on to convince himself he was a nice guy. When he was a hopeful adolescent and saw sexy young mums in the street, he used to say to himself 'She's done it once – she'll do it again.' He shook his head to clear the shameful thought and led Suzy off into the field by the road. So is this how a would-be stepfather feels? What if the real dad shows up? Can't. We buried him.

The further round the field they walked, the more uneasy Ned became. What was it Kate had said, about whether Suzy would 'perform' on a lead? Couldn't remember. But she showed no sign of wanting to do so. She trotted along beside him, occasionally glancing up at him but giving no sign that she wanted any privacy. He wondered whether to let her off the lead. What if he couldn't get her back? Imagine having to explain to Kate. Not just to her – the world! That he'd lost the late National Treasure's treasured pooch. Bollocks, he thought. She's trained to the nines. Off with the lead, my gel, and get on with it.

Turned out privacy was a factor. Not that Suzy hid behind a bush, but she certainly lingered until Ned was a little way in front. He looked back like Orpheus and caught her eye. She seemed embarrassed and wrinkled her bushy eyebrows, forcing him to turn away and walk on. Moments later she was back trotting alongside. She looked up. He patted her head. All well. Don't know why people make such a fuss. Dogs are a doddle when you know how.

'Did she do anything?' Kate asked, handing him a mug and remembering Saul.

Absolutely, Ned replied, realising they were having their first intimate conversation, albeit about a dog's toilette. 'Absolutely' wasn't apparently enough. Details would be good. Ned started to worry how to refer to the two options. It was important to get the tone right. The words were a dead giveaway: of one's vulgarity or excessive gentility or squeamishness. They were an instant measure of the degree to which you had really left home. And what sort of home it had been. There was as much danger of sounding as if one had been brought up in one's nursery by one's nanny as in a Sergeants' Mess. Then, just as it started to seem odd that he hadn't answered, he realised he didn't have a clue what Suzy had done. Just seemed to hunker down with her tail in the air. So that's what he said. Fine, said Kate, putting the cap back on the Thermos, and off they went again.

She took the route she knew. The sun didn't show up much but the witch was still at her till, still incomprehensible. As the hedges grew high on either side she started talking about Nick Parsons. Preparing Ned. By the time they crossed the big river, he'd started to wonder if there had been anything between them. Before they reached the whey-faced town he'd sort of decided there had not. Nick was clearly too much up himself to be attractive to Kate. He might be too much up himself to do what Ned needed him to do. How generous would he be? How relaxed?

It was dark when she nosed the Land Rover down Nick's track. They lurched terribly over slush-filled holes, bouncing the poor dog around until Kate slowed to a crawl. It was a much longer journey than she remembered, even allowing for the snail's pace. When the darkened house finally appeared she caught herself thinking he wasn't in. Must click back into the blind thing. Bad to piss him off. Bad to say: didn't think you were at home because all the lights were off. It took an age for him to answer the door. She wondered how he'd respond. With no phone, he had no idea they were coming. Eventually they heard footsteps and the bolt being thrown, and then the door opened.

'Hullo, Nick. It's me again – Kate. With Suzy. And I hope you don't mind; I've brought a friend.'

The bugger about the darkness was that Ned, momentarily uncertain if he'd been right about Nick and Kate as a non-event, couldn't see Nick's immediate reaction to her reappearance. His voice sounded pleased enough. He helped them in with their things, put the kettle on and lit the candles. That was nice of him, Kate thought. She fed Suzy who, as before, lay down near the range until the heat grew too much for her and she took herself out of the kitchen. Nick produced some bread and cheese and they supplied apples and wine and a cherry pie. And when they were finally settled and warm with mugs of tea all round, Nick asked why they had come. What could he do for them? Was it something more to do with Suzy? Kate looked at Ned, who thought for a moment before answering.

'I want you to teach me how to be blind, Nick, and how to be guided by Suzy. And to be able to pass for blind without anyone knowing I'm not. To do it so well, in fact, that my life could depend on it.'

10

THEY ARGUED INTO THE NIGHT. Or rather, Nick argued and Ned said as little as possible and Kate kept her thoughts to herself. It was like waiting for a bonfire to die down. When it was embers, they all went to bed. Kate slept in her old room, while Ned dossed down on the sofa. She didn't bother erecting more of her barricade than the blanket over the door. She didn't need to. She had Ned next door.

Nick didn't have just one argument. He had a string. When one failed, he moved on to another. He started off with the absolute impossibility of Ned being able to pretend to be blind. It was so easy to give yourself away by responding to something you could only have seen. Didn't they remember that great film that Sir Tommy was in? About the prison camp escape? In which one chap pretends to be deaf and dumb because he can't speak German, and they get caught in the café and the SS officer orders his men in English to take him out the back and slit his throat. And without thinking the guy makes a run for it and they shoot him. Ned said he didn't remember the film, but he could imagine the scene and had anticipated the problem. He knew he wasn't actor enough to carry it off without actually being blind, so blind he would be. Temporarily. Blind for the evening. Some sort of short-stay eye-drops. Ned made sure he didn't catch Kate's eye when he said this. Didn't want to clock her disapproval or, worse, her nonchalance.

Nick shook his head and moved on. This idea of using Suzy was just bonkers. Did Ned really think that he could learn how to use a guide dog in a couple of days? When Nick was doing this for a living it took four intense weeks with the owner plus follow-ups. It wasn't just learning a few shortcuts. The secret of achieving a good and effective team of visually impaired person with their dog lay in a combination of knowledge, experience, trust and authority. The dog was an equal partner in that process, but not in the relationship. The dog has to learn to respect his or her new handler. You can't just grab the harness and hope. It's complex stuff. If you don't get it right, not only will you give yourselves away – the stuff you learn won't be meaningful. And then you could both wind up under a bus. You have to get to know one another. It takes time and it goes both ways. Dogs get a feeling from their owners straight down the lead. If they get the wrong feeling, you're both buggered.

Kate was thinking as Nick spoke that this made really good sense. It was a crazy thing to be trying in the time. True, Suzy seemed to like Ned, but he knew nothing about dogs. Couldn't even tell if she was having a wee or a poo. Not a big problem in itself, but if your life depended on knowing your dog . . . She glanced at Ned. He wasn't getting red in the face thinking up clever answers. He was making notes.

'. . . just getting to know your dog's gait. A good one like Suzy sort of glides. You can tell, with experience, by the feel through the handle not only which way she's going but what sort of ground she's going over. You've got to be able to read her, and we're talking nuances. You're proposing to go into the Docks at night. Over cobbles and old railway tracks. Along quays with sheer drops. They're tricky places in daylight for a sighted person. Put out the lights and they become lethal.'

Ned spoke without looking up from his scribbling.

'What about intelligent disobedience? Would that help me?'

Nick snorted. He could tell Ned had been doing some homework.

But a little learning was dangerous. For people and dogs. It might save him. It might not. It wouldn't stop him from tripping over a kerbstone and bashing his brains out on an old anchor, or whatever else there was lying around. It wouldn't stop him slipping on wet paving and tumbling into the drink. And he'd be blind, remember. According to the great plan. The mad plan.

'When you were training, you presumably put owners and their dogs through tests? To make sure they made safe, viable teams?'

Absolutely. He did a host of assessments. How they handled the urban environment: traffic, crowded pavements, crossing roads, railway stations. On the bus. In the tube. At the park, with other dogs. The routes he or she habitually took. The streets around the person's home. Home itself. Sure.

'Fine,' said Ned. 'Train me with Suzy and then test us. If we fail, I won't go.'

There was quite a pause at this. Nick got up. Put a piece of wood into the stove. Got a pear off the dresser. Put it back. Sat down. Rubbed his hair vigorously with both hands. Shook his head. Went motionless. Ned and Kate exchanged glances. 'Wonder what he'll come back with'-type glances. They'd never have guessed.

'Right,' he said, as if he was the chairman of the board. 'I'll do it myself. I have the advantage here of actually being blind. I know Suzy and she knows me. I'd do anything to catch the bastard who murdered Tommy. *I'll* bloody do it.'

'Well, Nick,' replied Ned in measured tones, 'in a way you *will* be doing it. Nick Parsons will be doing it. Except I will be Nick Parsons.'

God, the spluttering. The preposterousness of the idea. And then the indignation. Enter Nick's vanity. How could someone impersonate him? And was it legal? What if he objected? What if any evidence Ned found wasn't useable in court because it was under false pretences, or entrapment or something? As this line played itself out Ned found himself agreeing with Nick's previous cliché that a little learning was indeed dangerous.

'. . . you think you can effectively convince someone that not only are you blind *and* a highly experienced guide dog trainer and handler, but that you are someone else? Me? Who do you think you are? Daniel Day-Lewis? Dustin Hoffman?'

In a remarkably calm voice, Ned pointed out to Nick that the people he would have to convince were at a vital disadvantage which made the subterfuge possible. They had never met the real Nick Parsons. They didn't know if he wore cowboy boots or Gucci loafers. If he spoke with a burr or a twang. If they had a picture of him it was ten years out of date. He and Nick were not that far off in age and vaguely similar in appearance. As to the dog handling, if he had a problem he'd say he was rusty. Hadn't been near a dog for a decade, and was just getting used to Suzy again. Anyway, Nick should know that the idea had come from Nick himself with the *Lorem ipsum* card. The only way he'd get into the place he needed to get into was by brandishing Nick's card and being Nick. Complete with the beloved old dog which Sir Tommy had willed to the man who had trained them both all those years ago. What could be more natural? And more plausible?

'Besides, there's no way I'm going to let you do it yourself. It's too dangerous, and whereas I'm not blind, there's no stuff you can stick in your eyes that'll turn you into a detective for a few hours. Not yet, there isn't.'

The next bit was surprising. Nick got up and came over to Ned, who was sitting in an ancient wing-backed chair which was losing its horse-hair stuffing. He knelt down in front of Ned and ran his fingers over his face. Several times. Kate was a little shocked. It seemed like a very intimate gesture between strangers, even if the one was bidding to be the other. Then Nick picked up Ned's hands, first the right and then the left, and felt them. Almost stroking them. Never mind what Ned had been wondering on the way there; Kate, for the first time in her life, felt a faint twitch of jealousy. And then Nick put his hands down and stayed there, his head inches away from Ned. Listening to his breathing, smelling him. It was more invasive than anything he had just done, and Ned and Kate were mightily relieved when it stopped. Nick got up and plonked himself almost sulkily back in his chair. He didn't say anything for a while, and then he launched into the most difficult argument yet.

'So you're me. And you're blind. And you've got Suzy. And you've got the *Lorem ipsum* thingy. And you need all of this to get you in somewhere you can't get in without. Open sesame. You're a . . . what? A Detective Chief Inspector, but you can only get in there by pretending to be me? Must be a pretty bad place. And you're not telling me what the place is, but you believe it to be connected to Tommy's death. His murder. So it's Murder Inc. or a vicious gambling or opium den, or a fight club to the death, or all of those things rolled into one. Or something equally unpleasant. And it's all connected to Sir Tommy. Somewhere he went voluntarily. So here's the problem. I loved that man. I'm sorry to repeat myself, but I loved him like a father. I couldn't bring myself . . . to expose him . . . to indignity or shame . . .'

Ned chose his words with great care. Much depended on it. He told Nick that what mattered was getting to the truth. That was his job.

'I never knew Sir Tommy, but I've met a lot of people recently who did, including you, Nick. And what you all have in common is that you loved and admired him for being extraordinary, life-enhancing, inspirational, compassionate. Only yesterday, I found myself staring at the famous photo of Tommy Best with Chippy: the one taken the moment after he found her as a baby in that sea of dead bodies in the Sudan. An amazing picture. An amazing person. He was a very rare man to inspire such feelings in so many others. All of us deserve the truth, and the rare are no exception. We owe them the truth too. And maybe a man like Tommy Best can take the truth better than the rest of us.'

Ned then had the good sense to shut up and not drone on, as he'd been told he always did by a girlfriend after they'd had a row in which he had happened – by chance – to be in the right. Well, by all his girlfriends, if he was being honest. It was a lesson that had taken long in the learning. Kate was mighty impressed, but she knew nothing of the back-story. And Nick too fell silent. That's when the fire started to go out, leaving embers that grew duller and duller until they lost all glint.

Kate wondered overnight if Nick would back-pedal the training so as to fail Ned. He seemed a bit subdued over breakfast, which worried her. He fiddled around in the barn, supposedly looking for a lead. Then he fussed for a while with Suzy's collar and harness. Then he insisted on having coffee, so they all had coffee. Ned and Kate got talking about something or other and it was a while before they realised that Nick wasn't in the kitchen. Neither was Suzy. They looked out of the window in time to see them disappearing down a path to the side of the lawn: Nick guided by Suzy. They discussed joining them, but Nick's untouched mug of coffee on the dresser suggested he probably wanted time alone with Suzy. Kate went upstairs to the landing and caught a glimpse of them walking along the narrow ridge her van had gone over. The ridge with a sharp slope on the far side down to the river. And then they passed behind a clump of trees and were gone.

She passed Ned halfway up the stairs, staring at the wild paintwork.

'Looks loony, doesn't it?' she said. 'Nightmarish.'

He nodded.

'The smell of paint. That's what it's about. He told me last time that there's no reason a blind person can't enjoy the smell of fresh paint, any more than a vegetarian can't eat horseradish sauce. If you're a veggy no one ever gives you horseradish sauce. So every now and then he grabs a pot of paint – he can't see what colour and he doesn't care – and he slops it on. Looks crazy, but it's not about how it looks. He says he enjoys doing it, too.'

She slipped outside while Ned studied the great gashes of colour. The memory of a book he'd had as a child came back to him. A book that had belonged to his father. It was a French story about two kittens who were painters. They had stripy overalls and ladders and brushes and pots and pots of paint. He couldn't remember their names, but at the end of the story they woke up one morning so happy that they tipped all the pots out and the colours ran into one another – yellow, blue, purple, green, red – and made new colours. In retrospect this can't have done much for their decorating business, but it looked like a hell of a lot of fun.

Ned had no sense that his childhood had been particularly joyous. Indeed, it had often been lonely and sometimes a bit miserable. But there were bits and pieces in it, like the painty kittens, which had a habit of connecting much later with things he saw or experienced. It wasn't spooky. These weren't premonitions. They were shortcuts from the past that provided refuge in the present. He really hated the blood and guts side of his job. Hated it as much as he loved the analysing, deducing side. Sometimes deep memories bailed him out, like waking yourself from a nightmare. And sometimes they just reminded him of the essential lesson for a detective: to be able to see things in different ways. Nick's walls were crazy, repellent psychedelia one moment, and entirely logical and sympathetic the next – if you understood them in terms of smell, not sight. And then they could be seen as expressions of joy. What two kittens do just because one morning they wake up happy and they've got all these pots of paint and there's no one to stop them. Bet that's another reason why Nick did it. Because he could.

When Nick got back, he was a changed man. He was excited. It was the first time he'd walked with a guide dog as a blind man. He'd blindfolded himself while training dogs – sure. But it wasn't the same thing. And Suzy was as incredible as he remembered, particularly given her age. She was so sure-footed and steady, so responsive and responsible. He admitted she'd just made him wonder if he'd been wrong all those years, not having a dog. Of course, Suzy wasn't any dog. Kate knew that and bent down to give her a cuddle. To Ned it looked as if she were restaking her claim to Suzy. As if she feared Nick might get possessive. But then Nick scotched any idea, real or imagined, that he or she 'owned' Suzy.

'Right!' he said to Ned. 'From now on, Suzy is yours. She's going to stick by your side, listen to you and do what you tell her to do. She will be with you when you eat and when you sleep. We aren't going to touch her or give her orders or even feed her. Suzy is now your dog.'

And with that, Nick held out the harness and Ned took it. Symbolic moment, Kate thought. 'Bugger me' was Ned's take. His own dog. He looked down at Suzy in a new light. She looked back at him, her head slightly to one side. She raised one brow, then the other. Then she gave a very big yawn. Ned glanced across at Kate, who was giving him a thumbs up. Yawns were evidently a good sign. From now on, it could only get tougher. And that's exactly what it did.

Nick asked Ned to sit down. He then moved up behind him, slipped a black blindfold over his eyes and fixed it firmly at the back. It smelled of mothballs. He'd stay in the blindfold, day and night until he'd done the test. Fair enough, thought Ned. How hard could it be? He passed over in his mind the night manoeuvres at the Greyhound Stadium. Not fair his memory dragging that in. It was entirely different. No dog there. Well, not in the VIP box. And Nick's blindfold made good sense. So too did his next instruction. Could Ned go to the Land Rover and bring in the bag of dog food from the back? A little exercise. Sure. Why not? Ned just wasn't quite sure how he was going to do it. He sat for a while, trying to remember his bearings. Hold on. Hadn't they got everything out of the Land Rover? How did blind Nick know they'd left a bag of dog food in the car? It crossed Ned's mind that Kate might have switched sides.

Now. Where's that dog gone? Suzy came at the call of her name. She moved very quietly. Must be some carpet in the hall, because he could hear when she entered the kitchen. Heard the tiny scratchy tapping of her claws on the flagstones. Good. He'd need his hearing as sharp as it possibly could be. No iPod for him this holiday. Or labour camp or whatever it was. Sure, now the dog was behind him, but which way round was she? He stretched out a hand and poked her in the bottom. Bad start. Fail. He could hear Kate stifle a laugh. Like to see her try. Up a bit. Bit more. What on earth is that? Oh. She seems to have turned. Where's the handle of the harness?

Ah! Got it. Now which way is she facing and where's the door? This'll only take a mo'.

In fact it took Ned nearly fifteen minutes to get the dog food from the car just seventy feet away. It would have been quicker, but for some reason he couldn't actually find the front door. It turned out there was another door right by it into the front room, and Suzy thought that's where he wanted to go. They wandered around there for a bit before he accidentally stumbled on what he thought was the way out. In his frustration he went ahead of Suzy and fell down a step into the larder. In doing so, he banged his head against a shelf and grazed his shin on a crate of cider. He stayed in the larder for a few minutes. The first was entirely devoted to cursing, and the second he spent trying to open his eyes under the blindfold just enough to glimpse his feet, on the basis that life was too short. Unfortunately the blindfold fitted too well. Then, almost in desperation, he asked Suzy to take him outside. Amazingly he suddenly felt her through the handle, like that moment in water-skiing when the tension is taken up, but before there's any pull. Next thing he knew they were outside. Piece of piss, as Spick would say. Ned didn't see the elation on Kate's face give way to pity as she clocked the nasty graze on his forehead. He couldn't see a thing.

He and Suzy started off fine down the path towards the Land Rover, but then she just stopped, firmly blocking his way. It was absolutely ridiculous of her. There was nothing there. He tried tugging and pushing, but she wouldn't budge. So he put the harness down and went round her, promptly tripping over what felt like a big bundle of bean-poles balanced on piles of flowerpots. He decided as he was falling that Nick couldn't have done this on his own. Ow! He'd deal with Kate later. At least he couldn't see the pitying, superior expression on Suzy's face, assuming dogs went in for that sort of thing. Certainly if they were ever going to, now was the time.

Things got a little better when Kate sat him down and put antiseptic on one shin and antiseptic and a plaster on the other and cleaned up his forehead. Wonderful chance to hone his awakening sense of hearing: her breathing and even – fleetingly, as she reached up past him for something – her heart. His sense of smell too: her breath again – fresh, warm, hint of mint – and from the rest of her, a heady infusion of cedar, soap, shampoo and fabric conditioner with what the wine writers would describe as faint notes of petrol and pet shops. Ah! Bonio Nouveau! It must have been Kate who put Suzy's food back into the Land Rover. Funny how much more you can deduce when you really use your senses. Then it was time for lunch. Odd how difficult it was getting minestrone into his mouth. He could pop a piece of bread in without difficulty, but something about using a spoon, whose length seemed to vary with every mouthful, made him glad he'd worn old clothes. His respect for blind people was growing immeasurably.

He spent the next few hours falling over less and learning more. It was probably because he had banged himself about in the morning that he was so receptive to Nick's teaching in the afternoon. All in all it was a fairly humbling day. Firstly, as he realised literally with a bump what it was like not being able to see to do the most ordinary things. Secondly as he started to understand how brave it was of Nick and Sir Tommy to carry on with their lives so independently, albeit in such diametrically opposed ways: Nick shunning everything and Tommy embracing everything. Thirdly, as he began to get an inkling of how extraordinary working dogs were. That made him think very hard both about Suzy and Kate.

Until the moment when Nick handed over her harness handle, Ned had seen Suzy as something to do with other people: Sir Tommy, Kate, the general public. She was after all the most famous dog in the country. He also saw her as not only fragile and wounded but crucial, like a Hitchcock heroine. She had seen what had happened. She knew the thing he did not: who the murderer was. In a Hitchcock film, she would now be the target of evil men, desperate to eliminate the only witness to their wrongdoing. Indeed, perhaps she was. It was precisely because she held the clue to Sir Tommy's death that they were doing all this, though whether the clue was extricable remained to be seen.

What Ned had not allowed for was the shift in perception and trust he would have to make in becoming absolutely dependent on Suzy. Up till now, he had sort of seen her as Kate's patient, like a sick dolly in a child's pretend hospital. What was it Chippy had done that had so angered Sir Tommy? Ah yes – dressed her up as a ballerina. And then there was dog as baby. The child of the single yummy mummy. She'll judge you by how you are with the thing she loves most. Get that right, or look as if you really want to learn how to, and she might love you next best. The rest is all to play for. And then he supposed he saw her as just a dog. The sort of waggy-tailed wooffly thing that other people had but he did not. Except he did now. And he needed the dog, not as part of a witness protection programme or a device to win fair lady, but for himself. Suzy now stood between him and grazed knees. Between him and bean-poles piled on flower pots. Between him and car bumpers. Between him and fatal falls over slippy quaysides. Who's your best friend now, Ned?

As for Kate, his new-found reliance on her stock-in-trade made Ned respect her all the more. His colleagues and subordinates, on whom he depended to do his job, were fallible and eccentric but at least he could talk to them, share ideas, discuss and argue. Kate, going into a booby-trapped bomb factory with Banshee, had to be able to do something incredible. She had to read and understand the mind, responses and communications of a totally different species. Get it right – lives saved. Get it wrong – bang!

Being plunged into the intricacies of dog behaviour was a bit like Take your Child to Work Day. The person you saw as one thing turned out to be something else completely. Ned remembered the day he spent with his father at the College of Further Education. Amazing! He knew all this stuff, and managed not to sound too pompous spouting it out. People actually seemed to take him seriously. Not just students, but fellow staff members. Listened to his opinions. Laughed at his jokes. And he seemed comfortable in his own context. Not scrabbling after something he'd never catch, like he was with Mum. Then again, perhaps the whole thing was a put-up job. Maybe everyone at the college solemnly agreed that on that one day they wouldn't make one another look like wallies. Wasn't in any of their interests to default on the deal. You don't need your child going home and saying to Mum, 'God, Dad's a real wanker.' Even – especially – if that's what she already suspects.

Dinner was polenta with wild mushrooms and rocket salad. Ned's aim seemed to be getting better – he could get the fork into his mouth pretty well. It was just surprising how often there was nothing on it. He kept wanting to watch Nick and see how he did it, but that was out. He became self-conscious about dropping stuff and having a messy chin. He kept dabbing at it with a piece of kitchen paper. Eventually the plate seemed to be empty. He swept the fork over it to see if it snagged on an uneaten mushroom. All clear. Relax.

'Enjoyed your meal?'

Funny. Ned had already said twice how good it was. And hadn't Kate cooked it? Then he realised there was a faintly reproachful ring about Nick's question. Think. Perhaps he should offer to wash up? Offer accepted, but tone still naggy. And what did Nick mean by '. . . if you've nothing better to do'? That could only mean Ned definitely had something better to do. Think hard! Ah yes, of course. Something he ought to have done immediately: take off Suzy's harness and feed her.

'Fair cop. Or, in this case, unfair cop.'

No one seemed to laugh at this, so he concentrated on feeding his new partner in crime-solving. He evidently didn't know he'd cut his finger opening the tin of dog food, because he came back into the kitchen dripping blood everywhere. Nick said he had quite forgotten about all the falls and scrapes. Early on apparently, Tommy had seriously contemplated wearing shin guards and his old motorcycle crash helmet. Kate sat Ned down and dressed the latest wound.

If all this was odd for him, it was even odder for her. It wasn't the fact that she was touching him. That was just bog standard first aid stuff, although it was funny having their bodies so close. His nearness felt very intimate, particularly that morning when she was cleaning up the bash on his forehead and his face was inches from her breasts. He couldn't see anything of course, with that blind-fold on. Probably only vaguely aware of her presence, with all that was on his mind. No, what was so very odd was seeing him at such a disadvantage.

She was used to Ned the winner. The youngest DCI in the force. Ned at the top of his game. The man who didn't mess up. Who didn't flail around. The judo black belt. Ned on his feet – not sprawled across the gravel with his face in a flower pot. OK for Bill and Ben but not for Mr Ned. She felt like the heroine in a film who has to watch the hero get beaten up. Do they always have to win for you to love them? Or can you read defeat and humiliation as proof of humanity? Maybe even evidence of that much-prized virtue in men these days: feminine sensibility?

Why did he care so much about solving the Tommy Best case that he would put himself through all this? Or did it have something in common with her job? She didn't care a jot for this terrace house or that remote farmhouse. But tell her there were explosives on the premises and she suddenly started to care a whole lot. Suddenly, that ugly building or dull warehouse really meant something to her. She didn't pitch up outside, say she didn't like the pointing or the colour of the gable ends – they weren't worth saving – and bog off home. She went in. She and her dog.

She thought about it, as he sat talking to Nick and drinking tea. Two blind mice. Perhaps she didn't mind Ned looking a little bit silly. Only she could see it, after all. And he was quite funny. Not laugh-aloud funny, but little-smile-inside funny. What she cared about was that – either way – things looked bad. If he passed Nick's test, then he was going to put himself at terrible risk. She dreaded him making that journey into the Docks. The visit to this Talmadge person. Retracing Sir Tommy's fatal last steps. That walkway. And if he failed Nick's test, then how was he going to find out what happened that night? He'd probably do it anyway.

All this was forcing her to wonder if she wanted to start caring this much about someone else, even though she knew it was getting a bit late for that. How would it be for them if they were together and she had to leave for a stint in some hot, angry country with little Jiffy, sniffing out dodgy parcels in dusty bus stations or suspicious mounds by the roadside? What would he say to her as she left for the airport with the dog in a travel crate and a bag of biscuits as hand luggage? 'Be careful'? And that made her realise that this wasn't really about Ned crashing into the furniture and looking a fool. It was about them.

The next day, Nick began by taking Ned through Suzy's key command words. He'd already chanced on 'Outside!' but there were many more, from 'Left' and 'Right' to 'Upstairs', 'Downstairs', 'Break' and 'Stay'. He had no idea a dog could have such a huge vocabulary. She beat Fatso, paws down. And she knew some that were particular to Sir Tommy. 'Dressing-room' and 'Off-stage' were self-explanatory. 'Firsts' would instruct her to get him back to his first position at the start of a rehearsal or a take. 'Cyril' meant take him to the car, and for some reason Nick had forgotten, at the word 'Zinc' she'd lead Sir Tommy to the studio bar. That, apparently, was their party trick. Big applause and treats all round.

The next lessons were about how to read Suzy's movements, so Ned would know when she was turning or stopping. There were loads of subtle differences, and trying to get used to them filled the afternoon. The small town nearby provided a perfect training ground. Not too many people. The occasional vehicle. And the sandbags provided useful obstacles on the narrow pavements. At first Nick had Kate lead Ned and Suzy through the streets. She'd dug up some high-visibility vests for them all to wear. Just as well, because what traffic did go through, went very fast. She nearly lost them to a huge articulated lorry that shouldn't have been on that road at all. By coincidence it belonged to Basle Club member Number 6, though the name meant nothing to Kate, and Ned couldn't see it to enjoy the irony.

For some reason, Ned struggled from the start and became irritated. There was a whole lot of very fussy stuff, like how and where Suzy should lie down in a café or restaurant. What to do when well-meaning members of the public wanted to pet her. How to deal with meeting other dogs, especially aggressive ones. It seemed over the top for what he needed. He wasn't actually a blind man looking for a guide dog to live and bond with. So he stopped outside what sounded like a school playground and told Nick not to bother about these niceties, as all he was planning on doing with Suzy was a brief stroll through some deserted streets at night; her table manners and PR skills weren't going to be put to the test, OK? Fine, said Nick. So what'll happen at this Mrs Talmadge's? Has she got a dog? Do you know what'll happen there? Do you want her realising that you aren't just rusty – you're totally incompetent? Ned let him go on a bit and then surrendered. He supposed Nick was right. Annoying, but right. It wasn't just a stroll. So Ned agreed to the gold star, de luxe version: full underbody wash with extra chillis and double hot fudge sauce . . . Bring it all on, my sightless and invisible tormentor. Bring it on.

Ned didn't say much when they got back to the farmhouse that evening. He removed Suzy's harness and fed her. He knew he ought to play with her a bit, but he was exhausted and worried. It hadn't gone well in the town. Neither the big things, nor the little. Suzy tried to lead him to the right around a corner, but he tripped forwards over her into the road. He heard a squeal of brakes and just hauled himself out of the gutter in time. He made a total hash of getting her back after a run off the lead in the dog area at the park. Kept calling her, then shouting, without realising she was sitting obediently in front of him waiting to have the harness put back on. They all went into a café and Ned didn't seem to be able to position her correctly. He couldn't remember if she was meant to be facing outwards or facing him, sitting up or lying down. Then he knocked over his cup and she couldn't get out of the way of the hot tea because he'd managed to wrap her lead around his chair leg. First he knew about it was a piteous yelp. Lastly, they failed to retrace their steps from the café to the supermarket car park – their first 'solo' flight – without getting lost. A woman with, from the sound of it, two small children took pity and insisted on escorting them.

Nick had encouraged Ned to ask the way as needed – it wasn't meant to be a guessing game – but the minute she left them in the car park, Ned turned in what he thought was the right direction for the car and nearly got them both run over for the third time in one day. The only thing Nick said on the way home was that it wasn't down to Suzy. Ned wasn't reading her and he wasn't trusting her.

Ned ate dinner in silence and his offer to wash up was refused. Out of pity, in fact, but it felt like more rejection. So he sat in the wing-backed chair and tried to arrange his body so it didn't co-incide with the places where the stuffing was falling out – either his or the upholstery's – and he closed his eyes. He was starting to drift off to sleep, lulled by Kate and Nick's voices, when he found odd phrases getting to him through the fog. He couldn't work out at first what they were talking about, but the more he heard, the more intrigued he became.

'. . . the force which keeps the working dog and the person in sync with one another and with their work . . . the phrase she used was "social gravity" . . . and she talked about there being a "moral congru-ence" between people and animals . . . I've got it here somewhere . . .' Ned heard Nick get up and open one of the dresser drawers. He pulled out some papers and went over to Kate before sitting down again.

'Here, it may be in this lot. The point for me is that the human and the dog share a common motivation in their work together, rather than it being the result of coercion or exploitation. The guide dog, for example, has such considerable latitude for initia-tive that there has to be some coincidence of mutual interests which provides the framework . . . which is what Vicki Hearne calls "moral congruence" . . .'

Kate evidently wasn't sure about this. Could the dog actually feel 'moral congruence', whatever that was? Or was this a human gloss on something the dog regarded as a game, not an exercise in morality? Certainly her experience with sniffer dogs was that they saw the search for explosives as a game, however serious the conse-quences were in reality . . . It was the dog's love of a game with set rules you had to appeal to, not the dog's moral sense.

'There are also big confusions over language,' Kate went on. 'We describe a dog as cheating, if it gives a real bite during play. Sure, the other dogs will shun one who repeatedly "cheats" like that, but because they don't want to play with a biter, not because they morally disapprove of cheaters. "'Cheating" is a loaded human word.'

'But it's also because the other dogs can't trust the biter,' Nick rejoined. '"Trust" is not just a loaded human word. It's a dog word as well. And it contains the idea that the dogs do not think the cheater is a "good" dog.'

'Yes, but "good" meaning "one who will not bite me". Not meaning virtuous. These aren't absolute moral values. The Nazis used GSDs and Rotties to guard concentration camps. Those dogs stayed loyal to their masters and did horrible things . . . or is that just "amoral congruence" . . . ?'

They talked inconclusively about whether animals could be said to be 'ethical' creatures and then about the range of emotions displayed by dolphins, birds and monkeys. Ned was surprised to learn, in his state of pseudo-slumber, that these included empathy, envy and a sense of fairness. Apparently, it wasn't surprising to be able to detect primitive forms of emotional states in animals. Where else did we get them from, given that we once clambered out of the primeval swamp on all fours?

He then became aware of a silence, broken by Nick.

'Is he asleep?'

Kate murmured that he was.

'Poor bastard was all over the place. Can't see him cracking it in the time.'

There was a pause before she answered.

'When I was little, I had this lovely auntie from Swansea. She was probably a great-aunt. When I'd been bad, she used to say to me at bed-time, "The Devil had you today, but the good Lord will have you tomorrow."'

Nick gave a little laugh, and then asked her if she was religious. No, said Kate, but sometimes she *was* good the next day. Her auntie took it as absolute confirmation of the existence of God. Kate saw it as the exercise of absolute free will. Or as she saw it aged eight: 'doing 'xactly what I want to do'. Ned only just managed not to smile.

She and Nick then drifted back into a long discussion about language: the huge vocabulary of trained chimpanzees, and the way human beings redefine the word 'language' so that no matter how many words animals learn, humans can still reassure themselves that they are superior. That all the animal is learning is a string of symbols – the use of which ensures good outcomes – and not language at all. Ned thought about Suzy, and the vocabulary Tommy Best had taught her to get around film sets and stages, to find the car, or the bar. Did it matter if this was in fact language or something else, as long as he could communicate with her, and she with him? But that didn't seem to be enough to explain what went on between a guide dog and her owner. Like the moment when he said the word 'Outside' and Suzy led him out. Perhaps what made that pay off was that he provided the command which she obeyed, and she provided the response which he obeyed. They had trusted one another. He was still her master, but he took her advice, and the next moment he was standing in the sunshine. Bingo!

Maybe trust was the clue to it. He had to surrender to the idea that the dog had her freedom and was placing it at his service, along with her sight and her skills. She was investing her freedom in a mutual, trusting, willing partnership; the harness was not a yoke. He would have to do the same. When he held on to the handle, he also had to let go.

And then he really did fall asleep. He didn't miss much, except that Kate found the bit that Nick was trying to remember, buried in the papers he had handed her. She remembered it from college. Then again, it was probably just as well that Ned didn't hear her read it out to Nick, given all that lay ahead of him.

'. . . with unique possibilities of congruence come also unique possibilities of incongruence and even tragedy, which is why the best dog and horse stories are about working relationships of one sort or another'.

* * *

Ned woke early – and in his sleeping-bag on the sofa. He wasn't sure how he got there, but vaguely remembered Kate was involved. Something to do with her smell and touch. Had she put her hand on his head as they went through the low doorway? Maybe. What was he wearing? Shirt and shorts. Bloody hell. Who'd taken his trousers off? He tried to remember, and couldn't. And then something definite did come back to him, but he had no idea at all if it was a genuine memory, or a dream, or just a powerful wish. He remembered her kissing him, ever so lightly, on the lips. Had it actually happened? If only he had Extra Bilge there! He could take a swab from his mouth and check it against Kate's DNA and then Ned would know for sure if she'd kissed him. Trouble was, so would everybody else. Extra Bilge was notoriously leaky with information. Ideas, emotions, even rumours were safe with him. But facts had to be disseminated. He couldn't keep them to himself. In Extra Bilge's world, facts were only validated by as many people as possible knowing them.

Ned lay snug in the sleeping-bag, face warmed by a squeeze of sunshine through the little window, wondering if he could just ask the Bilge to tell him if the DNA he found on this swab matched the DNA from, say, this wineglass. That's all, Bilgey Boy. Simple question, yes or no? Trouble was, how could Ned stop him running an internal cross-check? They were all on the system in order to factor out their own traces from a crime scene.

So he'd never know if she had kissed him and he could never ask; it would be much too intrusive, much too presumptuous. The longer he lay there thinking about it, the better he decided it was that he didn't know. It already felt ever so faint. Knowing anything more about it might crush the fragile life out of it. It was lovely just as it was.

Right. Shower time. But how could he wash his hair with the bloody blindfold on? That turned out to be easy. He went into the bathroom and took it off. There was no light in there, the window was blanked off and he always closed his eyes in the shower, so all he was doing was swapping one shade of pitch black for another.

And then he put the blindfold back. Still no one else up. Not even Suzy. He knelt down by her basket, and gently woke her with a cuddle. She stretched and rolled onto her back, letting him stroke her tummy. Then she sat up and licked his face. Damn. There goes the DNA. Don't know what Extra Bilge would make of a swab now. Yes, I love you too, Suzy. Time for our walk.

It seemed to be easier putting the harness on. Suzy stood very still, and his fingers seemed to know what they were doing. He stood and picked up the handle. He didn't hold onto it for dear life, nor was it casual. He held it, remembering what Nick had said: about how it was a bit like the diaphragm in a microphone, translating sound into vibration. In this case, it transformed sight – the dog's – into movement transmitted through the handle.

'Suzy, outside!'

He felt like a genie on a flying carpet. They seemed to glide out of the house into the garden, and out of the garden into the woods, and out of the woods into the meadows by the river. He knew the river was there not just from that lovely damp smell of weed and mist, but because he heard the chug of a slow old motorboat. It pottered up behind them and then ran alongside for a while before pulling ahead and away into the distance. Then he stopped and removed Suzy's harness, letting her run free like any other dog. He wasn't worried about getting her back; he knew she'd come. When she returned, he felt her drop something on his foot: a stick for him to throw. That's interesting. She does want to play, after all those years with Sir Tommy never throwing her a ball. They played until he evidently threw it into a tree, and she barked. Right, old dog. Time for our breakfast.

He put the harness on, and turned back the way they had come. After a moment or two her backtracking instinct kicked in; he could feel it happen through the handle. He did fall over rather spectacularly on the way, but that was because he missed a slight lateral move in the handle and tripped over a tree root. Anyway, so what? It was like skiing: no good if you don't fall over occasionally. Takes the curse off it.

Ned smelled the potatoes frying in onions and rosemary some way off. This was more like it. Rather – this was nothing like it. Nothing like how it had been up till now. This felt totally different. We are ready for the day, Mr Parsons. Suzy and I are ready.

Kate could tell something had changed. It wasn't just the fact that Ned looked so fresh and clean and that his hair had gone a little curly. It wasn't the mud caked on his jeans from what must have been a pretty hefty fall. Nor was it him remembering to remove Suzy's harness and feed her and make sure she had water. Something fundamental in their relationship – Ned's and Suzy's – had changed. Perhaps the key to it was the word 'relationship'. They now clearly had one. And a good one. That day working with Nick they made mistakes, but they seemed to make them together. And as the day went on, they made fewer and fewer. What started off as a refresher course for slow beginners segued into a masterclass. Nick was giving them tips and shortcuts, not basics. Somehow Ned had applied that great bonce of his. Curly hair and all.

By the end of the day, when Ned and Suzy were negotiating the shopping mall in the big town where Nick had been in hospital, Nick wasn't saying very much at all. He and Kate walked parallel to them as they backtracked through the throng of shoppers.

'I don't know what's happened,' Nick said to Kate, as she described how Suzy and Ned were weaving past trolleys and children and other dogs. 'But something's clicked. He's like a kid who's read the bloody exam paper.'

They went outside. It was dark now, and had started to rain. The car park was a mad place. People were dashing about, bunging bags into cars and abandoning trolleys where they pleased. There was no logic to the direction vehicles were coming from; no obeying 'one way' signs. Nick and Kate lost sight of Ned and Suzy. They hung around for a bit, then decided to wait for them in the Land Rover. It'd be funny if they beat us to it, she thought as they jogged arm in arm through the drizzle, but they hadn't. In fact she was just wondering whether to get out and look for them, when they turned up. Apparently they had found a lost child crying and had taken her back to the mall to page her parents. She'd held onto Suzy's collar until they showed up. Ned helped the dog into the back, removed her harness and started to dry her on an old towel.

'That's just the sort of thing Tommy used to do.'

'I'm a copper, Nick,' said Ned. 'It's just the sort of thing coppers do.'

As she drove back to the farmhouse, Kate could see Ned in the rear-view mirror, settling Suzy down, stroking her, talking to her. Big, big change.

The test next day was a bit of an anti-climax. It was a walk Nick did sometimes with his sister, along the riverside path beyond his house to the next village. It was sharply apt because it involved a waterside obstacle course including a walkway, but it wasn't as challenging as it should have been because Ned and Suzy had walked the exact same route that morning.

This wasn't altogether accidental. The evening before Nick had said the test involved negotiating a boatyard, with various quays and a café above a boatbuilders, which you got to via steep steps and a rickety catwalk. Sounded perfect. Ned hadn't planned on cheating – if it really was cheating – but he'd got up very early again and decided he and Suzy would go downriver instead of up. After a bit, he found himself walking alongside a sailing boat. Heard some creaking and the sails flap. He guessed it might have been one of those lovely old barges with rust-red sails. Anyway, a voice wished him good morning, and he said good morning back. And then he heard himself asking if they were going the right way for the café above the boatyard. The chap said they were, and did he and the dog want a lift? Ned balked at that. No point half-cheating by skipping the walk there. He picked up a few useful tips about distances and obstacles: which way to go round an old pill-box . . . then there's this little hump-back bridge over a ditch . . . and a bit further on there's a weir . . .

'Sure you're OK?' The voice rang out across the water as the boat started to edge away.

'We're fine,' he called back.

What was it Tommy Best used to say, according to that old boy at the funeral? Ah, yes. 'I got my dog . . . Who could ask for anything more?'

The man on the boat's distances felt optimistic, but it was another beautiful morning. Ned surprised himself a shade by not removing the blindfold. It crossed his mind: really check out the test route and maybe count out the paces. But that might be too obvious. He had heard Kate talking Nick through what Suzy and he were up to, and she didn't miss a thing. Besides, wearing the blindfold seemed to come under the heading of always telling your doctor everything. No point cheating himself.

He could tell when he was getting near the boatyard from the sound of halyards slapping against masts. He knew when he'd reached it by the change from muddy track to impacted gravel to patches of cobbles. He remembered what Nick had said about being able to sense the ground surface through the harness handle, but he couldn't. Not yet. He brought Suzy to a halt. This was getting a little bit dangerous. She had no more idea where she was going than he had. There were sounds of a band-saw and of hammering, and he thought he could hear what sounded like a donkey pump. Perhaps getting the water out of a sunken barge. No distant sounds of cups clattering or the snort of an espresso machine.

'Hullo. D'you need any help?'

The voice sounded very close. A girl. Late-teens perhaps?

'Is there a café around here? Upstairs somewhere?'

'Sure. I'm going there myself. Do you want me to take your arm or something?'

Ned said it would be fine if she'd just walk in front of them. And perhaps talk him through it as they went.

'Right,' she said. 'Follow me. I work there in fact, but I'm a bit late. You'll make a great excuse. Careful here down these two steps. Are you training her? Only with that blindfold, I didn't really think you were . . .'

Her voice tailed off. The B word was obviously taboo, even for a chatty, confident kid. No, said Ned. She's training me.

The route through the boatyard was tortuous. They made a series of sharp turns around sheds that sounded alive with boatbuilding. They also went over a couple of bridges, and across a small lock gate. Suzy would be doing well to get them out of there. Bad to have to ring Kate and be collected from the test course itself.

'Now these stairs are pretty steep. Are you going to be OK? She's really amazing isn't she? What's she called?'

'Suzy. But please don't distract her or pet her. She's a working dog.'

The form of words sounded priggish, but they did the trick.

'No worries. But she's just brilliant. Don't you get really pissed off with everybody staring at you?'

Ned didn't bother with this one.

'Oh no. Sorry. I'm being really thick. Four more steps to go. And then there's like a walkway thing. In a very strong wind it sways about a bit. Not as bad as those ones in the films that go across canyons. They always seem to break in the end, don't they?'

It was probably Ned's fault; he had asked her to talk him through it. But she was quite sweet. The café had tables outside or inside. Which did he and Suzy want? Only the sign said they didn't let ordinary dogs in, but blind dogs were OK. In fact, as long as she'd been there, they'd never had a blind dog. Sorry. Guide dog. Suzy was the very first. It was probably the stairs put them off. No, he said, he wasn't stopping. So how long was her day in the café? Till they closed at 6 p.m. Right, said Ned, and asked her for one more favour.

Suzy did a brilliant backtrack. She got confused just once, early on while they were still in the boatyard. Ned realised something wasn't quite right from the fact that the donkey pump was still to their right. It should now be on their left. He trusted to Suzy. She stopped for a moment, then turned round the way they'd come and set off again, leading him around three sides of a square – it felt like possibly some sort of jetty – and then back on course up the two stone steps. He stopped and gave her pats and praise. Good Suzy! Well done, Suzy! He felt her tail wagging through the handle as they set off back along the river.

They picked up the scents even further out than yesterday – successive waves of them. The smell of mushrooms frying in butter, garlic and parsley legged it all the way down to the river. The bread baking hit them as they turned onto the path by the lawn. At the door – fresh coffee. Kate had just picked the field mushrooms. It's all about trust, Ned thought, as he set Suzy's food down for her. Stay . . . take it! Dogs, people you can't see, people who can't see you, fresh mushrooms. Then again, was Kate eating them herself? She said she was. You see? Trust! We go together. Morning, Nick! Lovely mushrooms!

'Hullo, what a lovely dog!' said a familiar voice. 'What's he called?'

'It's OK. Don't bother,' said Ned to the waitress as they all sat down. 'They know we cheated.'

The girl laughed.

'Suzy a cheat? I don't think so. You were just practising, weren't you, darling? Oh, sorry. I know. No petting . . .'

It had gone fine along the river. In fact it had all gone fine. It was just that it had gone a bit too fine in the boatyard. How could they nip through the maze of sheds and jetties so fast? And how the hell did they know where to go?

'Have you ever brought Suzy here before?' Kate asked, as she and Nick stood waiting at the top of the rickety stairs.

No, Nick replied. The first time Suzy had been to his place was when Kate brought her a few weeks ago. She'd never been there as a puppy. Why?

'They've just reached a choice of three ways to go by a big crane,' she replied, 'and with hardly a hesitation they've plumped for the middle one, which is counter-intuitive, because the right turn leads in this general direction, although you can't actually get to here from there. And I can't see how Suzy can have known that unless she's been here before.'

Down below, the human half of the wonder team was fretting over the same problem. Ned felt it had all been too slick, but he didn't want to put in a fake wrong turn because he didn't want to confuse Suzy. Also, the whole point of the exercise was that they should get used to one another and sense one another's trust, and he didn't want to spoil all that by yanking on the harness and then having a bogus tug of war with her. Particularly as he knew she was right. Leave her to it. After all, Nick can't see and with luck if Kate susses it, she won't tell.

'You're a pair of cheats,' were the words she greeted them with when he and Suzy reached the top of the stairs.

'We didn't cheat,' Ned replied. 'Suzy and I took the test, only we did it a bit earlier. Anyway, dogs can't cheat, can they? Didn't a great dog expert once say that "cheating is just a loaded human word"?'

Live dangerously, thought Ned as Suzy led him over the swaying ropeway over the canyon. It didn't break, but just as they stepped off it, somebody gave him an almighty kick in the bottom, and he didn't think it was Nick. Fair enough, thought Ned. That's our first row over and done with. And then the dog-friendly waitress pitched up.

Lunch was a rather silent affair. Ned's gloss on it was that the judges were sulking. It was only when ordering coffee that he realised the judges weren't actually there. The waitress told him they sneaked away when he and Suzy went to the loo.

'I'm afraid we're both in the dog house, old girl,' he said to Suzy as they renegotiated the boatyard obstacle course. He'd already decided to take their time. No point hurrying into a storm. But then Suzy came to an unexpected stop just as the impacted gravel turned into the muddy track. There was clearly some sort of barrier, which called for a backtrack and rethink. As dog and man were pondering, an elderly gruff voice called out that there'd been a landslip and the path along the river was closed. Ned told the voice where they were trying to get to, and asked for an alternative route. He didn't bother asking the old boatman for a description of the exquisite Siren who had suborned him into blocking a public thoroughfare.

'If you're going up Nick Parsons's place, you best go by the road

197

as far as Swift Ditch, then cut down through Mangan's. Ask at the garage.'

Ned got the old fellow to take them to the road out of the boat-yard, and they then struck out on their own. Well, not quite on their own. Ned decided to keep his blindfold on, so he never saw the lithe Siren herself, carefully shadowing them out of Suzy's field of vision. She then turned into a guardian angel, and watched over them as they joined the main road and called into the garage. Once they were safely on the track leading down through Mangan's Farm, she jumped into the Land Rover and not surprisingly beat them home.

It turned out that keeping on the blindfold helped save Ned. Nick and Kate were sitting on the lawn when Suzy and he got back. As Suzy led him down the path, he heard Nick mumble something, to which Kate said: 'It's on. Still on.'

The next sound he heard was two people clapping. It was just as well he had the blindfold on. Didn't want Kate to see a tear in his eye, did he?

'Just before you take that thing off,' said Nick, 'there's one last thing for you to do. You wearing old clothes?'

At first Ned tried to paint the front room as if the final result mattered. As if it would be judged for its appearance and neatness. As the work of someone who could see. Gradually, he stopped caring, and started to take pleasure in the doing, in the sense of release. He lost all sense of direction, painting over half a window and a door. He hadn't a clue what colours he was using and he didn't care. Nick joined him in the slopping of paint and gradually the air became filled with splatters and laughter and the smell of distemper and emulsion, eggshell and gloss. Kate and Suzy wisely kept their distance, preparing dinner and generally behaving like grown-ups.

As the tide of unseen colours reached its height, and it felt as though there was as much paint on him as on the walls, the names came back to him: Sage and Image. They were the painty cats in the old French children's story. Ned didn't know if he was Sage or

Image. Certainly Nick had turned out to be a whole lot more Sage than he had guessed he would be. They sat together, exhausted in the sticky puddle that had once been a carpet, glasses of wine in hand, the last of the sunshine strained through windows heavy-lidded with paint. Ned could see the light slipping away, because he had finally taken off the blindfold. It felt very odd. Nice, but a bit scary, a bit exposed. His eyes were now unguarded. Seeing again had drawn a line in the sand. Lessons over – game on!

The sun bowed out and Ned closed his eyes. Nothing more to see. Kate gave them a ten-minute warning before supper. They both called out that they'd be along, but neither moved. They looked more like a Jackson Pollock painting than two men in a room. Then Ned felt Nick's hand on his arm, and heard his quiet voice.

'Don't tell me. Whatever you find out, please don't tell me. I don't want to know.'

11

THE ENVELOPE STOOD OUT FROM the others waiting in Ned's in-tray. It was long and narrow, and his name and address were written at right angles to the norm: the envelope was meant to be read vertically not horizontally. He could see why when he opened it. Inside was a long and narrow photograph of a lamp-post bent at an angle. At the foot of the post on the pavement edge were a bunch of wilted lilies and a jam jar containing greenish water and a few desultory daisies and dandelions. About three feet up the post, tied on with red ribbons, was a wreath. Across the wreath was a strip of white cloth with the words 'Chaz – Our Child' written in black marker. The ink had run, so that the letters seemed adorned with cedillas. It was a very pathetic sight.

He turned the photograph over. It was an invitation to a private show at 6 p.m. of 'Attrition by Tarmac – an exhibition of Nyanath Best's photographs.' Nyanath? Good name. Advanced Search . . . ah! Sudanese, meaning daughter of humanity. She's that alright, is our Chippy. Wonder what it's like, seeing that image of yourself as a baby in your father's arms become public property? A tiny, intimate moment between disaster and hope turned into posters on students' walls, screensavers on computers, printed onto mugs and T-shirts, splashed by Benetton across billboards, woven into a vast tapestry dominating the foyer at Unicef. Perhaps you stop being able to see yourself in the image. Perhaps you don't believe it is you. Are you proud of it? Proud of the millions it has raised for children's charities, famine relief and development in the Third World? Or does it make you resent the fact that you only exist because of someone else's chance act of charity? Because someone happened to bend down and pick you up.

Ned remembered a lecture at university, something from a wartime American study of the Japanese psyche. A researcher interested in the importance of 'face' had noticed the intriguing response of Japanese men to random acts of politeness in public. Apparently if their hats blew off in a wind, and were then retrieved and handed back by strangers, the Japanese gentlemen weren't at all grateful. They were resentful – because the little act of kindness had made them beholden to a stranger. Now they owed this person an obligation they had no likelihood of ever being able to repay. The resulting loss of face would last a lifetime. A long walk on a breezy day in Kyoto could see debts stacking up with every stiff bow, with every '*domo arigato gozaimasu*' forced through gritted teeth. Better to turn on one's heels and leave the bloody hat behind.

Across the bottom of the invitation Chippy had scrawled the words 'Come early.' He checked the date. It was tonight.

'Wotcha, cock!'

The doorway was suddenly full of Fatso. Fatso cheery. Fatso rampant. He'd just read Ned's plan. Clever, if a bit hairy. How was he going to avoid giving one to the tom? Make his excuses and leave? Pity Ned couldn't be wired, but it might look a little bit sussy when he took his kit off. If he went the whole hog. (Brilliant! They all treasured Fatso's unknowing references to the world of pigs.) Why couldn't it just end with them piling into Mother T's and reading everyone their rights? If Ned could get her to admit Sir Tommy had been there that night, what more did they want? Why was Ned going to go up onto the walkway? And what's all this about not wanting any close backup?

Ned was used to the Fatso quick-fire queries. The first time they had gone through an operation plan together was when Ned was a kid and Fatso could still glimpse his own toes. They'd had a tip-off about a bullion raid, and there were some tricky timing issues around making sure they nabbed the gang just as they handed the gold over to Mr Big in his Cessna. There was also their own nark to look out for, as well as the bloke at the warehouse who'd given the villains the insider information – and had then gone on holiday to Spain. It involved radios and aeroplanes and helicopters and infra-red and synchronised watches – and bullet-proof vests, because this bunch of jokers loved playing with guns. Fatso sat there while young Ned patiently demolished his entire catalogue of criticisms, and then came up with: 'Oi, cock. That's not fair. You've won 'em all so far. You got to let me have one.'

So Ned talked about Mrs Talmadge and avoiding entrapment and the tabloids, and about unresolved doggy mysteries, and Fatso paced up and down the office, listening and nodding and thinking and snorting. It was one of the things they all loved him for: the fact that he listened. They could have done without the snorting. Then he sat down opposite Ned and looked him hard in the eye.

''Ere, Ned the Yid. D'you know what happened to Tommy Best?'

Ned shook his head. He didn't know.

'But you got a pretty good idea, don't you?'

Ned nodded. He did, but it didn't fit the facts.

'Which facts in particular?'

Ned didn't answer, and Fatso didn't press him. He jumped to his feet with that odd athleticism, and spoke without looking back as he squeezed out through the doorway.

'Bet you a toffee apple the facts are wrong . . . an' watch yer bleedin' back on that walkway . . .'

I shall see nothing, Ned thought, least of all my own bleeding back.

'Hullo? Mrs Talmadge? Hullo. My name's Nick Parsons. Did Tommy Best ever . . . ? He did. Right. Yes . . . Yes. The Basle Club. Yes . . . Absolutely. How are you? . . . I've been meaning to call you . . . No. That's right. Way to hell and gone . . . middle of nowhere . . . Yes . . .

Bizarre coincidence ... No, it wasn't exactly the same thing, but similar. Rhinogenic optic neuropathy, they call it ... Blind as a bat is another way of putting it ... You're very kind ... Yes ... I just feel I'm following in his footsteps ... Yes ... Uh-huh ... No, I just couldn't face being with other people, and then when dear old Tommy died, I thought ... Well, I just feel I want to get closer to him ... No, he just said what a lot of fun he used to have when he came to see you ... Yes, you are so right ... Oh gosh. I don't know ... what do you suggest? I really just wanted whatever Tommy liked – whatever he had last ... I'm sure whatever was good enough for him would be more than good enough for me ... Like I say, just feel I'm following in his footsteps ... Actually, thinking about it, it should be the same ... Yes, rather than a different ... Yes. Exactly. Couldn't have put it better ... No, that'd be great. Fine. Eleven p.m. Great. Where is that exactly? ... OK. Yeah. Yeah. Lime Quay. No ... fine. Yes. Really looking forward to ... Yes ... The card? The green card? Oh yes, of course. I'll bring it with me. Sure. No, I quite understand ... Oh, one other thing, Mrs Talmadge ... OK. Fine. "Mother" ... Right you are. No, it's just that I'll have Suzy with me ... You know I trained her? ... Yes, well, she's back with me now ... Ha, yes, of course ... She'll know the way ... OK. See you then. Bye.'

In his cubby-hole, Extra Bilge switched off the recorder and started to fill out the log. Perched on a stool beside him, Span put down her headphones and came through to Ned's office. He was staring out of the window. She waited for a bit, and then asked him if he wanted anything from the canteen. He shook his head. When she reappeared ten minutes later, he hadn't moved.

'You did great, governor. She went for it 100 per cent. Defo.'

He didn't say anything. She put a rock cake on its little paper plate down on his desk and left.

Think it through, think it through. If this, then that. If that, then this. What if ... ? Then what do I do? And supposing ... ? Blind alley – back up. Think. Think.

Twenty minutes later, Ned looked round. Blimey – a rock cake.

Good old Jan Span. Must be Thursday again. Doesn't time fly when you're enjoying yourself?

Kate let herself into the house and was greeted by a very lonely, very pleased-to-see-her dog. They had decided that Suzy should live with Ned until after the night of 'The Walk', as they called it. Better for her to get really used to him. To continue seeing him as her master. She needed to get out in the middle of days when Ned couldn't get away early, and so Kate found herself in his home, among his things. He was really tidy. Clean washing folded neatly in a laundry basket. No bills lying about. Dishes done. It was almost as if he had anticipated how nosy she might be. Can't have, can he? He was so polite and gentle – how could he have had such nasty, suspicious thoughts about her? She snooped in the fridge, and in his walk-in cupboard. She peered behind the sofa, where there was a lovely old oil painting of sheep sheltering amongst crags from a gathering storm. Tiny, and in the distance off to one side, were the figures of a shepherd and his dog, out to look for them. The man was head down into the wind, but the dog was nose high trying to catch their scent. It was one of those pictures that the more you stare at it, the more you tumble into it, the more you want to know what happened next. The storm was gathering in the skies some way behind the man, but presumably the sheep had sensed its approach, because they were already huddled almost out of sight among the rocks. Did the dog ever find them? Did they get the sheep down off there in time, or did man, dog and beasts see out the storm together, shrinking into the mountainside, all tight together?

Bathrooms are really interesting places, if you're interested in their owners. What a lot you can tell about a body that is still unknown territory from the products on the edge of its bath, perched on the water heater in its shower stall, crammed in its mirrored cabinet. Is this a well body? A clean body? What's it worrying about? Does it suffer from dandruff or verrucas? And does it have this stuff because it still needs it, or are these empty ammo boxes from battles won? Are the implicit complaints under control or still running wild? Is it vain? How does it want to appear? Is it embarrassed about its streaks of grey, or its dry skin? Is it in the business of covering stuff up, rather than curing it? What, in and about this foreign body, do I have to fear? And, having taken a good gander at this lot, how unknown do I want it to stay?

Just a moment. If, nasty and suspicious as Ned would have to be to suspect I might snoop, he did the washing up and folded the laundry to give the impression of tidiness, how can I trust the evidence in the bathroom? The body washed and tended in here is suffering from no ailments, no embarrassing conditions. No tubes with white plastic nozzles for anal application. No camouflage kit for premature ageing. No jellies or ointments suggesting an interest in recreational lubrication. Indeed, no sign of the presence of an old girlfriend. No half-empty box of tampons of a make or size you'd never use. No girly stuff at all. Just natural soap. Shampoo for normal hair. Stripy toothpaste. Floss. Just the one toothbrush head, and that without the little coloured ring to distinguish 'his' from 'hers'. Who is he trying to fool? Is he just too good to be true?

What you see is what you get, Kate told herself as she carefully closed the bathroom door. Anyway, who's the detective here, and who's the dog handler? Stick to your thing, girl. The lead was where he said it would be, on the back of the door. She and the dog slipped out for a run in the park. It would do them both a world of good. Meanwhile, the shepherd and his dog strode out on their brave mission, no longer sheltered by the sofa back. Kate had left them leaning up on the cushions, wide open to the elements.

Ned didn't quite know why he was going. And that was partly because he didn't know why she'd invited him. Did she want to tell him something? Or was she flirting? Was that what 'Come early' meant? Had they already flirted? Ned re-ran the conversation they'd had while rummaging through Sir Tommy's shoe collection. He could recall nothing inappropriate on either side. Nothing to worry Chief Superintendent Larribee. Ned was not stupid enough to dismiss the idea by pointing out to himself that Chippy was only nineteen. That would have been like his mother discounting the possibility that someone was gay because he or she was married. Fancying girls half your age was an occupational hazard of being alive. Except he didn't fancy Chippy. He fancied Kate, and she was a whopping six years older than Chippy.

Blimey! Now you put it like that Ned, what the hell do you think you're doing? You're thirteen years older than she is! When you're mowing the lawn at Dun Nabbing, blasting pipe ash down your cardy and farting into your elephant cords, Kate will still be a head-turning, multiple pileup-causing, George Cross and no doubt bar-winning fifty-two-year-old. Really, Ned? Definitely, Ned. Well, Ned – sounds fine to me. I'll have all you can give me of that. Meanwhile our Chippy'll be an ancient forty-six-year-old. Now that's what I call inappropriate. No, he was going because he was curious, and because he did have a couple of questions for her, and because you never know.

'Excuse me, am I going the right way for "Attrition by Tarmac"? – Chippy Best's show?"

Anyway, he didn't just fancy Kate. That was simply the physical, juvenile, trashy, clammy thing he'd done before he'd got to know her. Before this little lot started. Before Sir Tommy stepped off the edge. Why did he do that, by the way? Thank God, Ned. You're finally back on track. 'Bout bloody time too.

'Yeah, I know I'm early. Thanks . . .'

The Art School had had the good sense to be designed by some great god of Art Nouveau, which had the effect of conferring dignity on anything hung there. Funny that. You might have thought it would further shrink the work of pygmies, but in fact a framed dish-rag looked good on those walls. And Ned went past one or two of them on his way up to the High Gallery. If you had talent – and Chippy, it turned out, had bags of it – then the building worked like a bloody great lens: blowing you up and showing you off. Chippy had the wit to make it work even harder for her, by projecting some of her images onto the walls and floor of the gallery.

When Ned tentatively pushed the swing doors open, the place

looked deserted. A dotted white line led away from the entrance; he was walking down a tarmac road. On either side were images of improvised road-side shrines to those killed in traffic accidents: wreaths and flowers and signs and photographs. They were often propped against or tied to the inanimate objects that had stopped the loved one dead in his or her tracks: posts, walls, trees. They were powerful singly; cumulatively they were very hard to take, perhaps because Chippy had personalised them: each had a face and a life story. Often a very short life story.

The inventor of motorbikes wasn't solely to blame, but he'd have been unlikely to get out of that exhibition with a clear conscience. Halfway down the 'road', Ned was given the fright of his life. His eardrums were split by the deafening roar of a bike which seemed to be coming up behind him. He turned and made an involuntary move to the side to get out of the way as the sound raced past him, ending a moment later at the far wall with a sickening clash and thud as the bike went from ninety to nothing in a split second. There was dead silence, and then the sounds of a country lane: birdsong, light wind in leaves, a bee. That was followed by a peal of laughter from the heavens as a gloating goddess claimed her latest victim.

'You OK? You look like you were shitting yourself. Was it too loud?'

High on a balcony behind a sound-mixing desk, Chippy looked down on Ned and giggled. He waved and went back to another photograph while she gave instructions to an unseen sound geek, and then appeared suddenly at Ned's side.

'I knew him. He was what started me off. He was in my year doing Fine Art.'

The face was washed out, reedy. Long blond hair. Wispy beard. A kid.

'He was hitching back from staying with his older sister, Heather. He died by this telegraph pole, at about seven o'clock in the evening. A guy in the lay-by opposite took the photo on his cell phone. He was just about to call his wife to say he'd be home late, when he heard a horrible noise. The brakes had locked up on this humongous truck from the Netherlands, and it slewed across the road and wrapped itself around the pole. Around Sammy. He died buried in tulips. Having a pee.'

She was on the point of tears.

'I asked him to spend that weekend with me, but he wouldn't. Heather had just had her first baby, a girl, and he was desperate to see them both. She told me he'd done some great sketches of the baby to show me.'

'Why didn't you go with him?'

Chippy shook her head, and didn't answer. They walked around for a bit in silence, and then sat down together on a radiator. Ned waited for her to say something, but she didn't. So he did.

'Must have been dangerous taking some of these photos.'

It was, she told him. Bloody hairy. The traffic in these places seems to go faster than elsewhere. On motorways, people always drive a tad slower for a few yards after passing torn bodies being filleted out of mangled wrecks, but on smaller roads where you find these shrines, stuff just hurtles by. To be fair, you're past them before you realise they're there, but some of the traffic's got to be local. Probably a point of honour for them not to slow down. Often, the best place to take the photo is the middle of the road. You take your life in your hand.

'My tutor said I didn't have to worry. Lightning never strikes twice and all that. Utter crap. Some of these places there's shrines within yards of one another. Major accident black spots.'

'You didn't do a photo of the shrine to your dad. At the foot of the walkway. It was pretty spectacular. Very moving.'

She knew people would think that. Didn't think anyone would say it. Trust a detective. Anyway, it wasn't tarmac. It wasn't a road accident. And he wasn't . . . it wasn't an accident, was it. She didn't get an answer, assuming she expected one.

'Here at Art School, they've taught us to have a framework. To set parameters for ourselves. No good just shooting off at a tangent. Throwing in any old bunch of wilted daisies.'

Chippy had suddenly gone pompous. Hiding behind Art School.

Hard to believe she was talking about her dad. Two can play at pompous.

'I don't think,' said Ned, looking around the gallery, 'anyone seeing this will fail to be reminded of the death of your father.'

'Fine.' She went the other way. 'Whatever.'

She was on her own playing sullen teenager.

People were starting to arrive. Ned could see them, the friends of Sir Tommy and Dame Angie, slightly distorted through the ornately engraved windows set in the ceiling-high doors: all dressed-up, wine glasses in hand, willing it to be simply marvellous, Chippy darling. Indeed, why wait till you've seen it? It already was simply marvellous, poor little latte-coloured adopted orphan babe of our darling Tommy.

'I think it's brilliant,' said Ned, getting his in first and meaning it. 'It's a really great idea, done fantastically well. You'll petrify them with those sounds. I thought I was going to be run over. You're going to make me drive more carefully.'

She looked very self-conscious, as embarrassed as she was pleased.

'I have a very few, very quick questions for you, Chippy. About your dad.'

Now she looked hunted. He pressed on. It was a really silly little point, but did Sir Tommy used to whittle toothpicks out of matches? He did. She'd watched him do it as long as she could remember. And what make did he use? Those Swan Vestas. He always left the toothpick one till last. And what happened then? If he needed a light, he used it. And he'd never sharpen a spent match? Never.

'Mum hated all that. Thought picking your teeth was what she called "the C word" – common. It wasn't really. It was just him doing exactly what he wanted. Like he always did.'

'That's all. I'll stop being a detective now. So, what was it turned you on to photography? Was it the amazing photo of you as a baby in his arms?'

'I don't know. Maybe.'

She looked uncomfortable.

'Maybe not.'

Ned asked his question anyway.

'What do you think when you see that photograph?'

She looked really uncomfortable.

'You can't really stop being a detective, can you? Look, I've got to go. They're waiting for me. It's why I asked you to come early. I knew this would happen.'

She dived away, as if relieved to be rid of him. He sat for a moment among the dead, with the rotting flowers and bent lamp-posts and skid marks all around him. With Sammy, drawings of his brand-new baby niece in his back-pack to show Chippy, having his final pee.

How did Chippy know they'd need more time? Time for what? What did she want to tell him? That she didn't like her dad? He had a temper, OK. He bollocked her for dressing the dog up. So what. It's not enough. Through the glass he could see the air-kissing, the patronage. As Ned reached the doors, they burst open and the throng spilled into the gallery. Chippy, carried past on the tide, threw Ned a pained, almost imploring look. He recalled her at Sir Tommy's funeral, a theatrical knight on either side, her thin arms white where they held her. Was it in fact support? Now, when he saw the image of them in his mind's eye, he saw it more as frog-marching. Making sure she was there at the funeral of the man who had bent down and lifted her out of the sea of dead. And that kidnap-victim look in her eye – was it the agony of grief? Or did it mean, don't force me to be grateful to this man forever? If she'd been one of those windswept Japanese men resentful as their hats are handed back, would she be saying, 'What hat? That's not my hat. I wasn't wearing a hat'?

'Leaving early, Chief Inspector?'

Only one voice like that on the planet. Cream on steel on feathers.

'Dame Angela. You're back.'

The vision in black and gold turned to tell Cyril she'd be an hour or so. No problem, ma'am. He wasn't about to stick the Roller in the municipal car park. They'd removed the chains so it could sprawl across the Art School forecourt. Royalty was in town.

'You'll understand how determined I was not to miss Chippy's first *vernissage*, Chief Inspector, when I tell you that I almost accepted a very sweet offer from John Travolta to fly me over himself. But I'd probably have had nothing to eat on the way but Big Macs and doughnuts.'

Ned walked back up the steps with her. She didn't seem surprised to see him there. Perhaps Chippy had told her she was inviting him. Or maybe it was a star thing. They were used to people just being there: chauffeurs, make-up artists, fans, Detective Chief Inspectors – all the same really. Grubby little mortals who live to serve. To hold open heavy oak doors.

'Thank you. In nineteen hundred and freezing cold, as Tommy used to say, I played my first lead for dear Frank Hauser at the Oxford Playhouse. I naturally expected my parents to be there on the first night and to come round after, but no. They'd left a message at my digs to say it was much too far for them to travel at night. A few years ago I had Cyril measure it. From their house to the stage door was 27.3 miles. Thank you.'

'Didn't you fear they'd had a car crash? When they didn't show?'

'You must be a terrible worrier, Chief Inspector. Not for a second. Deep down, I knew my parents. They didn't really care.'

On the way up to the High Gallery Ned told her how brilliant Chippy's exhibition was. Dame Angie said she hoped he'd told her so. She needed all the boost she could get. Of course, Dame Angela, of course. Then just as he was leaving her outside the gallery she turned back to him.

'You never rang me.'

He smiled. At the festival-jury-seducing way she submerged reproach into relief into a simple statement of fact. Inside the gallery, the motorbike hit the wall with its bone-shattering finality. Someone screamed.

'I'm still worrying at it, Dame Angela. Maybe next week.'

She raised an eyebrow. It was the exact look she had memorably given Robert Redford when he told her he'd just been for a walk to clear his head. Then the double doors opened and she was claimed by old friends and new pretenders.

In the Rolls, Cyril was watching football on television. Ned hurried into the soggy dusk in search of a bus.

Have a seat, said he, and the first thing Kate saw was that she'd left the bloody painting on the sofa. While Ned busied around making Chinese tea, she quickly stuffed it back where she'd found it. Then she nipped over to the floor cushion on the far side of the room, closely watched by Suzy. Wait a mo'. Supposing he'd already seen the painting on the sofa? He'd think it very odd if it suddenly vanished. While he clattered crockery, she retrieved it. At this point, Suzy got interested in what was behind the sofa. Must be something going on there. No, there isn't, dog of dogs. Nothing at all. You're no help to me; get back on your bed. Suzy! Kate thought he wouldn't hear her hiss under the kettle's whistle, but he did.

'Is she alright in there? She's not on the sofa, is she?'

No. She's not on the sofa. There's nothing on the sofa except some cushions and a flock of petrified sheep. Keep your wool on, all of you.

'Only I was reading that book you gave me and it was a bit down on them going on the furniture.'

He handed her a mug of tea and then noticed the painting. He murmured something about how the cleaning lady must have left it there. Big relief. He slipped it back behind the sofa, missing the thumbs up Kate gave Suzy. He sat and they sipped their tea. Then Suzy got up and ambled round behind the sofa and started sniffing. Kate suddenly become very interested in the tea-leaf buds opening like lily pads in her mug.

'Actually,' Ned said in a setting-the-record-straight voice. 'I don't have a cleaning lady.'

Suzy ambled back again, jumped on the sofa and made herself comfortable. Out of the silence Kate heard herself saying, similarly for the record: 'I'm not kissing you until after the Walk.'

And at that point the doorbell rang.

* * *

Doc Bones was not very happy. There were several reasons. For a start, he really didn't like meddling with the living. And *occuli* were jolly tricky bits. Then there was the fact that it was dear old Nedicus, of all people. And he was fearful of the plan. Not that he knew the plan, but that made it all the more worrying. The little he knew, he didn't like. Which brought him back to his part in it. Was it really a good idea to blind young Nedicus, and how sensible was it for him to wander about such a dodgy part of town in such a vulnerable state? When Ned told Doc Bones what he needed him to do, he'd made the point that being blind would protect him. Might even save his life. All very well, thought the Doc as he wrapped the phial up in cotton wool. But how safe can it be for Nedicus to be doing this with just an old dog for protection?

The door swung open and there was the brave chap himself.

'*Quid agis, medice*?'

'Evening, Ned old chap,' replied Doc Bones and went inside. Ned was a little disappointed. He'd spent some time working out a translation of 'What's up, Doc?' and was surprised not to have got so much as a smile. Either Doc was bluffing about his knowledge of Latin, or this was a whole lot more serious than Ned thought. On balance it was probably the latter, he decided as he hung up the Doc's heavy tweed coat.

If the Doc was surprised to see the *Scribilita Canis* curled up by the fire, he didn't show it. Actually, the Latin for a lady of dubious virtue was *scortillum*, but he couldn't bring himself to see this spectacularly winsome and correct young woman in such terms. A *scribilita* was, according to Pliny – and he should know – a kind of cheese tart, and that would do very nicely.

It all felt jolly cosy round at Ned's. A pair of pleasing young people. Bit of jazz bubbling away in the kitchen. Dog dozing on the sofa. The tea was a bit on the wild side. Looked like the pond at the back Mrs Bones had been on to him about clearing. Still, probably packed with vitamins. Bottoms up. Yes, seemed a pity to spoil it all by gouging out Ned's eyes. So to speak.

'So, Doc, how long does it take for the magic potion to take effect?'

Doc Bones reckoned twenty minutes to half an hour. He'd got it from his old squash partner up the Eye Hospital. It was developed as an anaesthetic for the optic nerve for some particularly tricky operation. Just four drops in each eye, the chap had said, and you'll be sightless for two or three hours. Usual caveats: don't combine with alcohol, don't use if you're pregnant, and operating heavy machinery is definitely contra-indicated. If you come out in a slight rash or feel at all light-headed, consult your GP immediately. If it's just nausea, vomiting, hallucinations and heart palpitations – they're normal, so don't bother him. Ha! Just a joke!

Ned looked at his watch. He had to be at Mrs Talmadge's at 11 p.m. The walk took . . . daylight saving . . . take away the number you first thought of . . .

'You couldn't just leave the stuff with us, could you, Doc? Kate here could pop it in for me, couldn't she? Otherwise you'll have to stick around for hours.'

'*Nulla problemata*, old chap. The young lady has a steady hand, I'll be bound. I'll just finish my tea and be off. So this is the famous hound, eh?'

The Doc swigged down the swamp and went over to give Suzy a pat. She rather liked him, which the Doc was a bit touched by. He handed the padded envelope to Kate, bade her farewell, made sure they had his phone number, and followed Ned out into the hall. While Ned was helping him on with his coat, Doc Bones suddenly remembered something he'd been meaning to tell him. Something about their mutual friend Cicero. You know, *Lorem ipsum* and all that. It seemed that in 46 BC old Cicero – and he really did mean 'old' – divorced his long-standing wife Terentia, the mother of his children, and married his ward Pubilia, who was fifteen. Forty-five years Cicero's junior. The marriage didn't last; apparently Cicero divorced her for being less than sympathetic when his beloved daughter died.

Ned leaned back against the wall, thinking.

'Doc, you know the *Lorem ipsum* passage?'

Doc Bones wound his scarf around his neck and nodded.

214

'What's he really saying? In a nutshell.'

Doc Bones pulled a face and pondered the question.

'I think he's telling us that if a pain leads to pleasure – in today's jargon – go for it. Taken with his penchant for young gels – not very nice . . .'

Ned nodded, and thanked him for everything. The Doc muttered something about being careful and strode off into the night. Ned looked around. The rain had cleared, but the cobbles would be slippy. Good soles needed. No wonder Sir Tommy favoured trainers for this one. He closed the door. Sir Tommy. The clincher about *Lorem ipsum* was that, by using the original Cicero rather than the usual printer's corrupt Latin, the great man showed he knew and cared what it meant: if a pain leads to pleasure, go for it. So whose pain? Whose pleasure? He'd know soon enough. Ned wasn't about to tell Kate, but his stomach was starting to feel leaden, and it wasn't the usual pre-op nerves.

They took Suzy for a last walk. There was a dog enclosure at the park, and they sat on a damp bench and watched a black Briard puppy try to get Suzy to play. They had a half-hearted go at not talking about the Walk, and then she asked him why he couldn't simply bail out as soon as he got Mrs Talmadge to admit Sir Tommy had been there that night. Ned said it wasn't enough. He had to follow it through. That admission by Talmadge wouldn't be enough. He had to find out what happened to Sir Tommy Best. This went beyond issues of guilt and innocence. It also, he thought to himself, went beyond Fatso's requirements. No guilty party, cock? Then just stick the stone back.

But the walkway wasn't some dark side, time-space fault line, Kate argued. Some fifth-dimension glitch. If he popped back up there, blind like Tommy and with Tommy's dog, events wouldn't necessarily repeat themselves. Why would they? While Ned was thinking about this, the Briard's owner came over for a chat. It turned out she was having a bit of trouble with the puppy running up to strangers – people and dogs – and barking at them. Kate suppressed her irritation at the interruption and gave her some tips.

'He may be barking because he's scared, not because he's aggressive. He may just be doing what he sees as his job. If that isn't the job you want him to do, then you'll have to remove the responsibility from him. Don't shout at him, or jerk at his lead. Lower your stress levels and his. Distract him. Keep him focussed on you, not on the stranger.'

The woman told Kate she ought to have her own television show.

As Kate and Ned walked back across the park with Suzy, she told him the importance of seeing apparently abnormal behaviour from the dog's point of view. The dog may know something you don't know it knows, and may be acting on it.

'There was a case where a woman asked an animal psychologist for help with her dog. Her husband often came home late, and when he came up to the bedroom, the dog would leap at him and bite him in the face. She couldn't understand why the dog didn't seem to recognise his own master. So the expert pointed out that the dog had heard the car. Heard the man's feet on the gravel. Heard him taking off his coat and heard him coming up the stairs. All totally familiar sounds. No way was that dog in any doubt who the man was. Quite the opposite. He knew only too well. The woman didn't need a dog psychologist; she needed someone to help her with why her dog felt she needed protecting from her husband.'

'Ah. Seeing it from the dog's point of view,' said Ned. 'It's what I did with Schrödinger's Cat – and nearly got beaten up for it.'

It was a lecture at university about a famous imaginary experiment. A lecture which ended in a near-riot after Ned's intervention.

'A cat is put in a chamber with a geiger counter and a tiny bit of radioactive substance plus a flask of hydrocyanic acid. If during the course of an hour one of the atoms decays, then the geiger counter will measure it and this in turn will trigger a hammer to shatter the flask. The cyanide will kill the cat. If no atom decays, then after one hour the cat will still be alive. The idea is that, according to the laws of quantum mechanics, until the door is opened, the cat is both dead and alive. Only the act of observing the cat after the hour has passed transforms the cat from this mixture of states into one in which the cat is definitely either dead or alive.'

Being a sensible person, Kate shook her head a little, and kept quiet.

'I argued – one man against the world – that the experiment should be seen from the cat's point of view. The cat, after all, knows if it's still alive. It is the event's only witness, and just being a witness makes you a player. Suppose the cat knocks over the cyanide? Or breaks the wire that would have triggered the hammer? Suppose it doesn't have enough air to last an hour, or pees on the geiger counter? The minute you introduce a cat, or a dog, into a set of unknowns, two big and opposite things happen. The unknown events become even more unknown to you, because you don't know what part the cat or dog has played in them, but conversely they become known to the animal. The trick is to find out what the animal knows.'

They turned out of the park and on to the end of Ned's street. It doesn't matter, he went on, whether the event is going on in a sealed chamber, or on a walkway at night in the Docks. It may be that the only way to find out what happened is to repeat the experiment, but this time to get in there *with* the cat.

'And what if the radioactive stuff triggers the smashing of the cyanide flask?' Kate asked. 'Where does that leave you?'

'It's only an imaginary experiment,' he replied lamely.

'Yeah, but what you're about to do isn't. Christ's sake, Ned! For a really clever man you can be amazingly thick.'

For the second time in his life, Schrödinger's Cat had got him in trouble. They didn't talk for a while. When they got back to the house, she plonked herself down on the floor cushion to study the label on Doc Bones's potion. He fed Suzy and went to take a shower. Can't pitch up grubby at a brothel. When he reappeared, clean and tidy, they were polite and business-like with one another. Just as they had been the very first time they'd met three years ago, preparing to go into the bomb factory.

Ned emptied his pockets. He checked he had no name tags in his jacket and coat. He took Nick's green *Lorem ipsum* card, unused and shiny. He took a library ticket and two credit cards he'd borrowed from Nick, along with his organ donor card and a small jiffy bag his sister had just sent him from Sydney, containing some sand, shells and seaweed. He took an envelope containing £1,000 in large notes whose numbers Span had logged that morning. He took some other things he'd kept in his desk drawer, waiting for this night. He took the clean pay-as-you-go cell phone he'd used to call Grace Talmadge. Extra Bilge had carefully put some plausible numbers into it. Nick's sister. His local taxi firms and supermarket delivery service. Then Ned gave Kate his personal cell phone and warrant card to look after. He called Jan Span from his landline. Then Spick. Then Extra Bilge. He looked at his watch. Then he ran out of things to do. Long, almost catatonic pause.

Kate broke it by dropping Suzy's harness in his lap. She watched him like a hawk, as if she had the power to ground him if he fumbled it, but he didn't. As he adjusted the little straps, he felt his pulse settle and the weight in his stomach lighten. Doing something. Operational at last. Cool. Level-headed. Relax. Relaxed. He straightened up and nodded at the phial and dropper Doc Bones had brought. He lay back on the sofa. Kate came and knelt by him. Hair falling about her face, that face. Body arched over him. So easy to reach up to. Reach around. His arms stayed resolutely by his side. Total professional. He didn't have to try to keep his eyes open, with that incredible vision floating above him. She brought up the eye-dropper and spoke for the first time since her outburst.

'You have the most beautiful brown eyes. Like Maltesers.'

'Do not pet me,' he replied, 'I am working.'

And then she squeezed the rubber bulb.

By the time they reached the Film Theatre he was blind. There had been a strange tingling in his eyes at first, and the feeling of liquids shooting through tiny, quivering tubes. Haze passed into fuzz, and then the fuzz got denser and denser. The last images were blurred streaks of traffic lights across his retina. Then there was nothing. It was very weird, and a little scary. He expected silence, like a fade to black in a film. No? Then how about suddenly heightened hearing: a pin dropping in an Alaskan haberdasher's? There was neither. Just the Land Rover engine rumbling and the usual accompanying chorus of squeaks and rattles. And Kate's reassuringly normal voice.

'We're just nearing the end of Brunswick Road. It looks like there's a gap about fifty yards before the Film Theatre. Is that OK?'

'On the same side?'

'On the same side.'

'That'll be fine.'

She parked the Land Rover, and kept the engine running.

'You're really sure about this?'

He nodded and unbuckled his seat-belt.

'And you know exactly where you are?'

'From fifty yards shy of the Film Theatre it's around . . . two hundred and eighty steps to the corner. There's a telephone junction box at waist height on the left as we turn right. On two hundred and fifteen steps to the Meriden Road bus stop. Glass shelter to the left sixteen feet long. Watch out for very uneven paving slabs over the next twenty paces. Keep going a further three hundred steps to the Whalley Way zebra crossing . . .'

'OK, OK.'

'. . . may not even bother taking the dog . . .'

Yuh right, Ned.

Kate went round to open the back. Dearest dog, sitting on her rug, harness on, wistful expression. She rubbed Suzy's tummy, and Suzy buried her head in Kate's coat. How much did she remember? Kate was torn between hoping it was everything – to solve the mystery and bring Ned and herself back alive, and nothing – to save Suzy having to relive old agonies.

'Changed my mind. The bit from Finland Road to Brunswick Quay's suddenly gone a bit blank. I'd better take her after all. Come on, old girl . . .'

As his mum would say: it's only a joke if everyone's laughing.

He helped Suzy down and checked the harness. Then stood, holding the handle.

'Are we at least pointing in the right direction?'

'You are.'

'Right then. We'll be off. Won't be long. See you at the far end of Canada Road, some time from 11.45 onwards. Don't come any further. And don't shadow me there, like you did with Nick. Promise?'

No reply.

'Promise!'

Her voice cracked very slightly as she answered him.

'Promise.'

And the man and dog walked away.

It took a few steps for them to get into their stride. He's holding her too tight, thought Kate, and then saw him relax. The lights were going out as they passed the Film Theatre and she lost them until they passed under a street lamp. Then into darkness again. All very well him knowing the distances, but he must follow Suzy's lead. He does remember that, doesn't he? They came back into the light as they reached the corner. She saw his left hand go out to touch the junction box as they turned – and then they were gone. It was all she could do not to go down to the T junction just to glimpse them again. All she could do not to drive straight there and bundle both into the Land Rover, whip them home and lock the doors. What was she going to do for the next hour? More to the point, what was Ned going to do? Crack the case? Get laid? Die? She sat for a moment, then did a U-turn and drove back the way she'd come.

Extra Bilge, sitting in Traffic Surveillance in front of the bank of monitors, watched his boss and the dog pass down a succession of ever-emptier streets. He had Ned's map of Sir Tommy's route in front of him, and tracked his progress along the dead man's footsteps. But that wasn't enough for Extra Bilge. He had his compilation of Sir Tommy and Suzy from the surveillance tapes hooked up on one of the spare monitors. He had pressed Play a little hastily – Sir Tommy reached the bus stop at Meriden Road fully five seconds ahead – but Ned was moving a little faster than the older man.

Ned had miscounted somewhere. He'd had his left hand up for about a dozen steps before he felt the cold glass of the bus shelter.

Then he forgot the uneven slabs and tripped badly, stumbling into Suzy and nearly sending her flying. Sorry, old girl. You all right? Concentrate, Ned. Don't lose it . . .

By the time they were picked up on the cameras at the start of Whalley Way, Ned had partly closed the gap with Sir Tommy. They were within seconds of one another on the zebra crossing by the school. And they were nearly level as they reached the corner where Sir Tommy spoke to the Harrisons before they parted. Extra Bilge found the sight of them stopping at almost exactly the same time really eerie. He didn't notice Fatso enter the room, and nearly jumped out of his skin when he heard the voice in his ear.

'What we got, cock? Ned on the left, Tommy on the right?'

Ned stood on the street corner, counting. Three minutes. It felt like forever. He stroked Suzy's ear, and told her she was a good girl. Sir Tommy hadn't done that, but who cares? . . . One sixty-eight, one sixty-nine, one seventy . . .

'Different men, same dog. Funny that.'

And Fatso sank his chompers into a cheese and onion pasty.

. . . one seventy-eight, one seventy-nine, one eighty. Let's go, old girl . . .

Side by side on the two screens, and within a second of one another, Sir Tommy left the Harrisons and Ned moved off.

'He's a clever bugger, is our Ned. Better than the telly any day, this.'

Extra Bilge resisted the temptation to brush the shower of pasty crumbs off the control panel. After all, Fatso was a Superintendent, and it wasn't Extra Bilge's control panel.

Ned slightly muffed the next bit. He stopped some way short of Sir Tommy . . .

'Whasis? Why's he stopping? Now the other pair's stopped and

221

all. Eh? Whas goin' on? Old boy having a slash? Ha! Come on, Ned, yer not trying. Where's your puddle?'

... and moved off early. More like thirty-eight seconds than forty-two.

Ned was already in Mission Street when the church clock struck eleven. Deep in the dark section, where the walls were gaunt and high, and the street lights petered out. This was the bit on the tape he'd pored over. He stopped as close as he could to where he thought Sir Tommy had stopped, and bent down as Sir Tommy had done. First time he'd walked it, Ned had re-tied his shoelaces. This time he gave Suzy a big cuddle. Neither was what Ned thought Sir Tommy had done at that point. He was sure there was a clue there in Sir Tommy's action, if only he'd been able to fathom it.

Suzy seemed to be panting a little. Was her heartbeat a little fast? What was a dog's heartbeat meant to be? Silly – should have checked. Extra Bilge would know. It's all right, Suzy. You're doing really well. There's a great big bone waiting for you at home when this is all over. He stood. It was even colder than before. The wind was howling up Mission Street from off the river. He waited another thirty seconds, patted Suzy one more time and then moved on. He knew he was moving towards the edge of the surveillance cameras' reach, and although he couldn't see a thing, he felt it getting darker.

On the monitors, Sir Tommy had made up the distance. He and Suzy dropped out of the bottom of the frame first, and then Ned and Suzy. The images on the monitors were static, apart from some spindly branches waving in the sodium light and the inexorable timecode. Then the timecode on the tape froze. After Mission Street, Sir Tommy's route was no more than conjecture.

'How long we got to wait?'

Extra Bilge shook his head and shrugged.

Stumbling on the cobbles and kerb edges, eyes useless and watering, anxious about Suzy's breathing, Ned forced himself on into the unknown.

12

AS SHE DROVE AWAY FROM THEM, Kate had a good go at shutting out her anxiety about Ned and Suzy. Trouble was, what rushed in to fill the gap was the memory of her last night with Banshee. Ned had wanted to ask her about it. He hadn't because he still didn't know her well enough, though he knew her well enough to know she wouldn't tell him. Large Sarge reckoned the only person who'd ever got Kate to talk about it was the Queen when she gave her the gong.

They had robots that night. Not the latest that are hypersensitive to TNT vapour and can climb stairs, but good, reliable versions of the old Wheelbarrows developed for fun and games in Derry and Belfast. They were fine for sweeping the ramps, but for diving down rows of parked cars – looking for the package, hunting the scent – a dog is best. Particularly against the clock, and the coded message was very specific about the timing.

The multi-storey car park was huge. A hell of a lot of ground to cover, and cover fast. It was late-night shopping, and the adjacent mall was emptying. People, children, trolleys everywhere. Popping out of this door, that lift. Behind this pillar, reaching for that shopping bag. Doors slamming. Cars moving. In the exercise they'd done the year before, oddly in that same car park, the uniformed branch gently shepherded the public away, the handlers concentrated on their dogs while senior officers calmly directed proceedings. Liaison with

223

the Bomb Squad was faultless. All devices, in helpfully identical sports bags, accounted for. No one killed. It went like clockwork. The night when it was for real, someone forgot to wind it up, or maybe they over-wound it and the spring went twang.

It was a nightmare's worst nightmare. Bomb Squad sent to the wrong car park. No senior officers on the scene until after the second device exploded. Nowhere near enough manpower to get the public out. Plus the warning covered the mall also, which meant that unlike in the exercise, people couldn't just be shoved back through the doors to do a bit more shopping while we sort these bombs. And these bombs, by the way, were in a variety of disguises: old cardboard boxes, supermarket bags, a bundle of old rags.

Kate found herself having to handle Banshee and mass panic at the same time. For twelve long minutes she was, it turned out, the only police officer on Level 7. Twelve minutes of fright and flame and mayhem. And the worst minute of all was when she sent Banshee ahead while she held tight to two small children, shielding them and restraining their hysterical mother. Amid the struggle and chaos she watched the dog trotting away from her. That jaunty, bouncy little trot into the gloom, with the fluffy tail like a wagging question-mark. Then fleetingly silhouetted by a flash, which was followed an age later by a body-slamming shock-wave and a brutal, explosive roar.

It was then Kate earned her gong: finding the last device and snatching two babies from the ball of flame rolling towards them and guiding people to safety as the floor above caved in on them. But, as she explained to Her Majesty, it wasn't difficult being brave. What was tough was doing it all *after* seeing her beloved dog blown away. A dog she'd had since a puppy. And such an adorable, sweet puppy. She'd trained her and loved her, and held her paw while she had her own puppies and they'd been through hell together. Kate didn't know if you could say 'hell' to the Queen, but she seemed OK with it, and so Kate told her about Banshee having just the coldest nose and the softest ears in the whole world. And to think of all that being ripped apart . . .

Her Majesty nodded. She remembered Banshee well. They'd met

when . . . Then she stopped nodding and shook her head a little. After that she slowly turned her back on Kate, seemed to look for something in a little bag on her arm, and then lifted a gloved hand to her face. Kate waited a bit, but the Queen didn't turn round. No one seemed to know what to do, not the Chamberlain chappy or the frog footmen, so Kate curtsied, went back to her seat and sat down.

It wasn't hard to see why her mind shunted back to that horrific night. The parallel was staring her in the face. Goodbye, Banshee; into the dark. Goodbye, Ned, goodbye, Suzy; into the dark.

The odd thing was that, the longer they walked along together, the more they got into the swing of it. Suzy really was brilliant. Ned wished he could see her weave and glide. He realised that the more he read her through the harness, the less he stumbled. He could feel her float over kerbs and bumps; all he had to do was follow. Clever old dog. He stopped being so anal counting his own steps, and gradually surrendered himself into her care and guidance, as he had at Nick's. Instead of him taking her on a walk, they were going together. Now he ticked off the waypoints as she led him to them, and she certainly seemed to know the way. Interesting, that. And following her freed his mind to think more calmly about the ordeal ahead.

There were two basic puzzles: who killed Tommy Best, and what was Talmadge's game? And then a third: were these riddles connected? The answer to the third might unlock either or both of the first two. This wasn't a linear problem; it was random access. Any single answer might be the way in to solve the rest. And the more Ned thought about it, the likelier it was that connecting the riddles would answer the big one: Sir Tommy's death. At this stage he ruled nothing out, including muggers and blackmailers. Hence the broken harness. Hence Suzy's distress. And the match? Does a man fighting for his life light up a cigar? Probably not. But we're assuming the match was dropped that night. It may have been thrown onto the old walkway as Sir Tommy sauntered away from Talmadge's on a previous visit. Which would make it pure coincidence that it landed at the very spot where he was later to fall . . .

He stopped to give Suzy a pat and let her rest. Her breathing was short, but her tail was wagging. Not just a clever old dog. A dear old dog. Come on, Suzy. We'd best be off, before we all change our minds. Funny. She didn't move away immediately. Just the faintest hint of hesitation. That's unlike her. Does she remember what this journey led to the last time? Why wouldn't she? If fish, according to Extra Bilge, can remember three months back, it would be odd if dogs couldn't manage rather less than that. And it would be odd if she could recall the exact route, but not the traumatic events that lay at the end of it. It's OK, Suzy. I'll be with you. We'll just have to stick together. It'll be absolutely fine, old girl.

They were on Canal Walk, nearing Lime Quay; Ned got a sudden blast of the sea from the great tidal river. He felt the rise at the approach to the canal footbridge at the head of the terrace. Stone slabs gave way to wood. Bit slippy. Bit steep. On the far side, it'd be onto the cobbles, bedded into their unique mix of iron oxide, ashes and lime. I'm joining the club, Tommy. I'll soon have the soles to prove it – if I ever get there.

At the top of the footbridge Suzy slowed and stopped. He coaxed her. Pushed her. Pulled her. Nothing. She really didn't want to go any further. His dad had a crappy joke about a bloke who bought a pony at a horse-fair for a knock-down price because it had this odd quirk: it sat on chocolate cake. Fine, thought the bloke. I don't even like chocolate cake. But then on the way home the horse suddenly sat down in the middle of a stream. Not a soggy crumb of cake in sight. He raced back to the dealer who was just packing up. Ah, said the dealer. Forgot to tell you; he also sits on fish.

That wasn't a great joke, but this wasn't any joke at all. For chrissakes, Suzy, let's go! How would it look if anyone came by and saw a blind man wrestling with his guide dog?

'You all right, mate?'

The voice came from some way off. Somewhere ahead of them, in Lime Quay itself. Bloody hell, that's all he needed. Try not hearing him. Come on, Suzy, please!

'Only you look like you got a problem.'

226

The 'only' at the front of the sentence sparked a memory, which Ned's nose confirmed: the smell of a roll-up. A short man in a green woollen pom-pom hat Ned had met down there almost on day one. The man who'd told him about the trick cyclists. At least the voice wasn't getting any closer, yet. Must be on his milk crate, peering over the wall. But he wasn't giving up interest.

'Your dog OK? Eh? Only it doesn't look it . . .'

Oh, God, thought Ned. I can't go on, even if Suzy takes the brakes off. Supposing he recognises me? Or her? Answer: fast retreat, now. He turned Suzy round and she led him back the way they'd come, easy as pie. The man called something after him, but it was blown away in the wind. Ned and Suzy walked back to the alley-way that joined Canal Walk to Merchant Street. They'd wait there in the dark, where no one could see them. He had no idea that they were standing under a wall-mounted street light.

Kate had a mug of sweet tea in the all-night caff by the bus station, after checking there were no patrol cars outside. The only familiar face she wanted to see was Ned's. No one else's would do. Needed him, needed the sugar. As she got back to the Land Rover she heard a phone ringing inside. An unfamiliar ring. Ned's phone. She'd left it on the ledge above the steering column. Fast fumble with the key, but not fast enough. She hit Missed Calls but didn't recognise the number. Then the phone rang again. Ned's voice-mail. A kid's voice. A hesitant kid. A kid wondering if she should even be ringing him. A kid with something to tell him, when he had a moment. Chippy.

Kate sat and thought. Given Chippy's timid voice, with its broken, unfinished sentences, either the kid was wondering how to tell Ned she loved him or this was important. With Ned out there at the sharp end, better to err on the side of caution and plump for the latter. Besides, the girl's voice had an edge, and it wasn't a tiny bit flirtatious. It was a tiny bit scared. But would she take a call from Kate? Would she spell out to Kate what she barely wanted to tell Ned? Would she trust her?

Large Sarge had a thing he'd say when they were heading

227

into trouble: 'If it was easy, everybody'd be doing it.' Kate checked the time and pressed Call.

The last thing Kate expected was that Chippy would know who she was. But as soon as she identified herself as a colleague of the DCI to whom he'd entrusted his cell phone, Chippy got her in one.

'You're the person who's looking after Suzy, aren't you? You were at the funeral. I remember you.'

Kate couldn't fathom that at all. The girl had seemed in floods of tears the whole time. Weird.

Chippy didn't want to speak to anyone but Ned. She wasn't even sure she wanted to do that. She needed a bit more time to think. Maybe the whole thing was crazy. Totally irrelevant. She had to think. When would he return? She could call back. Perhaps that was the best thing. She'd call back.

'It may be too late by then, Chippy.'

Dead silence down the end of the phone. Kate went on.

'I don't think we have much time. The DCI's really up against it, right now. If you know anything that might help him . . .'

Chippy's question that broke her silence was oddly intuitive. Almost psychic. Kate really couldn't figure her out.

'Where's Suzy? Is she with you?'

Kate thought quickly, and answered slowly.

'No, she's not. She's with him. They're together.'

'Oh, God.'

A shiver went down Kate's spine. A real horror movie tingler that left her heart pounding and her throat dry. Why 'Oh, God'?

'Chippy, why do you say "Oh God"?'

But Chippy had rung off. Kate called her back. It went to voice-mail. She left a message. Then she tried again. Chippy's phone was switched off. Now Kate was really, really scared. It started to rain. She sat in the Land Rover watching the drops settle for a moment before sliding down the windscreen, going over in her mind whether to race into the Docks there and then, find Ned and the dog, and pull them both out. Abort the whole thing. But he'd been so strict about her staying away. About them all staying away.

No unmarked van full of Spick's goons waiting at the end of the road. No surveillance teams. No wires. Nothing. If this is going to work, he had said at the final planning meeting, it will be because we are left quite, quite alone. A sealed experiment.

The rain came as a godsend to Ned. The nosy little creep in the green pom-pom would hardly stay perched on his milk crate in a downpour. It'd put his fag out for starters. Better wait till it is a downpour, though. So he stood – Suzy sat – geting wetter and wetter, lit by the dull glare of the street light. Couldn't leave it indefinitely. How long did Doc say the drops would last? Two or three hours, wasn't it? No point pitching up at Talmadge's after the potion's worn off.

Suzy heard the approaching footsteps first. Then Ned. Two people, maybe three, running. Getting nearer. Yes, he was a judo black belt. Yes, when he was at university he'd damn near made the Olympic Team. Yes, taking on three people wouldn't normally faze him. Unless he happened to be as blind as a bat. The feet pounded nearer. He backed up against the wall, deeper into what he thought was the gloom of the alley. They were close now. What if they were armed? This was not the moment to have a curly blonde Labradoodle in tow. This called for one of Large Sarge's German Shepherds. Brahms, perhaps. Or Handel. It was Handel who'd brought down that loony with a chainsaw in the Leisure Centre. Where are you now, Handel you old monster, when I really need you? In your kennel, dreaming of lunching on people's arms.

The footsteps seemed to slow as they drew close. This is it, thought Ned. Do something, or nothing? At the last moment he chose nothing. The footfalls reached him, went past and away round the corner. Ned gulped in air, realising he'd been holding his breath in fear. Why? Who were they? Was it a frightener? A quick pass, before they doubled back? Which way did they go? He and Suzy edged towards the opening onto Canal Walk. It was hard to say, but the footsteps seem to be going away from Lime Quay. Perhaps they were just joggers, caught like him in the rain. Breathe in. Breathe out. Come on, my old pooch. Let's have another bash at that footbridge. It may be safer in the bloody bordello than out here.

It was tipping down, but they must be there by now . . . Hold on, girl. Are you saying you'd rather the two you care for were tucked up in some evil witch's lair, than just getting rained on a bit? Distorts your values, worrying.

Up till the death of Banshee, Kate had been able to draw a nice fat black line between personal and work. She never fretted about what might happen if it was just her. Never thought about death. Not one of her hang-ups. She was as cool as a cucumber about it. She and Banshee had once been winched by helicopter onto the pitching deck of an Italian cruise liner in the Channel. Some fanatic separatist group was doing a better than average job of scaring everyone witless with tales of bombs in the hold under 428 passengers and crew. Turned out they weren't fibbing. Banshee and Kate found what they were looking for taped to one of the prop shaft bearings, deep in the keel. It was so dark and mucky down there she had to wear a head torch and carry Banshee much of the way. Just me and my dog. The crew hung back in the engine-room with the ship's security officer who couldn't stop throwing up. When Kate eventually got off the ship, a TV crew caught her unawares and asked if she'd been scared. The tape was immediately whipped away from them – no point plastering her lovely mug across the news – but it probably wouldn't have been useable: all she did was let out a bright, dismissive giggle.

Then Banshee. Now this: Suzy and Ned. That lovely, sad dog, having to go back into the past that had traumatised her. And that man. What if he were still just a DCI she'd been on a couple of ops with? Seen across the room during a few Fatso sessions. What then? How would she feel if she heard something had happened to him? Bad, of course. Bad anything happening to a colleague. But not bad like this. And then his phone rang.

'Hullo? It's me – Chippy. Is he back yet?'

No, he wasn't. Long pause. It didn't come naturally to Kate to talk a jumpy young woman down from her tree. Bit too close to home, perhaps. But she had to try.

'Look, I know you're wondering whether to tell me. That means it's really important . . .'

'That's the thing,' Chippy interrupted. 'I just don't know. It might be meaningless.'

'So tell me. Either way, I promise it'll go no further than me and – if I can get hold of him – the DCI. I promise.'

Another long pause. This had better be good, Kate thought, for all the knots it's tying in my stomach.

'OK. It's about the harness . . . About Suzy's harness. They said on the news it had got broken in the struggle. That the killers must have wrenched it out of his hand or something, and broke it. Or maybe it was while they were holding Suzy back so she couldn't help him – you know, go in the water after him . . . That's what they said . . .'

Kate tried her damnedest to sound calm.

'Yes, Chippy. They're right. I've seen it. The handle's definitely only attached on the one side.'

'Except it wasn't.'

Another horrid pause.

'It wasn't what?'

'It wasn't broken in a fight. It was already broken that morning. I noticed it at breakfast. He said the bolt had fallen out or something. He was mending it with a pipe cleaner. I asked him if he wanted some help, but as usual he said no, he didn't. He did ask me what colour the pipe cleaner was. I told him it was black. "Appropriately sober for a senior citizen," he said. He pushed it through the holes and twisted it round. He said it would hold well enough until he could get Cyril to fix it properly. He said Suzy didn't really need a harness. She just knew where he wanted to go . . .'

There was another pause in the conversation, but this time it was of Kate's making, as she grappled with the enormity of what Chippy had said.

'Do you think it matters? Is it important?'

'I think might be very helpful,' Kate replied in as even a voice as she could muster. 'I'll tell the DCI as soon as I can . . .'

Chippy didn't sound particularly relieved. She told Kate she'd hoped it wasn't important. That's why she hadn't come forward earlier. She nearly told him at her Art School show, but had bottled out . . . Even now, she couldn't really believe that Suzy hadn't been restrained. No, replied Kate. It seems hard to believe. Unless, Chippy went on, he had killed himself. But she'd talked to Mum, and they'd agreed that he was the least likely person in the whole wide world to take his own life. Yes, thought Kate, and that still leaves the question: what does a blind man do with his devoted dog when he wants to jump to his death? Tie it up to the railings somehow by a harness only held on with a pipe cleaner? And when the pipe cleaner breaks – it wasn't attached when she was found – wouldn't you expect the dog to go straight in after him?

'It's great you've told us this, Chippy. I'm sure the DCI will be able to work out what it all means.'

Only now did Chippy sound a little calmer.

'Mum said that he'll get to the bottom of it, if anyone can. She said he's really clever.'

She gave a little laugh.

'She told me not to get "drawn in" by him.'

I know, thought Kate. It can easily happen.

It called for lateral thinking. Literally. Ned didn't want to risk another mutiny on the bridge, so he went back up the side alley and took Suzy the long way round. His sense of the distances went out of the window but, tellingly, he knew the minute she came back on course; he could feel her anxiety through the harness. He could hear it in her short, agitated breathing. They were at the very far end of the terrace, and Ned hadn't a clue how many steps it was to Grace Talmadge's front gate. But Suzy knew. He fumbled around for the bell, and took several deep breaths – and then heard a noise from Suzy he hadn't heard before: a soft, high-pitched anxious whine. He bent down to give her a calming pat, and then the door opened, blasting him with arid heat and sickly room freshener.

'Mr Parsons? How very nice. We've been expecting you. Have you . . . ? Ah yes, thank you. Your little green card, I see, looks as fresh as a daisy. Do excuse the formality. Welcome. You're soaked. Come in. Come in. Lucy will take your coat. And wet shoesies off, I think.'

Her handshake was bone-dry and feather-soft. The kind so cherished by the Vice Squad Gaffer. She did not acknowledge Suzy. And shoesies? Who says a word like that, these days? The explanation lay in her accent. It was something from an old film: 1950s gutter girl made good – which was what she was. Ned wished he could see her. He wished he could see her home. But he would have to make do with sound and smell. And feel.

'Upsadaisy!'

He felt a hand around his ankle, lifting his leg, removing his shoes. He tried not to wince at the intimacy, but wasn't fast enough.

'Mr Parsons needs a little drinky, Lucy. Come inside, come inside.'

The madame's mantra. Inside they went, somewhere. It had a deep shag pile carpet, which Ned thought appropriate, and more of that sweetened air but now faintly cut with antiseptic.

'What'll it be, Mr Parsons?'

'Nick, please . . .'

'Nick it is, dear. And I'm Mother, as you know. And this is Tanya, who's going to get you a . . . ?'

Ned could hardly say that booze didn't go with Doc Bones's Blindness Drops. And he had to stop himself from blurting out, nothing thanks – I'm driving.

'A fruit juice would be lovely. Really. Thanks.'

The strange thing was that Ned had no sense of there being anyone else in the house but Mother Talmadge. He couldn't be sure that there was a Lucy; it might have been Mother removing his shoes. And equally, he had no sense that there was a Tanya. She never spoke, and an elephant could tango on that carpet and you'd never hear it. So his diminished world shrank still further. Mother's voice came at him as if through headphones, as if from inside his own head. Invasive, repellent, persistent. He held tight to Suzy's harness handle and stroked her neck, to try and remind himself of the world outside. Of rock cakes on Thursdays and Kate. But it was a non-starter.

'You know, Nick, I'm sitting here looking at you with Tommy's dog, and it's really quite unnerving. You send me back, dear, to the past. It's not that you look like him. No, you don't at all, really. But something about seeing you both. It's nice, dear. Not beastly. Very nice, really. Ah well. Chin chin.'

He had no idea if she was drinking. He knew he had to look as if he were relaxing. He sipped something sugary that could have been anything from pineapple to fig, stretched his legs out and sank back into a mass of cushions.

'That's better, dear, isn't it? Now before we go any further, I know you've got a little something for Mother . . .'

Ned produced an envelope from his jacket pocket.

'Tanya will just take that and verify the contents. We don't give receipts here, dear . . . Now, you said on the telephone that you wanted just exactly what Tommy had last time, bless him. Of course, she won't be in the same immaculate state she was for Tommy . . .'

And she let out a vulgar little tinkle of a 'boys will be boys' laugh. Ned joined in with a gentle chuckle. It didn't matter, Mother. As long as she was the same girl. Then he'd feel . . . you know . . . Mother did know. She knew exactly. She thought it was really tender of him. Sentimental, in the loveliest, old fashioned-est way. Ned gave an 'aw-shucks' bob of his head, and took another swig of syrup. So, had she seen a lot of Tommy over the years? He made it a 'making conversation' question. Airy tone as if, were she to be interrupted in her answer, he wouldn't bother to repeat it.

'Oh, yes, dear. We were very close. Since before the old king died. I couldn't do much for him, dear, with all those demands on him: the films, his charities, his family of course. But I could help him relax. Well, I helped them all relax. We took their busy minds off the world, even if it was just for an hour or two. It's so important for the men, I think . . .'

It was stifling, and not just the heat. Ned sat smothered in her cushions and her platitudes and euphemisms and illusions, and he nodded and smiled and frowned as required. Then she seemed to break off, as if someone had come into the room to give the thumbs up after counting the money. Although interestingly, Suzy, who was now lying down, did not move a muscle in response to a newcomer. After a moment of silence Mother said that everything was in order, and wasn't trust a precious commodity in this day and age of pin numbers and passwords? Long live old-fashioned, honest transactions between people. That's what she'd always cleaved to. Like a butcher's axe, thought Ned.

Truly terrible, he volunteered after another sip, about Tommy. He hadn't known him a fraction of the time she had, but he really was unnerved by it. Bereft, Mother said. She was bereft. It was as if the star had fallen from her constellation. Ned nodded. He couldn't have put it better. And how anyone could have brought themselves to do such a thing to him . . . Ah, said Mother. It's all such speculation, isn't it. The main thing is, he's gone. The how and why didn't matter to her so much as the bald fact of it.

'That's what we've all got to live with, dear. Not having the darling man. He was such company. Such a delight. He made me laugh so much, I actually – you'll have to pardon me, Nick, we hardly know one another – used to wet myself sometimes . . . We could honestly tell one another everything. And we did. You know his catch-phrase? From that show? I can hear him now – see him, peering round that pillar: "Who's your best friend, then?" Well, he never had to spell it out, but I always knew I was his. His best friend. Always . . .'

Her voice tailed off. Ned smiled sympathetically. Silence. The next thing he thought he heard was her crying. But he could have been mistaken. Then another silence. Then a tiny, faint nose blow. Then a pause and Mother spoke again.

'If you set us off thinking about Tommy Best, the girls and I just won't stop weeping at the sadness of it.'

Girls? Was it Lucy sobbing? Or Tanya? Was there a roomful of them? Or just Mother Talmadge?

'We'll be alright, dear. We just need the time for our grieving. The boys have been fantastic. We're hoping they'll come down and pay us a visit before too long. Not Mervyn, of course. We'll never see him here again, more's the pity. He's in a sorry way. Now, I don't know where you stand on this one, Nick dear, but Mervyn's an argument for mercy killing if ever I saw one. Have you seen him? No? Poor, poor darling. The girls and I went down to see him in his nursing home, and we honestly thought it would be the kindest thing just to send him to sleep there and then with one of his own pillows. We'd relax him first, of course, dear. He'd thank us for it. I know he would. But don't get me going on that . . .'

And she gave a snorting, unbiddable laugh.

What's really odd about this, Ned thought, is how Sir Tommy Best could stand being in her company, off and on, for over half a century. She was so appalling. So vulgar. So scary. If she was telling the truth about their relationship, then surely he'd got Sir Tommy badly wrong. He thought back to the Comic Relief show. Maybe Tommy Best just wasn't a snob. Maybe, as long as he got exactly what he wanted in life, he didn't give a shit who or what he got it from.

'Maybe you'd like to go upstairs soon, Nick dear. It's getting a tad past Lisa's bed-time.'

A tinkly, vapid laugh. Absolutely, Mother. No time like the present. He hauled himself out of the kapok, waded through the shag and felt a faint pressure on the small of his back steering him to the foot of the stairs.

'No, dear, leave the doggy down here with me. You know you don't go upstairs with your gentleman, naughty doggy . . .'

This was not the tone of a dog-lover, but Ned had no choice. He held out his hand and felt her take the harness handle from him. Suzy whined as she was led away. Ned was some way up the stairs when he heard distant words which shook him rigid.

'I see we've had our harness mended then, doggy. Got rid of Tommy's twisted pipe-cleaners . . .'

Ned stopped, his mind racing. If the harness was already broken, maybe that's why Sir Tommy had bent down in Mission Street: to tighten the pipe-cleaner holding it together. The last surviving evidence of the presence of a malevolent third party had just crumbled away. Fatso owed him a toffee apple. And if the harness was already broken . . . then Suzy was not being held back when Sir Tommy fell to his death. So what *was* she doing?

'I am in here.'

It was a very young voice. Bloody hell. They could set this one for the final exams at Staff College, he thought: the mystery drowning, the dog, the brothel, the legal pitfalls, the evidence and entrapment issues, the ethics, the health and safety implications . . . That'd keep them quiet for a few hours. Except Ned didn't have a few hours. He felt his way forward to an open door, and went in.

The second cup of sweet tea was too sweet, and she didn't finish it. Nearly 11.30 p.m.; time to make a move. Kate left the caff and walked across to the Land Rover. The rain had stopped: one tiny plus. But the rest was a frightening pile of minuses. And particularly the very last thing Chippy had told her: 'There's one more thing. He asked me at my show what I think when I see that photo of myself as a baby. You know, *the* photo, with all the bodies lying there. Could you say to him that I never look at myself in his arms. Or at him. I always look down at his feet, trying to see my real mother and father. I asked him once, but he just said he couldn't remember which ones they were. But over the years, I've worked it out for myself. My real mum's in white, just past his left leg. And my dad is in red, to the left of her. I decided it's them . . . I know it's them, because I looked at it on one of the computers at college, and zoomed right in. They're holding hands . . . Please tell him . . . He'll know what I mean . . .'

She was crying when she rang off. Kate tried to call her back, but she'd switched off her phone again. Kate started the Land Rover, did a U-turn, and headed for the Docks.

The whole of the conversation with Kate, Chippy hadn't once referred to Sir Tommy as her father. She said 'real mum' to distinguish her from Dame Angela. But she only had one father: a dead body in a red robe, twenty years and half a world away. There was something badly wrong there. Some gulf that Sir Tommy hadn't been able to bridge, or – worse – had opened up himself. Kate couldn't help wondering if this hadn't somehow had an effect on Suzy as well. Else why did Chippy say 'Oh, God' when she realised Ned and Suzy were alone together? The dog Nick had nearly rejected because she was too stressed. Because she took things too seriously.

Kate stopped at the end of Canada Road under a street lamp, and switched off the headlights. 11.41 p.m. It was a deep canyon of a place, with high brick walls on either side, topped with coils of barbed wire and stretching dead ahead into the darkness. The darkness of the Docks. The darkness from which Ned and Suzy would emerge any time from now. Wouldn't they?

Ned closed the door very carefully, and turned to face the girl. Luckily his anxious ignorance was as plausible for Nick Parsons as it was for a DCI on duty in a brothel with possibly a child prostitute. She led him to the bed and sat him down.

'Hullo. Would you like some music?'

Progress. Double progress. Firstly, he'd been worried where the girl might be from. Didn't know if they'd be able to communicate. In the event, she had an accent which might have been Russian, but she spoke English. Secondly, music: a chance to talk, without being heard below. Though if he was right about what had to happen next, it was vital that some sounds should travel downstairs. He might need her to lower the music.

The girl started to stroke his head, to blow in his ear. He stopped her as gently as he could, and smiled at her. Not yet, he told her. I just want to talk for now. It was fine, she said. A little talk.

'I want to talk about Sir Tommy Best. You remember him?'

He could feel her nod her head.

'Of course. He was with me, and then is dead . . . It is very terrible . . .'

They sat there quietly for a moment. He sensed she was upset, but couldn't be sure. No sniffing. No reaching over to a box of tissues. OK.

'Do you remember, when he was here with you, what you did together?'

'Of course.'

He couldn't tell if she sounded a little sharp because he was being stupid, or simply because she hadn't liked what had happened. Tricky thing, not being able to see her face. Or maybe that was what would make the whole thing possible. Not having to see her.

'How old are you, Lisa?'

'As young as you want.'

He forced a smile, and tried to sound as unlike a policeman as he possibly could.

'No, really, Lisa. I like to know. Tell me . . . how old you'll be next birthday? So I can send you a card.'

'Next birthday, I am thirteen.'

'Great,' he said, hoping his poker face was holding up. 'What I want you to do, Lisa . . .'

'Yes?'

'. . . is exactly the same thing now, that you did with Tommy.'

Yes, the girl said. Mother told her that this was the job. She knew this very well. But, Ned went on, he was not going to do what Tommy had done. He would just sit in the room and listen. She didn't understand. Who would be the man? No man, said Ned. Just you. Pretend the man is here. Make the movements. Make the sounds. The same sounds. Just like this is a film, and I am the director and I say you must do it all again. One more time. Just like before, when Tommy was here, but again. Like Tommy, he couldn't see anything. He was blind. He would just listen. The sounds were very important. Very important to him.

'They will relax you, Nick? These sounds?'

Her voice was turning the corner from puzzlement to seduction. Horrible.

'Yes, Lisa. They will relax me.'

There was a pause. She moved off the bed. He heard a drawer open. She got something out. She came back to the bed and dropped it in his lap.

239

'And this?' she asked.

Oh God. It was some sort of leather harness. He tried not to look shocked.

'Maybe, Lisa. But it's the sounds that are so important to me. Whatever sounds you made before, you must make again. But I will not touch you. Do you understand me? You make all the sounds, but I will not do anything.'

The girl leaned right over to him. He felt her breath on his face. Lavender cachous.

'And that is all you would like? Yes?'

Yes. Nothing more. As long as it sounds exactly the same, that'll be perfect. And the music . . . ?

'Not so loud. Just a little . . .'

She turned the music down. And then she led him off the bed and rather tenderly sat him down in a small armchair. He heard a rustle of clothing. He buried his head in his hands, and listened.

It was the most painful experience of Ned's entire life. He had no idea how long it lasted. Perhaps fifteen minutes, perhaps forty-five. Whoever, whatever, however old Lisa was, she was an extraordinary actress. Her attention to detail, her ear for it, was unnerving. He sat, frozen and horrified, imagining and finally believing that Sir Tommy Best was in that room with him. Abusing her, and terrifying her, and making her scream. It had nothing to do with sex that he could hear. Not sex in any sense that Ned understood it. No doubt the Vice Squad Gaffer wouldn't have batted an eyelid, but he could see why Large Sarge had burned himself out. It ended in an agonised mockery of an orgasm, enacted for the benefit of someone – the late Sir Tommy Best – who had no concept of pleasure without pain.

'*Lorem ipsum quia dolor sit amet, consectetur, adipisci velit, sed quia non numquam eius modi tempora incidunt ut labore et dolore magnam aliquam quaerat voluptatem.*'

And through it all, through the whimpers and the cries and the thrashing about, Ned could hear, down below, the dog bark. Then fall silent, and then bark again.

* * *

The darkness at the end of Canada Road was unbroken. Kate knew what he'd told her, but she wasn't prepared to wait a minute longer. She got out of the car and started walking. If there was no one else involved but Suzy and Sir Tommy, then she had to get to Ned and tell him. She couldn't let him go up on the walkway. She broke into a run. Halfway down the road she wondered why she hadn't brought the Land Rover, but it was too late. She checked her torch was working, and ran into the darkness.

Mother helped him on with his shoesies and wet coat. He didn't know if she could tell how shaken he was; he tried hard to act like a satisfied customer. A 'relaxed' customer.

'Hearing you two going at it hammer and tongs tonight took me right back to when Tommy was here. It almost sounded to me as if you were finishing off something he'd started, it really did. Like you were completing his circle. I'll tell you honestly, Nick dear, it's been delightfully nostalgic for me, having you with us. But just a teensy bit poignant. Like having a final visit from him. It's as I said before, you don't look like him, but I can tell you have the same tastes. And that's what binds close friends together, isn't it? Tanya's got the doggy waiting for you. She got a little anxious when you were upstairs with Lisa, but then she was like that with Tommy. Particularly towards the end.'

The hand that passed him Suzy's harness felt like the hand he had shaken when he first arrived. Mother's. The door was opened. A sudden blast of icy air.

'You know, I somehow don't think we'll be seeing you again, dear . . .'

Don't count on it, he thought.

'. . . I sense you've had what you came for and no more.'

He told her she was very wise. That she really knew people.

'That's all I've been trying to do all my life, dear. And I was so lucky that the one person I really managed it with turned out to be the most important.'

241

The pride of a whore, Ned recalled, surpasses that of a ploughman in his best clothes.

'He was a one, was Tommy Best. Such a one. I used to say to him, "May you be in heaven half an hour before the Devil knows you're gone!" And he was, dear. I'm certain of it, if I'm certain of anything. He's up there now, smiling down at us . . .'

The door closed. Almost before Ned had turned, he felt Suzy's pull. With greater certainty than she'd shown all evening, she led him away down Canal Walk. Wolves behind, sheer drop ahead.

Fatso rumbled awake, prodded from his snoring by Extra Bilge alerting all units. The camera they had mounted on the warehouse at the end of Canal Walk showed signs of life for the first time in an age. Ned and Suzy were on the move.

High in the cab of matey's crane, Span picked them up with a night vision scope: two green shapes slipping through an eerie green landscape towards the dark green of the basin.

Spick gave the orders to start closing in on Canal Walk.

Large Sarge, his moment to settle an ancient score finally come, lumbered out of the warm car and put on his coat.

Extra Bilge worriedly re-checked the tables; the tide was now on the ebb.

Kate, running fast, had lost her way in the maze of alleys and found herself staring in the direction of the basin across a canal with no bridge in sight. In the distance she could see the twin walkways snaking behind warehouses, past the crane, over railway line, walls and water. No sign of Ned and Suzy yet, thank God. Unless it was too late. She dived back the way she'd come, panicking and desperate.

Ned reined Suzy in a bit. She wasn't going to set the pace. There were things to do. Issues. Questions. First, had Span made sure the gate to the old walkway was open, and if so, would Suzy go right onto it, or left onto the new, safe one? He'd know soon enough. Another twenty paces. Her breathing was short and sharp again. And he heard a faint throaty choke as she strained against the neck strap. Easy, old girl. Easy. Five paces. Any moment now. He felt her rise onto the first step. He put out his left hand. If he felt brick, he was on the new walkway. If he felt two sets of railings, she'd led him onto the old. His fingers touched the cold, cold metal of the two strips rising. Interesting. Worrying. He felt his heart-beat race. Take it calm. Up we go. On the walkway proper now. Mustn't miscount the steps to the hole. That'd be bad. What's next? Ah yes.

The wind was gusting, and somehow it felt colder in the lulls. Ned reached into his pocket. His fingers felt the aluminium tube and the box of Swans. Must have been stiller up there the night Sir Tommy did this last, or he'd have found a pile of dead matches by the hole, not just the one. They walked on, under the crane, past the window Ned had climbed out of onto the old walkway that first time, while Sir Tommy's body lay on the mud below.

Two hundred and ninety, two hundred and ninety-one, two hundred and ninety-two. He stopped. Pause. Think. The hole must now be right in front. Resist the temptation to feel ahead with the feet. The dog must believe she is still responsible for your safety. It would take both hands to light the cigar. He'd have to let go. Just as Sir Tommy must have done. Feeling like a sailor casting off from a safe shore, Ned gently laid the harness handle down, brushing the back of his hand fleetingly on Suzy's fur. Straightened, feeling naked without the umbilical link to her. Try to relax, Ned. Take your time. Just as Sir Tommy must have done.

He pulled out the tube and removed the cigar. Its cedary smell was a welcome corrective to the saccharine and carbolic mixture at bloody Mother Talmadge's. He put it in his mouth. Strange, organic, leathery, musky. Not unpleasant, but alien to Ned. Like everything else Sir Tommy did. What had the National Treasure thought at this same moment? That more than anyone in the whole world, he richly deserved this fine cigar? He had, after all, been wallowing in his own glory all day. From news of the Burma visit for Unicef to playing Pius Thicknesse to adulation at the Film Theatre to violence against a twelve-year-old. Resounding endorsements of a magnificent career, succeeded by a virginity surrendered in pain. And now, just room for a tiny bit more luxurious oral gratification. The perfect ending to a perfect day. He owed it to himself.

Ned lit the match. God – his sight must be starting to come back. He saw a glare! Nothing else, just a flash as the match lit. Suck. Draw. Was it lit? Seemed to be. One more match to make sure. The glare again, like a yellow streak across a night photo on a long time exposure. He sensed the clouds of smoke around his head. Tasted the best Havana could offer the man who had everything. So this was it?

Yes. This was it. Crunch time. He had imagined the moment for so long. Almost since the first day. Crazy as the premise had been, one by one the objections to it had fallen away. Not just the practical ones, dismissed by a pointy match, a £1,000 child prostitute and a harness held on with a pipe-cleaner. But also the psychological ones. The premise had moved from the possible to the likely that night when he listened secretly to Kate and Nick discussing dogs and intelligent disobedience and 'moral congruence'. If there could be moral congruence between man and dog, then there was the possibility of moral incongruence. Moral dissonance. But he still couldn't be sure. To know for certain what had happened to Sir Tommy, he'd have to take a step forward. Would Suzy stop him? Or – Lisa's cries ringing in her ears – would she let him fall?

He puffed on the cigar. Could she smell the smoke? Even if it didn't convey the precise message of her master's smug self-satisfaction, was it one more detail that told her history was repeating itself, and therefore she'd know what was likely to happen next? After all, she had led him onto the old walkway. He listened. He couldn't hear her. He couldn't feel her against his leg. Perhaps she wasn't there. Or perhaps she'd moved ahead, across his path, guarding him from the hole. Only one way to find out. He took the step.

She wasn't there. Nothing was there. He fell through the hole, banging his leg and then his shoulder against its jagged rim, into the air between walkway and basin.

High above him, Span, transfixed, had seen them stop just short of the hole. The trouble was, from her angle, Ned was masking the dog. She couldn't see if Suzy was between him and oblivion. She saw the sudden greeny-white glare of the first match. Watched the way the smoke shimmered and faded in the infra-red glow. Realised Ned was going to go through with it. Guessed that if the dog were in fact blocking his path, she would see it from up there. So if she couldn't see the dog, it must be because she had moved to one side. That meant Suzy wasn't going to stop him – and Span couldn't. She'd never get down there in time. Then she saw the second puff of green smoke, and a flurry of movement, and Ned wasn't there anymore. And then the strangest, greenest splash. Horrified, she leaped out of the cab and started down the cat-ladder through the icy wind.

Ned fell into water and sank into mud, and then fought his way back to the grim, stinking surface. He couldn't breathe, had swallowed some of the freezing, filthy liquid. Called out, before he sank again, one word: 'Suzy!'

Up on the walkway, the dog heard her master's cry. Hesitated for a moment, then barked loudly and scrambled through the hole into the darkness after him. He felt something take hold of his shoulder. Pulling him up and up. They broke the surface, and he heard her bark again for help. Then she clamped her jaws onto his arm and pulled him towards the edge of the basin.

Kate, running as if for her own life around the warehouse, heard the barks echo from the basin. By the time she reached the edge and found them with her torch, Ned was lying on the mud, half in and half out of the water, coughing up yuck with Suzy panting beside him. She clambered down a rusty ladder, jumping the last part, sinking up to her knees in the swamp. She waded over to them, flinging herself the last few yards, relieved beyond words to find he was still breathing, still alive. He reached an arm around her, and they lay there together, listening to the converging chorus of sirens, both stroking the dog alongside them. That dearest of dogs. Then Kate lifted her head and carefully rested it on Ned's, forehead to forehead, and the longer they stayed like that the less they heard the world beyond, and the less they cared about it. The dog breathed on heavily for a while but then grew quieter and quieter and quiet.

Epilogue

KATE KNEW A PLACE. He didn't ask where and as usual she drove. It seemed to be out of the city. Large Sarge had asked if she needed support. He said they'd turn out mob-handed; she only had to give the word. No, she said. I'll be OK. I'd be happier on my own. She didn't say anything about Ned going with her. It wasn't anyone else's business. Anyway, Ned's time was his own; he was signed off sick. She glanced across at him. He gave her as much of a smile as he could dredge up, and then turned away.

'There's a line people come out with which always makes my blood run cold . . .' she said, breaking the silence which had lasted since she picked him up. Since he took a long look into the back of the Land Rover at the much folded-over, heavily taped-up body bag. Since he said, 'Oh dear' under his breath several times before climbing into the passenger seat.

'It's when they say, "We had a dog once, but . . ."'

No matter how the sentence ended, she thought to herself, it was always badly. Was that how it was for them? Had she and Ned had a dog once but . . . ? She supposed they had. Suzy was theirs if she was anybody's, and buts don't come any more final. He was thinking pretty much the same thing, but said nothing. The city tapered away; the road started to climb. How would this go? he wondered to himself. Would she dissolve into tears? Would he comfort her?

Or would they stand by the grave he'd dig, and not know when the moment was over? Would it be like those mad Soviet events at which everyone applauded Stalin for hours because no one wanted to be the first person to stop? If he turned to her before she turned to him, would it look like he didn't care? Or would it be the sign of grown-up people supporting one another to move on? Would that be when they'd finally have that first kiss?

'We're lucky,' she said. 'It's rained up here.'

It was the harbinger of something he'd not prepared for and that he still didn't sense even as he heard the grounded tone in her voice: that she would be the strong one. They pulled off the road at the cattle grid, just as Kate had done on that first visit to Nick. They got out and took a little walk and she told Ned about it. How this was the first place – maybe the only place – where she'd seen Suzy totally relax into being just a dog. Gambolling about. Sniffing. Listening. Feeling the sun on her back. He talked about the one time she did that with him. The morning at Nick's when she brought him the stick to throw. Except he never actually saw her free and easy: he'd kept his blindfold on. Damn. Wished now he'd peeked. Turned out he was first with the damp eyes. She put an arm round him for a moment or two, then slipped away.

He gradually became aware of the sound of digging, and then a clang of spade against rock snapped him out of his thoughts. He hurried across to her, making 'Here, let me do that' noises. Kate said she'd keep going a bit longer. Wasn't a good idea to stress himself. Doctor's orders, remember. And these were proper doctors, not Doc Bones. Anyway, the ground was soft, and it didn't need to be that big a hole. He watched her. She never seemed to play the little lady. Never struggled so others would come to her rescue. So beautifully self-contained.

Kate knew all about Ned's feelings of guilt. He'd told her about them late at night in the hospital. The nurse said they'd pumped out his stomach and given him a sedative, so he'd probably be asleep but she could just look in on him – her being police and that. Oh, and did she know she had some smears of mud on her forehead? He was still awake and very relieved to see her. She took his hand and they sat without saying anything for a while. Then it all came out. First his stomach, she thought, now his conscience. He hadn't the right to take Suzy to the Docks that night. He'd had the choice but the dog wasn't given any option. It wasn't even as if he didn't know her feelings on the subject; she'd made them perfectly plain when she refused to take him across the footbridge at the top of the terrace. He had argued for seeing the experiment from the animal's point of view, but in fact he was just using her as a lever, exerting pressure on her to crack a mystery. When push came to shove, he hadn't really cared about the fate of the animal: Schrödinger's Cat, Ned's Dog, same difference. He had put his tunnel-visioned sense of duty over Suzy's life. He sank back a little into the pillow, beaten-up and empty.

She squeezed his hand and then told him something of the night she lost Banshee. She tried not to make it sound as if she was capping his story: I killed a dog long before you did, so there! She talked about Banshee's tail curled like a question-mark and the juddering roar and the heart-stopping realisation. About the grief she'd always dreaded but couldn't prepare for. That was the risk they took using animals for police work. She felt desperate sadness and loss, but no guilt. In fact she'd never felt guilt in her whole life. She was no slouch at feeling bad about herself, but that had nothing to do with how she'd treated others. It was just between her. Nothing hardened her quite as much as others dumping guilt on her. It was simply a way of trying to control her and it had been years since she'd taken that from anyone, thanks very much, Mum and Dad.

Ned smiled for the first time that night. Thank God, she thought, and hoped he'd leave it at that. Time for a rest now. But it wasn't. Not quite yet. He just wanted to make the point that maybe, as she had once said, the explosives dogs treated it as some kind of game, but Suzy knew it wasn't. None of it was a game to her. That's what Nick had said, wasn't it? That she took everything deadly seriously. Maybe it was OK with Banshee because they were saving lives, but you couldn't use that argument with Suzy. And – afterthought – he wasn't like her. He'd been reared on guilt; it was an old, inseparable enemy.

Her turn to smile. Well, she said, tonight it was Ned – 6, Guilt – 0. She told him about the child prostitution racket busted. About the underage girl from the house crying on Jan Span's shoulder for an hour and then giving her chapter and verse. Other girls. Other men. Arrests. The Basle Club behind bars. He listened, shaking his head and then settling back a little comforted.

They sat in silence, his eyes flickering shut. He looked like a brass-rubbing she had once done of a young knight who had died in battle. His fit, ramrod-straight body was delineated all the more sharply under bed-clothes pulled taut on either side by his bare, muscular arms. The colour had come back into his cheeks. In that moment he was just the sexiest thing she'd ever seen.

After a while Kate handed Ned the spade and let him do a bit of digging while she went off somewhere. The hole looked OK to him, but he dug down a bit deeper all the way round to show willing. When she came back, he realised she'd only got him to dig to save him having to bring Suzy over from the Land Rover. The terrible thing was how much she could feel the dog through the heavy plastic. He saw the look in her face and took Suzy from her and then he felt her too and held her tight for a moment before laying her gently in the hole. They put the earth back with tears streaming down their cheeks, and stood together beside the little mound.

He no more said Kaddish than she said the Lord's Prayer, though oddly both their thoughts were turned eastwards. She wondered how she felt now about taking Jiffy into some arid tinderbox to root out roadside bombs. About whether Suzy's death left her with any reservations, which she decided it hadn't. About the beating sun and a hot, thirsty dog and a suspicious lump in the sand. And he thought about lines his father used to quote: 'For lust of knowing what should not be known/We take the Golden Road to Samarkand.' That's why he'd done it: for lust of knowing. It was less a sense of duty to others that drove him, than his own curiosity. Fatso, Dame

Angie, Kate – they'd all have voted for him not going the extra mile, but he had to know what really happened to Tommy Best. And however awful he felt about Suzy, he knew he'd do the same again. Then he looked down at the fresh earth and remembered what lay beneath it: that sad, serious, dearest of dogs who had saved his life. He gave up analysing and just wept.

He had no idea she had left his side until she slipped up from behind and wrapped herself around him. Then she gently turned him away from the grave so they were in each other's arms. Definitely and at last. Ah, he thought, drying his cheeks on her hair. About that first kiss. Then he decided to say it out loud.

'Too late,' she said, drying her cheeks in his neck. 'We've done that already.'

'I don't remember it.'

'That night in hospital. After you fell asleep. Oh, and there was a time at Nick's when I put you to bed. I'm afraid I've been taking advantage.'

'It doesn't count then. Not for me.'

'Don't whinge about it,' she told him. 'Get even.'

And he did.